THE FIRST CASUALTY

THE FIRST CASUALTY

Ben Elton

BANTAM PRESS

LONDON · TORONTO · SYDNEY · AUCKLAND · JOHANNESBURG

TRANSWORLD PUBLISHERS
61–63 Uxbridge Road, London W5 5SA
a division of The Random House Group Ltd

RANDOM HOUSE AUSTRALIA (PTY) LTD
20 Alfred Street, Milsons Point, Sydney,
New South Wales 2061, Australia

RANDOM HOUSE NEW ZEALAND LTD
18 Poland Road, Glenfield, Auckland 10, New Zealand

RANDOM HOUSE SOUTH AFRICA (PTY) LTD
Isle of Houghton, Corner of Boundary Road and Carse O'Gowrie,
Houghton 2198, South Africa

Published 2005 by Bantam Press
a division of Transworld Publishers

A catalogue record for this book is available
from the British Library.
ISBN 978 0593 051115 (cased) (from Jan 2007)
ISBN 0593 051114 (cased)
ISBN 978 0593 051122 (tpb) (from Jan 2007)
ISBN 0593 051122 (tpb)

The author and publishers are grateful for permission to reproduce the following extracts:
'In The Twi Twi Twilight', words by Charles Wilmott and music by Herman Darewski ©
1907, reproduced by permission of Francis Day & Hunter Ltd, London WC2H 0QY;
'It's A Long Way To Tipperary', words and music by Jack Judge and Harry Williams ©
1912, reproduced by permission of B. Feldman & Co. Ltd, London WC2H 0QY; and
'Pack Up Your Troubles (In Your Old Kit Bag)', words by George Asaf and Felix Powell
© 1915, reproduced by permission of Francis Day & Hunter Ltd, London WC2H 0QY.

The publishers have made every reasonable effort to contact the copyright owners of the
extracts reproduced in this book. In the few cases where they have been unsuccessful
they invite copyright holders to contact them direct.

Typeset in 11/15pt Sabon
by Falcon Oast Graphic Art Ltd

Printed in Great Britain by
Clays Ltd, Bungay, Suffolk

1 3 5 7 9 10 8 6 4 2

Papers used by Transworld Publishers are natural, recyclable products made
from wood grown in sustainable forests. The manufacturing processes conform
to the environmental regulations of the country of origin.

This book is dedicated to the memory of my much-loved
grandfathers, Victor Ehrenberg and Harold Foster,
who served on opposite sides in the First World War.

1

Ypres, Belgium, October 1917, before dawn

The soldier was laden like a pack mule.

Besides his knapsack and his water bottle, he carried on his back an iron bar around which was wound a mass of barbed wire that must have weighed a hundred pounds. Hanging from his belt and webbing were two Mills bombs, a hatchet, a bayonet, a pouch of ammunition and various entrenching tools. In his hands he carried his rifle. In addition, the man was wet through and through, every stitch of cloth and every inch of leather as sodden as if it had been deliberately immersed in water, so that it all weighed three times what a uniform, coat and boots ought to have weighed. Of course, every man in Flanders was as wet as that, but not every man carried a reel of wire on his back and so not all of them staggered as this man did or made such slow time.

'You there,' cried a voice, trying to make itself heard above the roar of artillery that thundered up from the guns at the rear. 'Military Police! Make way. I must get past. I simply must get past.'

Perhaps the man heard, perhaps he didn't – but if he did, he did not make way, but continued to plod steadily towards his goal. The officer could do no more than travel in his wake, cursing this ponderous beast of burden and hoping to find a point where the duckboard grew wide enough to let him pass safely. It was doubly frustrating for him to be so obstructed, for he knew enough about the nature of an attack to see that this fellow would not be advancing in the first wave. His job would be to follow on, using his wire and tools to help consolidate the gains made by the boys with the bayonets. The impatient officer did not expect any gains to be made. No gains of any significance anyway. There had not been any in the battle before this one, nor had there been in the one preceding that. Still, even gains of a few yards would need consolidation, new trenches to be dug and fresh wire laid. And so the pack mule plodded on.

Then the mule slipped. His heavily nailed boot skidded on the wet duckboard and with scarcely a cry he fell sideways into the mud and was gone, sucked instantly beneath the surface.

'Man in the mud!' the officer shouted, although he knew it was already too late. 'Bring a rope! A rope, I say, for God's sake!'

But there was no rope to hand. Even if there had been one, and time to slip it around the sinking man, it is doubtful whether four of his comrades pulling together would have had the strength to draw him forth from the swamp that sucked at him. And there was no room on the duckboard for four men to stand together, or even two, and so slippery were the wire-bound planks that any rescue attempt would have resulted in the rescuers sharing the same fate as the man they hoped to save.

And so the man drowned in mud. Dead and buried in a single moment.

2

Some time earlier

Douglas Kingsley was an unlikely candidate to join the ranks of conscientious objectors, in that he had killed more men than most soldiers were ever likely to do. Not directly, of course; he had not plunged in the knife or pulled the trigger but he had killed his quarry no less certainly for that. It was a point he readily conceded at his trial.

'It is true that I have no small acquaintance with matters of life and death, sir,' Kingsley said, addressing the judge, 'and have been forced to examine my conscience accordingly. I have, how-ever, slept soundly in the knowledge that those men and the three women who were condemned to death as a result of my investigations were all heartily deserving of their fate.'

It was a very public trial. Most conscientious objectors were court-martialled before military tribunals, but such was the notoriety of Kingsley's case that somehow the authorities had intrigued to bring him before a civil court. Kingsley cut an in-congruous figure in the dock, not least because he was impeccably turned out in the dress uniform of an inspector of His Majesty's Metropolitan Police. His buttons shone, his badges sparkled and the ribbons at his breast were an unlikely decoration for a man who stood accused of cowardice. Tall and proud, almost arrogant in his stance, Kingsley was steady and commanding in voice and manner. His tone clearly irritated the judge, who seemed to feel that some humility on his part would have been appropriate.

'You think yourself a better arbiter of moral worth than His Majesty's Government?' he demanded.

'In the circumstances under discussion, how could it possibly be otherwise?'

'Do not curl your lip at me, sir!' the judge barked.

Kingsley's lip had indeed curled, but involuntarily. All his life those who knew and loved Douglas Kingsley had found themselves making excuses for what often seemed on first acquaintance to be an insufferably superior manner. Kingsley did not set out to patronize people but the truth was that every line on his face was wont to display evidence of his absolute conviction that he knew better than them. He was constantly surprised to discover that the fact that he usually *did* know better in no way mitigated people's irritation at his all-encompassing assurance.

'I will not be sneered at in my own courtroom!' the judge added, raising his voice.

'I do not mean to sneer, sir, and was not aware that I was doing so. I am sorry.'

'Explain yourself then! How is it that you imagine yourself so much more morally astute than those who govern us?'

'In general I would make no such claim, sir. I am merely seeking to point out that I have known every single person whom I have sent before the hanging judge and known them intimately. I have examined every available detail of their character and their actions. His Majesty's Government knows none of those whom it kills, be they Germans, Turks, Austro-Hungarians or our own men.'

This last comment drew cries of shame from the packed gallery of the courtroom.

'You're a traitor, Kingsley,' an old man shouted, 'and a dirty German too!'

This jibe was a reference to the fact that Kingsley's grandfather had been born in Frankfurt and his family name had been König.

'Traitor or German, sir?' Kingsley enquired. 'If I *were* German, which I am not, then I could hardly be called a traitor for refusing to fight them.'

Kingsley's lip again curled, and a hail of abuse descended upon him from the gallery. Above the noise of it he could hear in his head his wife's voice scolding him for making patronizing comments. Comments she used to repeat to him angrily on their way home from dinner parties at which he had imagined himself to be the soul of reason and reserve. 'You think yourself so clever,' she would chide, 'and I'm sure you are, but you don't know everything and nobody likes a smart Alec.'

Certainly Kingsley was making no friends in the courtroom.

'Coward!' shrieked a shabby-looking woman who was dressed in conspicuous mourning.

'Filthy snivelling coward!' the ex-private soldier beside her added with equal venom.

Kingsley had noticed this man earlier. He had been carried into the dock by his family, for he had no legs on which to walk.

Kingsley thought of his brother Robert, missing since the first morning of the Somme and long since pronounced dead. If Robert had merely lost his legs instead of being vaporized by shells, could it have been him sitting there in the gallary? Hurling abuse, his face a mask of fury?

The judge called for silence but he issued no rebukes. It was clear that he sympathized with the sentiments of the crowd.

'This courtroom will not provide a platform for slanders and treason, Mr Kingsley! The British government does not kill its own men. The enemy kills our soldiers to further its wicked aims and our valiant soldiers are prepared to sacrifice themselves in order to stop it. You dishonour the memory of the fallen with your fatuous sloganeering.'

'I assure you I had no such intention.' Kingsley pressed on quickly. 'The point I am trying to make is that whilst I am entirely

11

satisfied that the human souls I sent to the gallows in pursuance of my duties as a police officer were wicked ones fully deserving of their early dispatch, His Majesty's Government is unable to judge the moral merits of ending the life of even a single one of its victims.'

The judge seemed about to shout but instead he gripped his gavel and paused to collect himself. His was a position of great authority, the dignity of his office the bedrock of the criminal justice system, and clearly he realized that he was in danger of allowing himself to be provoked. He must attempt to meet Kingsley's arguments calmly and leave baying to the mob.

'Inspector Kingsley, this is childish! The German soldier represents the will of his government, a government whose moral merits we know only too well.'

'We know them because they are similar to our own!'

Again there were roars of protest from the gallery. Kingsley bit his lip, aware that every word he uttered must increase the contempt in which he was held. All his common sense told him to be silent and yet he could not stop himself. He wanted people to understand that he was *right*. Not necessarily right morally, for to his mind that was a matter of personal conscience, but right *intellectually*. All the arguments were irrefutably on his side.

Somewhere in the distance a military band struck up 'Goodbye Dolly Gray'. It was a warm day and the high windows of the courtroom had been opened an inch or two, so the music could be heard despite the noise in the room.

> *Goodbye Dolly I must leave you,*
> *Though it breaks my heart to go . . .*

The old Boer War favourite had been a popular revival in the early days of the war, sending many a troop train of the British Expeditionary Force on its way from Waterloo and Victoria. The song had been heard less frequently in recent years and Kingsley wished that they would not play it now. It was a favourite of his

12

son's, and many times Kingsley had watched as the little boy marched about their cosy sitting room while his wife sat at her beloved piano and sang.

Kingsley tried to put thoughts of his family from his mind. He had tried to do this every waking moment since he had been arrested, but he always failed. In happier times Kingsley had believed that nothing on earth could ever mean more to him than his family, yet he had sacrificed them for a cold, dry principle and a part of him loathed himself for it.

'I do not approve of the Kaiser!' Kingsley said, raising his face to those who sneered down upon him. 'I think him vain and aggressive and believe that he must take much of the blame for the catastrophe that we all now face . . .'

'Well, I am sure we are all delighted to hear it.' The judge's voice dripped with sarcasm. 'No doubt General Haig will see fit to pass on your comments to the army in an order of the day, that they may be emboldened in their task.'

'Nonetheless,' Kingsley pressed on, 'whatever his faults, the Kaiser leads an industrialized, imperial, Christian nation! Just as does his first cousin, His Majesty King George. It is true that we are a democracy and Germany is an oligarchy but it is not for that reason that we fight. Indeed, our ally Russia was until recently every bit the absolute monarchy that Germany is. I can see no reason why all these most similar European nations have pronounced the death sentence upon one another's populations.'

'It is not your business to look for reasons, sir!'

'I consider it to be more than my business, I think it my duty.'

'If you knew anything about duty, sir, you would be in France!'

Cheering broke out at this and it seemed to Kingsley that the judge would be happy to allow the spectators to descend from the gallery and lynch him there and then.

'You are a citizen and a subject!' the judge thundered. 'If you wish to influence national policy you have your vote. If you wish to influence it further, then for a small deposit you may stand for parliament. You have lived all your life in comfort and prosperity

13

under the protection of parliament and the Crown. You have happily embraced the rights and privileges of British citizenship. What right have you now to avoid its responsibilities?'

Kingsley struggled to meet the judge's eye. The hostility in the room was intense and despite his confident manner Kingsley was horrified to be the focus of so much aggression. For a moment it seemed as if the fight was draining from him.

'I have no such right, sir,' he said quietly.

'Speak up, man!' the judge demanded.

Kingsley raised his head once more and looked straight at the judge. He knew the case was drawing to a close.

'I have no right to avoid my responsibilities. At least not unless I am prepared to accept the consequences. But you see, sir, I am. That is why I am here. To face the consequences of the position which regrettably I have felt obliged to adopt.'

At this something approaching a hush fell upon the courtroom, which only moments previously had threatened to become a bear pit. The baying mob was briefly taken aback by this sudden appearance of humility on Kingsley's part. The judge also took a quieter tone. It seemed that, beneath the bluster and the anger, Kingsley troubled him.

'Inspector Kingsley,' he said, 'you are aware that I am empowered under the law to exercise tolerance of pacifism if that pacifism is grounded in a genuine moral or religious abhorrence at the taking of human life?'

'I am, sir.'

'Those individuals who come before me burdened with such principles may expect to be obliged to labour for their country in some peaceful capacity, but in general they will escape a prison sentence.'

'I understand that.'

'And yet you do not seek to claim such principles in your defence?'

'I am not a pacifist, sir. Nor do I believe that all human life is inalienably sacred. I believe that there are circumstances under

14

which killing may be justified. Perhaps even on the industrial scale currently under way on the fields of Belgium and France, although it is difficult to imagine what those circumstances might be. The reason I stand before you today is that I do not think those circumstances are met by the guarantees this country made to Belgium in the London Treaty of 1839.'

The moment of calm was short-lived. Once more the gallery began to stir. Kingsley could hear his wife's voice warning, *Nobody likes a smart Alec.* Why bring up the treaty? Why mention the date? It was snooty and bookish and could only further alienate an already deeply hostile room. But Kingsley would not be browbeaten. Facts were important. They were *all* that was important when justifying a war. Kingsley knew his facts, and he was damned if he was going to water down his arguments simply to satisfy the preference of the mob for dogma and ignorance.

'You think it wrong then,' the judge enquired, 'that a great and mighty nation such as ours comes to the aid of a small, brave one like gallant Belgium when that country is brutally attacked and occupied?'

'If that is the reason for our current expedition then I think it strange that we felt no similar obligation to the peoples of the African Congo whom "gallant" Belgium has happily attacked, subdued and fiendishly brutalized in a manner which I dare say exceeds any current German excesses on the Continent.'

'You compare the fate of savages with that of Christian white men?'

'Yes, I do.'

The judge seemed momentarily taken aback. It was certainly true that the particular cruelty of Belgian imperialism had provoked much criticism in Britain a few years earlier. Criticism which had been quietly forgotten in the circumstances of Belgium's currently celebrated martyrdom.

'The Belgian Congo is utterly irrelevant to your case.'

'I don't see why.'

'Because you are a British citizen and we are discussing British policy, Inspector Kingsley, and it is not for the individual to pick and choose what articles of national policy they care to subscribe to. That is called anarchy. Are you an anarchist, sir?'

'No, I am not, sir.'

'I am glad to hear it. It would be a strange thing indeed if a man who has seen fourteen years' service with the Metropolitan Police were to be an anarchist.'

Kingsley knew that he was getting nowhere and suddenly he felt tired. The months since his arrest had been taxing in the extreme, the trial itself terrifying and exhausting. He decided that he must try to assist in bringing the proceedings to a close.

'Sir, I am sorry to have caused you and this court so much trouble. I truly am. I recognize that there is no legal defence for my position and that there is only one verdict that you can deliver. All I can say is that in the current international circumstances I am forced, with the greatest reluctance, to renounce my obligations as a subject of the King. I cannot shelter behind any deeply felt moral or religious principles. I accept that there are men I would be prepared to kill. I accept that there are wars I would be prepared to fight. All I can tell you, sir, is that the German Army does not contain those men and this war is not one of those wars.'

'Damn it then, if your objections are neither moral nor religious can you please tell me in simple terms what they are?'

Kingsley paused. He knew that his answer would not sit well with the judge, the gallery or the wider public outside, but he could think of no other.

'Intellectual, sir.'

'Intellectual! Thousands of brave men are dying each day and you speak of your *intellect*?'

'Yes, sir, I do. It is intellect that sets man above the beasts.'

'It is *conscience* that sets man above the beasts.'

'The two are surely connected, sir. It is intellect that informs a man what is right and conscience that determines if he will act on that information.'

'And your intellect tells you that you should not fight this war?'

'Yes, sir, and my conscience forces me to respect that advice. This war is . . . stupid. It offends my sense of logic. It offends my sense of scale.'

3

A visitor

Shortly before the supper bell on the evening before his sentencing, Kingsley was told to expect a visitor. It would be the first time he had seen his wife in almost three months.

Being more than usually dedicated to his work, Kingsley had waited until he had passed the age of thirty before endeavouring to find a wife. It was generally acknowledged amongst his colleagues that Agnes Beaumont had been worth the wait and that in winning her Kingsley had made the finest catch in all his celebrated career.

From the moment that he first set eyes upon her over the egg sandwiches and Victoria sponge at a police charity cricket match in Dulwich, Kingsley's heart was entirely lost. He knew instantly that he would devote every fibre of his being to her pursuit. They made a disparate couple. Her soft golden curls, blue eyes and rosy cheeks were in sharp contrast to his own somewhat stern, headmasterly appearance but, as Agnes was wont to point out, opposites are well known to attract.

'It's Darwinian, I think,' she would tease. 'If beautiful girls did not marry hideous men then their hideousness would go unchecked down the generations and before long a race of gargoyles would be produced.'

More than ten years his junior, Agnes truly was a daunting goal for a middle-ranking police detective with no fortune whatsoever. Not only was she vivacious and beautiful but she was also the daughter of Kingsley's ultimate superior, Sir Wilfred Beaumont, Commissioner of Scotland Yard.

'If you want a successful career in the police,' Kingsley's friends had assured him at the time, 'there is only one rule: never, repeat *never*, lay a finger on the Commissioner's daughter.'

But in love, as in so much else in his life, Kingsley made his own rules. He *knew* that Agnes Beaumont was the right girl for him, and when Kingsley knew that he was right all further argument was useless.

A celebrated débutante, Agnes had been presented to the King in the 1910 season, during which her looks and personality had ensured that she outshone numerous girls of far more elevated rank than her own. The Beaumonts were a Leicestershire family who, although never quite noble, could trace their lineage back to before the Reformation. They had their own pew in the church at Willington and over the generations had built up a large estate in the surrounding county. Agnes's grandfather had been a junior minister in the second Salisbury government.

Outside the aristocracy itself, stock did not get much better than the Beaumonts.

Kingsley's father, on the other hand, had been a physicist at Battersea Technical College and his mother a newspaper sketch artist. It was said that it was from his mother that Kingsley had inherited his uncanny eye for detail.

It was true that in terms of rank and status Kingsley had got the better of the match but Agnes did not feel that way and, after initial doubts, nor did her family. This was the twentieth century, after all. The Chancellor of the Exchequer himself was a Welshman of lowly stock, who, in partnership with the aristocratic young Home Secretary Winston Churchill, was ushering in a new age of egalitarian social reform. Who could tell what such a man as Kingsley might achieve? The early years of the century had seen a massive expansion in the work of the Metropolitan Police. London was by far the richest city in the world, a polyglot metropolis of some seven million souls, the centre of the largest empire the world had ever seen and the principal home port to a merchant fleet that carried more than 90 per cent of the world's trade. This was a town with plenty of scope for crime and consequently an equal measure of opportunity for energetic and ambitious police officers. The tall, handsome and (as he would tell you himself) rather brilliant Kingsley was just such a man.

And his foreign antecedents? Well, as Agnes loved to point out, were not the Royal Family themselves recent German immigrants?

Kingsley was already seated when Agnes entered the visitors' hall.

Ever since the first time he had made her blush, Kingsley's private name for Agnes had been Rose, and if a rose is beautiful when set within the beauty of a garden, how much more beautiful is it when found within the bounds of prison walls? Kingsley's whole being shook with misery as he watched his wife make her way across the long grey room with its heavy stone floor and forbidding grille, behind which the inmates of Brixton Prison were privileged to share precious moments with their lawyers and their loved ones.

Agnes was dressed soberly as befitted the times and the sombre situation. She had forsaken the modish, calf-length dresses which, to show off her shapely ankles, she usually wore with high-buttoned boots. She had instead chosen a floor-length skirt of dark brown wool with matching jacket. Her starched white blouse was buttoned high up under her chin and her hair was pinned severely.

Despite this gloomy ensemble and an uncharacteristic pallor, she turned every head as she passed along the ranks of other visitors who sat before the grille. Such beauty was rarely glimpsed in the bleak community of HM Prison Brixton.

Agnes sat down in front of Kingsley but declined to meet his gaze, preferring instead to fix her eye upon the bench.

'Father is waiting with the car,' she said. 'I shan't keep you long, Douglas.'

Kingsley had not looked for any sign of warmth or sympathy and so he was not surprised when he found none.

Devastated, but not surprised.

Secretly he had always allowed a tiny part of himself to hope that she might yet forgive him, but in truth he knew she never would. In the long months since he had first told Agnes what he intended to do, she had left him in no doubt as to how she felt about it. Probably the hardest moment of his journey to trial had been the night when Agnes had forsaken their marriage bed, leaving in her place an envelope containing nothing but a single white feather.

'Now that you are convicted I shall seek a divorce,' she said.

'Is a conviction sufficient grounds?' Kingsley asked. 'It's not an area of law I am familiar with. I thought that adultery was required.'

'I might have forgiven you that,' Agnes replied, tears suddenly starting in her eyes. 'Adultery is at least a crime committed by a man!'

Kingsley did not reply, for he could think of nothing to say. Intellectually he considered his wife's attitude simply ridiculous, pathetic even. Emotionally it was a hammer blow. There had been a time when Agnes's simplicity and lack of seriousness had charmed him; now that it stood between her and any possible understanding of what he was trying to do, it made his heart ache.

'Yes,' she continued, 'I could have forgiven you much but not this shame, Douglas. Not this shame!'

'Ah yes. The shame.'

Kingsley knew that this and this alone was his crime as far as Agnes, second daughter of Sir Wilfred Beaumont of the Leicestershire Beaumonts, was concerned. Not cowardice. He knew that she did not believe him to be a coward. Part of the charm that had swept her off her feet in the hot and romantic summer of 1910 had been Kingsley's obvious devil-may-care gallantry. He was not a modest man and he had certainly not been so foolish as to keep his three citations a secret from her wide-eyed admiration, and of course his dashing but level-headed handling of the Sydney Street Siege had been much reported, particularly as it made such a contrast with the rather over-excited reaction of Churchill, the young Home Secretary, who had been much criticized for irresponsibly putting himself in the line of fire.

'If only you had been a coward,' Agnes continued, 'then at least I might have understood.'

But it was clear to Kingsley that Agnes would never understand. How could she? How could any wife understand that at a time when women of every type and class were giving up their husbands, brothers and sons to the slaughter, her husband, her handsome, famous husband who was neither coward nor moral zealot, had refused to go? She had found it difficult enough during the period of Kitchener's volunteer army, when men at least chose their fate. Kingsley's position in the police and his relatively senior age of thirty-five had partly excused his absence from the forces, but now that conscription had been introduced and still Kingsley would not do his duty the shame was simply too much.

'You know that I am cut off by all our friends,' Agnes said.

'I imagined that would be the case.'

'Nobody calls. I receive no invitations. Even Queenie has given notice.'

Kingsley's conscience ached for Agnes. To be snubbed by her own cook would have been a hard blow indeed for a proud woman like Agnes, but Queenie's departure was inevitable for she was a woman of fiercely jingoistic disposition. Kingsley recalled her telling him proudly of having camped out all night on a pavement in order to witness the funeral of Edward VII. She claimed that it had only been the lumbago she was sure this adventure had induced which prevented her from doing the same thing for the Coronation of George V.

'In two years' time your son will be six,' Agnes continued. 'What prep school do you imagine will take him?'

'How is George?'

'Why would you care?'

'That is unworthy of you, Ro— Agnes.'

'You do not destroy the lives of people you care about,' Agnes snapped. 'At least we don't do it in Leicestershire.'

Silence fell. For a moment Agnes's manner softened very slightly.

'He misses you. He speaks of you constantly. You're his hero, you know that.'

This heartbreakingly ironic observation provoked further silence, which again was broken by Agnes.

'Fortunately his age protects him from our shame but that will not always be the case.'

Kingsley drew deep breaths and gripped tight the chain that linked the cuffs at his wrists to those at his ankles. Forsaking his son had been the most difficult part of his whole dreadful undertaking. It was almost unbearable for a man to bring disgrace upon his family, a fact of which the Ministry of Information was clearly well aware. Every railway and Underground station carried the current crop of posters designed to play upon the most vulnerable part of a man's conscience. 'Daddy? What did *you* do in the Great War?' – that was the phrase which some brilliant propagandist had coined. It was accompanied by a haunting portrait of a small boy putting the question to his comfortably seated but hollow-eyed and guilt-ridden father while his tiny sister looked on, innocent of Papa's awful shame. It was not a question which Kingsley's son was ever likely to have to ask, for what his daddy had done in the Great War was currently in all the newspapers.

'I'm sure we could all have forgiven you,' Agnes said, 'had you been a genuine pacifist. But this . . . to ruin yourself, to bring down your family for mere matters of dry argument . . .'

'I do not approve of this war,' Kingsley said gently.

'Yes! So you have assured me a thousand times,' Agnes hissed back. 'Do you think I approve of it? Do you think Lady Summerfield, who has two boys dead and another blinded by gas, approves of it? Nanny Wiggen, whose only brother fell in the first week but who still devotes herself to George whilst you skulk in here, does *she* approve of it? Our friends? Our neighbours? Douglas, we have *scullery maids* whose husbands and lovers are making the sacrifice that you are unwilling to make. Do you think a single one of them approves of it?'

'Then they should join me here, for if they were all to do so along with their husbands and lovers then no further sacrifice would be necessary.'

'Yes, and we should all be overrun by bloody Germans! Is that what you want?'

Kingsley had heard Agnes swear only once before in his life and that had been in the agony of labour.

'No,' Kingsley said finally, 'it's not what I want. You know I love my country.'

'But you will not fight to defend it.'

'This war is destroying it. Don't you understand? This war is actually *destroying* the very Britain we are fighting to defend. It will destroy all of Europe. It's a stupid war.'

'It is *not your place to say that*, Douglas.'

'I wish it wasn't but it is. It's everyone's place. I tell you this war will ruin everything. It is Europe gone mad.'

Agnes rose to go but then almost immediately sat down once more.

'I loved you, Douglas.'

'I still love you.'

'I don't want your love. I do not want the love of a man who brings down his family for an idea! Who would sacrifice his wife and son not for his heart but for his head. You think yourself too good for this war, Douglas. It offends you. You set yourself above it. You think it beneath your mighty intellect because it's messy

24

and cruel and utterly terrible, whilst other men die for those very same reasons! Stupid men no doubt in your view . . .'

'You know that I don't think . . .'

'Yes, you do! You think that if only the politicians had as much sense as you they would never have started this business, and if only the people were less foolish they would refuse to see it through. What is that but thinking yourself above it all? *Cleverer* than the rest? As I say, if only you truly were a pacifist, Douglas, one of those awful blaggards one sees speaking at Hyde Park Corner who claim to understand the word of Jesus better than the rest of us and seem to think that the Germans are all sweet and kind and terribly misunderstood . . . But you're too *clever* to be a pacifist. You prefer to *choose* the wars you would fight and oh, isn't it such a shame, this one isn't good enough for you!'

The bitter sarcasm masked Agnes's pain but now the tears came. She pulled a handkerchief from her cuff and blew her nose, then she slipped the wedding ring from her finger and slid it discreetly beneath the grille that separated them. Kingsley stared down at it.

'Take it,' Agnes said quietly.

He picked up the ring and put it on his little finger.

'I still love you, Douglas,' Agnes added, almost whispering now, 'and I always will. I think that is the hardest thing of all.'

Then she rose to her feet once more. This time she would clearly not be sitting down again.

'We shall not speak again, Douglas. You shall hear from me via Mr Phipps at the Downey Street Chambers.'

'Very well,' Kingsley replied.

'When we are divorced, will you allow George to take his grandfather's name? My name?'

'Yes.'

'Thank you. Goodbye.'

Agnes hurried from the room as quickly as her fast-dissolving dignity would allow. For a moment Kingsley was visited by the recollection of her turning and running from him in happier times, in the summer of their courtship. It had been at the Gardens at Kew, which they had visited for a Sunday picnic. He had begged a kiss, a kiss which she most clearly intended to grant him but not before a suitable chase had ensued. He had chased her for fully half an hour before winning his prize. Agnes had never been easily won over in any part of their lives together.

Kingsley watched her disappear from the room, wondering if his heart would break. Logic informed him that of course it would not. The heart was no more than a muscle, a pump which distributed blood about the body; it had nothing whatsoever to do with a man's emotions. But if that was the case, why did it ache so?

4

The Lavender Lamp Club, London

On the same evening that Kingsley was receiving his visitor at Brixton Prison in south London, in Frith Street just off Soho Square a very different kind of reception was under way. Captain Alan Abercrombie, late of the London Regiment (Artists Rifles), was bidding farewell to a few friends at the end of a short period of leave from the Western Front. He was not in uniform – uniforms were banned at the Lavender Lamp, or Bartholomew's Private Hotel to give it its proper title. Soldier patrons were invited to remove their tunics and don one of the beautiful silk dressing gowns that hung from hatstands in the entrance hall of the club.

The Lavender Lamp had got its name from its proprietor's preference for gas lamps, which he liked to shade with lavender-coloured screens imported from Italy.

'Gaslight is so much softer and more romantic,' Mr Bartholomew explained to guests who enquired how it was that such a wealthy establishment had not yet gone electric. 'One cannot make love under electric light, it's so terribly *brutal*. It leaves *nothing* to the imagination, dear. I doubt that *Mr Edison* was a very romantic soul. Although I must concede that it is to his genius that we owe the happy fact that I may still hear the voice of *dear* Oscar, although Oscar himself has long since left us.'

An early wax-tube recording of Oscar Wilde reading 'The Ballad of Reading Gaol' was one of Mr Bartholomew's most treasured possessions. Mr Bartholomew always claimed to have been, in his youth, intimate with the great writer but nobody really believed him.

Inspector Kingsley would certainly have heard of the Lavender Lamp Club, which was an exclusively male establishment. He would have been aware that some of the things that went on in the upstairs rooms by the light of Mr Bartholomew's gas lamps were highly illegal, and had Kingsley been a witness to them he would reluctantly have been forced to make an arrest. But the police never visited the club (with the exception of one or two highly placed officers who went there on a non-professional basis), for this was no low brothel but an exclusive social club where gentlemen of status who shared certain tastes met privately behind heavily barred doors. Nobody got past Mr Bartholomew and his sturdy porters whom Mr Bartholomew did not know personally or who had not been personally recommended to him. At the Lavender Lamp Club patrons were free to drop the constant, grinding pretence that they wore like a cloak in almost every other circumstance of their lives. For a happy hour or two, they could be themselves.

Mr Bartholomew knew Captain Abercrombie, of course – or Viscount Abercrombie as he had been in civilian life – for the young captain was a celebrity, a published poet and decorated soldier, a famous wit and bon viveur and a highly valued patron of the club. As were the friends with whom Abercrombie was sharing magnums of Veuve Clicquot '06 and dishes of cold partridge with water biscuits and chutney, all being consumed in an atmosphere of the greatest hilarity.

'I think I shouldn't mind a bullet very much,' Abercrombie remarked as he busied himself pouring champagne. 'It takes you either straight to heaven or back to Blighty, which surely must be nearly as blissful. Unless of course one was hit in the tool shed.

That I simply couldn't bear. If ever young *Private* Abercrombie was unable to come to *full attention* I think I'd stick my head above the parapet and let Fritz finish me off there and then.'

'Well, don't go waving it about at the front,' one of his companions remarked. 'From what I recall it would make one a devil of a target.'

'It would, my dear, it would,' Abercrombie replied with mock sorrow. '*Fearfully* easy to hit, I'm disgustingly proud to admit. When brother Boche finally throws in the towel I intend to run a flag up it!'

The laughter was loud and the champagne flowed. Abercrombie was not the only soldier whose leave was up that night and the party had a determined wildness to it, as any party might when a number of the guests present are well aware that it may be the last party they ever attend. Guests who in the morning would venture forth to do their duty by, and perhaps give their lives for, a country which despised them.

'I say, do you suppose,' a major in the Blues and Royals in a gown of emerald and turquoise enquired, 'that after the war, what with them talking about giving women the vote and Home Rule to the Paddies and God knows what kind of autonomy to the wogs, they might start going a bit easier on us poor old queens? Eh? Any chance, d'you think?'

'Not a bit of it,' another replied. 'If there's one thing the average Englishman cannot abide it's a sodomite and there's an end to it.'

'Which is most puzzling,' Abercrombie added, 'when one considers how many average Englishmen *are* sodomites, or damn well wish they were.'

This sally provoked more laughter, more bottles were ordered and one or two younger men who were not the viscount's guests but were known to Mr Bartholomew joined the group, and there was dancing and flirting and cuddling in corners and one or two couples began to drift towards the staircase that led to the rooms above.

'Play "Forever England",' a young man called out to the piano player.

But Viscount Abercrombie was not happy with the request.

'Damn it, anything but that! I forbid it!' he said firmly.

The young man looked crestfallen.

'I'm sorry,' he stammered. 'I thought you'd be pleased.'

'My dear sweet boy,' the Viscount replied, in a softer tone, 'have you any idea how often I have to suffer that wretched dirge? It follows me about the place like some jilted lover. Everywhere I go it's a step or two behind me and I have to smile and nod and pretend I'm delighted. A nightmare, dear boy. A bloody nightmare.'

'Oh, I'm sorry, I had no idea. Don't you like being famous then?'

'Well, I like being lionized and admired and petted, of course, but you can't turn it off, you see. I dread to dine out because I know that by the time my soup's arrived there will be a giggling gaggle of moon-faced flappers hovering behind the pastry trolley and I shall have to smile and write my name on their menu cards until my food has gone stone cold.'

Viscount Abercrombie pressed a glass of champagne into the young man's hand and called for cognac and sugar to make a proper drink of it.

'It's worse for me, being a *bachelor*,' he added, taking the man's hand and leading him to a velvet divan. 'All the fat mamas push their revolting skinny little darlings on to me, hoping to make a famous match. Little chance of that, I fear, despite the pleadings of one's *own* mama.'

Abercrombie laid his hand upon the young man's knee.

'So who are you then, young scout,' he enquired, 'apart from a charming boy who has no taste in music but looks delightful in silk?'

'I'm Stamford,' the man replied, his voice shaking with nerves.

'Well, Stamford, what brings you to Bartholomew's Private Hotel?'

'I heard about it from a fellow I fagged for at Harrow . . . We kept in touch and he told me that I'd be . . . welcome here.'

'And he was right.'

'We were . . . "friends" at school.'

'You mean he used you shamelessly, the beast.'

'I didn't mind.'

'I'll bet you didn't, my primrose pal. And here at the Lavender Lamp we can all pretend we're still at school, eh?'

Abercrombie leaned over and kissed Stamford on the cheek. The young man went red and smiled brightly.

'I was so hoping that I'd get a chance to meet you,' he said. 'We're to be in the same regiment, you know.'

'Well, darling, what a coincidence! Perhaps we shall share a puddle together. You can massage my trench feet and I shall rub yours.'

'Is it truly terribly awful? I've spoken to other fellows who say it's pretty grim.'

'And they were honest men, young Stamford, pretty grim is exactly what it is except grimmer.'

They were closer now. Abercrombie had his arm around the shoulders of the younger man and had poured them both another champagne and cognac.

'It's all right for you,' Stamford said, 'you're so terribly brave.'

'Terribly, darling. I *drip* with medals. I'd rather thought of having a couple made into earrings. Wouldn't that look smart on parade?'

'You see, you can even joke about it. I'm sure I never shall. I'm scared that I shall funk it and let everybody down.'

'Tell you what,' Abercrombie said, 'let's not talk about it, eh? Let's pretend that there is no beastly rotten war at all and that the only interest we need take in soldiering is cruising for a compliant Guardsman outside the palace when we fancy something rough.'

Abercrombie kissed Stamford again but this time on the mouth. When their lips separated the young man grinned nervously and took up a little leather manuscript bag that lay on the velvet cushions beside him. Abercrombie's face fell instantly.

'Sweetums, please, please don't say that you have poems in that satchel.'

Now it was the turn of the young man's face to fall.

'I . . . Well, yes,' he stammered. 'I've written one about . . .'

'Your feelings on going off to war?'

'Yes, exactly!' the young man replied, looking pleased again.

'Just like poor old Rupert Brooke, silly Siegfried Sassoon and brave Viscount Abercrombie with his simply thrilling and stirring "Forever England"?'

'Well, I would never class myself in—'

'Are you proud, young Stamford? Do you hope to do your best? Shall you miss the country of your birth but nonetheless are content to go and die for it if needs be?'

The young man was crestfallen.

'You're laughing at me.'

'Well, come on, am I right?'

'That's what I wrote about, yes.'

'What's it called?'

'It's called "England, Home and Beauty".'

'Good. No need to read it then, eh? Put away your satchel, little schoolboy, and dance awhile with me instead.'

'I think you're very cruel,' Stamford said, tears starting in his eyes. 'I'm a poet, just like you. I thought that you might respect that.'

'I'm not a poet, darling. Not any more. Bored with it. Such a yawn, don't you know. Haven't written a thing in months. Not a bean. And by the way, have you any idea how many people come up to me and want me to read their silly stuff? They send it to me in the bloody post! Simply *everyone*'s a poet these days, darling! I think that's why I've chucked it in, just *too, too common for words*.'

'So you won't read my work?'

'No, little poet, I will not.'

'I see.'

Stamford put his satchel aside.

'Can we still be friends?' he enquired. 'Even though you think me contemptible?'

'Darling! Contemptible? Whatever gave you that idea? I think you're sweet and lovely and very, very beautiful and honestly if I were ever again to read *anyone*'s poems I should read yours first and only yours but, you see, I shan't, ever . . . and tonight, well, wouldn't it be more fun to dance?'

The pianist was playing a waltz and Abercrombie took Stamford by the hand.

'Come along, sweetie,' he said. 'I'll be Albert, you be Doris.'

Together they waltzed as best they could in the limited space available in front of Mr Bartholomew's little bar. Two or three other couples shared the floor and they all danced together until, one by one, they drifted towards the staircase.

5

A bath in a brewery

Just as Kingsley was watching Agnes disappear and Viscount Abercrombie and his young friend were dancing a waltz together in the tiny bar of the Lavender Lamp, across the Channel in the small Belgian village of Wytschaete a large group of private soldiers of the 5th Battalion East Lancs were awaiting their first bath in many weeks.

Wytschaete had been a tiny village with few comforts and amenities even before it had been engulfed by the various battles of the Ypres salient. Now, three years into the carnage, there was very little left of it. Its buildings were all ruins, its singled cobbled street no more than a muddy ditch, its church spire had been atomized and what trees and flowers had ever grown there grew no longer. The little village did, however, have one supreme advantage to recommend it to the men of the 5th Battalion of the East Lancashire Regiment. It stood (or had once stood and now lay) a whole two miles from what was currently the Wipers front line. This was why the regiment had selected it as one of the locations in which it attempted to provide brief respites from the line for its exhausted soldiers.

The Wytschaete army bathhouse was located, as was often the case with army bathhouses, in an old brewery. This one had been partially shelled out, but the sappers had done a decent job of putting in a replacement roof and the brewery plumbing within had been efficiently converted to provide a communal shower.

A group of about fifty men stood outside it amongst the shattered walls of the next-door building, their towels flung across the shoulders of their filthy uniforms. They smoked their fags and waited for the fifty men within to complete their wash.

'I can remember when we went in only twelve at a time,' one man grumbled, 'and we had baths then, proper barrels filled with lovely hot water, and five minutes all alone to soak. Not like now where we stand on duckboards and the army pisses all over us. Might as well stay in the trenches and wait for rain.'

'Wouldn't 'ave long to wait,' another man joked. 'Not in bleeding Wipers. I reckon your Belgian civvie is part fish.'

'*And* you kept your own clothes then,' the grumbler insisted. 'They was numbered before you went in and medical orderlies brushed 'em and ironed out the seams for bugs while you were 'aving your tub, and they give you back your own uniform when you come out again.'

'You mean you got the *same* uniform back?' a teenage conscript asked, aghast that such luxuries had ever been possible on the Western Front.

'Yes, you did. That was before Kitchener died, of course. It all changed then, when the old man went down and yer conscription come in. Too many bleeding soldiers to give 'em a decent bath *or* their own tunics.'

The fact that men who were detailed for showers were then expected to take pot luck and grab any supposedly laundered uniform when they emerged on the other side was a source of enormous resentment amongst the private soldiers.

'I always hangs on to my own,' said another. 'There's no less bugs in the one I got on than the ones they hands you back and at least I *knows* my lice. They're family.'

'It's disgusting,' an angry-looking soldier asserted, 'expecting free-born men to put on any filthy old uniform the army hurls at us and then asking us to take pride in our units! Bloody generals should try it themselves and see how proud they feel.'

This soldier's name was Hopkins and he was not a popular man. He was known to be a Communist and a follower of something he called the International, and although most of the men were always happy to vilify the much-despised General Staff they did not hold with Bolshevism.

'Piss off to Russia then and see how you like it' was the usual reply to Hopkins's diatribes.

'You're all mad, bloody mad,' Hopkins shouted to anyone who would listen. 'Look at us. We're sheep, that's what. Sheep to the bleeding slaughter. We can't win this war, not the poor bloody infantry. We just sit around hoping to cop a Blighty so's we can stagger home crippled, grateful not to be dead.'

As usual Hopkins was stirring up more resentment than support.

'What do you mean we can't win? You lying bastard!'

'I mean what I say. We can't win it and *they* can't win either,' Hopkins insisted. 'Not the common man.'

'Who are you calling common?'

'The only people who will win this war, who *are* winning this war, who have already *bloody won* this war are the people who make the shells and guns that working men lob at each other.'

'Ay, that's true enough,' a man named McCroon who was the unit's other Bolshevik chipped in. 'Like the slogan tells you, a bayonet is a weapon with a worker at both ends.'

'And we should lay down ours and refuse to fight,' Hopkins cried. 'That's what we should do, vote with our feet like the Russians are doing. Tell those bloated capitalists we won't die for their profits.'

'Well, why don't you then, you Bolshie bastard?' a voice cried out. 'Piss off so's we don't have to listen to you bangin' on no more.'

'Because they'd bloody shoot me, that's why, you Tory prick! Socialism doesn't want martyrs, it wants solidarity. If one man goes or a handful they just shoot 'em but if we *all* walked off they'd have to think again, wouldn't they? Solidarity forever!'

'Don't you *ever* give it a rest?'

At that point Hopkins was forced to stop because bath time was called and the men took off their uniforms and under-garments and trooped naked into the brewery, where they stood on duckboards as the water was turned on over their heads. Some of them had managed to keep a bit of soap safe for the occasion.

'I had a lovely bar of Pears my missus sent,' a man said. 'Fucking rat ate it. Just fucking *ate* the whole bar. Would you credit it?'

'Won't his shit smell beautiful!'

There was plenty of joking and some singing too, for bare though the arrangements were, to soldiers who had lived in ditches for weeks even this brief communal shower was a treat. The joking and singing was of course filled with the bitter irony which was the Tommies' only real defence against the nightmare in which they had found themselves.

> '*If you want the old battalion,*
> *We know where they are,*
> *We know where they are,*
> *We know where they are.*
> *If you want the old battalion,*
> *We know where they are,*
> *They're hangin' on the old barbed wire.*'

The one drawback of rest periods for soldiers who lived cheek by jowl with death was that they provided unavoidable evidence of the unremitting bloodletting of the line. Men standing in a bath queue or assembling a team for a kick-about could not help but dwell upon who amongst their comrades had been present at the last rest and was not present at the current one.

All too soon the shower was over. Another fifty men were

standing naked outside and it was time to go out once more and find a uniform.

'Lovely, that. Just the ticket,' men shouted as they slipped about on the soapy boards. 'I almost imagined for a moment I was human.'

'Just wait a few months,' less cheerful souls warned. 'Come December when you're out there starkers in the snow and there's ice on the duckboards, you won't be imagining *nothing* then. You'll just be hanging on to your balls to stop them disappearing altogether.'

Outside the bathhouse the men picked with disgust at the louse-ridden khaki threads that awaited them. Suddenly it was all too much for Private Hopkins. He had put on the underwear supplied to him but on inspecting the tunic that was offered he hurled it down in disgust.

'I'm not wearing this!' he shouted. 'I want my own uniform back and I want it clean of lice! I am a *man*, not an animal.'

Some men cheered, others sniggered, many looked on with some sympathy. Hopkins was not popular but there was no denying he had a point. An officer of the Royal Army Medical Corps approached.

'Private, pick up that tunic and put it on,' he said quietly.

'I will not put it on!' Hopkins replied, standing shaking in his underwear.

'Private, I do not wish to have to punish you for I am no fonder of the arrangements in which we must all live than you are. Now pick up that tunic which is the King's uniform and put it on.'

'Let the King wear it then! I want my own back.'

No one was sniggering now. Hopkins was refusing to obey an order, which was a capital offence. The forty-nine other men grew silent, pausing in their efforts to find the best uniform available. The next group of men, who had already entered the shower, knew nothing of the drama going on outside and, as Hopkins and the medical officer stared into each other's eyes, their joking and singing rang across the yard.

'We are Fred Karno's army, the ragtime infantry.
We cannot fight, we cannot shoot, what bleedin' use are we?
And when we get to Berlin we'll hear the Kaiser say,
"Hoch, hoch! Mein Gott, what a bloody rotten lot are the ragtime
  infantry."'

'What is your name, Private?' the officer asked.

'Hopkins, sir.'

'Well, Private Hopkins, I shall give you one last chance to save yourself from a very great deal of trouble. Pick up the tunic you have discarded and put it on.'

Hopkins stared at the officer, his lip quivering. He said nothing. The officer could hesitate no longer: to offer further quarter would be to condone mutiny.

Hopkins was arrested and marched away, still wearing only his underwear.

6

A visit to the prison governor

Kingsley was sentenced to two years' hard labour and dispatched in chains to Wormwood Scrubs. It was there that the violence which he had known awaited him since first he had been arrested finally began in earnest.

'A lot of your old pals live here, Inspector *sir*. Isn't that jolly?' the warder gloated as Kingsley was stripped, searched and disinfected. 'And they's all most anxious to see you again. Oh yes they is. Most anxious. Planning quite a welcome party some of 'em is, I've 'eard, *quite* a welcome.'

Kingsley was kitted out in a filthy and flea-ridden prison uniform and told that he was to be brought before the governor.

In order to get there the warder conducted Kingsley on the longest possible route, parading him in chains across the floor of the main hall of the prison. At the sides of the huge hall numerous steel staircases rose up to connect the grilled walkways which were stacked up, tier after tier, towards the roof. It was a perfect amphitheatre in which a sacrificial beast might be displayed. Those prisoners who were out of their cells stared down and jeered; some spat, and one or two tin mugs were thrown. Some warders even unlocked cell doors to allow inmates with a particular interest a first glimpse of the new house guest.

'Oh yes,' the warder repeated, 'all jolly old pals *most* anxious to reacquaint themselves with you, sir.'

Kingsley had not expected sympathy from any quarter but he was nonetheless taken aback by the venom he encountered. It seemed that the prison staff considered him as loathsome a figure as did the inmates, and with a shiver of fear Kingsley realized that he would not be able to look to them for protection against the vengeance he must now expect from those criminals who had once been his prey.

A voice rang out from the growing din.

'They should have sent you straight to Passchendaele, you malingering bastard!'

Kingsley knew the name of course, who didn't? Just one more obscure village whose existence for centuries had been known only to those who lived there and to the cartographers of the Brussels Bureau of Ordnance, but which now and for evermore was burned into the hearts of mothers, wives, sons and daughters the length and breadth of Britain, Australia, New Zealand and Canada. Just one more French village whose name, against all odds, would be written in stone in a thousand other villages and towns, on sombre monuments throughout Britain, the Empire and the Commonwealth. Passchendaele, that elusive prize which lay just a few hundred blood-soaked yards beyond the Ypres salient.

'I did not send your brothers to Belgium!' Kingsley shouted into the din and was rewarded with a slap across the face from the warder.

'We have a policy of prisoner silence here, *Mr* Kingsley *sir*,' the warder said, although he had to shout himself in order to be heard above the cacophony.

Kingsley's mind reeled, and not as a result of the blow. Could it be that they were blaming *him* for the national tragedy that was decimating their communities? Kingsley was a shrewd judge of human nature and no stranger to the numerous hoops through which a man's conscience will leap in order to apportion blame to anyone other than himself, but he truly had not expected this. It defied all logic. He wanted to scream that he *alone* amongst that crowd was blameless. That he *alone* was attempting in his own small way to stop the war. But Kingsley was fast learning that within the collective madness that gripped the nation any attempt at rational argument was useless. Worse than useless, for clearly it provoked rather than defused strong emotion. Now that he was brought so low he was discovering that his greatest asset, his intellect, was the thing most likely to see him torn apart by the mob.

Finally Kingsley found himself in the governor's office, standing on the threadbare Axminster, waiting while the governor himself sat behind his great oak desk making an elaborate show of ignoring Kingsley and continuing to work through the papers that lay before him.

After a silence which lasted fully five minutes the governor spoke to Kingsley, although he still did not deign actually to look at the prisoner.

'I see that this war "offends your logic",' he said, turning the pages of the court reports in an old copy of the *Daily Telegraph*. He held the pages by a corner, gripping them disdainfully between his thumb and forefinger as if the very newsprint itself might infect him with the bacillus of cowardice and effete intellectualism.

Kingsley was coming to regret having used the word 'logic' to explain his position at his trial. It had been widely reported and seemed to have had a particularly incendiary effect, being held up as clear evidence of the innate snobbery and moral corruption of the pacifist mind. On the other hand, how else could he have answered the damn-fool questions he had been asked? And why should he apologize for being right? There was no other word that so clearly summed up his objections.

'Yes, sir. It offends my logic.'

'You consider patriotism illogical?'

'No, but neither do I think it a sufficient excuse to act in an obscenely illogical manner.'

'In an obscenely illogical manner, SIR!' bellowed the warder who stood behind him, bringing his nightstick down hard on Kingsley's shoulder.

'In an obscenely illogical manner, sir,' Kingsley repeated, through gritted teeth.

'You don't think it a sufficient *excuse?*' the governor parroted in exasperation. 'What excuse does an Englishman need for patriotism? What the hell are you talking about, you bloody prig?'

'Slaughtering millions of men in pursuit of no discernible strategic or political goal seems to me both illogical and obscene, no matter how honourable the sentiments behind it.'

'Our goal is victory.'

'That may well be our goal, sir, but I believe it is a deceptive goal.'

'You believe we cannot win? Is that why you won't fight?'

'I do not think that "winning" is the issue any more. To my mind it is self-evident that any so-called "victory" will be as destructive for the victor as for the vanquished. Every nation involved will be left exhausted and crippled.'

'Good God, man! You speak as if you believe it doesn't matter whether we win or the Germans do!'

'Logically I do not think that it does very much.'

The governor leaped to his feet, shaking with sudden rage. He scrambled around his desk, knocking over his inkwell in his haste. Coming before his prisoner, the governor suddenly raised his fist and Kingsley thought for a moment that he would strike him.

'You swine! You bloody swine, sir! Pacifist is one thing, traitor quite another! You are a bloody traitor.'

Kingsley remained silent, knowing that once more he had provoked far more anger than was necessary. He had had his say and nobody had listened. Now he was in prison. Why keep saying it? Once more he had failed to shut up and was paying the price for his intellect and his ego.

'My son fell at Loos,' the governor spluttered. 'He led his men into the teeth of the German machine guns. Those Hun bastards mowed him down at a distance of two hundred yards! Him and virtually every man that followed him! And you stand there and tell me that it doesn't matter whether the Germans win or we do.'

Kingsley managed to resist the temptation to reply. It was a hard lesson for him to learn and he was learning it much too late. Only days before, even that morning, he would have been unable to resist answering. He would have been unable to stop himself from insisting that the death of the governor's son was *not his fault*. It was the man's own fault. It was the government's fault. It was every person's fault who failed to protest at the insanity of the war. The one person whose fault it was not, was him.

Now the governor was holding the photograph of his son in front of Kingsley's eyes. Kingsley had seen the photograph before. Not that particular picture, not that actual son of that actual father but numerous other near-identical ones. It was the same as ten thousand photographs, a hundred thousand. Millions. You saw them everywhere, on people's mantel shelves, in their lockets, on top of pianos, crowded together on occasional tables and in the black-edged pages of the newspapers. Always the same picture. A young man in a photographer's studio, his expression held stiffly so as not to blur the image as the light entered the shutter. Officers would often be sitting, their gloves and sticks upon their knees; other ranks would stand, perhaps in pairs or groups of three, brothers, cousins. Pals. Sometimes the livelier souls would have placed their caps at a jaunty angle, and occasionally the figure might carry a gun or wear a sword. But despite these small differences, all the photographs were essentially the same. Young men frozen and stiff in life just as they would shortly be frozen and stiff in death.

Beyond the photograph Kingsley could see the governor's face, contorted with fury.

'Does my son's death *offend* you, Mr Kingsley? Does it bother your *intellect*? Do you find its *scale* inappropriate?'

Kingsley did not reply.

'Answer me!' the governor barked. 'Does it offend you?'

'Yes,' Kingsley answered. 'As a matter of fact it does.'

Once more Kingsley thought that the governor would strike him but instead he retreated back behind his desk and began mopping up the ink he had spilt.

'Take him away,' he said, his voice faltering. 'Get the bastard out of my sight.'

7

A *welcome dinner*

While Kingsley was spending the first evening of his sentence at Wormwood Scrubs, Viscount Abercrombie was taking his first dinner with the officers of his new battalion. A formal dinner had been arranged to welcome new arrivals. It had been rather a splendid evening, considering the circumstances under which the banquet had been organized. The battalion cooks, in conjunction with the various officers' servants, had put in a heroic effort, scouting far behind the lines on bicycle and on foot, back beyond the devastation, back to where as if by magic the world was normal again. A world where there were crops in the fields, animals in the pens and fresh butter every morning. It felt so strange to venture outside the land of mud, to cross that blurred line only an acre or so wide which ran north/south through Belgium and France and travel to where the world was in colour once more. To cross in a few short steps from a brown and grey existence to one of vivid greens, reds and yellows. To purchase (at exorbitant prices) good clean wholesome things and carry them back across the thin divide, back into the hell that man had created. But carry them back they did and, with the addition of what their masters could donate from the food parcels they had received, a magnificent dinner was prepared.

There had been two types of soup, roast goose, roast pork, a magnificent salmon and to follow cherry tart and treacle pudding, plus cheese, water biscuits and savouries. Decent wines had been acquired, also port, brandy and Scotch whisky. Viscount Abercrombie's welcome contribution had been an enormous box of very large and very fine Havana cigars.

'I sent my man to Fortnum's for 'em,' Abercrombie explained loudly as he sent them round with the port. 'I said I want 'em big as Zeppelins! Big as a Hun hausfrau's howitzers!'

Abercrombie was different now to how he had been at the Lavender Lamp Club. A little louder and a little coarser. He was wearing his mask.

The dinner had taken place in a ruined school hall which had been requisitioned as the officers' mess. Many candles had been lit and a portion of the regimental silver had somehow been brought out of storage in order that the loyal toast might be made in fine silver-plate goblets instead of the usual tin mugs. The candlelight twinkled on the shiny service as every man stood and saluted the King Emperor.

Prior to the loyal toast the colonel had made a hearty speech of welcome to those officers who had joined the battalion since last it had campaigned.

'Some of you fellows are still wet behind the ears and some of you are old lags come to us from disbanded formations elsewhere on the line,' he said. 'Either way you are East Lancs now and I hope you're as proud to be with us as we are to have you!'

There was much cheering at this, in which Abercrombie joined enthusiastically. Opposite him at the table, across a centrepiece artfully contrived from paper flowers arranged in an upturned German helmet, sat Stamford, the young subaltern whom Abercrombie had befriended at the Lavender Club. Stamford was not cheering. Looking rather sad and serious, he was trying to attract Abercrombie's eye, as he had been doing all evening with little success.

'Now, as you all know,' the colonel continued, 'we don't hold

47

with snobbery in this battalion. Officer and man, we're all in this together. However, I would like to offer a special welcome to one particular officer. You have all heard of Viscount Abercrombie, of course. Something of a hero at the Somme, but then we've got a fair few of that sort amongst us and we certainly don't crow about it, eh? A medal or two's all very fine until you see how many those damn Staff wallahs have on *their* chests and realize it's all rot anyway!'

Hardly surprisingly, there was renewed cheering at this and some banging of spoons, over which the colonel was forced to appeal for silence.

'What we've never had amongst us before, however, is a published poet, of all the damn things, and a famous one to boot. Now I have to say that as a rule I don't hold much with poetry. To be quite frank, I think pretty much everything written along those lines since Tennyson has been absolute bilge. Complete tommyrot. However, I don't mind telling you that I make an exception for the work of our brother officer here. "Forever England" really moved me. I remember when I first heard it, it brought tears to my eyes.'

'But then again, sir,' Abercrombie interjected boldly, 'so does mustard gas!'

There was huge laughter at this quip, in which the colonel was happy to join.

'Damn right, Captain. Damn right. And most poetry *is* bloody gas, if you ask me. Well anyway,' the colonel continued, 'there you are. Well done and all that, and since by reputation you fight even better than you write, let me say, Abercrombie, that we are proud and excited to have you amongst us. What's more, from the chitter-chatter I've heard from various WAACs, lady drivers and nurses about the place, and God's blood, *can't* they chatter!' – more laughter at this, of course – '*they're* pretty proud and excited to have you amongst us too! Eh? Eh? Lucky dog, Abercrombie! Why, even my own damn wife has written telling me to be sure to get you to sign a copy of your damn book!'

'Happy to oblige her ladyship, sir!' Abercrombie said, making a small bow from his seat. There was still more laughter at this and a voice called out that fellows should be careful not to let Abercrombie near their sweethearts, for he would no doubt steal them away.

After this, the colonel called for silence and his expression became more serious.

'Now I know, Abercrombie,' he said, 'that like many other fellows around this table you have come to us because your previous mob was pretty badly shot up and had to be disbanded after the last big show. Most of the Pals' outfits have gone that way and most of us have seen many chums and fine comrades go with them.'

Abercrombie nodded. Perhaps it was the memory of his departed comrades that caused his hand to shake a little and upset a glass, which fortunately he had only that minute drained to the dregs.

'But the sad demise of the London Regiment (Artists Rifles),' the colonel said, 'has been the 5th Battalion East Lancs' gain. So good, that's it. Well done you. Honoured to serve with you and well done all.'

Somebody began to beat the table at this and there was prolonged applause, with all eyes centred on Abercrombie, who stared at his untouched cheese plate and smiled shyly as if to say that he wished they would not make such a fuss.

When the applause had finally subsided it was possible for the colonel to finish his speech, which was a surprise to his audience who had thought he'd already finished it.

'Now I don't think it's any secret that things are hotting up around here,' he said. 'Brigade has been brought up to strength and you've all seen the amount of ordnance that those damned noisy fellows in the Royal Artillery seem to be stockpiling. Well, if there is to be another show soon, and I don't think I'm giving away any intelligence secrets when I tell you that it seems pretty ruddy likely, I could not wish to go forward with a finer body of men. Enjoy yourselves tonight, for tomorrow we are back in the line. Gentlemen, the King.'

The company rose to their feet and raised their glasses to George V, and soon afterwards the party began to break up. It had been a wet summer and most of the officers present had not slept in a dry bed for weeks, so they were naturally anxious to make the most of their last night in billets, even though for the most part this small luxury represented little more than a straw mattress on the floor of a ruined cottage.

Abercrombie, who had only that day arrived from England and was hence not so anxious to sleep, went outside to smoke a final cigar in what had once been the village street. It was there that Stamford was finally able to speak to him.

'Hello, Alan,' he said.

'Don't call me Alan, Lieutenant. My name is Captain Abercrombie.'

'Of course. I'm sorry, Captain. It's just that . . . Well, I tried to speak to you at Victoria and then on the boat over and in all those endless trains today. It feels rather as if you're ignoring me.'

'Don't be ridiculous. I don't ignore brother officers. If you wish to speak to me you only have to present yourself.'

'I've tried to catch your eye but . . .'

'Catch my eye! Catch my eye, man!' Abercrombie barked. 'What are you, a chorus girl? This is the army, not the bloody hippodrome. If you wish to communicate with me, come to attention, state your name and explain your business.'

The moment this conversation had begun, Abercrombie had started walking away from the mess and towards the edge of the village. He had set off at a considerable pace, causing the younger man to scurry after him. The little hamlet was so small that the two of them were already on the outskirts.

'You seem so different,' Stamford pleaded as they passed the last of the houses, outside of which a couple of officers were lounging in the damp air, smoking their pipes. 'I thought that we were friends.'

Abercrombie did not answer immediately. Instead he waved with exaggerated good cheer at the pipe-smoking men.

'Just off to show this young 'un a real firework display,' he called out. 'Sounds to me as if the guns are going to put on quite a show tonight.'

'Every night is Guy Fawkes night, eh?' one of the officers replied.

They laughed together as Abercrombie, followed by Stamford, disappeared into the darkness. When Abercrombie judged that he was sufficiently clear of the last ruined dwelling not to be over-heard he turned furiously on his pursuer.

'Now listen to me, you bloody little fool! I am *not* your friend. I am a senior officer, do you understand? I do not *know* you . . .'

'But we—'

'We shared a drink together,' Abercrombie interjected firmly. 'We shared a drink together with other officers on the night before we departed. We drank in the bar of the hotel in which we were both staying. *That*'s what we did. As prospective members of the same battalion it would have been ridiculous not to. However, that does not mean that you can presume an in-appropriate familiarity with your superior. Is that clear?'

'Inappropriate!'

'And it certainly does not give you licence to go about the place making moony eyes at me like some silly flapper.'

'Captain Abercrombie, two nights ago you buggered me from midnight till dawn . . .'

Abercrombie slapped Stamford across the face.

'Now you listen to me!'

A sudden explosion of ordnance above them lit up both their faces. Abercrombie's was both furious and fearful, while Stamford's had tears streaming down it.

'Whatever may or may not have happened in London *remains* in London. Do you understand? People are put in prison with hard labour for doing what you are suggesting we did. If even a rumour of it is heard in the wrong circles a man may expect to be ruined.'

51

'I would never say anything, I swear . . .'

'Your bloody face is an open book, man! Every inch of you *screams* pansy and you look at me as if you were in love.'

'I am in love!'

'Don't be absurd. You met me three days ago.'

'I loved you before I met you.'

'Listen to me, Stamford.' Abercrombie's tone softened, but not by much. 'Out here, you are a very junior subaltern and I am an experienced captain and something of a lion. It is not possible for us to be friends in anything other than a comradely fashion which is above all appropriate to our ranks.'

'But . . . I love you, Alan. And what's more, I'm scared. I need help, I'm not brave like you . . .'

'I am not brave! I have told you that!'

'But your poetry!'

'I've told you I don't write poetry. Not any more.' Abercrombie turned away. 'Please remember what I've said, Lieutenant. Good night.'

Abercrombie began to walk back towards the village, leaving Stamford to weep alone.

In consideration of his rank and aristocratic status the viscount had been given a room of his own in what had once been the house of the village priest, a house that had miraculously remained standing whilst the adjoining church had been reduced to rubble. Abercrombie lit the oil lamp which his new servant had thoughtfully procured for him and, taking out paper, pen and ink from a small leather music case, he began to write a letter. A letter to the mother of a fallen comrade, with whom he had been in correspondence ever since the death of her son. In his letters Abercrombie told her how cheerful and how wise her boy had been, how brave he was and what an inspiration to his men. A *golden boy* in fact, and that was how he must always be remembered, as a *golden boy* who shone as brightly as the sun and shed a happy light on all who knew him and on Abercrombie most of all. In reply the boy's mother would tell Abercrombie about the equally sunlit childhood her son had spent, the happiness he had brought to his parents and to all who knew him. What promise he had shown and how big and bold had been his dreams. She told him also how often the boy had mentioned Abercrombie in his letters to her, and how much comfort she and her husband took from the knowledge that the two friends had been together when their son had died.

Abercrombie unscrewed the lid on his ink jar and filled his fountain pen. A beautiful pen on which were inscribed the words 'Love always'.

Dear Mrs Merivale, he wrote.

But try as he might, Abercrombie could write no more and it was tears instead of ink that marked the page that lay before him. What more could he say? He had told this grieving mother everything he could about her boy and told it many times. Except for one thing. The only thing that mattered and the one thing he could never say. That he had loved her son as dearly as she had loved him and that his love had been returned in equal measure. That never before in all the long history of love had two people loved each other as he and her son had loved. That he and her son had sworn to be together until death did them part and that when death did part them, when Abercrombie cradled her son's body in his arms for the final time, Abercrombie had died also. Died inside. Never, he believed, to love or even to *feel* again.

Finally Abercrombie gave up his efforts to write to the mother of the man whom he had adored. He screwed the tear-stained sheet of paper into a ball and threw it to the floor. Then, having taken a moment to collect himself, he took a fresh sheet of paper from his little leather case and began a second, very different letter.

8

Cold shoulders and a cold supper

The supper that Kingsley endured on his first evening in prison was in stark contrast to the friendly welcome which Captain Abercrombie had enjoyed. Whereas on his first public exposure to the wider prison population he had provoked a cacophony of derision, now on entering the mess hall shortly after leaving the governor's office he was met with a sullen silence. Every head seemed to turn as he made his way into the room. Every eye seemed to follow him as he shuffled towards the vats from which the evening stew was being served.

'What do you want?' the prisoner who had the task of serving the food enquired.

'My meal,' Kingsley replied.

'Warder!' the prisoner shouted. 'Warder, here, please, sir, if you would, sir, please.'

A uniformed warder approached the bench on which the stew urns stood.

'What's to do here then, Sparks?'

'I don't see as how I should have to serve a coward, sir.'

'I know how you feel, Sparks, but the man's got to eat.'

'He's a traitor, sir. I won't serve him, sir. Stick me on the Mill if you will, sir, I don't care.'

The warder turned and addressed the assembled hall.

'Will any man serve this prisoner his stew?'

Of all the hundreds of men sitting on the benches at the long thin tables not a single one spoke. Kingsley was utterly alone, the object of such contempt and derision as he would not have thought possible. A copper and a coward. In the minds of the population of Wormwood Scrubs in the late summer of 1917 a man did not sink any lower than that.

'Perhaps I might be allowed to serve myself?' Kingsley suggested quietly.

'And perhaps you might be allowed to shut your fucking face until I ask you to open it.'

'You have a statutory obligation to feed me.'

The warder's fist smashed into Kingsley's mouth.

'Try eating with no teeth in your head,' he shouted as Kingsley staggered but managed to remain upright. 'Prison rules states prisoners *be served*! Not serve themselves! If I lets you get hold of that ladle who knows what mischief you'll make of it! Why, you might use it as a weapon or else a spade to tunnel out with. A fellow as clever as you, *Inspector*, could probably turn it into a flying machine.'

'You cannot let me starve.'

Once more the fist flew out and this time Kingsley was knocked properly to the ground.

'I – said – shut – your – fucking FACE,' the warder snarled. 'We has food provided, that's our duty, that's our job. We has food aplenty but you can't serve it. No you can't, them's the rules. And if you can't serve it and no man'll serve you, well, then you might very well starve and personally I don't know as how there's a way around it.'

A loud, deep voice rang out from across the room.

'Ah'll serve yon prisoner his vittles, sir.'

The man spoke with the unmistakable accent of the Clyde.

Staggering to his feet, Kingsley peered across the hall to where he saw a man stand up. A huge man with quite the most

55

startlingly orange hair he had ever seen. Kingsley recognized him instantly, for this man had once been almost as significant a press hate figure as were the leaders of the Irish Republicans. 'Red' Sean McAlistair, regional secretary of the dockworkers' union, a man whose influence in the vast Port of London probably exceeded that of the chairmen of the P&O and White Star lines combined.

McAlistair had been seated at the far end of the dining hall amongst about a dozen serious-looking men. They were slightly separate from the rest, and the chairs immediately beside them were unoccupied: clearly these people, like Kingsley himself, were set apart. Socialists and trades unionists, strikers imprisoned by a society that was taking an increasingly dim view of those it considered to be putting class war before Great War.

McAlistair began to cross the hall and prisoners stood aside to let him through. His vast bulk was his protection, that and the group of silent men he had been sitting with.

Arriving before the bench upon which the vats of food stood, McAlistair held out his enormous hand.

'May Ah trouble you for the ladle, Warder.'

'You want to give comfort to a coward and a traitor?'

'Currently Ah see only a fellow soul in distress, Warder.'

With much ill grace the warder handed the ladle to McAlistair, who, taking up a tin bowl, served Kingsley with stew and placed a hunk of bread on top of it.

'There ye go now, wee policeman. Here's your supper.'

'Thank you.'

McAlistair turned to go and Kingsley spoke after him.

'May I join you at your table, sir?'

McAlistair stopped and turned, staring at Kingsley for a moment.

'No y'fuckin' can't, ye disgusting little English flatfoot.'

His words hit Kingsley harder than the warder's fist had done.

'Ah'll see y'gets your food just now because it's yer right and *unlike you*, Inspector, Ahm a man who's powerful bothered about a fellah's rights.'

'Please, I—'

'But do Ah look like the sort o' man who would break his bread with a fellah who thinks himself too good t'fight alongside the coupla' million British working men currently wearing the King's colours?'

The hall was still silent. All eyes remained upon Kingsley, witness to his humiliation.

'Ye wore a uniform o' His Majesty y'sel' did ye no, Mr Kingsley? Police blue so it was. Ye wore it at y'trial. Ah saw it in the *Illustrated London News*, a warder showed me so he did. A police inspector, stood in the dock for reasons of his conscience. An' Ah got t'thinkin' how a man like you whose conscience never troubled him in all the years o'police brutality agin the common man had suddenly found one now? All the years o' strike-breaking and spying, the mounted thugs on their big horses sent agin starving miners. How in all those years of lockouts when coppers in that same blue uniform o'yours stood at factory gates to stop union men from going to their work, all those years o' great platoons o'men in blue protecting scabs brought in from miles away by absent bosses to break the local union. How in all those years, Mr Kingsley, o' belonging t' an organization whose principal reason for existence is not to uphold justice but to protect the *properties* of the rich who leech upon the labour of the common man who has no *property* to protect. How is it that your conscience never troubled ye then? The "logic" o' killing soldiers *offends* you, it seems, but the logic o' killing working men, miners, dockers, weavers, printers and the like, that appeals to ye no doubt.'

McAlistair spoke in a loud, commanding manner, for he was used to addressing crowds at dockside wharves, factory gates and pitheads. He knew how to hold an audience and so, although the ranks of prisoners were again eating their stew, they remained silent and listened.

'I have never killed a working man,' Kingsley replied, 'save those I have caused to be hung. And I do not believe that the police have killed above a handful.'

'Oh, Ah think you'll find it's more than that, Inspector. And that's not including them as die in misery and need for want o' the rights that are denied them. So no, I shan't sit with ye, sir. I wouldn't piss in your mouth if your tongue was on fire. Good day.'

The big red-headed man turned on his heel and went back to his table, where his companions quietly applauded.

Kingsley took his stew and sat in a vacant space, causing those nearby instantly to gather up their bowls and move away. Alone with his thoughts, he knew that the big trades unionist had had a point: Kingsley had lived all his life in a society in which there were any number of *logical* contradictions. Britain's power over the populations of its Empire. Capital's power over labour. Men's power over women. Kingsley had spent his life sworn to protect so much that was unjust, immoral, illogical, why was this war so different? Once more Kingsley could only give the answer of pro- portion, of scale. He could accept the *exploitation* of a generation whilst he could not accept its murder.

Of course, for Kingsley all such considerations had become entirely academic. He was lost to the world where his thoughts and opinions mattered and from this point on the only issue that would occupy his mind was survival.

9

Old acquaintances

After his lonely supper Kingsley was taken to a cell. A cell he was to share with three other men.

The men had been hand-picked by a senior warder, a man named Jenkins whom Kingsley had met before.

'Remember me, Mr Kingsley?'

Kingsley peered at him through the gathering gloom.

'Ah,' he said with sinking heart, 'Sergeant Jenkins.'

'Not sergeant any more, Mr Kingsley. It's Warder Jenkins now, *Senior Warder* Jenkins.'

'Congratulations, Senior Warder Jenkins. You have clearly thrived in your new profession.'

'Yes. It seems that not everybody thinks themselves too good to work with me.'

'I did not think myself too good to work with you. I merely thought that your skills were not best suited to the work of criminal investigation.'

'Oh, is that so? Well, we're not so bloody high and mighty and damn yer eyes now, are we, *Inspector*?'

Kingsley did not recall being high and mighty with the man or indeed damn yer eyes, he could only remember being . . . logical. He had found himself burdened with a detective sergeant whom he considered a slow, dim-witted brute. He had therefore had the man removed from his department and recommended that he be found work of a more menial nature. It did not surprise him to learn that the man had ended up in the Prison Service.

'I was finished in the police after you wrote me up, Kingsley. They recommended that I lose my stripes.'

'I am sorry to hear it.'

'You weren't then, Inspector, but I'll bet you are now. Oh yes, I'll bet you are now. And you're going to get a lot sorrier, mark my words. Strike off the prisoner's chains,' Jenkins ordered. 'Unlock the cell.'

The chains were removed from Kingsley but he took little relief from it as the cell door opened.

The three men with whom Kingsley was expected to co-exist grinned with evil intent as he entered the tiny room. What teeth they had between them shone and the five good eyes sparkled in the smoky light of the warder's paraffin lamp. Electricity had yet to come to this particularly dark corner of Wormwood Scrubs.

'Hello, Inspector. Remember me?' said the first shadowy figure.

Remember me? It was a question which Kingsley had suddenly come to dread.

'Yes, I remember you. I remember all of you,' Kingsley answered.

It was only now that the full horror of his situation truly dawned upon Kingsley. Up until this point there had been so much else to think about. The loss of his family, his job, his world. The endless efforts to explain himself. The white feathers in the streets, on his pillow. Up until this point his life and the protest with which he had ruined it had mattered. His existence had had some purpose.

Not any more.

Now, he had no life. The man he had been only the day before had effectively ceased to exist. What existed in its place was a cornered human animal. Bare-toothed prey caught in the steel jaws of the most vicious of traps. Kingsley had been cast, alone and utterly defenceless, amongst his most bitter enemies. He had come to live with the men whose lives he had destroyed. Surely the devil himself could not have designed a worse predicament, and yet Kingsley knew that he had designed it for himself.

'Good evening, gentlemen,' Kingsley said, inwardly computing what, if any, defence he might put up against these men as the first one stepped forward. 'Good evening, Mr Cartwright.'

Cartwright had murdered his wife and Kingsley had nearly got him hanged for it. He would have done so had Cartwright not contrived also to murder his daughter, who had been the only witness to the crime.

'You owe me fifteen years, Kingsley,' Cartwright snarled.

'Mr Cartwright, you and I both know,' Kingsley replied, 'that by rights you should have hung.'

'You can't look down on me, you yellow-bellied bastard,' Cartwright sneered. 'Not now. I'd rather be a killer than a coward.'

'It is quite possible to be both, Mr Cartwright, and you are.'

It was not that Kingsley was without fear; he was as horrified at his immediate prospects as any man might be. It was only that even in these desperate straits his logical instincts prevailed. He *knew* that there was no profit to be had in pleading for mercy and experience had taught him that any strength, even if it is only a refusal to be cowed, can be of advantage in a fight. Therefore he resolved to make a show of courage and contempt. He was utterly alone in his fight for life: once he gave up on himself there truly was no hope left for him.

The other two men, a burglar and a pimp, stepped forward.

'Evening, Inspector,' they said. 'Remember us?'

Kingsley braced himself. Placing his back against the door he dropped to a fighting stance with his fists raised and his knees bent. He was tall and fit and an excellent boxer – he had won a Blue at Cambridge – but his three antagonists were strong also. For all Kingsley's skill, might prevailed and he hit the floor in less than a minute. He curled up in the foetal position as the blows rained down upon him until, coughing on his own blood, he lost consciousness.

10

Field Punishment No. 1

On the morning after the welcome dinner in the officers' mess, Captain Abercrombie faced the first duty of his new command. It was his unpleasant task to preside over a punishment detail involving a man from his section.

A gun limber had been brought to what had once been the Wytschaete village square and now served as an improvised parade ground for the 5th Battalion. A small party stood before it: Captain Abercrombie, four officers of the Military Police and the prisoner Hopkins, who was cuffed at the wrists.

A cold drizzle was falling and it seemed that what summer there had been in Flanders that year was already over. Abercrombie stepped up to address the prisoner.

'I do not know you, Private Hopkins,' he said, 'and I had not taken up my post when the offence of which you have been found guilty was committed. I therefore take no pleasure in what is now required of me. However, the army code leaves me no choice.'

Hopkins attempted to hold his head up and stare Abercrombie down but his whole body was shaking with fear.

'We all have a choice,' he mumbled. 'Don't assuage your conscience with me.'

If Abercrombie had heard the man, he ignored his comment.

'You have been found guilty of disobeying a direct order.'

'I didn't refuse to fight! I refused to put on a lice-ridden jacket! Would you have put it on, *Viscount*?'

'You disobeyed an order. Repeatedly. You could by rights have been shot. Do you have anything to say?'

'Yes.'

'Speak then.'

'Your poetry's shit, Captain. "Forever England"? What a lot of lying shit. I've heard *boys* quote it, Captain. Sixteen-year-old *boys* parroting that shit as they marched off to their deaths. Forever England? Forever shit. Shit shit shit.'

Abercrombie stood for a moment as if he had been struck. The colour drained from his face. It seemed to the policemen watching that the captain had to make some effort to collect himself.

'Is that all, Private?' he asked finally.

'Yes, and more than enough.'

'Field Punishment Number One!'

Two of the military policemen removed Hopkins's handcuffs and dragged him towards the gun limber. Then they lashed him across one of its wheels, spreading his limbs wide like the male figure in Da Vinci's famous sketch, a copy of which Abercrombie had had pinned upon his wall at school.

Hopkins hung upon the wheel all day.

11

An uncomfortable convalescence

Anyone who imagined that Kingsley had refused to be conscripted in order to avoid danger and pain would have been quickly disillusioned had they attended the medical room of Wormwood Scrubs in the early hours of the first night of his sentence. There he lay upon a hard wooden bench, unconscious and entirely caked in blood, while the prison doctor, woozy and boozy after being called from a fine supper, attempted to ascertain whether Kingsley's back had been broken.

As it turned out, no permanent damage had been done although the victim had been badly beaten. He regained consciousness in time to hear something of the doctor's report. Kingsley could smell the brandy and cigars on the doctor's breath as the medical man stood over him.

'There has been considerable bruising and a few cracked ribs. Clearly the wretch has also been quite severely concussed, which means I shall be required to keep him here for further observation,' the doctor said.

'How long?' Kingsley heard the voice of Jenkins enquire.

'A day or two for certain, concussions can be dangerous things. I've seen a man get up and walk out as happy as a sandboy and an hour later – bang. Seizure. Dead.'

'It would be no great loss. Send him back to his cell immediately.'

'No thank'ee, Mr Jenkins. No thank'ee indeed. I like a quiet life and that means doing things by the book. By the book, sir! The only rule for them as likes a quiet life. I don't mind 'em dying. Oh no, happy with that, sir. Happy to be rid of 'em and good riddance say I. But if they are to die then they must die by the book. By the book, I say! Which in the case of concussions means they must have been appropriately *observed*. If they die *during* appropriate observation then all well and good. If they die *after* appropriate observation none will be happier than I. What I can*not* have is them dying in the *absence* of appropriate observation, for then they would not have died by the book and I, sir, should not wish to answer for that. The prisoner stays here, Mr Jenkins, until such time as he has been sufficiently *observed*.'

The senior warder grunted in a resentful manner.

'It's a fine thing indeed that a fellow like this lies here at his ease while the boys he's betrayed sleep and die in mud.'

'I grant you that is so,' said the doctor, his full belly straining his waistcoat, rich food and wine seeping from his every pore, 'but the book is not concerned with what is just or right, it is concerned with what is *in it*. That is, what is legal and prescribed. And in this medical room, sir, the book is law.'

'Well, perhaps it's for the best,' Jenkins conceded. 'Could be questions asked if he didn't make it through his first twenty-four hours in our care.'

'In *your* care, sir. The prisoner was brought to me in this state and that fact will be duly noted, sir. In the book.'

Even through his swollen eyelids Kingsley could see that Jenkins was a little troubled. Every nerve in Kingsley's body was testimony to the savagery of the beating that he had endured. He was clearly fortunate to be alive. A senior warder would not wish to be held responsible for his death, for Kingsley was a high-profile prisoner. He might have been disgraced but he was still the son-in-law of the Commissioner of the London Police. Kingsley judged that for the time being he was relatively safe. Safe at least from being murdered, for no matter that he was now persona non grata, neither his family nor the authorities would be able to ignore his sudden death. Later on, things would change, the memory of his disgrace would fade, he would eventually pass from people's minds . . . and then, well, if it were announced that he had fallen from some high walkway while taking exercise, who would question the passing of a coward and a traitor?

'Take your time. Let him have a week,' Jenkins concluded. 'Patch him up a bit. Then we'll hand him over to some other "old pals" of his.'

'Yes, well, Mr Jenkins,' the doctor complained, 'I would be obliged to you if you could arrange to have him assaulted at a slightly more social hour next time. I do not appreciate being called from the due conclusion of my vittles. It impairs digestion and is most inhibiting to the maintenance of properly regulated bowels.'

The warder and the doctor then departed, leaving Kingsley alone with his thoughts. And grim thoughts they were. It was clear to him that his already desperate situation was only going to get worse and that it could lead to only one conclusion. He was going to die, not immediately but quite soon. Unless of course he could find a way out.

'So would yiz loik a shot o' morphine, moi foin pacifist friend?'

Kingsley could not turn his head to look but he presumed that this was the voice of a medical orderly.

'Oi could see yiz was conscious while those two bastards was gabbing on,' the voice continued. 'Jesus wept, yiz mosst be in a terrible load o' pain. Oi can give yiz a bit o' relief for that easily enough.'

It was the first offer of kindness Kingsley had received for some time. It made him feel weak and emotional, as if he wanted to cry, something that he had not done since he was a child. Not even when he found the white feather on his pillow. Not even when he had returned home to find that his son had been removed from his corrupting presence. As the tears seeped between his swollen eyelids, causing the cuts to sting with the salt, Kingsley wondered whether he was crying for those things now.

'Thank you,' he whispered through swollen, blood-clotted lips, wincing in pain as the movement caused the splits in them to open up and bleed afresh.

'You're welcome.'

'Not many in here are concerned about my comfort.'

'Not many at all.'

'But you are.'

'Well. All God's creatures, eh?'

'Why do you not despise me?'

'Woi would Oi dispoice a man whom de King sees fit t'incarcerate?'

An Irishman. And a Republican, of course.

'Any fockin' fellah dat annoys his precious Imperial fockin' Majesty is foin boi miself. Now d'you want dis shot o' morphine or don't ye?'

Strange to be finding comfort from such a source. How many times had Kingsley heard that same soft accent hurling hatred and abuse at him? Police relations with the Irish in London were almost uniformly hostile, particularly since the Easter Rising of the previous year, and it was an unfamiliar thing indeed for him to find himself on the receiving end of Irish good humour.

'No thank you,' he said. 'But thank you all the same.'

Kingsley did not want morphine. No matter what pain he was in he knew that above all he must keep his wits about him; they were literally all he had left. Besides which, years spent trying to police the bestial horrors in the labyrinths between the Strand and New Oxford Street had given Kingsley a morbid horror of drug addiction.

'Suit y'self,' said the orderly. 'Oi hope yiz won't mind if Oi do.'

Moments later Kingsley made out the tiny sound of a syringe being depressed, followed by an audible sigh.

'Oh, very noice. Very noice indeed,' said the orderly, his voice now slightly abstracted, 'and all accounted for boi de book. Oi shall tell de doctor dat yiz had your shot as properly prescribed, so Oi's hope yiz won't be goin' an' contradictin' us.'

'No, I shan't.'

'Good.'

'Perhaps you could give me a little water?'

After the orderly had placed a cup to his damaged lips and then departed to enjoy his dreaming, Kingsley once more fell to considering his position and what if anything he might do about it.

First of all he considered escape.

People had got out of Wormwood Scrubs before and Kingsley flattered himself that his mind and eye were sharper than most. But to escape he would need all his strength and agility. Currently, beaten black and blue as he was, he had neither and was unlikely to recover them, for once he was released from the sickroom and back in the bosom of the prison population Jenkins had already made it clear that he would be attacked once more and then attacked again.

With the option of escape only the most distant possibility, Kingsley tried to think along other lines.

Surely he could not be the only pariah in the building? Reason told him that there were others like him who were outside the normal run of prisoners. Not conscientious objectors, he knew that. His had been a special case: those other objectors who had been dealt with by military tribunals had, if imprisoned, been sent to far less brutal establishments than Wormwood Scrubs. Only Kingsley had been treated as a common criminal.

But were there others with whom it would be possible to form an alliance? Could he seek out those who were also threatened and form a non-aggression pact in which each would leap to the defence of the other if attacked? Even in the bleakness of his pain Kingsley could not help but reflect that it had been arrangements such as these that had brought all the dominoes of Europe crashing down together and created the disaster which was now consuming them. For a little while his thoughts drifted into a crazy vision in which the entire prison population was involved in a giant punch-up in the name of collective security. Chairs were smashed, pies thrown and suddenly the doors burst open and the room was filled with grotesquely gurning American constables hitting each other with comically ineffective truncheons. Like most people, Kingsley enjoyed visiting the new picture palaces and in happier days he and his little son had laughed along with everyone else at the antics of Mack Sennett's Keystone Kops. Now, in his delirium, they provided a brief diversion from his current misery. When clarity returned once more, he mused that even if there were others like him in the prison, existing in fear on the fringes of the community, of what use would they be to him? Other persecuted individuals would be as defenceless as he and impossible to organize. Besides, the idea of seeking out the child-killers, rapists and other pariahs in an attempt to enlist their support in a defensive alliance seemed as obnoxious as it was hopeless.

Kingsley needed to join a group. An established band within the prison that had the power to act collectively in mutual self-interest. But who? He had already discovered that the Socialists would have nothing to do with an ex-policeman. Were there any others amongst whom he could cast his lot?

The orderly returned.

'Oi heard yis laughin', mate. Oi do tink dat's hoily fockin' commendable.'

That accent once again. The accent of the outsider, the pariah. an Irishman in England knew all about what it felt like to be despised.

'I was dreaming about the Keystone Kops,' Kingsley whispered.

'Ah yes. Hoily amusin', Oi must say. Although if truth be tol' Oi don't foind watching policemen of any description a source of entertainment.'

The orderly helped Kingsley to some more water, his hand less steady now as the morphine which he had injected worked its way through his system.

70

'Excuse me,' Kingsley said when he had drunk his fill, 'but would you by any chance know any Fenians within the prison?'

The orderly set down the cup. Addled though his brain might be, 'Fenian' was not a word that he could ignore.

'Does Oi know any of de Brotherhood?'

'Yes.'

'And woi would yiz be askin' me that?'

'Because, like me, they are incarcerated not for greed but for a principle.'

'And you'd be an Oirish Nationalist then, would yiz?'

'I don't pretend that we are incarcerated for the *same* principles but they are principles nonetheless.' Struggling to ignore the pain from his bruised and battered flesh, Kingsley attempted to concentrate his thoughts. 'I wish to appeal to them for protection.'

'And woi would de IRB give a fock about helping you, moi friend?'

'I have told you. I am a fellow idealist.'

'Doze are hard men t'be messin' wit, Inspector.'

It was a desperate idea and Kingsley knew it, the longest of possible long shots. If English trades unionists despised an ex-policeman how much more so would Irish nationalists? They certainly would not be inclined to help him out of pity. Was it possible that he could convince them he had something to offer? Names? Intelligence? Even a short period under their protection might give him time to recover and search out some means of escape. And if they turned on him, what did it matter? He was a condemned man anyway and at least the IRB were patriots, soldiers in their own way. Prisoners not of greed but of conscience. Better to die at their hands than be kicked to death by pimps and thieves. Kingsley felt confident that the IRB would at least dispatch him cleanly.

'Oi hope yiz knows what yiz is doin',' the orderly added.

'Not really, no,' Kingsley replied. 'But in my current position I don't think it matters much, do you?'

12

Ypres salient, zero hour, 31 July 1917: the dawn of the Third Battle of Ypres

Abercrombie could not seem to stop his throat from swallowing. Over and over again it gulped involuntarily as if some great object like a cricket ball had lodged itself inside and nothing could be done to shift it. He and his platoon had come up to the front shortly after darkness had fallen on the previous evening and had spent the night in this foremost trench of the British line.

The hours of darkness had been terrible but splendid. Abercrombie, like every man in that line, had watched transfixed as the dark sky exploded and the German horizon ignited and burned under the force of three thousand British guns, each one hurling shell after shell after shell at the enemy. All night long the men of the Royal Artillery, who laboured just to the rear of Abercrombie and his men, had pushed themselves to the very limits of physical exhaustion in order to create a barrage that it was hoped would cut the German wire and pulverize their forward defences.

Every soldier recognized the strange and awesome beauty of the night-time barrage; no Chinese firework master could ever have imagined such a show as the airborne inferno which exploded over Ypres on the evening of 30 July 1917. The thunder of it bludgeoned the eardrums and its lightning dazzled the eyes. Men crouched beneath it, numbed and battered, as the pressure changes created by the thumping explosions in the air around them deadened their senses whilst at the same time fraying their nerves. And all night long Abercrombie and his men, along with nine full divisions of British infantry, sheltered beneath this sulphurous sky. Hiding in the dirt, sandwiched between the monstrous majesty of their own guns and the snarling teeth of the German wire that they knew they must face at dawn. For no one in all of Flanders could now have been in any doubt that the next big British push was about to begin.

In the hour or so before dawn, the guns grew quieter and it was possible for those who wished to speak to make themselves heard.

'Better place a lookout for submarines, eh, sir,' Abercrombie's platoon sergeant quipped. It was an old joke in the waterlogged swamplands of the Western Front but never more relevant than on that morning, for all night the rain had poured as if Mother Nature, offended by the carnage, was trying to douse the violence of the British guns.

Abercrombie did not answer. On any other morning in his military career so far he would have answered. He would have given the sergeant a smile and produced some bit of dry wit to comfort his men, showing them that their captain was cool and in control. But on this morning Abercrombie could not answer; the cricket ball which he seemed to have swallowed had now grown big as a football. He was having trouble breathing, let alone trying to speak. His wit, which was his greatest weapon and also his trusty shield, had, at this moment of supreme testing, been denied him.

Abercrombie wanted to be strong but his strength was draining from him, down through his waterlogged boots and into the mud below. During the night he had managed to collect himself for a moment and find the strength to give support to a subordinate. Stamford had passed along the trench escorting an observation team from the artillery. The young man's face had been a picture of terror, enduring as he was his first artillery barrage. Abercrombie had offered him his hand and as Stamford had taken it, Abercrombie had squeezed it gently and their eyes had met as they had not done since their night together in London. Stamford had smiled and seemed a little calmed.

Abercrombie was glad that he had managed to give some comfort to the boy who loved him but now he doubted he would ever be able to give comfort to anyone again. Least of all himself, for he feared that he would not have the strength to give the order to advance and so would be disgraced. Something had changed inside him. He had heard that this was not uncommon amongst men who had seen a year or two of constant service. Some brave men just stopped being brave. Abercrombie feared that he was such a man.

He hugged himself to mask the shaking, and the football in his throat just kept getting bigger.

13

Silence after battle

It was evening once again. The evening at the end of the first day of the Third Battle of Ypres, a battle that was to rage with increasing hopelessness for the next two months. General Haig had set the objective for that first day as the village of Passchendaele, some four and a half miles from the British starting point. Instead, about a single mile had been covered and at cruel cost. Nonetheless this represented a greater advance than almost any previous British assault of the war and the General Staff at least had pronounced the day a qualified success.

Abercrombie was in no position to celebrate this small victory, for he found that he had been struck dumb. Eight hours earlier he had managed with a supreme effort to dislodge the ball in his throat sufficiently to give him enough voice to count off the final minutes before the assault began. The rum ration issued to every man in that last half-hour of waiting had done its work and loosened his choking throat, and he had been able to blow his whistle and wish his men luck before forcing himself upwards over the parapet ahead of them.

But after that he was silent.

He had done his duty and led his men into the withering machine-gun fire, proceeding in an orderly fashion towards the enemy line. He had taken one or two flesh wounds but had escaped serious injury, unlike the majority of his company, who had fallen around him.

He had arrived at the German wire with the bedraggled remnants of the British first wave and had been involved in the bayonet work and hand-to-hand fighting which occurred as they took the forward line of enemy trenches.

He had fought a decent enough battle, but now, however, sitting in the field dressing station to which he had staggered after the position he had occupied had been relieved, he knew that he was finished. Incapable of further action of any sort, he could not speak, he could scarcely hear and, as the organized chaos of blood, men and bandages proceeded around him in the crowded dugout, he wondered if he would even have the strength to walk towards the medical officer when his turn came to be diagnosed.

'So, Captain. Lucky and not so lucky for you, I'm afraid,' the MO said when finally he was seen, and an orderly was applying disinfectant to the shallow bullet wound he had taken in the shoulder. 'Lucky, in that five inches to the left and this bullet would have killed you, unlucky in that three inches would have scored you a Blighty. As it is, back in the line tomorrow, I'm afraid.'

But Abercrombie knew that he would not be in the line to-morrow. He took up a wax pencil which the doctors used for marking flesh to guide the operating crews and wrote upon his hand that he was mute.

Later still, in the small hours of the morning on what would be the second day of the Third Battle of Ypres, the colonel who had welcomed Abercrombie into the battalion with such enthusiasm only three days earlier stood beside the regiment's senior medical officer to discuss the surprising and distressing development.

'I suppose even heroes get shell shock,' he said with genuine concern. 'Poor fellow, he'll take this very hard when he comes to understand it.'

Abercrombie had walked back a further two miles to an

RAMC operating centre, a vast tent in which ten teams of surgeons and nurses worked simultaneously on the ever-lengthening queues of stretcher cases which were being carried back across the mud. Each patient had been previously marked for cutting with the wax pencils at the forward dressing centre. The surgeons had to trust to the diagnosis of their colleagues at the front, for there was no time now for further examination: every wound was seeping through its bandages, disease hung in the air and crawled upon the floor, and every man was in danger of dying if not sewn up immediately. The teams around the tables took no more than a brief glance at each newly sedated body before setting to work. The Royal Army Medical Corps was proud of the fact that during this third year of the war they were able to send almost 80 per cent of the wounded men they processed back to the front or at least into some form of useful war work. The men groused that the RAMC were getting so good that the only way to be permanently excused from the army was to die.

In a corner of the vast tent, set slightly apart from the crimson mayhem, Abercrombie sat alongside a number of other dazed-looking cases, amongst whom was also Private Hopkins, the man whom only two days earlier Abercrombie had ordered lashed to a gun carriage. The two men looked at each other but did not speak. Neither was capable of it.

'So the fellah can't talk to us?' the colonel enquired.

'Not at the moment. Muteness is a pretty common symptom of shell shock,' the doctor replied. 'It doesn't tend to last long but until it wears off we won't know much about his real mental state.'

'D'you think he's gone loopy?'

'Probably not. I should think it's just nervous exhaustion. Most cases are, although if I'm frank I know pretty much bugger all about it. Not many people do really. The army never considered such matters before. But then battles didn't last so long in the old days, did they? From my experience those who do claim to know about shell shock always sound pretty bonkers themselves. That's why I stick to a knife and a needle and thread, you know where you are with a patient from the neck down. Anyway, we'll send him back to Beaurivage and see what they say.'

'Damnable business really.' The colonel sighed. 'I hear he did awfully well today, got quite a few of his chaps right up to the wire.'

He looked sadly towards Abercrombie then turned away, limping slightly as his boots touched the sticky coating of blood and gore that covered the floor of the tent.

'Just a scratch, bit of shrapnel nicked me. Not a Blighty, I fear,' he said as he began to hobble away. 'Shame that, could have done with a break. I hear the grouse are particularly thick on the moors this season. Not surprised, nobody left but women and clergymen to shoot at 'em, I suppose.'

'One thing, Colonel,' the doctor added. 'Abercrombie wrote me a note. He says he wants his satchel brought back from his trench. A leather case with papers in it. He was most insistent, not bothered about anything else but very concerned about his blessed papers. Could you arrange for it to be brought down?'

'What? Yes, yes, of course.'

'Fellows in his condition can get very fixed ideas and it's generally easier all round if we can give them what they want.'

'Right. Absolutely. Leather case. Papers. Will do.'

'Thank you.'

The colonel shook his head sadly. 'Splendid chap like that, eh? What a rotten shame. I suppose we all get a bit worn down in the end, don't we? Damnable business.'

He turned and made his way back through the mayhem of ten operating tables, at times having to step over the discarded limbs that littered the floor.

14

A potential ally

On the evening that the colonel left Abercrombie sitting mute amongst the wounded and the dying, Kingsley was sleeping fitfully in his prison hospital bed. It had been nearly a week since he had approached his Irish orderly for help and neither of them had mentioned the matter since. Kingsley had resigned himself to the assumption that he could expect no aid from that quarter. What was more, he knew that he was recovering slowly and although he could not yet be moved he was uncomfortably aware that the day must soon come when he would be returned to the body of the prison where only beatings, and almost certainly fatal beatings, awaited him.

He was woken from sleep by a hand over his mouth. Opening his eyes, he saw above him a man in prison uniform who held his finger to his lips for silence. Kingsley nodded gently to indicate that he understood and the man removed his hand from Kingsley's mouth.

'Raise him up a little,' the man said.

'Yes, sor. Certainly, sor,' the Irish orderly muttered, clearly terrified of the prisoner who had woken Kingsley. He stepped forward and propped pillows beneath Kingsley's shoulders so that he might see about the room.

There were three men present besides the orderly, the one who seemed to be in charge and another two standing near the door. All were in prison uniform but they did not look like the prisoners Kingsley had so far seen. With the exception of the drug-raddled orderly they stood straight and, as far as Kingsley could make out in the flickering gaslight, their eyes were sharp. That was all he could see of their faces, however, for they were all masked, with rags knotted across their noses.

'My friend here tells me that you've an interest in speaking to loyal Irishmen,' the one who was in command said softly.

'I've an interest in speaking to anybody who might be prepared to help me,' Kingsley whispered through his bruised lips.

'How do you think we could help you?'

'You have power. That's plain enough to see or else how could you have left your cells to come to me tonight?'

'It's true that we have a bit of influence about the place,' the man replied. 'Paddies everywhere, you see. Can't get rid of us. We're like flies on shit, so we are. Some doors are open to us. Sadly not the front one.'

The man did not have the thick Dublin accent of the orderly and, despite the coarseness of his language, his voice was soft and educated. Kingsley imagined that he might be a product of Trinity College, whose professors did a fair line in nurturing enemies of the British state.

'You know who I am,' said Kingsley. 'You know what I am here for.'

'Yes. You're the fellah who objects to the war because he thinks it stupid.'

'Illogical.'

'That's right, illogical. Tell me, Inspector Kingsley, how do you feel about the logic behind the war the British have been waging against the people of Ireland these past thousand years or so?'

Kingsley had of course expected this.

'I regret that in the past I have not considered it as much as I should.'

'But you're considering it now?'

'Yes.'

'Being as how there's not an Englishman left who'll give you the time of day, you thought you might try your luck with the Micks.'

'I suppose that is a fair summation of my position.'

'How do you feel,' the man continued, 'about the "logic" of them dragging Paddy Pearce and the rest of the boys from the Post Office in Dublin at Easter last year and hanging the lot of them for having the temerity to believe that Ireland should be run by the Irish?'

'I think it was highly illogical. The British created another half-dozen martyrs to inspire your cause.'

'Well, I must say that's very comforting. Especially coming from a fellah who was happily in the employ of the murderers at the time.'

Kingsley had no answer to this and so he remained silent.

'Well, now we should get down to cases, I think,' the man said. 'Can't be out of our cells all night, you know. Wouldn't do to push our luck. You are looking for protection, I believe, Inspector? The idea being, I presume, that we let it be known that any fellah as hurts you will shortly thereafter have to reckon with the Mad Micks? Is that right?'

'I would appreciate such an arrangement very much.'

'Us scary crazy Irish that steal babies from English mothers in order to feast on their flesh?'

Once more Kingsley did not answer.

'And what,' the man continued, 'I hope you'll forgive me for being so crass as to enquire, would be in it for us?'

'I . . . I can tell you something of what I know.'

'And just what *would* a flat-footed London peeler know, Mr Kingsley?'

'I was at one point with Special Branch. I still have contacts.'

'Do you know the identities of any undercover officers?'

'Yes, I do.'

'Will you reveal them?'

81

'For you to murder? No.'

'At least you're honest, Mr Kingsley. Fortunate for you, for I know a little about you and most certainly would not have believed you if you had said yes.'

'Before 1909, before we had a proper secret service, it was the police who were your principal opponents in London.'

'Yes, Mr Kingsley, I know that. I didn't come here to listen to a lecture. What do you have for me?'

'I can tell you something of what we know . . .' Kingsley was improvising desperately. 'We know that the IRB has infiltrated the Gaelic League. I am sure that Eoin McNeill would be surprised and horrified to learn how many of his precious Irish Language Conversation groups were in fact tutorials for bomb-makers and gunrunners. And also the Gaelic Athletic Association? How many of your men have been secretly recruited and trained whilst you all pretend to play football? Half the fellows who took part in the rising must have come to you that way. We know because we have men amongst you.'

'You do, do you?'

'Yes. That was how we learned of Casement and his mission to Germany.'

'Inspector, it was in the bloody papers.'

'We knew where he was landing. We knew where to grab him.'

'Sir Roger Casement was a bloody idiot who couldn't keep his mouth shut if his lips were bolted together. His capture was no loss to us and small credit to you. Now then, let me ask you this. If you have British spies and coppers playing Gaelic football with the lads of the GAA in Donegal, will you give me their names?'

'No.'

The Fenian smiled.

'Why not?'

'Because I will not condemn them to die.'

'Or, more to the point, because these spies do not exist.'

'You may hope so.'

'Inspector Kingsley, I expected better of you.'

'I am sorry to be a disappointment.'

'Neither the police nor your precious new Secret Intelligence Service have ever infiltrated the IRB in any significant manner.'

'If we have, then surely you would be the last to know.'

'If you had, then surely the British authorities in Dublin would have had some foreknowledge of the Easter Rising, Mr Kingsley. But they didn't, did they? It took them totally by surprise.'

'How can you be sure? We crushed it, didn't we?'

'Yes, you crushed it as you were always going to crush it, but not because of any brilliant intelligence work on the part of your spies, my friend, but because you are the fucking British Empire and you have a big army and we are a bunch of farmers and bank clerks equipped with the kind of shitty nineteenth-century ordnance which that fool Casement managed to beg from the Germans! And even if we hadn't gone at it half-arsed like we did, putting only a thousand men on to the streets when we could have fielded ten times that, you *still* would have crushed it. Now then, Inspector Kingsley, let us dispense with your desperate fantasies and see if you have anything for us that is worth us saving your life in this prison. I shan't ask you to betray your own because I know that you wouldn't but you can betray some of ours if you've a mind. You were with the London Special Branch, what say you give me the names of half a dozen Irish informers, eh? That'll buy you a bit of protection, my friend. Tell us the names of six traitorous Micks, laying pavements, digging holes and stirring tar in London, who all the while are keeping an ear open on behalf of the police.'

For a moment Kingsley considered making up names; perhaps it would buy him time. The thought, however, was only fleeting. A man did not need to have worked for Special Branch to know that you did not play games with the Brotherhood. They were violent, angry men and would never suffer a slight such as that. However, Kingsley could not tell the truth either, for although he most certainly did know the names of a number of men who dug the Underground and paved the roads who were police informers, to reveal them to the IRB would be no more or less than murder.

'I shall not name our informers.'

'Mr Kingsley, these men are scum. You have your spies, we have ours. They know the risk and they take those risks for no better reason than gold sovereigns. I shall give you one more chance. Give me the names of six Irish informers in the pay of Scotland Yard or the SIS, three even, and we will see to it that you come to no harm from the thugs in this prison.'

Kingsley struggled for a moment with his conscience. Here was an offer of the protection he so desperately needed. And for what? The names of traitors. Men who sacrificed their countrymen out of pure greed. Surely his life was worth easily three of such men? Their *business* was betrayal, they worked simply to betray their comrades. Why should he not betray them?

Because he could not. No logic on earth could be twisted to justify such a course and Kingsley knew it. Whatever their moral worth they were servants of the Crown; the information they provided might even have saved innocent civilians from terrorist attack. He had no right to murder them.

'I cannot give you names.'

'Well then, Inspector, you have lost me half a night's sleep on a fool's errand. When O'Shaughnessy said that you wished to parlay I imagined that you must at least have *something* to offer us.'

'The Gaelic League . . .'

'Please, Inspector. Any reporter on the *Irish Times* knows of our recruitment strategy. You know it. We know you know it and we don't care that you know it, for even the English cannot arrest a man for playing football. You have brought us nothing, sir, and we will give you nothing in return.'

'Please!' Kingsley gasped. But the men of the IRB were already gone.

15

A shot in the night

That evening, across the Channel in France, near Merville, at a
grand old château close by the beautiful River Lys, other men lay
in hospital beds, suffering no less anguish of mind than Kingsley
was doing.

Each evening these men retired to their beds but found that no
rest or peace was to be had in the long watches of the night.
Everywhere in that big old French house there were screams and
shouts as men gave conscious and unconscious voice to the nightmares that besieged them whether they slept or were awake. Some
men writhed about, others lay still as corpses, eyes wide open but
seeing nothing. Some slept but while they slept they ducked and
dodged the shells that in their dreams rained down upon them.
Some men railed against the Boche, others pleaded with him for
mercy, some conducted quiet conversations with comrades who
had been blown to pieces years before. Some said nothing at all
and made no sound while all the time, behind their open, staring
eyes, they screamed.

All nights were the same in this place where each day more and
more men arrived, shattered by battle, in search of peace that could
not be found, and after the first two terrible days of the Third Battle
of Ypres the grand old château was filled to bursting point.

In one room Private Hopkins lay, and there amongst a group of other men he shouted that he would not wear lice-infested clothes that were not his own. He told the night that he was a soldier and a man and he would die wearing his own tunic. Then in his mind policemen lashed him once more to the wheel of a gun limber and once again the flies sat upon his eyes in clusters, crawling on his mouth and in his nose.

In another room two men lay together, holding each other in a lovers' embrace. They kissed each other urgently and passionately. Once, not long before, the older one had been in charge, the wiser one, the stronger and the more experienced, but now all that had changed. The younger man spoke most between the kisses, offering comfort and love, whilst the older man could only whisper in reply.

A little later in that house a shot rang out. Nobody heard it. A million shots rang out in each man's head that night. Another million could be heard for real up and down the length of France and Belgium and in Turkey, Greece and Asia Minor, the Balkans, Persia, Mesopotamia, Africa, Italy, deep in the heart of Russia and upon the dark waters of the Atlantic. One shot more or less could hardly matter and nobody paid it any mind.

16

Bad news at the Carlton Club

Lord Abercrombie had breakfasted at the Carlton Club, as was his custom on days when he was scheduled to attend the House of Lords. He had eaten heartily, having worked up an appetite earlier that morning riding in Hyde Park, and had now repaired to the reading room in order to digest his sausage and kedgeree over several pipes and the morning papers.

Lord Abercrombie did not like being disturbed and when first the club servant had appeared at his elbow, bearing a silver tray on which lay a card of introduction, his lordship had waved him angrily away.

'This is the *reading room*, damn you,' he hissed, for there was a strict code against speaking in such a place. 'I come here to avoid people, not have them chase me about with their bloody cards!'

The servant looked as if he wished the ground would swallow him, for Lord Abercrombie's temper was legendary. Nonetheless he stood his ground, refusing to move until the angry lord was forced to read the card. Having done so, Lord Abercrombie grunted angrily, cast aside the copy of *The Times* in which he had been reading news of the current bloodbath at Passchendaele and stumped noisily from the room.

'Well, what is it?' he demanded rudely of the young man who awaited him in the grand entrance hall of the club. 'What does the Home Office want with me that's so important it requires the sending of an undersecretary, no less, to interrupt my morning pipe?'

The young man was about to speak but Abercrombie gave him no opportunity. Like all good parliamentarians, he was accustomed to answering his own questions. 'If I am to be lobbied once more over these damned engineering strikes then you have disturbed my digestion for nothing. Mr Bonar Law has made it quite clear that the Conservative Party does not negotiate with strikers, particularly a gang of bully-boy shop stewards who do not even have the backing of their own leadership! Let them return to work and then perhaps we might . . .'

There was something in the undersecretary's face which made Abercrombie pause. He was not the most sensitive of men but even he could see that the young man was deeply troubled.

'It's Alan, isn't it?' he asked suddenly. 'You have news of my son.'

'Perhaps we might adjourn to . . .'

'Damn adjourning, you bloody fool! Is he dead?'

'Yes, my lord, I am afraid that Captain Abercrombie is dead.'

The old man gripped at the porters' desk for support. The shock was terrible, although in many ways he had been expecting it. Like millions of other parents up and down the country and right across the globe, he and his wife lived in daily fear of receiving the news that their son had been killed.

For a few moments the two men stood in silence in the hallway whilst Lord Abercrombie attempted to collect himself.

'How did he die?' he enquired finally.

'It is stated that he died in battle, sir.'

'It is stated?' the old man said sharply. 'What the devil do you mean by "it is stated"?'

The undersecretary seemed to study the carpet.

'It is stated, sir. The army has released a statement that your son died at Ypres. He is a hero fallen.'

A cloud of doubt began to creep across the old man's grief-stricken features.

'Follow me,' he ordered and led the unfortunate undersecretary into a private smoking room.

'I spoke to my son last night,' his lordship said when the door had been closed and he and his visitor were alone. The undersecretary did not reply.

'He was not at Ypres,' the old man continued. 'He placed a telephone call to me here at the Carlton Club from a French château. He had been sent there to recover, having temporarily lost the power of speech.'

Still the young man remained silent.

'Ypres is in Belgium,' Lord Abercrombie insisted. 'The château from which my son telephoned was in France. He was anxious that his mother should know that he was all right. He was convalescing.'

Once more the room fell silent. The wretched undersecretary refused to meet the old man's eye.

'How can a man who was convalescing in a château in France have been killed in action at Ypres? Did he put down the telephone and rush across the border into Belgium and up to the front in order to take part in a night raid?'

'Your son is dead, sir,' the undersecretary reiterated. 'It is stated that he died in battle. He is a hero fallen.'

17

A slow recovery

'He shall be treated by the book, Mr Jenkins, which means those cracked ribs must be bound and he must be observed. *Observed*, I might add, Mr Jenkins. By the book.'

The doctor placed his hand upon Kingsley's chest, causing the patient to cry out in pain.

'Please, doctor, my lungs!' he gasped.

'The beating he took's done more damage than I thought,' the doctor continued. 'I don't think your prisoner is likely to survive very long in your cells and I fear I must formally notify you that it is my opinion he should be kept in solitary for his own safety.'

'Is it necessary that you put that warning in writing?' Jenkins asked.

The doctor considered this for a moment.

'Well, I should have to check the book but it seems to me that a verbal observation will suffice to cover my responsibilities.'

'And you would only make mention of that verbal observation if you was approached? By the authorities, so to speak?'

'Certainly it is no part of my duties to go pestering my superiors with unasked-for observations. Of course if I were to be *approached . . .*'

'You will not be approached.'

So that was it. There was to be no paper trail to implicate those who were clearly intent on shirking their duty of care and allowing him to be quickly beaten to death. The sadistic Mr Jenkins, who was responsible for his safety, wanted him dead and the doctor did not mind in the slightest as long as his own back was covered. A nod and a wink were to be his death warrant.

'Patch him up, like I said, to within the limits prescribed in your blessed book, doctor, and when he is well enough to stumble to the door, hand him back to me.'

In fact Kingsley was already well enough to return to the cells but for want of a better plan he had, since his failure to enlist support from the IRB, been dissembling wildly and had managed to convince the doctor that his ribs had been cracked.

When Jenkins had departed, the doctor, aided by a medical orderly, began the work of changing the bandages on Kingsley's chest. Kingsley could see by the light at the window and the fob watch that hung by a chain across the doctor's portly stomach that it was morning. Despite the earliness of the hour, the doctor still stank of brandy; clearly it was not only after supper that he was half-drunk but all day as well. Kingsley gasped loudly in pain as the hapless doctor struggled inexpertly with the bandages, at one point even resting his weight on Kingsley's chest, which gave Kingsley an excuse to cry out all the more.

'Be quiet, man!' the doctor snapped. 'These bandages should not be wasted on you but sent to the front where they might be of service to a soldier, not a coward.'

'Doctor,' Kingsley whispered through clenched teeth, 'I have not read your book but I do not believe that forcing damaged ribs into the lungs of your patients is described there as part of your duty of care. If you continue in this manner I may die here on your bench and what would your book say about that?'

The doctor stood back.

'Damn you then for an ungrateful swine! I am not in any way obliged to dirty my hands with you! The book requires that I attend your sickbed and make my diagnosis. So much have

I done, sir! And done damn well. You have three cracked ribs and each has been duly noted, annotated, listed and written up with the required copies made and filed! I have done my duty, sir, and no man may say I haven't! Your treatment I may now legitimately leave to an orderly. I do not think that it is any part of the Home Office Code of Practice pertaining to the duties of HM Prison Medical Officers that I be submitted to slurs and insults from conscientious objectors such as yourself. I bound your wounds as an act of Christian charity but if my ministering does not suit you then the devil may take you, for I wash my hands of you. Orderly! Attend this prisoner!'

With that, the doctor withdrew his bottom from the bench on which it had been resting and marched self-importantly from the room.

18

The Carlton Club once more

Lord Abercrombie's face looked as if he had been struck a blow. Whatever explanation he had expected when he lobbied the War Office for further information about the death of his son, it had not been this one.

'Murdered? It can't be,' he insisted. 'Who could possibly wish to murder my boy? He was loved. Loved by everybody.'

There were no undersecretaries present now. The Secretary of State for War himself had hurried to speak with Lord Abercrombie the moment he had discovered that the Opposition Chief Whip was refusing to accept the official explanation for the famous poet's death.

'I'm afraid he was murdered, my lord,' the minister insisted. 'The Prime Minister has asked me to convey his deepest sympathy and . . .'

'Damn his sympathy!' the old man spluttered. 'This can't be true. Alan's a soldier. What am I to tell his mother? There's been some appalling mistake and I shall see that whoever is responsible never—'

'I'm afraid there has been no mistake,' the minister interrupted. 'We have the news directly from the Military Police and it has been confirmed by the Secret Intelligence Service. Captain

Abercrombie was most certainly murdered.'

'The SIS? What the hell have that gang of thieves and snoopers got to do with it?'

The Minister for War sighed. When first he had heard the news of the murder of so famous a man he had understood instantly, as had the other senior ministers who had been informed, that this was a matter of the highest delicacy.

'Lord Abercrombie,' he said, 'I am afraid that I am going to have to ask you to give me your word that what I tell you will go no further than this room.'

'I will give no such assurance, sir!' the old man thundered. 'How can I? I have no idea what you are talking about except that my son is dead and it seems that for some reason you have sought to lie about how he died.'

'We believe that your son was murdered for political reasons. His killer was a revolutionary. A Bolshevik.'

'A Russian! A bloody Russian shot my son!' Lord Abercrombie barked and for a moment his astonishment appeared to overcome his grief.

'No, sir. An Englishman, an enlisted man but nonetheless a disciple of Lenin.'

Lord Abercrombie sank down on to a leather couch, the fight all knocked out of him.

'What am I to tell her ladyship?' he almost whispered. 'What will his mother say?'

'Sir, I do not believe that you *should* tell her ladyship. Your son was a hero, he has the right to be remembered as such. Imagine what effect it would have upon morale if it were to become known that he was murdered by a fellow countryman! Viscount Abercrombie fought with distinction for two years, and wrote often of his desire to die in action. Surely his mother has a right, surely the *people* have a right, to believe that wish to have been fulfilled? It's not the viscount's fault that he was cruelly murdered whilst honourably recovering from battle, a battle in which he could quite easily have died. Is it not best for everybody, and particularly for your son's memory, that the truth of this dreadful incident should never be known?'

The old man sat in silence, looking tired and defeated.

'Yes,' he said finally. 'Yes. You're right. It wouldn't do for a man like Alan to be remembered principally for the grubby manner of his parting.'

The minister readily agreed.

'His songs and poetry would never be seen in the same light again. His legacy would be forever tainted.'

'I shall not tell his mother. Better she should think he died as he lived. A hero.'

'I am grateful to you, my lord,' the minister said. 'Our nation is currently going through a period of greater industrial unrest than at any previous time in the war. The man who has been arrested was a fairly prominent trades unionist. A scandal such as this one, should it ever become public, could only be horrendously divisive. There will always be those who wish to think the worst of the government, of the army. An aristocrat has been murdered by a working man, what is more, a Communist. In this year of all years, with Russia going all to hell, we do not want this incident to become an issue of class division.'

'What will you do with the swine?' his lordship enquired.

'He'll be tried in camera and no doubt shot,' the Secretary of State replied. 'His family will be told that he too died in action. That is the army's regular custom with those who have been shot for cowardice.'

'Just so long as he's shot,' his lordship replied, despair and anger etched in equal measure on every line of his fierce old face.

19

A radical assembly

The conversation had quickly grown heated.

Lord Abercrombie was not the only person who was angry about Viscount Abercrombie's death. Nor were the senior figures in the Cabinet with whom the Tory peer had discussed the matter the only people of power in Britain who were concerned with the fate of the man accused of the murder.

Heated debate was hardly unusual at the home of Beatrice and Sidney Webb, that almost legendary Socialist salon on the Embankment near the Tate Gallery in which dark injustice had been angrily debated on an almost daily basis for some three decades or more. Yet again Fabians, trades unionists and Labour politicians had gathered in the Webbs' cosy sitting room in order to consider a collective response to the iniquities of the ruling class.

'You say that this man Hopkins was arrested and has now simply disappeared? Accused of a murder which the army say never happened?' The speaker was Ramsay MacDonald, former Labour Party leader and implacable opponent of the war.

'That seems to be what has occurred,' Beatrice Webb replied. 'Some terrible incident took place at the château in which both Hopkins and Abercrombie were convalescing. Now Abercrombie is trumpeted in the press as a hero who fell in battle while the army continues to hold Hopkins for his murder.'

'How do we know this?' enquired Arthur Henderson, who had replaced MacDonald as leader of the Labour Party. 'I am personally highly suspicious of the tendency of some comrades to see conspiracy wherever they look. Perhaps the army is telling the truth.'

'Ha!' MacDonald snorted.

'Hopkins was no ordinary soldier,' Beatrice Webb insisted. 'He was a Communist, well connected within leftist circles amongst the rank and file. A comrade of his, one Private McCroon, has made an appeal to Hopkins's trades union which has been forwarded to me. I have made what enquiries I can and only two things appear to be clear: Abercrombie is dead and Hopkins has disappeared. He is not listed as killed, missing or deserted but neither is he with his battalion. I can only presume that the army are holding him.'

'Lies and deception!' MacDonald stated. 'This lad's been pinched for being a Communist, that's what, for speaking out against the war. The government's making the same mistakes the bloody Tsar made and they'll reap the same whirlwind.'

Henderson winced at what he clearly considered was MacDonald's inelegant turn of phrase.

'I urge a cautious reaction,' the party leader insisted. 'The public adored Alan Abercrombie. Imagine what harm it would do to us in the Labour movement if we were to announce that he did not die a hero, and were instead to take the part of a Communist activist who may well have killed him.'

'You *would* urge caution, Arthur!' MacDonald retorted unkindly. 'After all, you wouldn't want to upset your old paymasters, would you?'

Until recently, Henderson had represented Labour in Lloyd George's coalition Cabinet. He was seen by many as having supped with the devil and having liked it rather too much.

'You're little better than a Liberal yourself these days,'

MacDonald continued. 'Sometimes I wonder why you don't run off and join them.'

'Now hang on, Ramsay,' Henderson retorted. 'I'm a bit sick of this damned sneering. If I hadn't been in Cabinet exercising a restraining influence, things might have gone a lot harder on the Clyde last year and—'

'Scottish strikers do not need *protection*, Arthur, they need *representation*!'

'I am not a meeting of Glasgow dockworkers, Ramsay,' Henderson replied, 'so please don't address me as one!'

The teacups perched on the knees of both men rattled in their saucers as they jabbed their fingers at each other.

'Now then, now then, now then!' Sidney Webb intervened. 'Really, you two. Am I to fetch a bucket of water and throw it over the pair of you?'

'More tea, Arthur?' Beatrice Webb suggested soothingly. 'Perhaps another scone, Ramsay? It's the last of the butter.'

The fierce-eyed Scot accepted a scone with little grace and consumed half of it in a single emphatic bite, as if it was his Socialist colleague's head that he would have preferred to be biting off.

'We really must stick to the point,' Sidney Webb insisted. 'I'm afraid it is a natural tendency of us Socialists to try to solve *all* the problems of the world each time we meet, a tendency which often leads us to solve nothing at all.'

'All the problems of the world emanate from a single system,' MacDonald grumbled.

'Ramsay, please. I think we may take it as read that we all disapprove of the excesses of capitalism.'

'The point to which we should be sticking,' Beatrice Webb insisted with gentle-voiced but steely firmness, 'is that something very strange has occurred and the authorities are lying about it. Perhaps the government's agenda is one which we can support, perhaps not. However, before we can make a decision on that score, surely the truth must be uncovered. We must insist that the army explains itself and if it will not, we shall make public such information as we have. If Britain is fighting for justice then that justice must be visited upon all equally, without fear or favour, even upon Communists.'

And for a moment within that famous sitting room there occurred a most strange and unfamiliar thing. Consensus. Grumpy, irritable and grudging consensus perhaps, but consensus nonetheless.

20

A lifeline

Kingsley lay in the hospital room for another week, nursed, after a fashion, by the Irish orderly, who saw Kingsley as a gift sent from heaven to feed his morphine addiction.

'Oh, he's still in a terrible amount of pain, sor,' the orderly would explain, whilst Kingsley groaned loudly when the doctor paid his brief daily visit to the room. 'He suffers terribly from his cracked ribs.'

'Morphine,' the doctor would duly announce, 'and be sure to note it in the book.'

Kingsley was in fact nearly recovered but the doctor had continued to accept his deception and so the orderly received his drugs. Kingsley was left alone with his increasingly desperate thoughts, knowing that even with such a poor physician he could not dissemble forever.

At the end of the second week of incarceration in the medical room, Kingsley awoke from a fitful sleep in which as usual he had dreamed of Agnes and his son, to find that he was being examined by a very different orderly from his usual drug-addicted companion. This was a serious and softly spoken man, who inspected Kingsley's chest with expert care.

'Not cracked at all,' he said, 'just badly bruised and definitely well on the mend.'

'I know,' Kingsley replied, 'but I thought it best not to contradict the doctor. I hope you will not feel obliged to note your observation in his book?'

'Don't worry about that, Inspector.'

'What is your name?'

'Names don't matter here. We are all numbers. Except for you, of course – everyone knows your name and hates it.'

'Yes, I'm afraid that they do and it will be the death of me.'

'It's pretty clear that the senior warder intends that it should be, which is why you must listen to me very carefully.'

Kingsley's ears pricked up. There was something about the man's manner which for some reason gave him hope. Before speaking further the orderly checked that there was no one outside the door.

'Inspector Kingsley, let's face it, your death warrant is signed. There are twenty men under this roof who have sworn to kill you. It is openly discussed and there have already been fights about who's going to have the pleasure of being your executioner. Men have laid bets on how long you have left to live and the brutal truth is that no odds, no matter how generous, will draw bets above a month or so from now. Most of the lads don't even give you another week. You must escape.'

'Ah yes. That would be a clever move, wouldn't it? Sadly, I fear there is no escape route available to me.'

'Not every door in this prison is locked when it should be locked.'

'How do you mean?'

'Tonight the door to this room and that at the end of the room beyond will not be locked.'

'You'd do this for me?'

'The doors will be open, that is all I can say.'

'You will be blamed.'

'No, they will be locked when I leave and the locking duly

noted in the book, but they will be open again later tonight. That is all you need to know.'

'Why are you helping me?'

'The doors will be open tonight. After that you're on your own,' the man insisted.

With that he departed, leaving Kingsley to sweat out the rest of the day and make what preparations he could.

When night fell, Kingsley gritted his teeth against the pain and, swinging his legs off the bench, lowered himself to the floor. He had attempted some exercise over the previous week and was fairly fit to walk, although perhaps not to carry out an escape from prison. However, he had no choice. Fate had thrown him one single card to play and clearly he must play it that night. Whoever his mysterious comrade might be, Kingsley doubted that he would be able to leave doors unlocked indefinitely. Staggering across the room, he turned the handle of the door and it opened. He found himself immediately in what might be described as the heart of the prison hospital, although it would have taken a leap of the imagination to think of such a cold, bare stone garret as a heart.

Two doors led from this second room in addition to the one through which Kingsley had entered. The first carried a board on which were written the names of several prisoners. This door was heavily bolted but through a grille cut into its steel panels Kingsley could hear the groans and weeping of men in pain. A heavy, sweetish smell hung in the air also, a smell Kingsley knew well from his journeying amongst the sinks of London where injuries were common and medicine pitiably rare. The smell was gangrene and Kingsley knew that some poor soul beyond that bolted door must either have it cut from him in its entirety or have his blood fatally poisoned. Since the only medical expertise available was supplied by the appallingly casual and self-indulgent doctor and his 'book', Kingsley doubted whether the man would still be groaning one or two nights hence.

The second door was located at the far end of the room. It was not bolted and, if the orderly had kept his word, it would not be locked either and would lead from the medical wing out into the body of the prison. Before trying it, Kingsley sought to arm himself from what supplies he might find in the medical cabinet. He had only the vaguest idea of how he was to proceed once he had left the security of the medical wing but he felt certain that at some point he would encounter guards.

The cabinet was locked but Kingsley saw that it was attached to the wall by a bracket: it would be a simple matter to lift the entire thing from the wall and gain access from behind. Having done so, he found himself pitying the poor prisoners whose health relied on such dismal supplies. Few modern drugs seemed to have found their way on to the doctor's procurement list but there was morphine aplenty, and chloroform. It was clear to Kingsley that the pursuit of cures was not the objective in this particular hell-hole, and that the sole purpose of the drugs available in the so-called 'hospital wing' was to subdue troublesome patients until they either recovered or quietly died.

Kingsley took the bottle of chloroform and, having wrapped a rag torn from his prison shirt around the neck of the squat little container, stuffed it into his pocket. Then he approached the second door in the room and turned the handle.

As promised by the orderly, this last door was open. It led out on to one of the numerous iron landings overlooking the great well of the prison. Kingsley had suspected that this would be the case, but as he had been carried unconscious into the hospital wing he could not have known for sure. Trying not to gasp from the pain of his bruised ribs and the unaccustomed movement of his limbs, Kingsley began to make his way along the silent corridor towards the first stairwell. To his left were cells packed to bursting point with sleeping prisoners. To his right was the great well of the prison, across which through the anti-suicide mesh he could see the mirror image of the walkway he was on, and beneath it another, identical one and beneath that four more. This much he had expected: what he had not expected was the absence of guards. It seemed to him that, apart from the prisoners who could be heard snoring and grunting behind their cell doors, he was alone in all that vast, cavernous space. Could it be that once the cell doors were locked the warders simply retired for the night? It seemed incredible but, as Kingsley made his way along each corridor and down one stairway after another, he could think of no alternative explanation. There was not a soul about.

Having finally descended to the floor of the great hall, Kingsley peered through the gloom for the exit, the door through which he had been brought on his first evening, to be paraded before the prisoners on his way to the governor's office. He could see it now, on the other side of the hall, so he made his way towards it across the dining area where he had eaten his solitary supper. Kingsley was astonished to discover that this door, too, was unlocked. He had had no idea of how he was to engineer a way through this barrier but he had certainly not expected to have simply to turn the handle.

He closed the door behind him and paused momentarily for breath. He was beyond the great hall and in a small internal courtyard, which he recalled crossing when he had first been brought to the prison. He knew that the reception area could be found in the building opposite and beyond that lay the prison gates. So far no alarm had been raised and he had encountered not a single soul, but he knew his luck could not last much longer. Surely escaping from His Majesty's prisons could not be as easy as this?

He stepped from the doorway and began to cross the cobbled yard. He had scarcely gone three steps when he found himself staring into the light of several electric torches.

'Good evening, Inspector,' a voice said from behind the light. 'Leaving us so soon?'

The door behind Kingsley, which he had just closed, opened once more and he heard footsteps behind him.

'It would seem not,' Kingsley replied.

The man stepped out from behind the torches.

'Run,' he said.

'What?'

'I said,' and with this the man raised his pistol, 'run!'

Now the torches parted and beyond them Kingsley could see another open doorway, the one that led to the reception area of the prison, the door to which he had been heading. He struggled to make sense of what was happening. They wanted him to run. Why did they want him to run?

Suddenly Kingsley knew their game. They wanted a neat finish. No untidy paperwork. No further investigation required. They wanted him to be shot whilst escaping.

They wanted to kill him by the book.

'I will not run.'

'Run!'

'I will not. If you wish to shoot me you must shoot me where I stand.'

The figure before him raised an arm. Silhouetted as he was by the torch lights behind him it was difficult to make out any detail, but from the man's position it was clear to Kingsley that he was facing the barrel of a sidearm.

'The prisoner Kingsley is running!' the shadow shouted. 'All here stand witness to the fact. Does any officer or warder here take issue with the fact that this man is in the process of escaping and I have no option but to shoot him down?'

Silence.

'Speak now,' the man called out, 'or forever be silent!'

Still there was silence.

'Prisoner Kingsley, I command you to stop! Stop, I say, or I shoot!'

Kingsley did not move. Nobody spoke.

The man fired directly at Kingsley's head and there he fell.

21

The Kingsley family home, Hampstead Heath, London

Agnes Kingsley, or Agnes Beaumont as she now called herself, was in her drawing room engaged in embroidery when her maid informed her that an officer, a certain Captain Shannon, wished to see her. She had been most surprised, for she was not expecting a visitor. As she had explained to her husband at their last meeting, nobody called upon her any more. Nonetheless she bid her maid bring the captain in and, having asked him to sit down, ordered tea.

'Mrs Kingsley,' the captain began.

'Beaumont, Captain,' Agnes corrected. 'I call myself Beaumont now. It is my maiden name. My husband and I are shortly to be divorced.'

'I am afraid that considerations such as that are no longer necessary, Mrs Beaumont. It is my painful duty to inform you that your husband . . .'

Agnes's hand froze in the act of raising a teacup to her lips.

'Mrs Beaumont, Inspector Kingsley is dead.'

She was wearing very little rouge or powder and so the draining of colour from her face was quite startling in its speed. The rosy cheeks that Kingsley loved so well turned white in an instant. An observer would have concluded that, whatever she thought of her husband's views on the war, she loved him still.

'Dead?'

'I am afraid so. I am truly sorry.'

'But how can this . . .'

At that moment a small boy ran into the room, a lively-looking lad in a little soldier's uniform.

'Not now, George, please.'

The boy's face fell.

'I heard you talking, Mummy. I thought it was Daddy.'

'No, darling . . .' She was struggling to keep her voice steady. 'I have told you, Daddy is away . . . He will be gone a long time, a very long time . . .'

Now the boy was looking at Captain Shannon.

'You're a soldier, aren't you?'

'Yes, I am . . . It's George, isn't it?'

'That's right. Are you very brave?'

'Oh, I don't know so much about that, George.'

'My daddy's brave, he's got three ci . . . ci . . .'

'Citations, darling,' Agnes said, and now she was hiding her tears behind a handkerchief. 'Run along . . .'

'He's very, very brave. Can I see your gun?' George asked.

'I said run along, darling.'

'I'm afraid I do not have it with me, George,' the captain replied with a smile.

'What sort of soldier doesn't have a gun?' George enquired.

'A rather poor one, I suppose,' Shannon answered.

Agnes rang for the maid and asked her to take George to his nanny. When the boy had gone she took a moment to collect herself.

'I'm sorry, Captain Shannon. Forgive me, but there must be some mistake. My husband is in prison.'

Shannon reached across the tea things and patted her hand. He was a strikingly handsome man with what seemed to be a genuinely sympathetic manner.

'No, he's not, Mrs Beaumont. He's dead. Shot while trying to escape. I'm so very sorry that on top of all your trouble you should be burdened with this.'

For a moment it seemed almost as if Agnes's distress would overwhelm her, but then she looked puzzled.

'Why . . . why have you come with this news, Captain? Why is this an army matter? Douglas had nothing to do with the army. That's why he was in prison.'

'I'm with, well . . . I'm with what you might call intelligence. Whilst in prison your husband was contacted by Irish nationalists. We do not believe he told them anything but we had to look into it. I was on my way to the prison to interview him when he attempted to escape. In his way your husband was a brave man; personally I admired him. I volunteered to bring you the news immediately since it will without doubt be in the evening newspapers.'

'Thank you, Captain. Thank you for that.'

Once more Captain Shannon patted her hand.

'Thank you, Captain,' she repeated.

'If there is ever anything I can do . . . anything at all.'

Agnes stood up.

'I think that George and I shall manage very well together, Captain. And I have my father.'

'Of course.' Captain Shannon rose to leave. 'Well, goodbye, Mrs Beaumont.'

'Mrs Kingsley, I think, Captain,' Agnes replied.

22

A journey to Folkestone

'Shot dead while escaping. Not many men have taken that route out of Wormwood Scrubs.'

'Yes. And still fewer have been shot dead while escaping and survived.'

Once more Kingsley found himself listening to disembodied voices whilst he lay wounded, although this time he was not in a strange bed but in a motor car, a big one, and well upholstered – perhaps a Daimler, he thought, or a Roller, judging by the leathery smell and the big, heavy, dependable sound of the engine. Kingsley's head ached more than he would have imagined it possible for a head to ache, and the bumpy movement of the car made him feel sick. Nonetheless he was clearly alive, which, considering what he remembered of events when last he had been conscious, seemed to him a considerable bonus.

'Exceptionally brave fellow,' the first voice said. This voice came from his right, and it appeared to Kingsley that it belonged to an older man. 'To stand there and face it like he did.'

'I don't know so much about brave,' the man on Kingsley's left argued. 'Intelligent certainly, intelligent enough to see that he was done for. He could either run or stand, same result both ways. Bang. Cheerio. Ta-ta. Goodbyeee. He knew that. Less trouble to stand, I'd say. Is that courage? I don't know. Does a dog that gets hit by a stick show courage?'

'Well, I hope I show as much bravery if ever I find myself facing a pistol at point-blank range.'

Kingsley wanted water desperately but decided that he would not yet alert the speakers to the fact that he was awake. Something very strange was occurring and Kingsley thought he might learn more if the men were not aware that he was listening. 'Poor fellow had a hell of a night, eh?' the man on Kingsley's right said. 'How long do they say before he'll be operational?'

'Well, the good news is Castle says his ribs aren't broken after all, despite what the prison sawbones said. So it looks like we'll be able to get him to the front far sooner than we'd feared.'

'Not bad for a dead man, eh, Shannon?'

'Yes, not bad at all,' the man called Shannon replied. He had a more brutal, arrogant tone than the older man, a tone that Kingsley did not much like.

'We won't know for sure, of course, until a decent doctor's taken a look at him but I must say he seemed pretty fit to me.'

Kingsley attempted to take stock. Who were these people? How had he come to be in their car? What could they possibly want?

He considered their voices.

He had heard voices like theirs many times before. Languid, relaxed voices, effortlessly confident and commanding. Kingsley had been listening to these voices all his life, voices that simply assumed the authority which men who spoke in different accents had to earn. Kingsley remembered those voices from his youth, when his grammar school rugby team had faced one of the nearby public schools. When some progressive-minded headmaster from Harrow or Winchester had thought it proper that his boys should mix briefly with the sons of the next class down. Kingsley and his friends had to hide their jealousy as a horse-drawn charabanc arrived from the station full of adolescent boys who spoke as if they owned the country. Which of course they did, or would do when their papas died.

So, these men who had taken possession of him were upper class and English.

What else could he discover? The back of Kingsley's hand was resting against the older man's trouser leg. Kingsley struggled to discover what type of cloth it might be. The back of the hand is not a sensitive instrument of touch, particularly if the owner is fearful to move it, but Kingsley thought that the material was thick and roughish. This was not the sort of fabric that would normally be used to make the trousers of men who spoke in voices such as the ones he had been listening to. Unless, of course, the material was khaki . . . And they had spoken earlier about getting him to the front.

Had he been kidnapped by the army? It was an extraordinary thought.

'Do you think he'll cooperate?' the older man was saying.

'Oh yes, I think so,' Shannon said. 'After all, what choice does he have? He's dead already, or so the world believes. Nothing to stop us popping him off for real, after the fact, so to speak.'

Kingsley struggled to make sense of what they were saying. There was something that these arrogant, supercilious men wanted him to do. Somehow they had spirited him from gaol by faking his death and now they were casually discussing killing him in earnest if he refused to cooperate with them.

'I think that Inspector Kingsley will weigh all the options, apply his famous logic, add a dash of that derring-do for which he has also been so rightly celebrated and come round to our way of thinking. What do you say, Inspector? Am I right?'

It was a shock but Kingsley managed not to flinch. Was it a trick? Or did Shannon really know that he was conscious?

'Inspector, I have been listening to your breathing. I considered it before you regained consciousness and I am considering it now. I asked if you thought that you might come round to our way of thinking.'

Kingsley attempted to open his eyes but realized that there were bandages across them. For a moment he feared that his eyes had been damaged when they shot him. But they did not feel damaged. It seemed more likely that he had simply been blindfolded.

'I have absolutely no idea what your way of thinking is,' he whispered. 'But if you are the man who shot me in the head with something that did not kill me and has left me wishing I was dead then you are clearly mad. So no, sir, I doubt that I shall come round to your way of thinking.'

'That's a shame. It was a bullet made of rubber, by the way. I constructed it myself actually, tested it on stray dogs. Killed three before I got the consistency right. Wanted something that would lay you out, bust the skin enough to look convincing to a casual onlooker but leave you fit to fight another day. Worked a treat, though I hate to crow. You went down like a sack of coal, all the guards saw it happen, that appalling old drunkard they use for a doctor pronounced you dead on my say-so and here you are. A dead man with a splitting headache.'

'Why?'

'We need you.'

'Why do you need me?'

'All in good time.'

'Does the world think that I am dead?'

'My dear fellow, what on earth would have been the point of constructing such an elaborate fiction if we were not to make it public? Of course the world thinks you are dead. You were shot while trying to escape from prison.'

'And you arranged for that escape?'

'Ah-ha, the penny drops.'

Now Kingsley understood the reason behind the ridiculously easy manner in which he had made his way through the prison.

'Are you the SIS? The Secret Intelligence Service?'

'Not supposed to talk about that sort of thing, old boy . . .'

'Kell's men or Cumming's?' Kingsley insisted, and for the first time Shannon seemed to lose the tiniest degree of his irritating sangfroid.

'I must say you are well versed, Inspector.'

'Not really. Your secret service isn't as secret as all that, you know. An awful lot of chattering goes on in the pubs and clubs around Whitehall.'

'Well then, Cumming's,' Shannon conceded, whereby Kingsley knew that he was dealing with the foreign section of military intelligence. This confused him even more. He had assumed that anything they might want from him would involve domestic counter-intelligence. He was after all a policeman, not a soldier.

'Then you have gone to a great deal of trouble for nothing, Mr Shannon,' Kingsley said, 'for I will not be a part of this war. Not in any capacity, secret or otherwise.'

'Well. We shall see, eh? Discuss it tomorrow when you feel a little better, eh?'

'I shall not join your war.'

'We do not intend to ask you to. Not *join* it, just trot along beside it for a few days.'

'Does my wife believe that I am dead?'

'Of course. She was the first person we told. There is a proper process to these things, you know. We're not without human decency, old boy.'

'Damn you!'

'Well, there's gratitude.'

'And my son?'

'Oh, don't worry about him. He's four, isn't he? Good time to lose a father, hasn't had the chance to get too attached. Besides, it only puts him in common with thousands of other little boys across the country, doesn't it? Good heavens, there's precious few lads about the place these days who *haven't* lost their father. He'd have felt quite the odd one out with you above ground.'

Kingsley struggled to master his emotions.

'Sir,' he said finally, 'I do not like your tone. You have clearly preserved my life for a purpose, please do not make the mistake of thinking I am grateful.'

'What on earth makes you think I'd value the gratitude of a

113

malingering, traitorous toad like you, Kingsley? Quite frankly, you make my skin crawl. Agnes Beaumont could have done *so* much better. Perhaps she will.'

'Don't you dare mention my—'

'Oh, do put a sock in it, you two,' the older man interrupted. 'We've miles to go and I can't stand bickering.' After that none of them spoke and soon the older man could be heard snoring. Then, despite his racing mind and his anguish at the thought of his family being so deceived, Kingsley himself fell into a fitful sleep.

23

Expressions of sympathy

Agnes Kingsley knew that she would not sleep that night.

For months the silver tray upon which were deposited the cards and notes that had once arrived throughout the day had lain empty. Now, in a bleak pantomime of the life she had once led, the tray was full again. Today, however, the cards were black-edged and the notes contained no jolly invitations to parties and soirées as of yore when the Kingsleys had been a fine catch for any hostess; now the cards carried no more than brusque expressions of sympathy. Curt and cold. The London in which the Kingsleys had once moved observed the niceties – there was, after all, a code – but the disgraced family remained unforgiven.

That was not why Agnes wept. Once, she had thought that the niceties mattered but now she recognized that they did not. She shed no tears that day for her loss of standing or for the indifference of people she had thought of as friends. Instead she wept for her son, whom she had just told that his daddy had gone to heaven. And she wept for herself and for the loss of her husband. She had believed him lost to her months before but this day's news had taught her that in her heart she had not truly lost him at all.

Until now.

24

Captain Shannon

Perhaps they had drugged him or perhaps it was just the physical and emotional exhaustion but Kingsley did not recall any more of that confusing car journey or indeed its end, and when he finally awoke once again he found himself in yet another strange bed. How many more times, he wondered, was he to regain consciousness in a new and unfamiliar environment? This one at least was considerably more comfortable than the previous ones. The linen was crisp and the room smelt very clean.

'Why don't you try opening your eyes?' said the voice which Kingsley remembered as Shannon's. 'We've removed the bandages.'

Slowly Kingsley opened his eyes. The light that smashed brutally into his retinas seemed to redouble the pain in his head.

'Where am I?' he asked.

'In a safe house.'

'As I came to I heard ships. The window is open and I smell salt on the breeze. Have you taken me to France?'

Shannon laughed.

'No, no. But we are by the sea. At Folkestone.'

'Ah, Folkestone.'

Kingsley knew, as any well-connected police officer might

know, that much of the apparatus of British military intelligence was centred at Folkestone – as, indeed, were the secret operations of a number of the Allied powers, the French, of course, but also the Belgians and, it was rumoured, the Russians, although whether the tottering Kerensky government was still sufficiently in control to consider spying on its western allies was highly dubious.

Now that his eyes had adjusted he was able to look at the man who had taken him prisoner. He had known in the car that Shannon was the younger of his two captors but he had not expected him to be *quite* so young. He could scarcely have been more than twenty-five. It was the voice which was deceptive. That effortless public-school tone scarcely changed in a man from twenty to sixty.

'You're young to be a captain,' Kingsley said.

'Young man's war, this,' Shannon said cheerily. 'Not many fellows get a chance to grow old.'

Kingsley got straight to the point.

'I don't know what you want, Captain, but whatever it is, you have come to the wrong place. I have told you that I will not work for your war. I also told you that I suspect you have gone to a great deal of trouble for nothing.'

'Look here, why don't you get up, have a bath and then we can have lunch, eh? I expect you could use a walk?'

Kingsley had longed for a bath, and for some fresh air. 'Actually, I should like a walk very much, particularly as I suspect you will shortly be returning me to Wormwood Scrubs.'

'Can't do that, you're dead. They're going to bury you this morning, confines of the prison and all that. Something of a disgrace, I fear. Your wife has declined to attend. Good thing really, considering they're burying a coffin full of sand.'

'You find it easy to be flippant about the ruination of a man's life, don't you?'

Shannon smiled.

'As a matter of fact I do, old boy. A few whiffs of gas plus a dead comrade or ten and a fellow quickly learns not to give a damn about very much at all. Besides which, I didn't ruin your life, Inspector. You ruined it, by being such a pompous prig. We just brought a sequence of unfortunate events to a neat conclusion. I thought we might eat down on the seafront. There are one or two quite good hotels.'

'Aren't you fearful that I will be recognized? I may not be Lord Kitchener but I have been in the newspapers. Being dead, I should hate to give an old lady a heart attack.'

'Oh, I think you'll be fine, old boy. That beard of yours is coming along nicely, you have a bandaged forehead and I brought you these.'

He handed Kingsley a pair of thick, horn-rimmed spectacles. Kingsley's eyesight was excellent but these were fitted with clear glass.

'You were a dapper sort of cove, weren't you?' Shannon continued. 'I'm afraid that the Secret Service doesn't run to much of a costume budget. When you've bathed you can put these on.'

The clothes that he gave to Kingsley were not remotely of the standard that he was accustomed to. Shannon was right in that Kingsley had always been rather elegant in his dress and would never have dreamed of wearing the shabby tweed suit that was now presented to him.

Having washed and dressed, he surveyed himself in the mirror. It was true, he was extremely unlikely to be recognized. He could scarcely recognize himself in the dowdy, bearded, bespectacled fellow who stared back at him and he was fairly confident that nobody else would either.

Thus emboldened, he and Shannon walked out together.

It had not been much of a summer and despite the fact that it was still August, what summer there had been was almost gone. Nonetheless, it wasn't a bad day for a stroll, particularly viewed from the perspective of a man recently sprung from prison. The air was chilly but the skies were blue. The sun shone, it was bracing and Kingsley realized how much he'd missed the open air.

Together he and Captain Shannon strolled along the Promenade. Shannon turned many female heads as they went, looking splendid in his uniform, with his medal ribbon, his swagger stick, his polished Sam Browne belt and riding boots. He sported a small, rakish Douglas Fairbanks moustache and impeccably brilliantined hair, on which his cap was perched at a jaunty angle. He had bought a toffee-covered apple from a stall and was munching it ostentatiously as he strolled along. In Kingsley's view, Captain Shannon was a cocky, showy bastard but not a man to be underestimated. Beneath that smooth exterior Kingsley sensed the soul of a violent man.

They passed a small Pierrot theatrical troupe who were drumming up business for their afternoon show by performing a truncated version of it on the Prom. Shannon stopped to watch, forcing Kingsley to do likewise.

'I say, woof woof!' Shannon exclaimed, referring to a tall, willowy creature who was doing some solo high kicks in a tiny white skirt with jolly multicoloured pompom buttons down the front. 'Splendid, eh? Very splendid *indeed*. That's the stuff to give the troops, eh? Not half! And then some. I do love a showgirl, don't you? I absolutely *love* a showgirl. Well, they know the score, don't they? Of course they do. Little teases. Oh, they know the score all right.'

The girl finished her dance. Shannon clapped loudly and was rewarded with a demure smile all to himself.

'See, told you.' Shannon grinned. '*She* knows the score.'

The girl retired to join the others at the side and the men tumbled on in their white Pierrot suits to perform an execrably unfunny, mimed sketch about a platoon of soldiers falling in and shouldering arms, in which the only joke (such as it was) seemed to be the inability of the soldiers to place their rifles on the same shoulder at the same time.

'Shame!' cried Shannon, showing none himself. 'Bring back the girls!'

There were no young men in the troupe, of course. A young

man cavorting about on the Folkestone Prom in a baggy white Pierrot suit with coloured pompoms would have been given short shrift by the crowd that season. There were just old men with horribly dyed hair and too much pancake make-up and eyeliner performing with the young girls.

'That's the job to have,' Shannon observed. 'Male Pierrot in the age of industrial war. Not a dashing young chap left standing and all the gorgeous ingénues in their smart little skirts and tights left to granddad's toothless drooling. I don't know why we don't send the old fellas over the top and give the young lads a decent shot at the bints. After all, it doesn't take a lot of youth and vigour to stroll ten yards then get shot to bits by the Boche, does it? You could do it with a walking frame. I really think I might write to the newspapers about it.'

Then the whole troupe assembled for a musical finale, ending, inevitably, with 'Forever England'. Shannon joined in lustily with the crowd.

Afterwards, as Shannon and Kingsley were about to continue their walk, the leader of the troupe approached them, his face furious beneath its thick cake of dark yellow Five and Nine make-up.

'I would have hoped,' he blustered, 'that a gentleman who holds the King's Commission might have behaved with more decorum, particularly in front of enlisted men.'

'Well, you would have hoped wrong then, wouldn't you?' Shannon replied. 'Now push off, you sad old queer, before I pull off your pompoms and stamp on 'em.'

The old man was clearly horrified but he attempted to bluster it out.

'I see your regimental badge, sir. I shall write to your commanding officer.'

'Do you know, old chum, so many of them are dead I think I may even *be* my commanding officer by now. That would be a lark, wouldn't it, putting myself on a charge?'

Shannon took Kingsley's arm and turned away. 'That "Forever

England" ditty they sang,' he said as they resumed their walk. 'You are perhaps aware that the fellow Abercrombie, who wrote the words, is dead?'

'No, I was not aware. I have not been in a position to follow the news over the last few weeks.'

'Try not to dwell on the past, old boy. Look at you now, sunning yourself on the Prom at Folkestone and watching jolly little Pierrettes jump through hoops.'

'You were pretty unpleasant with that old man. Do you enjoy bullying people?'

'Oh yes, absolutely,' Shannon replied. 'Capital sport. As for him, well, to tell you the truth I'd kill him for thruppence and enjoy the job. No, honestly, I really would. The only Englishmen worth a damn these days are in France, in fact most of them are *buried* in France. This trash back home, putting on patriotic airs and singing bloody stupid songs, should be digging latrine ditches for the comfort of the boys who fight. If they can lark about on the Prom they can dig bogs.'

The two men continued along the pavement in silence.

Kingsley turned to Shannon, who was happily winking and waving at the girls on the beach.

'All right, Captain,' he snapped. 'I'm a patient man but my patience is wearing damned thin. What the hell do you want with me? I demand that you tell me or I tell *you* I shall walk away from you right now.'

'Oh yes?' Shannon enquired with casual sarcasm.

'Oh very much yes, Captain. I know something about disappearing, you know, and I swear I could lose you in five minutes, bruised ribs, bashed head and all. Then you'd be stuck, wouldn't you, my supercilious friend? Because I am officially dead and once I'm gone there will be no one to look for, will there? A dead man leaves no tracks and I know every bolt-hole in London, aye, and the means to get a passage on a neutral ship from Tilbury if I need to. So if you don't want to find yourself getting a postcard from a corpse that has relocated its cold dead bones to South America, stop playing your bloody silly spy games and tell me what the hell it is you want.'

'Yes,' Shannon mused, suddenly thoughtful. 'They all say you're a useful sort of a chap. You'd better be . . . Ah! Here we are.' Shannon's cheerful demeanour returned instantly as he stopped outside a smart-looking hotel. 'The Majestic. Excellent brunch, I'm told, highly recommended by our codebreakers and, let me tell you, codebreakers are absolute sticklers for having things *just so*. Boring bunch of blighters but they know their tucker. Eggs, bacon, bubble, devilled kidneys, very fine black pudding and, I'm assured, some of the prettiest skivvies on the Prom.'

'Damn your brunch, Captain, and damn your fatuous gawping at the girls. Say what you have to say and let's be done with it.'

Shannon made a face of mock disappointment.

'Surely you don't object to us conversing in comfort and on full stomachs, Inspector? I confess I have a pecuniary motive for bringing you here. If I eat with you I may keep the receipt and the War Office will reimburse me the expense. If I eat alone then I fear I must stump up the cash myself, and I do hate laying out my own coin if I can be making free with John Bull's.'

Reluctantly Kingsley allowed himself to be led into the hotel, again reflecting that there was no advantage to him in alienating Shannon, and remembering also that he had not eaten since his last revolting supper in the prison hospital.

25

A rushed funeral

Agnes Kingsley raised her veil to stare down at the coffin. Her beauty was once more in stark contrast to the grim surroundings of a prison, just as it had been on her visit to Brixton when she had told Kingsley she was to divorce him.

Shannon had lied to Kingsley about Agnes. She had in fact elected to attend his funeral and would never have dreamed of doing otherwise.

They had given her scandalously short notice, forcing her to rush to Regent Street with barely an hour to assemble the appropriate widow's weeds. She had had to change at the shop and walk out wearing her new black gown with the hem all done up with pins, and with the clothes she had arrived in wrapped in paper by the shopgirl and put in a bag. It was uncomfortable and unseemly but Agnes Kingsley had no intention of allowing the prison authorities to see her as anything other than a proud, upstanding English widow. Her life might have collapsed utterly but that was no excuse for lowering her standards.

She had arrived almost exactly at the appointed hour and as she passed through the huge front door of the prison had demanded that a warder run on ahead to the little courtyard and tell them to pause for a moment, till she arrived.

'I will not run to my husband's funeral,' she said. 'They must wait or, mark my words, they will *never* hear the end of it.'

They did wait, and Agnes was able to stand before the grave and bid her final farewells during a brief service, in which the funeral rites from the Book of Common Prayer were read out at breakneck speed by a prison chaplain who would clearly rather have been elsewhere.

'Manthatisbornofwoman . . .' the chaplain jabbered. 'Webringnothingintothisworld . . . Ashestoashes . . . TheFather theSonandtheHolyGhost . . . Amen.'

There were no added readings, no poetry or music.

After the service, such as it was, had ended, the chaplain stepped back and bid the gravedigger begin immediately to fill the grave. Agnes raised a hand to stop them.

'Wait,' she said. 'I wish to read.'

The governor, who had attended the funeral in deference to the rank of Agnes's father, took Mrs Kingsley's arm.

'I am afraid, Mrs Kingsley, that we are a busy prison and do not have time for—'

'Unhand me, sir! I wish to read,' Agnes said firmly, pulling her arm away. The governor bowed reluctantly and Agnes took a paper from her bag.

'This poem my husband read often to my son, who is only four years old. It is "If" by Rudyard Kipling.'

The chaplain, the governor, two warders and the gravediggers sighed audibly, but Agnes Kingsley did not read for them.

When she paused at the end of the first verse, it was clear that the governor was itching to intervene and stop the recital but had not quite the courage to do so. It was now obvious to everybody that Agnes intended to read the entire poem, all thirty-two lines of it, and, what is more, to read it slowly, with firm and plodding meter. The governor could only stare up at the sky and count the syllables as she read the third verse and then the fourth. Finally she finished and having done so she dropped the poem into the grave, then she lowered her veil once more in order to hide her tears.

'Thank you for your patience, Governor,' she said.

'You are welcome, Mrs Kingsley.'

'I must say,' she added as he escorted her out of the prison, 'it seems that you were in quite a hurry to dispose of my husband's remains.'

The governor denied it but Agnes insisted.

'Is it customary then to bury a man the very next day after he dies? It certainly is not so in Leicestershire.'

The governor explained that this was always the way when bodies were buried within the confines of the prison, since sadly they had no mortuary facilities available to them.

'And why is he buried in a prison at all? He was not a murderer.'

'Those were the instructions that the Home Office gave us, Mrs Kingsley.'

Agnes had thought about protesting; she was a proud woman and was certain that the authorities had gone far beyond their rights in disposing of her husband's remains in this unseemly and underhand manner. It was clear to her that they wished to be rid of the whole ghastly scandal as quickly as possible. But what would have been the point of making a fuss? Douglas was dead and were she to have insisted on arranging for a proper funeral who would have attended?

Perhaps, after all, this was the best way. Kingsley himself had always maintained that when a man is dead, he is dead and that she might chuck him in the Thames for all he cared. Agnes returned to her car and was driven away from Wormwood Scrubs.

26

Brunch at the Hotel Majestic

'I say, *what ho*! Proper little piece, eh? That's the stuff to give the troops, don't ye know!'

Shannon and Kingsley had entered the dining room of the Majestic and been ushered to a table in the window by a young waitress who was indeed, as Shannon observed, a delightful-looking girl.

The table was the most secluded one available, partly separated from the body of the room by a cluster of rather large potted palms. A string quartet was situated close by, which, although not loud enough to inhibit their conversation, would serve to mask it from the other tables.

Like most string quartets in hotel dining rooms, they were playing a selection from Gilbert and Sullivan and had arrived at a rather mournful piece from *The Yeomen of the Guard*. Shannon sang along under his breath for a moment as he stared out through the salt-stained window.

> '*Heigh-dy! Heigh-dy!*
> *Misery me, lackaday dee*
> *He sipped no sup and he craved no crumb*
> *As he sighed for the love of a la-dye.*'

Perhaps it was the music but he seemed suddenly to have fallen into a reflective mood. 'Nannies with babies,' he mused, 'old bastards with sticks, fat old bags of matrons and their lapdogs, brats rolling hoops, Jack tars with their girls or more likely strutting about hoping to find one. God's bones, it's a peaceful sight, what?'

'Yes, it is.'

'How far is it from here to Passchendaele, I wonder? Fifty miles? Rather less than that, I think. Less than fifty miles and a billion too. Here and there could be on opposite sides of the universe, couldn't they? Rather bizarre, don't you think? A fellow might take tea here in the morning and if he gets a move on he can have it blown out of his guts in Belgium before he's had a chance to digest it. If that's not bloody bizarre then quite frankly I don't know what is.'

'I'm sure you're right.'

'Do you think any of the people strolling along out there so damned pleased with themselves could possibly have any concept, even in the wildest parts of their tiny imaginations, of the scale of carnage taking place *at this very minute* just fifty miles away?'

'The casualty lists are public information. Those people out there who you seem to despise are mothers and fathers, sisters, brothers, husbands, friends. They know what's going on and I doubt many of them are feeling very smug or pleased about it.'

Shannon stared at Kingsley for a moment in silence, his face filled with contempt.

'But of course. *You* haven't been there either, have you? I was forgetting.'

'No. I haven't been there.'

'Ha. You're like them. Oh yes, you know that men are dying, dying in their thousands day after day. Everybody knows *that*. But you don't know *what it's like*. You could spend the rest of your life trying to imagine it but you'd never get even close. Nobody could who hasn't been there. You'll never join our club.'

'I do not wish to join your club. I wish your club had never been formed.'

'A mincing machine. That's what they all say. And it is a mincing machine. But that's not what it's *like*. All a mincing machine does is mince things up. Let me tell you, Kingsley, nothing, no words in the English language or any other bloody language for that matter, could *ever* describe what it's like.'

The string quartet were taking a short break and in their place Shannon began to sing, softly, under his breath. He sang to the tune of an old hymn. Kingsley knew the tune well but the lyric he had heard only once before. It was a soldiers' lyric and he had heard it late one night at Victoria Station, sung quietly by a group of walking wounded awaiting dispersal.

> '*And when they ask us*
> *How dangerous it was,*
> *Oh we'll never tell them*
> *No we'll never tell them.*'

'And they won't tell you now,' Shannon concluded. 'For they haven't the wit to do so, nobody has. That's why everybody's a bloody poet these days. Everybody *wants* to tell, everybody's scribbling away, but it's no good. Nobody will ever find a way to bridge the gap between those who were there and those who weren't.'

Now it was Kingsley's turn to quote.

'*Leprous earth, scattered with the swollen and blackened corpses of hundreds of young men. The appalling stench of rotten carrion.*'

'What's that bilge?'

'Part of a letter which T. S. Eliot sent to the *Nation*.'

'Bloody poets again, eh? What the hell would he know anyway?'

'It's not his, it's a quote from a letter he received from an officer at the front. I learned it off by heart to quote at my trial . . . *Mud*

128

like porridge, trenches like shallow and sloping cracks in the porridge – porridge that stinks in the sun. Swarms of flies and bluebottles clustering on pits of offal. Wounded men lying in the shell holes among the decaying corpses: helpless under the scorching sun and bitter nights, under repeated shelling. Men with bowels dropping out, limbs blown into space. Men screaming and gibbering. Wounded men hanging in agony on the barbed wire, until a friendly spout of liquid fire shrivels them up like a fly in a candle . . . But these are only words and probably convey only a fraction of their meaning to the hearers. They shudder and it is forgotten. Like you say,' Kingsley concluded, 'he was trying to describe it but knew he never could.'

'Yes. And like I also said, everyone thinks they're a bloody poet.'

'It seems to be a common theme, this frustration that nobody will ever understand,' Kingsley observed. 'Sassoon made the same point, didn't he? In his letter?'

'Ah yes, Sassoon. What a *despicable fucking bastard.*'

Kingsley was shocked at the venom.

'You disapprove of what he did?'

'That whining little shit. That windy *turd.* And him an MC too! They should tear it off him. Sneaking home with a bit of shell shock and letting the side down. We can do without war heroes turning conchie on us. Bad enough when famous detectives do it but Sassoon was one of *us.*'

Everyone knew of Siegfried Sassoon and his protest. A bona fide hero, he had become utterly disillusioned and whilst invalided home had written to the newspapers resigning from the army and denouncing the war as wicked and pointless. As he was something of a celebrity, his letter had caused a sensation. He had very nearly been court-martialled, but after a number of strings were pulled and attention drawn to his numerous battle credits he was sent to a hospital to be treated for shell shock.

'They should have shot him,' Shannon said.

'For stating the obvious after eighteen months in the line? That seems a little harsh, Captain.'

'Oh, don't get me wrong, Inspector. We all know that he's right, the war's gone mad, nothing could possibly be worth the price we're paying, but they should have shot him all the same because, you see, we *have* to win this war. We just have to. And I can assure you, whatever a revolting conchie like you might think, most of the fellows agree. We're the British Empire, for God's sake, we can't go through all this and *lose*.'

'We've already lost. Everybody has already lost.'

'That's just rubbish! We may be ruined, we may be crippled but we haven't *lost*. There is a difference, you know, but the more people like you and Sassoon go about the place undermining the very bloody easily underminable the closer we all get to packing up and going home and then we *will* lose. The French very nearly did just that, you know.'

Kingsley did not know.

The extraordinary mutiny of the French Army (which had never recovered from the epic slaughter of Verdun) was not yet common knowledge. News of it had been kept as quiet as possible. There were stories and rumours, of course, but the true extent of the mutiny had been suppressed.

'Terrible business,' Shannon went on. 'Just what we did not need with Russia going to hell in a basket. Did you know that at the end of last May at Chemin des Dames *thirty thousand* French soldiers mutinied?'

'I had no idea.'

'No, and neither have most of our Tommies, thank God, or perhaps they'd get up and do the same. On the first of June at Missy-aux-bois French infantry took over a *whole town*. They actually established their own anti-war "government". That's just two months ago. The bloody revolution had actually started *in France* and the entire line was on the verge of collapse.'

'But it didn't.'

'No, but only because the Germans had no idea of the

opportunity they were missing. If they'd pushed then, the whole bloody lot would have caved in. But they didn't and the rebellion was crushed but, let me tell you, nobody's expecting another offensive from the French any time soon. That's why we're so heavily engaged now. It's all down to us till the Yanks arrive, and God knows when that will be. But I can assure you that when Pétain realized he had a mutiny to deal with he didn't send the bloody ringleaders to hospital for shell shock. He court-martialled nearly *twenty-five thousand* of them, handed out over four hundred death sentences – won't carry them all out, of course, but the point was made. It's the only way in war. I have a lot of sympathy for mutineers but I'd shoot them just the same. Particularly Siegfried bloody holier-than-thou Sassoon.'

The food arrived and Shannon seemed instantly to forget the grim themes he had been pondering in order to flirt with the pretty waitress.

'Sugar, sir?' she enquired, holding the little silver tongs in her dainty hand.

'Ah, sweets from the sweet.'

The girl went a little pink.

'I shall tell General Haig on you,' the waitress admonished but it was obvious that she was pleased.

'And what will you tell him?' Shannon enquired with easy arrogance. 'That you like to walk out with officers?'

'No. I shall tell him that I'm a good girl.'

'That's no protection from the army, miss. General Haig would do what he always does and order me to advance.'

'What *can* you mean, sir?'

'The British soldier knows no other way. Advance, advance, advance! Storm the enemy's strongholds and occupy them.'

Now the girl really was blushing, to Shannon's evident enjoyment.

'But an efficient advance requires good intelligence. So let me begin to gather some now, pretty miss. What's your name?'

'Not telling.'

'When do you finish work?'

'I shan't say.'

'Come now, my dear, this is a military operation. I order you to tell me.'

'Well then, I'm Violet if you must know and I get off at half past three but I'm on again at six.'

'In which case, Violet my dear, I must be prompt. If I were to attend the lobby of this hotel at three thirty-one precisely, might I take you for a stroll by the sea?'

'Well, you *might*. Why don't you attend and then you'll find out, eh?'

'Good girl! That's the spirit! Well said, Vi! Three thirty-one it is. And then, over the top, eh!'

'You officers! You're worse than the men.'

'It's our duty. We are instructed to lead by example.'

The waitress laughed and scurried off.

'Three thirty till six,' Shannon observed. 'Two and a half hours. A lot can be achieved in two and a half hours. We took twenty thousand dead in not much longer than that on the first day of the Somme. Your brother Robert was one of them, wasn't he?'

'Yes, he was.'

'Well, I'm sure I can turn a good girl bad with a similar window of opportunity.'

'Captain Shannon, if I wanted to watch a dog on heat I would hang about in an alley.'

'Well, you know something, Inspector, I know I'm being rude but, you see, I have a rule and I never break it.'

'Rule?'

'Shannon's credo. Any drink. Any meal. Any girl. Any time.'

'I was under the impression that you are on duty?'

'There is a higher duty and that duty is to make hay while the sun shines because, you see, Kingsley, the sun will not shine for long. I am bound soon to die.'

'You're sure of that then?'

'Certain to, my number's been up for a while now, don't ye know. I was a rowing Blue at Oxford. Race of 1912. Of all the men I sculled with I'm the only one left. Think of that: every one of them popped his clogs, isn't that extraordinary? Even the poor little cox, who got hit by a sniper on Vimy Ridge – and incidentally that Hun must have been an extraordinary shot because, believe me, our cox was the tiniest, skinniest little bloke you could ever hope to meet. I shan't be long joining them, that's for certain, borrowed time and all that. If I hadn't been seconded to the SIS I'd be dead already, what with the bloody mess that's going on at Ypres. That's why I have my rule, you see. Grab it while you can. Get it while it's good.'

'Always?'

'Always. Any drink. Any meal. Any girl. Any time. Without fail. Do not falter. Never let one single opportunity to eat, drink, sleep or bed the ladies go by and hang everything else. So when that bullet finally finds its billet, or I'm gassed, or shit myself to death with dysentery or I'm blown to bits or drowned in the mud or just keel over with plain funk I shall know that there never was a single girl I could have had that I didn't have, nor any drink, nor any grub nor any other comfort either which came my way and which I did not grab. Not a bad rule, eh? Come on, you must admit.'

'I suppose it does make a lot of sense.'

'Damn right it does. But look here, I can't sit here jabbering with you all day. What say we get down to business?'

'I think it might be for the best.'

'But first, of course, the rule!'

Shannon attacked his eggs and kidney with vigour. He also had bacon, sausage, mushrooms, black pudding, grilled tomato, a thick pork chop and all the toast including Kingsley's. He drained the teapot and ordered another with a shot of Scotch to pour into it, and only when not a single scrap of food or drink remained anywhere on the table did he finally light a cigarette and get to the point.

'So. We mentioned the sad news about Viscount Abercrombie?'

'That he's dead.'

133

'Yes, he died in France. He was murdered.'

'He didn't die in action?'

'No. That's what people think happened but in fact he was murdered.'

Kingsley considered this for a moment.

'Whatever that means,' he said finally.

'What do you mean, whatever that means?'

'I'm not sure I know what murder is any more, particularly in France.'

'Oh, do *please* put a sock in it, Inspector. You're a policeman. You know damn well what murder means, it's when one man kills another illegally.'

'In my view Haig has become a murderer, Lloyd George also, the Kaiser is a murderer . . .'

'Yes, we all know what you think about the war, Inspector. You have made it absolutely bloody clear. You don't like it. You think it's utterly insane. Well, here's some news for you. *None* of us likes it, we *all* think it's insane, *particularly* those of us who have actually fought in it. But we don't all feel the need to *bang on about it* all the time.'

'You were speaking of Viscount Abercrombie.'

'Well, as you might imagine, his death has been something of a shock to people. A very great shock. He was one of the last of the real romantic heroes, a hero who still *was* a bloody hero. A Rupert Brooke, not a Siegfried Sassoon.'

'Rupert Brooke died of an infected mosquito bite on his lip.'

'On his way to fight. His poetry inspired people, it did not rub their noses in the horror they had to live with anyway. It lifted them up.

> *'If I should die, think only this of me:*
> *That there's some corner of a foreign field*
> *That is for ever England.*

'Don't you think that's beautiful?'

'Yes, I do. Beautiful and deeply poignant.'

'Abercrombie's poetry was like that.'

'Abercrombie wrote verse, not poetry. He was no Brooke.'

'People loved it because it was simple and heartfelt and noble.'

'What has Viscount Abercrombie's death to do with me?' Kingsley enquired.

'Well, as I told you, he was murdered. Killed, it seems, by a disaffected private soldier. They were both invalided out of the line with shell shock and were under assessment prior to treatment. The soldier shot Abercrombie and was discovered with the gun. He's under arrest awaiting court martial and I hope they hang, draw and quarter him. To think of a brave fellow like Abercrombie, an inspiration to us all, ending up in some grubby little murder. Do you remember what he said in "Only remember me"?'

'I don't think I do.'

> 'I hope to lead my men across
> That bloodied battleground forlorn
> And lay my body down for them
> And for the place where I was born.'

'I am pleased to say that I do not know Abercrombie's work well.'

'Yet you memorized every bloody word of that foul letter Eliot thought so bloody important. Good God, man, we all know it's muddy and maggoty and unutterably bloody frightful. The beauty in this war is in the human spirit, its capacity for honour and sacrifice. That's what Abercrombie was about and some nasty, spiteful little private shot him for it.'

'Again I ask what has any of this to do with me?'

'You're a policeman. We want you to investigate it.'

'The SIS?'

'Good lord, no. The top nobs, bigwigs, high-ups. How should I know? Lloyd George himself, I shouldn't wonder.'

'So this is not to be an SIS investigation?'

'Why should it be? It's police business. All we were told to do was to get you out of Wormwood Scrubs with no questions asked and deliver you to London.'

'London? Then why have you brought me to Folkestone?'

'We thought you had three cracked ribs. Honestly, that prison doctor, it's a scandal. We thought you'd be laid up for another week and you'd be safest down here with us.'

'But why would you need me at all? If they have made an arrest, isn't it rather too late to begin a police investigation?'

'Well, you'd have thought so, wouldn't you? It looks open and shut to me, but that's what they want so that's what we'll do. I've telegraphed London that you've been passed fit for duty and—'

'I do not intend to perform any duties.'

'I've told you, this has nothing to do with the military effort. It's police work, police work which your government requires of you. We expect you to at least listen to the detail of the task we want you to perform.'

Put like that, it did not seem unreasonable.

'Very well. I shall listen.'

'Right. Well, first you're to return to London.'

'You'll tell me nothing more now?'

'No, I'm just a poor foot-slogger. You're to be briefed at a much higher level than my poor status allows.' Shannon handed Kingsley a slip of paper. 'You're to report to this address at Whitehall tomorrow morning at nine sharp.'

'You won't be with me?'

'Oh yes, I shall attend, but what about between now and then, eh?'

'What about it?'

Shannon lit another cigarette and offered one to Kingsley, which he gratefully accepted.

'Well, here's the thing,' Shannon said. He drew deeply and then expelled the spent smoke. 'I have a proposal to make to you, you know, just between ourselves.'

'Go on.'

'It concerns my rule. My credo.'

'Any drink, any meal, any girl, any time?'

'Exactly. You see, I'm *supposed* to stay with you between now and tomorrow morning . . .'

'And?'

'Well, it just seems rather pointless us hanging about together, don't you think? You don't like me and I certainly don't like you. What's more, I'd thought I'd have a whole week skulking about beside the sea making a beast of myself while you recovered. Now it turns out you're disgustingly fit and my cushy little nursemaid's billet has come to an abrupt end when it had scarcely begun. Dashed disappointing. So what I'm saying is, why don't we just split up and agree to meet in London?'

'You'd trust me not to abscond?'

'Well, I really don't see why you would want to. You have no identity and if you tried to reclaim your old one you'd simply be sent back to prison. You're penniless and homeless and we are offering you the prospect of gainful employment. I rather think that a logical fellow like you will see that sticking with us, at least until you know fully what we want, is your best bet.'

'You'd actually let me wander off alone, having gone to all this trouble to secure me?'

Shannon was smoking so ferociously that he was already forced to light another.

'Think about it for a moment, Inspector. It's nearly noon. That means I have twenty-one hours before I am expected to deliver you to my superiors. Nearly *a whole day* in which I'm not dead and not under fire. Have you *any idea* what that means to a man who's served two years in the trenches?'

'But all the same . . .'

'When I am returned to the line and shortly thereafter am no doubt lying dead or dying in some muddy Belgian crater I should *hate* to look back and think that I had *twenty-one hours* in Blighty and I spent them talking to a shit like you.'

'Instead you wish to apply your cardinal rule.'

'It's three and a half hours until I meet gorgeous little Violet and then she's back on at six. If I work hard and flash my Military Medal about I reckon I could bed three girls just here in Folkestone before getting blind drunk on the last train to London and having a crack at the 'dilly in the small hours.'

'And for that you would forsake your duty as my keeper?'

'I've told you, the walking dead like me have a higher duty. A duty to what's left of their short lives. Besides, as I've also made clear, Inspector, I believe you'll come to the meeting, and if you don't I shall simply say that you gave me the slip. Believe me, Kingsley, I care far more, *infinitely* more, about pleasuring myself than I do about you or the damn-fool mission that my boss has planned for you.'

Kingsley did not like Shannon much but he certainly found him intriguing.

'You really think you could seduce three women and still get to London tonight?'

'Inspector, this is wartime and not just any old wartime either. It's Great War time. Most of the young men are dead and those that aren't will be dead tomorrow. Rest assured, girls have adjusted their point of view accordingly. And if they won't come across, I just have to find a way to persuade them, eh? Believe me, if I wish to bed a girl, I *do* bed her.'

Despite the distaste that he felt for Shannon, Kingsley could not help but be impressed with his self-belief. He himself was a man of enormous confidence but this young, amoral captain was in an entirely different league.

'Where will you start?'

'Perhaps with that lovely Pierrot. Or down on the beach. I might take a stick and effect a slight wound. Girls love all that. Offer them a nip of brandy against the wind and hello, Prince Wilhelm, hands, knees and bumps-a-daisy!'

'Aren't you worried that I'll be recognized?'

'Oh, you'll make sure you're not. As I say, if Inspector Kingsley *were* to come back to life the best you could hope for would be prison . . . But of course you will understand that that would hardly be an option for us.'

Shannon had placed his cigarette in the ashtray that lay amongst the clutter of his meal and was looking hard into Kingsley's eyes. Of course Kingsley did understand. He could see that, having faked his death, the SIS could scarcely afford to have him come back to life.

Kingsley stroked his beard. He had never in his life been inclined to grow facial hair, not even in the days of Edward VII when it had been something of a fashion in the police.

'I shall remain anonymous. At least until I fully understand what is expected of me.'

'Excellent fellow.'

Shannon called for the bill, gave an ostentatiously large tip, courtesy of the taxpayer, and instructed Violet not to forget the promised rendezvous. Then he and Kingsley left the hotel together, and as they prepared to separate on the pavement outside Shannon issued a final warning.

'Remember, Inspector, that your sudden appearance in the land of the living would put all of us in a fearful mess. If you blow your cover either by design or by mistake I shall kill you, it's as simple as that.'

'You already have my word. There is no need for threats.'

'Yes, but I find they never do any harm. Anyway, we'll say no more about it, eh? Instead I shall advance you one pound for travel and tonight's board in London. I'm afraid I shall have to ask you to sign for it.'

Shannon held out a Foreign Office expenses chit, which flapped about in the sea breeze.

'What shall I sign? The only name I have belongs to a dead man.'

'Good point. Do you know, I hadn't even thought of that, and me a secret agent! I *am* an ass, ain't I? We were going to set up your new identity tomorrow. Who's your favourite author?'

'Shakespeare.'

'Too showy. How about Marlowe?'

'I think that will be fine.'

Kingsley signed himself Christopher Marlowe and took his pound.

'You do know that Christopher Marlowe was a spy, don't you?' said Shannon as they parted.

'He was also a poet,' Kingsley replied, 'and I'm not that either.'

'I've told you, *everybody*'s a poet these days.'

27

A free afternoon

Having checked on the times of trains to London, Kingsley began his afternoon by asking the way to the public library. It felt wonderful to be his own master once more, walking through the quiet streets of an English port. Of course the guilt he felt over his estranged and deluded family did not go away, but nonetheless a lunchtime stroll was an unexpected and luxurious respite from the hellish turmoil into which his life had of late descended.

He found the library, a decent old pile, testimony to the late Victorian zeal for public education, and entered its hushed environs. It was very full: everywhere men and women sat in reverential silence, hunched over books or the day's newspapers, each of which was mounted on a tall, unwieldy stick. Kingsley was surprised at how well the place was patronized, reflecting that perhaps in these terrible and crazy times people sought comfort in the wisdom of the past. Certainly there were plenty of black veils and armbands to be seen. Kingsley was particularly touched and saddened to note that children, some as young as eight or nine, were there also, sitting about quietly reading, the mark of mourning on their arms. One little girl had a copy of the *Rainbow* comic and by rights 'The Jolly Adventures of the Bruin Boys', a popular cartoon about a boarding school for animals, should have made her laugh, or smile at least, but as he passed her, sitting on her little child's stool, he could see that she was crying. The girl's mother sat beside her upon another child's stool. She had black crêpe trim on her threadbare dress and there was a magazine upon her lap but she wasn't reading it; she was staring into the distance while she gently stroked her little girl's hair. Kingsley wondered whether Agnes wore black that day and what, if anything, she had said to George.

He found an empty writing desk and sat down. It had been his intention to write a letter to Agnes, a letter which he would ask to be sent to her in the event of his death. But try as he might, he could think of nothing to say. He had no idea what was to become of him and so could give her no information on why she had been so cruelly deceived. And as far as commenting on the past was concerned, everything that could be said had already been said. She had dismissed him from her life and there was an end to it. She had not even attended his funeral.

Kingsley fell to considering the sad death of Viscount Abercrombie. A man whose murder the authorities wished him to investigate. A man whose death had, temporarily at least, saved Kingsley's life.

He looked up the reports of Abercrombie's death in what newspapers were available. The library did not keep an archive of the national papers, holding them only for a day or two, but they had all the past editions of the local journal. This had reported the hero's death in some detail, although not with any accuracy, for as far as the newspaper was concerned Abercrombie had died in action:

HERO DEAD

It is with great sadness that we must report the death of Viscount Alan Abercrombie, DSO, aged 25, only son of Lord Abercrombie, Conservative Chief Whip in the House of Lords. The young viscount's fame eclipsed even that of his distinguished father by dint of his illustrious war record and the highly popular patriotic poems that he wrote. Whilst he was still at Oxford, his verse cycle Country Lane and Village *was much admired. The best-known part of it, 'Cricket on the Green and Tea', has been compared to Brooke's famous 'Grantchester' for its evocation of the England for which we are all fighting. Abercrombie enlisted in 1915 (a bout of pleurisy had kept him out of the first year of the war) and first saw action at Loos, where he led his men in an heroic charge against the machine guns. He won his DSO on the Somme a year later, by which time he had been promoted captain. He was decorated for his actions in rescuing a wounded comrade under heavy fire. Viscount Abercrombie published two volumes of patriotic verse that have brought much comfort to soldiers and civilians alike and which, before the advent of conscription, were a feature of many recruiting concerts. He will perhaps be best remembered for his poem 'Forever England', which was inspired by the late Rupert Brooke's 'The Soldier'. 'Forever England' has, of course, been set to music by Mr Ivor Novello and has proved a rival even to the success of Novello's 'Keep The Home Fires Burning'. Captain Abercrombie was killed in action, dying as he lived, a hero and a leader of men. We reproduce Viscount Abercrombie's best-known work below:*

> *Forever England. Home and hearth.*
> *Valley, dale and country path.*
> *Lonely cottage. Village green.*
> *Cricket, hunt and church serene.*
> *Forever England. When I die*
> *I pray beneath your turf I'll lie.*
> *But if instead, I die abroad*
> *Cut down by bullet, bomb or sword*
> *To mark the sacrifice I gave*
> *Put 'Forever England' on my grave.*

Try as he might, Kingsley, who beneath his brusque exterior was not an unemotional man, could not bring himself to see this appalling verse as anything other than juvenile drivel. He felt sorry for the young man and his family and admired his bravery, but to his mind England had not lost a poet.

Kingsley found his thoughts turning to Captain Shannon. Why were the SIS involved in this case? He doubted that their part in it really was as simple as Shannon claimed.

Thinking of Shannon caused Kingsley to reflect on the man's plans for his afternoon and evening. Kingsley felt sorry for the girls who crossed his path; Shannon was not the sort of man whom anyone would wish their daughter to associate with. Kingsley thought of Violet, the little skivvy from the Hotel Majestic, who hadn't looked more than seventeen. Suddenly he felt a chill of fear. He recalled the cruelty with which Shannon had handled the old man on the pier. He remembered the words Shannon had used when asked if he was sure of his prospective conquests: '*And if they won't come across, I just have to find a way to persuade them, eh? Believe me, if I wish to bed a girl, I do bed her.*'

At the time Kingsley had not read much into this, but now he wondered. Looking at the wristwatch which he had been given along with his clothes, he noted that it was nearly three o'clock. He got up and hurried from the library.

28

A soldier demands his comfort

After a pleasant interlude at a guest house with the willowy Pierrette, who did indeed know the score, Shannon proceeded back to the seafront and along it towards the Hotel Majestic. His blood was up now, his stride less jaunty but his pace just as fast and his stance aggressive. He pushed his way through the afternoon strollers without apology. His easy smile had become a cross between a leer and a snarl. He was on the hunt.

Violet was waiting for him outside the hotel. Instantly Shannon's style changed once more, back to its old easy nonchalance.

'Well, well, Violet! You came. How splendidly kind of you,' he said, taking her arm.

'Well, you were very sweet, weren't you, Captain,' the girl replied. 'You never should have left a tip like that! The other girls were green!'

Violet was clearly delighted to be in the company of such a handsome and dashing officer. She glanced through the windows of the hotel dining room as they passed, thrilled that all her colleagues could see her in the company of such a gorgeous catch.

'Let's take a bus along the front,' Shannon suggested, and together they sat on the open top of an omnibus with the wind blowing in Violet's hair and making her cheeks red and Shannon showering her with witty compliments and making her giggle and reddening her cheeks all the more.

They took the bus right to the very end of its journey on the edge of the town and then Shannon led her down on to the beach.

'Why've we come here?' Violet enquired.

'Oh, you know, I do hate crowds,' Shannon said with a boyish smile. 'What with all the noise and horror of life at the front it's nice for me to get a little quiet, particularly in such charming company. Not many lovely girls where I've been, you see, or any peace.'

Thus charmed, Violet allowed herself to be led further along the empty beach before Shannon found a little fishing jetty and suggested that they shelter beyond it as the wind was picking up.

'I have to be back by six, you know,' Violet reminded Shannon.

'Oh, I shan't need to keep you that long,' Shannon replied.

If Violet thought this a strange thing to say she did not show it, and together they sat down in the shelter of the jetty.

'Well now, isn't this nice?' Shannon declared.

'Lovely. Really lovely,' Violet agreed. 'Here, I say! Do you know what, Captain, I don't even know your name yet.'

'I'm the fellow who's going to show you a bit about life, dear,' he said and put his arm around her. For a moment she didn't resist, even briefly laying her head on his shoulder, but when he pulled her down on to the sand and began to kiss her on the lips she protested loudly.

'No! No, Captain!'

He took his mouth from hers as she pushed at his shoulders.

'What? What do you mean, no?'

'I mean no! Gosh, you're fast! None of that now. I only met you a minute ago! You can hold my hand if you like but no more kisses. Not kisses like *that*, anyway!'

'Hold your hand,' Shannon repeated. '*Hold your hand?* Do you really think I've brought you all the way out of town to *hold your damn hand?*'

146

Suddenly the girl was scared. Shannon did not look at all like the man he had been only moments before.

'I'm only sixteen,' Violet protested, 'and I'm a good girl. I told you . . . I told you.'

'I don't care how old you are or what you think of yourself, dear. I'm going to fuck you.'

Violet was instantly terrified: she had scarcely even *heard* the word before, let alone been threatened with it.

'No!'

'Yes! Now lie down quiet and let's get on with it.'

'Please, Captain, no! I don't want to, I never have . . . please.'

'Well, if you've been saving it up, then who better to give it to than a soldier of the King? Eh? EH? Or ain't I *good enough* for you? Who do you think you are, you little slut? Too good for a British soldier, is that it? Come on, answer me, you hussy!'

'No. I never said . . . !'

'All the young men are dying and little tarts like you are back· home *saving it*! Saving it for what? Some big rich American? Is that it? Is little missy hoping to whore herself a Yankee?'

'No!'

'You ungrateful little tart. Your countrymen are *dying* for you. Do you understand? If you had any decency at all you'd offer your skinny little body to every single serviceman you met! You'd whore for them at the dockside! Fuck a platoon a day and think yourself honoured! *Lord Kitchener wants your cunt!*'

Shannon's face was contorted with spite and venom. The girl was weeping, shaking with fear and distress, snot running from her nose. Shannon grabbed her wrists and forced her back down on to the sand.

'I am a British soldier,' Shannon shouted into Violet's sobbing, sopping face, 'and I want my comfort! *You* are a British whore and you shall damn well give it to me!'

Shannon began to pull up the girl's skirts. She shrieked in fear but, too terrified and confused to offer more resistance, she did not struggle further.

'Please . . .' The snot turned into bubbles at her mouth as she tried to utter the word 'don't'.

The brief struggle was over. Shannon had subdued her with his brutality. Now he forced one of her arms across her face to wipe the tears and mucus on to her sleeve, and then once more he pushed his mouth down on to hers whilst pulling up her skirts and tugging at her underwear.

Just then Kingsley emerged from behind the jetty.

'Unhand that girl this instant,' he commanded.

'What the devil . . . !' Shannon exclaimed, looking up from the girl, his hand still pulling at her clothing.

'I said take your hands off her, Captain, or I shall take them off for you.'

Kingsley's tone was forceful; he was a man used to giving commands. So, of course, was Shannon and for a moment there was a stand-off. Then Shannon smiled and, letting go of Violet's dress, he raised himself from her.

Kingsley leaned forward and, offering the girl his hand, he pulled her to her feet.

'Are you all right, miss?' he enquired.

'Yes, sir,' Violet sniffled, still shaking with fear and shock. 'I think so.'

'Did you *follow* me, Inspector?' Shannon asked, brushing the sand from his clothes.

'Yes, I did, Captain Shannon. I don't know what moved me to but I suddenly thought that I would. It's being a policeman, I suppose. You come to *smell* wickedness.'

Shannon smiled and then suddenly jabbed out a blow towards Kingsley, a nasty, powerful rabbit punch that might easily have broken his nose. Kingsley, however, was as fast as Shannon, faster even, and deflected the blow. Violet screamed and cowered by the jetty.

'Shall we fight then?' Kingsley enquired. 'Understand that I'm ready for you.'

'No, better not,' Shannon replied, as instantly easy and languid as he had been instantly ferocious. 'I'm supposed to deliver you in one piece and ready for service.'

'What makes you think that I wouldn't be in one piece after fighting you?' Kingsley asked.

'Touché, old boy. Tou-ruddy-ché.'

Kingsley had spoken with a confidence he did not entirely feel. He knew that Shannon was a killing gentleman and he himself had never been that type. He turned back to Violet.

'Will you be all right to make your way home?' he enquired.

'Yes, sir, I think so . . . I have to go back to the hotel.'

'Do you have your bus fare?'

'Oh yes, sir.'

'Well then, dry your eyes, pull yourself together and go back to the town. Have a cup of tea and try not to dwell on what has happened. You've had a very nasty experience but it has turned out all right, hasn't it?'

'Yes, sir.'

'Goodbye then.'

'Goodbye, sir.'

Violet turned to leave.

'And Violet, not all men are like this one. Remember that.'

'Goodbye, dearie,' Shannon sneered. 'Perhaps I shall come looking for you some other night.'

The girl ran away as fast as she could manage.

After she had gone the two men stood facing each other on the sand.

'Do you intend to follow me around all day in order to protect the virgins of southern England?' Shannon asked.

'I just had a feeling about that one. She seemed . . . vulnerable.'

'Mmmm. Well, don't worry, I don't normally bother with kids. I like a bint who knows what she's doing. I just set about that one because she was pretty and well . . . because she was *there*. Can't let them pass. Feel I owe it to myself.'

'And you have a taste for violence.'

'Do you know, I rather think I do. Awful thing really. For a

149

gentleman. But there is something bracing about taking a helpless little bird and breaking its wings, don't ye know. Shall we return to the bus stop?'

'I think we'll give it a few minutes if that's all right by you. I think it would be a shame to terrorize that girl further.'

'You are *such* a prig, Kingsley.'

29

Gothas

Having finally caught a bus back into town, Shannon and Kingsley parted.

'See you in the morning, old chap,' Shannon said. 'I shan't forget you ruined my sport.'

'Believe me, it's not an incident I'll forget either, Captain. Something tells me that some day you and I shall have a reckoning.'

'Can't wait, Inspector.'

Kingsley's train for London did not depart for another two and a half hours, so he decided to make his way back to the library and perhaps find an hour's solace in books.

As he retraced his steps through the town, an unfamiliar sound began to fill the air. Quietly, almost imperceptibly at first, a droning had begun.

Kingsley had never before heard this sound and yet he knew it instantly. He could have guessed it just by looking at the faces of the people in the streets.

Gothas. German heavy bombers, each carrying nine bombs and far more deadly than the Zeppelins that had preceded them. Folkestone had been hit before, in May. Twenty-three Gothas headed for London had lost their way in cloud and some bombs had landed by the sea. Now it seemed that Folkestone was to be hit again and this time deliberately.

The droning grew louder and soon the planes appeared, nine of them in the sky above. Nine little crosses amongst the clouds. Everyone was staring upwards; there was nowhere to run to for nobody knew where the bombs would fall. Then down they came, a long whistle followed by a terrible bang. Eight bombs hit the town and each was followed by a cacophony of shouts and screaming.

One landed quite close to the library, blasting bricks and glass about in a shower of flying clubs and knives. Kingsley rushed forward to see if he could help. The street was littered with civilians, some lying still and others crying out in pain and shock at the slashes that had appeared suddenly in their flesh.

Kingsley saw a sight that he would have given anything except the life of his own son not to see. The little girl whom he had seen in the library, weeping over her comic, lay bleeding in her mother's arms, blood pumping from the severed artery in her neck. Someone with a Red Cross armband was trying to help but Kingsley knew that no pressure could staunch such a ghastly wound. In minutes she would join her father as a victim of the Great War, and her mother would have to face the future with nothing left at all.

30

A domestic interlude

Kingsley felt his isolation keenly that evening.

Having arrived at Victoria Station, he secured himself a room in a small hotel nearby and set out to walk off his melancholy and perhaps find a chop house for a solitary dinner. Lost in his thoughts, he found himself heading north, first past St James's Park, then around the palace and across the eastern fringes of Hyde Park. With no real appetite to make him search out supper, he simply walked, and although he had not started his journey with any destination in mind, he began to realize where his feet were leading him.

How strange it felt to be abroad once more in the city which, apart from three years at Cambridge, had been his home for his whole life. To be in London but not to be a part of London felt miserable in the extreme. He had *always* been a part of it, more than most men ever are. He had been responsible for its safety, he knew its underside, its dark secrets: the city had been *his*. But now his home was no longer his home, his beloved place of work was barred to him, probably forever. Those who had once known him believed him dead. Dead and disgraced. With his beard, his spectacles, his hat pulled low and his shabby suit, he had no fear of being recognized; in fact he no longer recognized himself, so utterly unfamiliar was the sensation of walking through streets which he knew intimately and yet having no connection to them whatsoever. He passed shops, hotels and pubs, inside which he knew would be people with whom he was acquainted, some friends even, all strangers to him now. The big police station on Seymour Street, near Marble Arch, had been at one time a home from home for him, for he had drunk brown ale with the friendly desk sergeant many times. The sergeant would no doubt still be there, as he was far too old for military service. The sergeant would be there, but Kingsley was not. He was not there at all. He did not exist.

He started to make his way up Baker Street. He knew where he was going now, although he did not know what he would do when he got there. He skirted round the western edge of Regent's Park up towards St John's Wood and from there up Fitzjohns Avenue.

He was going home.

It was not that he had any intention of making himself known to his family but he had to be near them, if only for a moment. He could not help himself.

It took him nearly two hours to walk from Victoria Station to Hampstead Heath and by the time he arrived at the big houses at the end of Flask Walk the long late-summer evening was over and night had fallen.

As he walked along the elevated pavement, his collar turned up and the brim of his hat pulled even further down on his forehead, Kingsley noticed a special constable eyeing him with some suspicion. He realized that he was walking like a fugitive so he straightened up, reminding himself that the first rule of disguise and deception was confidence. He sang out a cheery 'Good evening, officer.'

The special gave him a wave. She was a woman; they were all women now, or old men. Shannon would probably have observed that being a special constable was as good a job as joining a Pierrot troupe in terms of gaining an unfair advantage with the girls. The constable walked away, clearly relieved not to be forced to investigate a tall, bearded rough-looking fellow. Kingsley knew these 'specials' to be the subject of much derisive humour, celebrated in music-hall sketches and in song. Everybody knew that '*You can't trust yer specials like yer old time coppers/When you can't find your way 'ome*', but Kingsley had always admired them for their enthusiasm and pluck, if not for their efficiency.

These thoughts provided him with a momentary distraction from the fierce beating of his heart as he approached his old home. How many evenings had he walked up Flask Walk since his marriage in 1912? So many, many evenings. Always the same, up in the lift at Hampstead Tube Station, then left past the newspaper seller, picking one up if he hadn't done so already. Often also some flowers from the stall on the high street, occasionally some chocolate or a cake from the fancy patisserie. And then home, home to the arms of his beloved Agnes who was always so happy to see him, always so anxious to hear what feats of cleverness and derring-do he had accomplished that day. And little George! It was a rare treat indeed to be home in time to see him before bed, but on the occasions when Kingsley thought that he would arrive in time, how he rushed. How he cursed the grim and inexplicable stoppages of the Tube train, the long queues for the lift made up of crowds of other men all as anxious as him to get home to the bosom of their families. When he could not get home in time, the first thing he would do after embracing Agnes would be to creep up to the nursery and kiss George while he slept. Sometimes the boy would stir and whisper, 'I love you, Daddy,' through his dreams. Those were the moments that Kingsley had lived for; those were the moments he had thrown away.

Now he stood before the gate in the gloomy shadows away from the nearest gas lamp some ten yards further up the road. His gate. His house. He had bought it (or at least a part of it, for Agnes's family had helped), he had carried Agnes through that gate on the day they returned from their honeymoon, and he had never ever thought to leave it. Now it was the gate of Mrs Beaumont, widow and mother. It was her gate.

The street was empty, not a soul about. Lights were burning in the windows of his house, burning down in the basement where no doubt the scullery maid would be doing the dishes from supper, burning in the front hall where perhaps Molly the housemaid was tidying the boots and coats, and burning in the drawing room, where Agnes would be sitting. Reading, or at her needlework, or simply sitting. Alone.

Without giving himself time to consider the consequences, he opened the gate and crept into the garden. He made his way to the house, avoiding the front path and sticking to the shadow of the great elm that stood in the middle of the front lawn, the tree in which he had promised George he would one day build a house and never had and now never would. The lace curtain of the drawing room on the ground floor was drawn but the heavy drapes had not yet been pulled for the night. The room within was brightly illuminated, for the whole house was fully electric, to the delight of Agnes, who had grown up in a big, old country house on which the modern world encroached only slowly. The light within the room would allow Kingsley to see in through the lace and yet, reflected on the delicate white cotton, prevent Agnes from seeing out. If he remained still and silent, he might stand before the glass and look in. He might see her.

The night was silent, with only the distant sound of revelry at the Flask Inn to disturb the stillness of the air. Checking once more to ensure that the street was empty, Kingsley gently gathered up a wrought-iron chair from the little suite of garden furniture that stood beneath the elm and made his final approach. The drawing-room window was above head height, so he placed the chair against the wall to provide him with a step. Carefully he mounted it and slowly raised himself up before the window, unable to prevent his mind from noting that the sills would need repainting within the year.

She was there, as he had known she would be. Sitting before the empty fireplace. The first fire of the autumn had not yet been lit and in its place stood the summer screen with its fine equestrian portrait that Agnes had brought with her from her drawing room in Leicestershire. She was in her chair. The one opposite his, which was now no one's chair, empty, its cushions fully plumped. She had a magazine upon her lap; Kingsley fancied it was the *Lady*. Agnes loved her magazines and definitely favoured those that were filled with romantic short stories, fashion items and gossip, but these she kept as a guilty pleasure in her bedroom and dressing room and on the little Queen Anne table in her water closet. Downstairs in the drawing room she kept only the sort of magazine which she would wish callers to *think* she read, *Country Life*, the *Tatler* and, of course, the *Lady*. Not that she received callers any more, not since he had ruined both their lives for principle's sake.

Agnes was not reading the magazine. It lay on her lap and she was staring into space, an expression of distant melancholy on her beautiful face. Kingsley had never seen her look this way before. Angry, yes, many times, for she had a fiery disposition; sad, petulant, bored certainly, but never melancholic. Agnes's was a light and easy spirit, or at least it had been, before he had crushed the spirit out of her. As he watched he saw her sigh. It was a long-drawn-out sigh, the sigh of a person with a long, empty night ahead of them. Then she rose and turned towards the window. Every instinct told Kingsley to drop away from the pane, but intellect told him to be still, that sudden movement would be detected. Only stillness would keep him hidden. She began to walk towards the window, towards him. Now she stood before the lace. Suddenly not three feet from him, separated only by a pane of glass and a scrap of embroidered cotton. If she moved the lace to look out she would probably die of fright and he would end up at the bottom of the Thames with a Secret Service bullet in his brain.

She did not move the lace. She stepped forward to draw the heavy curtains for the night and for a moment they were face to face, he staring into those exquisite pale-blue eyes framed with golden curls that had first captivated his heart at that cricket match in Dulwich seven years before. Except now he noticed amongst her curls a colour that had not been there before, a streak of grey. She was scarcely twenty-four. Every fibre of his being longed to hold her, to wrench up the sash, reach out for her and cover her sweet face with burning kisses. He did not care that she had in a sense betrayed him, that she had not had the strength to rise above the common herd and be proud of him for what he had done. He had always known that Agnes was not the stuff of which that kind of hero is made. She was brave enough and had stood the pain of childbirth with a courage that left Kingsley in awe, but Agnes loved society far too much to have the strength of will ever to stand outside it. But none of that mattered to Kingsley. He had married her for what she was, because he loved her for what she was, and he would not wish to change her in any way.

Now she stepped aside to unleash the cord that bound the curtains. First one side, then the other. Kingsley watched as she reached a hand behind the curtains, searching for the sash. He wanted to cry out, 'Don't pull it! Stay with me a moment longer!' but he did not and her arm came down and with that movement the curtains closed, blotting out the light.

Kingsley stepped down from the chair, devastated. Utterly wretched and alone. Perhaps it was this desperation that led him on. Considering the matter later, he wondered if he was not willing himself to be caught. He imagined that it would mean death at the hands of Shannon or his like but at least he would have seen her again. And George. The only creature on earth whom he loved as he loved Agnes.

Kingsley looked up at the great dark edifice of the house. Four floors plus a basement. At the top were the servants' rooms, housing two maids, a nanny and Cook. Below that was a guest bedroom, the servants' bathroom and convenience, a music room and what had been Kingsley's study and Agnes's sewing room. The first floor contained a large master bedroom which had been his and Agnes's, and a beautifully appointed modern bathroom with a separate showering cubicle with glass walls that Agnes's mother had considered rather racy. Also a dressing room, a nursery with a small bathroom and water closet attached, and George's room.

The bedrooms were at the front of the house, two of the big bay windows for the master bedroom and one for George's room.

George's window. The window through which, together, father and son had often watched the moon and stars before story time. George would be inside that room, in his little bed which he had only just graduated to when first Kingsley was forced from his home. The window was open.

Something almost primal inside Kingsley compelled him now. He simply had to see his son. He took hold of the thick iron drainpipe, one of several that snaked down from the guttering on the roof above, and began to climb. The pain in his ribs was considerable but Kingsley paid it no heed at all and in a few moments he found himself hanging spider-like from the wall outside his son's window. It was a sash window, open only a few inches to allow fresh air into the room. Holding fast to the pipe with one hand, Kingsley reached out with the other and placing his hand inside the opening he pushed. The window slid open noiselessly. He did not give himself time to consider the possible consequences of what he was doing; for a rare moment in his life his heart was leading him and not his head. Placing one foot upon the bracket that attached the pipe to the wall, he stretched out the other until he had it on the window sill. Then, in one single movement, he hauled his body across. Now he was squatting on the sill, a hand holding either side of the frame, his knees pushing against the curtains. Kingsley glanced behind him: the elm tree masked him from the road, he was still unobserved.

Slipping between the curtains, he entered the room.

Lowering a leg to the floor, he just stopped himself from stepping on a rubber figure of a clown. Kingsley knew that clown. When squeezed, it made a noise that was supposed to sound like laughter, although to Kingsley's mind it sounded more like chronic wind. He reminded himself that George's room was likely to be littered with possible booby traps that squeaked, rattled and squawked. The previous Christmas Eve, whilst attempting to load George's stocking, he had nearly been given away by a jack-in-the-box that popped open with a shriek when you dropped it.

Carefully lowering himself to the floor, Kingsley parted the curtains behind him so that moonlight could illuminate the room. It was all just as he remembered it: the toys on the floor, the little basin in the corner, the pirates on the wallpaper and the little boy asleep in the bed with the fairy-patterned coverlet. George was his usual sleeping self also, his sheets and blanket kicked away, his little body stretched at an extraordinary angle, pointing the wrong way in the bed, his back arched and his head hanging over the side in a rather alarming manner.

Kingsley did what he always did when looking in on George at night. Stepping forward, he gently picked up his son and laid him out properly, with his feet pointing towards the foot of the bed and his head upon the pillow. Then Kingsley pulled the sheet and blanket up under George's chin, arranged them neatly and tucked everything in.

'There, there, little boy. Snug as a bug,' he whispered and, leaning forward, kissed him.

The boy stirred a little, his eyelids flickering, but he did not wake.

'I love you, Daddy,' he murmured through his dreams.

Kingsley could not raise his head in time to prevent two tears from falling on to George's little face.

'I love you too, Georgie Porgie pudding and pie.'

Then Kingsley heard a noise upon the stair. It was Agnes come to check on George. Her tread was different: before she had flitted lightly about the house and now the step was slow and weary, but from her sigh he knew that it was she. There was no time to retreat; he must hide instantly. In one corner of the room stood a hatstand on which hung George's dressing-up costumes, a pirate, a prince, a knight, a maharajah, a soldier and, of course, a police constable. Kingsley knew those costumes well; he had hidden behind them before when playing hide-and-seek with George. Now he hid behind them under very different circumstances, ducking deep into the shadows just as the door opened.

Once more he saw her, or at least her outline, silhouetted in the light of the doorway. He had not expected this second encounter and the pain was even more intense; it felt so unmanly to be cowering in his own child's bedroom, afraid to face his wife. Agnes paused for a moment where she stood, clearly perplexed. She was looking at the open window. She took a step back into the hallway.

'Elsie! Elsie, would you attend me a moment, please,' she called.

Kingsley did not recognize the name. Agnes must have taken on new staff. Clearly his wife had not been exaggerating when she had told him that some of the servants were ashamed to work for her. A young woman appeared beside Agnes, dressed in the black skirt and white pinny of a housemaid.

'Yes, Mrs Beaumont?' Of course, she had resumed her maiden name. How it pained Kingsley to hear his wife thus described.

'George's window. Did you open it and draw his curtains?'

'No, ma'am, I did not.'

'Are you quite sure?'

'Quite sure, ma'am.'

'Very well. Perhaps he opened it himself to look at the moon – he's getting so clever and independent all of a sudden. Imagine if he had reached out and fallen! He always likes to look at the moon before he sleeps, it's what he did with . . . what he did before.'

'Yes, ma'am. Shall I shut it?'

'No, I shall see to it. We must arrange to have a lock fitted. We will speak to Mr Pierce when he comes to clean the gutters.'

'Yes, ma'am.'

'Thank you, that will be all.'

Agnes sounded so lonely, chattering to her housemaid for want of other company. Not that she was ever brusque with the servants, but on this occasion she was sharing more of her thoughts than had been her habit in the past.

The girl left and Agnes entered George's room once more. She crossed to the window and closed it but fortunately did not slip the latch; had she done so, she might have been left wondering in the morning how it came to be undone. She reached up to draw the curtains but then, turning to see George asleep in bed with the moonlight on his face, she thought better of it. He looked like an angel at his rest. Agnes crossed to the little bed and kissed the boy.

'No need to tuck you up tonight, sweetums? You must be having gentle dreams.' She kissed him again and turned towards the door.

'Mummy,' said the boy, still half asleep.

'Yes, darling?'

'I dreamed I saw Daddy.'

'Oh darling, did you?'

'He was here. He kissed me.'

'If he was here I'm sure that's exactly what he would do.'

'When is he coming back?'

Agnes gulped and steadied herself before replying.

'Darling . . . You recall what I told you. Daddy has gone to heaven.'

She was struggling to control her voice, fighting back the tears.

'Yes, I know, Mummy, but when is he coming back?'

'Well, you see, precious, people don't come back from heaven, I'm afraid. They wait for you to come to them. It's awfully good fun for them but boring for us to have to wait to see them . . .'

'I think he will come back.'

'Well, perhaps, darling. Perhaps.'

'I miss him, Mummy.'

'I miss him too . . . Very, very much.'

Kingsley thought his heart would burst. Had Shannon and the whole of the Secret Intelligence Service been before him at that point he would happily have shot them all for playing such a cruel trick.

But even in the midst of his misery he could not help but feel a small thrill.

She missed him. She missed him very, very much.

Having dabbed her eyes and mastered her emotions, Agnes kissed George for a final time.

'Good night, darling. I am sure we will both dream of Daddy tonight.'

Agnes stepped back from George's bed but she did not leave the room. Instead she stood watching as the little boy drifted back to sleep, while through the shadowy folds of George's dress-ups Kingsley watched her.

Then she spoke once more.

'Oh Douglas.'

Kingsley almost cried out, so shocked was he. Did she know he was there? Had she been aware all along?

'Oh Douglas, Douglas. How could it come to this?'

She was speaking to herself.

'You've really left me now. Gone. Gone forever.'

Tears were streaming down her face and Kingsley's too. It took him every effort of will not to step forward, but what could he have said? A bruised and bearded spectre from the grave who was now the creature of the Secret Service?

Shannon was a killing gentleman and he had not made his threats lightly.

Then, still staring at the boy, Agnes began to sing to herself, in a quiet small voice, almost a whisper. A song that she and Kingsley had often sung together, as they strolled on Hampstead Heath with George in his perambulator on summer evenings.

> 'In the twi twi twilight.
> Out in the beautiful twilight
> We all go out for a walk walk walk
> A quiet old spoon and a talk talk talk

That's the time we long for.
Just before the night
And many a grand little wedding is planned
In the twi twilight.'

Finally she turned away and left the room. Kingsley heard her cross the hallway to what had once been the bedroom they shared. She was weeping, great long sobs of anguish and despair.

Scarcely able to bear it himself, Kingsley emerged from his hiding place and went to stand before his son's bed one final time.

'You're right, George,' he whispered. 'I will return. I promise.'

Then he stole from the window and, having closed it and the curtains behind him, he disappeared into the night.

31

A protest meeting

The following morning Kingsley breakfasted indifferently on
kippers at his hotel, paid his bill and set out to walk to Whitehall.

Once more he passed the palace, noting that the Royal
Standard flew above it, which meant that the King was at home.
A troop of Horse Guards was riding out, much to the delight of
the small boys assembled at the gates. The guards were all in
khaki, having forsaken their splendid red tunics and breastplates
for the duration. They seemed terribly drab to Kingsley's eye, and
the gleaming sabres that they held upright as they rode looked
silly set against the dull, functional uniforms of modern war. It
was as if the army itself was in mourning, which of course it was.

The recently erected Victoria Memorial was festooned with
American flags and many more hung all along the Mall. This
would be in honour of the arrival of General Pershing, the
American Commander in Chief, whom Kingsley had noted in
the paper over breakfast was that day to have a special audience
with the King. He was only a general, not remotely a head of
state, but such were the hopes which the exhausted Allies were
placing in their new comrades that no honour was deemed too
good for them. When the Americans had entered the war many
months previously there had been enormous rejoicing, for the

majority of people had assumed that a vast army of doughboys would instantly materialize in the trenches. The reality, now fast sinking in, was very different: the USA was entirely unprepared for war, it had no air force at all and only a tiny standing army. Its navy was more formidable but ships were not what was required in the bloodbath of the Western Front. Even a glance at the reports in that morning's paper of Pershing's tone and comments so far told Kingsley that the American general saw his current mission as one of dampening hopes rather than fulfilling them, and that the King need expect no glad tidings from the New World. Once more, and for the fourth time, the war would most definitely not be over by Christmas.

Kingsley made his way along the Mall. As he did so, he found himself glancing backwards occasionally. He felt uneasy. He wondered whether he was being followed. If there was a man behind him, he was good at his job because Kingsley could detect nothing in the sparsely populated street to confirm his suspicions. He did not feel unduly worried. Cast adrift as he was with nothing left to lose, he was able to take a fatalistic view of what-ever might be in store for him.

As he approached the end of the Mall, Kingsley heard the sound of a crowd ahead of him, and passing under Admiralty Arch he saw that a demonstration was in progress in Trafalgar Square. Having a little time to kill, he crossed over the road and strolled up past Nelson's column to investigate. Above a speaking platform on the steps of the church of St Martin-in-the-Fields, a banner announced 'the National Labour and Socialist Convention'. A fierce old man with a long beard was con-gratulating the Russian people on the overthrow of the Tsar.

'The Russian worker has seized the day!' he shouted hoarsely through the great coned megaphone he held in his hand. 'He has seized the day!'

The crowd was pretty evenly divided between those who supported the rally and those who did not. A couple of soldiers on a spree called from the back for the old fellow to bugger off to

Russia if he didn't like good old England or, better still, go to Germany where they knew what to do with traitors. There was some cheering at this, to which one or two serious-looking fellows shouted back that in a Socialist utopia it wouldn't matter where you lived because everywhere would be equally blessed.

Kingsley felt a tap on his shoulder. It was a surprise, for he had not felt anybody so close behind him. His body tensed as he turned, ready for whatever might appear. However, he found himself confronted by nothing more dangerous than a fresh-faced schoolgirl, her hair in long plaits. She wore the sailor uniform made so popular by the former Tsar's beautiful young daughters.

'My father is fighting the Hun,' she said. 'Take this.'

The girl held out to him the familiar white feather.

'I hope no harm befalls him,' Kingsley replied, letting the feather fall to the ground between them.

'Hope's no good,' said the girl. 'You should get out there and jolly well help him.'

'Young lady, until this madness is finished hope is all we have.'

'You're a rotten coward!' the girl snapped. 'If I was a man I should knock you down.'

'Goodbye, young lady.'

Kingsley turned away and the girl stamped off, in search of other recipients for her feathers. Up on the platform the writer and philosopher Bertrand Russell was being introduced.

He took up the loudhailer to speak with admiration of the 'thousand pacifists who languish currently in prison. Clifford Alan! Stephen Hobhouse! Corder Catchpool, and Douglas Kingsley, of whose sad death we learned yesterday!' This brought cheers from the rally's supporters. Kingsley was shocked to hear his own name, and beset with the most curious sensation of attending his own funeral. 'Brave men all, not cowards!' Russell shouted.

'Bloody cowards!' the Tommies shouted back, and although it was only mid-morning Kingsley suspected that they had been drinking.

'No!' shouted Russell. 'Heroes! By their refusal of military service, conscientious objectors have shown that it is possible for the individual to stand against the whole power of the state. This is a great discovery! It enhances the dignity of man!'

At this point Bertrand Russell's own dignity was seriously assaulted as a rotten cabbage knocked his hat off. One or two scuffles broke out and the handful of special constables present looked nervous. Kingsley decided the time had come to leave; if the real police were to turn up it was just possible he might be recognized by an ex-colleague. Unlikely with his beard, glasses and shabby clothes, but possible.

Kingsley drifted away and, having still a little time to kill, went to order coffee and a fruit scone with margarine in a Lyons Corner House at the west end of the Strand. The girl who served him reminded him of Violet, the waitress from the Folkestone hotel whom he had saved from Shannon. Young, pretty and forced to grow up fast in a world that was changing beyond all recognition. Kingsley hoped that Violet had not been too deeply upset by her experience. Shannon's tone, or what Kingsley had heard of it as he had hurried forward across the sand, had been fearful in its violence and cold contempt. Kingsley imagined that a young girl would find such a voice difficult to expel from her nightmares.

If ever a man had been corrupted by the horrors of this terrible war, it was Captain Shannon. He appeared to believe that what he had endured gave him the *right* to visit pain upon others. For men like Shannon, humanity was no longer worthy of respect; the war had taught them that weakness was contemptible and only strength mattered. Kingsley imagined that there might be quite a few like Shannon left knocking about Europe when the war was finally done with.

He glanced at his watch: the time had come to make his way to his meeting. He drained his coffee and left the café to search for the address he had been given.

He passed Downing Street, where a single policeman stood

guard outside the most famous door in Britain. Glancing towards the house, Kingsley imagined Lloyd George inside with the War Cabinet and the Chiefs of the General Staff, all wearily facing another day in their so far fruitless search for a way out of the deadlock in which Europe was mired.

Just then Winston Churchill, the new Minister of Munitions, bustled past him, deep in conversation with Admiral Jellicoe. They were no doubt on their way to see the PM and were most animated in their talk, Churchill gesticulating fulsomely as he spoke. Kingsley knew, as all the country knew, that Churchill had just returned from months of active service in France. Having found himself out of office after the Dardanelles debacle, he had elected to go into the trenches. He seemed, however, to have got over his fall from grace and thrown himself back into public affairs with his usual energy. Kingsley was always surprised at how openly British government continued to be conducted, with generals and ministers wandering freely around Westminster and even the Prime Minister, on fine days, walking to the House of Commons. Considering that the war had begun with an assassination, Kingsley's policeman's instincts could not help but question the wisdom of this casual attitude to the safety of great men. On the other hand, it was certainly an attractive feature of an open society.

When he had walked another quarter-mile down to the shabby end of Whitehall, Kingsley's search took him into a small mews that still seemed to carry the faint smell of the horses who had vacated it a decade or so before. Here he was to meet Sir Mansfield Cumming, head of the foreign section of the Department of Military Intelligence, known as MI1c.

As he turned into the mews he noticed Shannon leaning languidly against a railing, smoking a cigarette.

'Good morning, Inspector,' Shannon said, managing even in so few innocent words to give an impression of amused superiority.

'Good morning, Captain. Rape anybody last night?'

'Oh, come now, Kingsley. Do let's not harp on little Violet, eh?

Most girls are delighted to make my acquaintance. Perhaps even Violet might have come round to it in the end if you'd given me the chance to knock the cobwebs off her. They like it rough, you know, these girls, although they always say they don't.'

Kingsley stared at Shannon for a moment but he did not comment further, walking past him into the mews.

'You dropped this, by the way,' Shannon said. He held out a white feather. 'I promised that little girl I'd see you got it.'

Still Kingsley did not reply, but he was forced inwardly to acknowledge that Shannon must be an expert tail for he had been unable to catch sight of him.

'Oh yes, I've been with you since you paid for your kippers,' he sneered. 'Anyways, I've already been in and told the boss you're coming so I'll leave you to it,' and with that Shannon strolled back out into Whitehall, while Kingsley approached the door of the little ex-stable to which he had been directed.

32

At the heart of the SIS

The building was extremely shabby, which did not surprise Kingsley overmuch; long experience had taught him how penny-pinching the British government could be when it came to the working conditions of its employees. The waiting room into which he was shown boasted one or two goodish pictures and the furniture, what there was of it, was either Georgian or excellent reproductions, but it was cramped, the carpet threadbare and the walls in need of new paper and paint. Kingsley was to discover that the whole department consisted of little more than the reception area in which he sat, Cumming's office, a map room and a small library. That this should represent the heart of the British Empire's overseas intelligence and espionage network surprised even Kingsley, a man well versed in the often amateurish, public-school manner in which the affairs of a great nation were conducted. It was so ridiculously inadequate to the needs of the modern world, Kingsley half expected a bookcase suddenly to slide back and reveal a stairway leading to a vast subterranean nerve centre bustling with telegraph operators, codebreakers and photographic laboratories.

'Yes, we don't put on much of a show, do we?' said Sir Mansfield, when Kingsley was ushered into his office. 'Budget, you see. Always budget. I swear if I want to feed a carrier pigeon I must first draw up a special seed requisition order, in triplicate, copy it to the War Office *and* the Foreign Office and then await authorization from both! By which time of course the poor bird has died from hunger.'

Kingsley nodded sympathetically but said nothing. His host was a man of whom he had heard much during his time with Special Branch but about whom he knew little of any substance. He imagined Sir Mansfield took trouble to keep things that way. The foreign intelligence supremo was, Kingsley judged, in latish middle age but still looked very active. His grey hair was cut short and he was clean-shaven. He wore naval uniform and sported a monocle, which gave him a slightly flippant appearance. Kingsley felt quite certain there was little else that could be considered flippant about Captain Sir Mansfield Cumming.

'The Cabinet doesn't like spies, you see,' Cumming went on. 'The Civil Service like us even less. Don't think it's the *done thing*, think it's something that *foreigners* get up to, which is of course precisely the point. *They do*. Which is why we have to. Do you know, I'm supposed to run an overseas intelligence operation and yet our own bloody *ambassadors* won't have us in their embassies! They don't think it's *British* to spy on your host. Where else are we to stay? Can't afford hotels, not on our allocation. Need whatever we've got to bribe the locals. Anyway, enough of that, not your problem, eh? Expect you had similar constraints at Scotland Yard. No bore like a budget bore, eh? Tea?'

Kingsley accepted the offer and was only slightly surprised when Cumming went to a little gas ring set up in the corner of the office and started to make the tea himself.

'They would give me a girl, I suppose, but I've neither the time nor the resources to vet one. It'd be a poor lookout if my tea lady turned out to be a Boche Brünnhilde who sneaked all our secrets back to Germany in hollowed-out biscuits, wouldn't it? Less trouble to make the tea myself. Condensed milk all right?'

'That would be fine. Thank you.'

Cumming opened a can using a little multi-tooled scouting knife which he produced from his pocket.

'No sugar, I'm afraid, but this stuff's tooth-rottingly sweet anyway . . . I've got Camp coffee if you'd prefer it?'

'No, thank you. Tea is fine.'

'I rather like Camp – only the British could have invented it. Tried it on Marshal Foch's liaison chap last week, the fellow thought I was trying to *poison* him! Of course coffee's a positive *fetish* for the French, which isn't healthy in my view. Took me ages to explain that we British simply do not set the same store by the stuff. Tea's the thing, eh?'

Kingsley was in fact one of those Englishmen who did take his coffee seriously, roasting and grinding his own beans, which he bought wholesale from an Italian café owner in Wardour Street. But that had been in another life and he had not come to Whitehall to discuss refreshments.

'Tea is fine,' he repeated.

'Good. Excellent.' Sir Mansfield carefully warmed the pot, emptying the spent water into a dead aspidistra. 'First and foremost I must apologize for the unorthodox manner in which you have been brought to us – although from what I hear it's lucky we *did* get you out. Apparently you had been beaten almost to death?'

'Things are never going to be comfortable for a policeman in prison.' Kingsley shrugged, not wishing to appear in any way in the debt of people who might have saved his life but who had done so by abducting him and certainly not as a favour. 'Why have I been brought to you?'

'Ah-ha. The rub . . . Well, no doubt Captain Shannon has explained that it has to do with the death of Viscount Abercrombie.'

'That is what he told me, although I only believe it now I hear it confirmed by you, Sir Mansfield. Captain Shannon is not a man whose uncorroborated word I would ever be minded to accept on any subject at all.'

173

'Yes,' Cumming said, opening a tin of biscuits. 'I'd heard you were a good judge of character. Garibaldi?'

'Captain Shannon is an unbalanced sadist and a dangerous lecher,' Kingsley said, declining the biscuit. 'It takes no great leap of judgement to see that.'

'Mmm. A bastard indeed, but *my* bastard, which is all that matters really, isn't it?'

Cumming sat down in one of the two armchairs that stood before the mean little unlit fireplace and indicated that Kingsley should take the other. Above the mantel hung a rather fanciful painting of Napoleon's surrender at Waterloo. The spymaster stared at it for a few moments as if seeking to draw inspiration.

'The problem is,' he said finally, 'the death of Viscount Abercrombie is making waves. Damned fellow got murdered, you see, and what with him being who he is, HM Government decided to lie about it. Probably a mistake as it's turned out but at the time it seemed a good idea. This is a modern age, you see, an age of celebrity. And in particular just now, the celebrity *poet*. You've probably heard about the trouble that blighter Sassoon has caused with his damned anti-war letter to the press. If he hadn't been a poet, a *celebrity* poet, *The Times* would never have published it.'

Cumming had been dunking his garibaldi in his tea for too long and half of the biscuit broke off, falling back into the cup. He swore creatively for a moment while fishing about in his cup with a teaspoon.

'Where was I?' he said, having retrieved most of it and eaten it off the spoon, a process which Kingsley found rather unpleasant to witness.

'Celebrity poets,' Kingsley prompted.

'Ah yes, more popular than cricketers these days. They'll be putting them on cigarette cards next. Brooke started it, of course, with all his Little Englander romantic tosh:

> *'Stands the Church clock at ten to three?*
> *And is there honey still for tea?'*

'Bloody rot if you ask me. I've been to Grantchester and, let me tell you, it's boring. Not surprised the clock stopped, lost the will to carry on, I imagine.'

Kingsley sipped his tea and kept silent. No doubt the master spy would get to the point eventually.

'Well, anyway, here's the thing. At first Abercrombie's death looked like an open-and-shut case: the Military Police arrested one Private Hopkins and charged him with the murder. The obvious thing to do was to keep it all as quiet as possible and let the people's memory of their fallen hero remain pure. Unfortunately, certain circumstances and witness statements have emerged which must at least give us reason to doubt Hopkins's guilt, and some people here in London – *influential* people – got wind of it. Lord Abercrombie, the dead chap's father, had been happy that Hopkins be quietly shot and his son's reputation remain unscathed. However, the other side started crying foul and now *everybody*'s clamouring for further explanations. If things develop unchecked, either one side or the other is bound to start talking. It will all come out, including the government's original lies, and we shall have a scandal and a trial on our hands to rival the bloody Dreyfus case. Divided nation and all. Working man pitted against aristocrat, Labour fighting Tory, with the poor old Liberal government stuck in the middle. What we need, and need quickly, is for the thing to be properly investigated and, if humanly possible, for the truth to be established. If that could be achieved and the evidence placed privately before the warring parties, the matter might yet be quietly laid to rest.'

Of course Kingsley could see where all this must be leading. He was not, after all, being told this for nothing, but he could not understand why they needed him.

'Surely this is a job for the Military Police?'

'Well, you'd have thought so, wouldn't you? But of course the

Labour lot won't have it; they don't trust the police at all. They say they've already been compromised by leaping to judgement.'

'Then surely your department . . .'

'Ha! If Labour and the unions don't trust the police, they trust us less. I have been told that when the War Office suggested that the SIS take over the investigation, Ramsay MacDonald actually laughed. I can see his point, of course; we do have something of a reputation for harassing revolutionaries. The funny thing is, the Conservatives don't really trust us either, convinced we've been infiltrated by Bolshies. Who'd be a spy, eh? No, I'm afraid neither the police nor the SIS will do. What is needed here is a *disinterested party*, a figure of proven *integrity* and high moral credentials who also happens to be a brilliant criminal detective.'

The fact that this was flattering did not make it any less astonishing. 'You mean that Bonar Law and Ramsay MacDonald have been discussing *me*?'

'Oh, don't be so modest, Inspector, you know damn well that you were the Yard's best man . . .'

'Well, yes, I was but . . .'

'And all this conchie business, hateful though it may be to most people, has shown that you are a man of unassailable principle. Honestly, you couldn't be better suited to help break this dead-lock if we'd designed you ourselves. It didn't take long for your name to come up. In fact, looking at the secret minutes, it seems to have been the Prime Minister himself who suggested you.'

Kingsley sipped his tea, pretending to take this with a pinch of salt but secretly rather thrilled.

'Well, well. The Prime Minister, eh?'

'Yes, although that may simply have been him trying to take the credit. He is rather prone to that, you know. Great men often are, I find.'

'So the Prime Minister himself asked for me?'

'Absolutely. There was, however, one problem.'

'My being in prison.'

'Exactly. There was talk of granting you a pardon or at least a stay of sentence but that was scarcely practical, given the notoriety of your offence and the public opprobrium in which you were held. More to the point, people would have wanted to know *why* you had been released and then the whole thing would have come out anyway. We needed your skills and your reputation, but we did not need *you*.'

'Hence my death.'

'Exactly. There was a meeting in camera *at the highest level* where the proposal was put to those politicians who have currently taken such an interest in this case. They were asked whether, *if* a way could be found whereby you, a brilliant ex-police officer, proven to be of high moral integrity, could conduct an investigation *anonymously*, those politicians would abide by the conclusions you drew. They agreed.'

Despite all his troubles, Kingsley could not avoid a feeling of satisfaction.

'I'm most gratified.'

'And so we were briefed to produce you anonymously and here you are. Dead, but all present and correct to do an enormous service to your country. Solve this murder mystery before it drives a bloody great wedge right down the middle of our fragile wartime consensus.'

Kingsley lit a cigarette. It was an astounding story and yet he could see the logic.

'Well,' he remarked, after he had exhaled the deep draught of tobacco smoke, 'it is true that both the police and the intelligence service are hopelessly compromised.'

'Hopelessly. We might as well all pack up and go home. *Only you* can do this, Inspector. *Only you* can serve your country in this matter.'

Cumming was no fool when it came to judging a man's character and he could see that the biggest chink, probably the *only* chink, in Kingsley's intellectual armour was his vanity.

'I certainly do appear to be the logical candidate.'

'So you're game?'

'I didn't say that.'

'Of course, if you don't think you're up to the investigation . . .'

'Don't bother with that old trick, Sir Mansfield. I'm a little too long in the tooth to be cajoled with such simplistic psychology as that.'

But of course Kingsley wasn't. The suggestion that he might not have the confidence to attempt the challenge had raised his hackles, no matter how much he might try to disguise the fact. Cumming continued to twist the knife.

'I'm just saying that I'd understand if you thought you couldn't crack it. The trail's pretty cold after all.'

'My decision has nothing to do with whether I can "crack it" or not,' Kingsley said, with some irritation. 'If anybody can "crack it", I can. Therefore were I to attempt to "crack it" and fail I would know that the case was not "crackable" and hence there'd be no shame in my having failed. I am merely taking time to consider the parameters of your proposal.'

'Consider away then, always remembering that each minute increases the probability that whatever evidence and witnesses remain will be blown to Hades.'

'I'd need authority to conduct inquiries, particularly in a military zone. I presume your plan would be to equip me with a new identity. A policeman?'

Cumming could see that he had hooked his man.

'Absolutely: Captain Christopher Marlowe of the Royal Military Police.'

'And if I *did* take on your job . . . at the end of it, what then?'

'You and your new identity depart these shores, Inspector. For good. Australia, we think. Lots of openings for energetic men there, particularly considering how many they've lost in France and Turkey. Not a lot of questions asked either.'

'My wife and son?'

'Inspector, they were lost to you anyway. You would never have survived your prison sentence.'

Kingsley was under no illusions about the value the SIS would place on his life at the end of an assignment like the one proposed. Alive, he could cause a great deal of embarrassment.

Cumming could read his thoughts.

'His Majesty's Secret Intelligence Service does not deal in murder, Inspector.'

'Millions are being killed. Why trouble yourself over one more?'

'I suppose I must simply ask that you trust me.'

Kingsley stared at Cumming as the master spy busied himself clearing up the tea things. Perhaps it was best not to dwell on the future but to consider the present. He was a man whose old life had been over anyway. What did it matter what he did?

And then, of course, there was the thrill of the chase.

Kingsley took out a little spiral notebook and pen that he had bought at WH Smith and Sons at Victoria Station. He could not help himself, he was a born policeman.

'You spoke about "circumstances and witness statements" which give you reason for doubt?'

Cumming smiled. A policeman with his notebook was surely getting down to work.

'Well, the first question to be asked is what was this great hero doing in an NYDN centre in the first place, and what a coincidence it is that Hopkins was in the next-door room.'

'NYDN?' Kingsley enquired.

'Royal Army Medical Corps acronym for Not Yet Diagnosed – Nervous.'

'You can't be serious.'

'I'm entirely serious. That's what the army calls these places. They don't like the term "shell shock", don't like it at all.'

'And just how "nervous" was Viscount Abercrombie?'

'Well, this is the point: nobody knows. He'd only been at Château Beaurivage a week before he was shot.'

'Was he in a ward?'

'Sadly not. A few witnesses would be nice, but being aristocracy and famous to boot he had his own billet.'

'And the theory is that Private Hopkins went in and shot him?'

'Well, that's how it *looks*. God knows he's got the motive and he was found later with the gun, but as I say nobody actually saw him do it.'

'So where do the doubts come in?'

'Well, the first point is that Hopkins swears blind he didn't do it.'

'In my experience most murderers tend to take that line. What else?'

'Rather more disturbingly, we have two eyewitness reports that suggest *somebody else* was in Abercrombie's room shortly before he was found dead.'

'Who?'

'An officer, that's all we know. He disappeared and has not been seen again.'

'Are these witnesses reliable?'

'One's reliable and the other's pretty dubious. The dubious one's a private soldier, chap called McCroon, who had also just been admitted to Beaurivage and had in fact spent much of the earlier part of the evening with Hopkins doing raffia work. It seems to have been this fellow who first cried foul and got word of Hopkins's arrest to his union.'

'Did nobody else at the centre speak out when it was announced that Abercrombie died in battle?'

'No, the incident had happened at night and only a few of the medical staff were aware of it. They are all military personnel and hence subject to military law, and they had been told to keep quiet.'

'You say that this McCroon was a friend of Hopkins's?'

'Probably more of a comrade.'

'You mean a political friend?'

'Yes, McCroon was a political comrade. They were both avowed Socialists, in fact Bolsheviks.'

'Well, such a figure might easily make up a story about shadowy officers to help a comrade and confuse the authorities.'

'True, but the other witness is less easy to dismiss. A nurse.'

'Male or female?'

'A girl. Steady sort, only twenty-two but with over a year's service behind her. All at the sharp end too, as close to the guns as girls are allowed to get, which is pretty close these days.'

'The police told you that?'

'No, we conducted cursory inquiries ourselves. Shannon has been over and spoken to her. We wanted to be able to provide you with as much information as possible in the short time available.'

'You say that Hopkins had a motive for killing Abercrombie?'

'Well, apart from him being a Bolshevik and Abercrombie being an aristocrat, a few days previous to the murder he'd got Field Punishment Number One for disobeying an order at the bathhouse.'

'Field Punishment Number One?'

'Most unpleasant, being lashed to a gun limber, and Abercrombie was in charge of the punishment detail.'

'I see.'

'Of course the same motive Hopkins has for killing Abercrombie gives the military a very real motive for wanting to railroad him straight to the gallows. As you know, the situation at the front is pretty desperate; nobody knows if the British army will go the way the French did, or, worse still, the Russians. General Staff are certainly very nervous. For them, the fewer Bolshies like Hopkins in the trenches the better.'

'Are you saying that people think the army would execute an innocent man in order to rid themselves of a pithead revolutionary?'

'Believe me, people will believe *anything*. What about the Angel of Mons, eh? The human capacity for superstition and theories of conspiracy is endless. *Particularly* if there's a foundation for them, which in this case there is. Any number of people knew that Abercrombie was in that NYDN centre. Officers and men alike, there's plenty of them wondering how a man with shell shock came to be killed in battle. Rumours fly around and before you know it the truth gets lost altogether – which can be all to the good – but in the meantime the tittle-tattle in the ranks is that Abercrombie was murdered, murdered by another officer. They believe that the toffs know the truth but won't hang one of their own; far better and more convenient to frame the Bolshevik next door who's suffering from shell shock.'

'I can see that it might be an attractive theory to war-weary soldiers.'

'Yes, well, fortunately at the moment these ideas are confined to the troops at the front. We control the press and currently the wider world believes that Abercrombie died a hero. They've never heard of Hopkins. But if we shoot an innocent man and it ever comes out, God knows what might happen. Don't forget that Hopkins was a miner. Have you any idea what the miners could do to the war effort if their union decided to turn nasty? Practically the entire fleet is still coal-fuelled.'

'You're not trying to tell me they'd strike, surely?'

Cumming was about to respond but instead a loud and commanding voice answered from the door. A loud and commanding voice with a strong Welsh accent.

33

Illustrious company

'Oh, I don't think they'd do that. I bloody 'ope not anyway, boyo! Do you see?'

Kingsley looked round and nearly fell off his chair with surprise. He was lucky not to upset his tea. The figure who had entered the room was the most instantly recognizable person in Britain, after the late Lord Kitchener and the King himself. A man who had dominated the House of Commons for over a decade, first as President of the Board of Trade, then as a revolutionary Chancellor of the Exchequer, a Minister of Munitions and finally, after Asquith's career had been machine-gunned along with the flower of Kitchener's army on the Somme, as Prime Minister. David Lloyd George was Britain's most famous politician since Gladstone: '*Lloyd George knew my father*,' the troops often sang, '*Father knew Lloyd George.*' Or 'Lord' George, as the old and the poor had called him after his famous 'People's Budget' had introduced to Britain the concept of state pensions and social security. Other names were whispered too, for it was generally accepted that Lloyd George's famous energy did not stop at politics; he was the most incorrigible womanizer to hold high office since Henry VIII.

'I must say, the rather splendid thing that this war 'as

demonstrated so far,' the great man continued, entering the room – 'No no, don't get up, lads, I'm not the bloody Pope, am I now?' but Kingsley and Cumming had already jumped to their feet – 'is that the British working man and 'is brother at the front puts 'is country before class. Mind you, last year you could 'ave said that about the Russians, couldn't you? And look at them now! Confound the lot of 'em. This is Thompson, by the way. Say 'ello, Thompson.'

'Hello, sir. Hello, sir.'

Lloyd George had been followed into the room by a rather harassed-looking young woman with ink on the cuffs of her blouse and her hair coming out of its fastenings. She was struggling to carry paper and pencils, a portable typewriter and a heavy briefcase.

'One of my secretaries, do you see? Thought we might need some notes taken. Although perhaps this is all too 'ush-'ush for that, eh, Cumming? I say, Thompson girl, have you an *invisible ink* ribbon for that typing machine of yours, ha ha!'

The young woman, who was flushed and perspiring slightly, made a half-hearted attempt at a smile while the great man laughed at his own joke. Cumming finally found a moment to stammer his greeting.

'Good morning, Prime Minister,' he said. 'I had rather supposed you would require me to bring Inspector Kingsley to you. I do hope you have not been inconvenienced.'

'Not a bit of it, Sir Mansfield.' The short, grey-haired man with the twinkling eye and bushy moustache was relieving his secretary of some of her burdens and placing them on Cumming's desk. 'Winston finished his daily *lecture* early. Now there's a first, eh? I think that fellow's the only chap in the country who's more long-winded than I am. I often think we should 'ave a contest, 'im and me, see who can blow the most hot air! I reckon we could float a Zeppelin between us! Ha ha!'

The Prime Minister threw himself down into the armchair recently vacated by Kingsley and proceeded to prove his own point.

'God love 'im, Winston does meddle so! 'E'd brought Jellicoe round to talk convoys, do you see? I swear 'e still thinks 'e's First Lord. I says to 'im, I says, "Winston, these days you're Minister of Munitions, do you see? You *makes* shells, t'aint your job to worry *where to fire 'em*." But 'e won't be told. Aristocrats never can stand that, can they? That's what made this country great and also what's buggered it up in the process. Ha ha! Pardon your young ears, Thompson, I keep forgettin' we've a *lady* present. Anyway I fancied a stroll so I thought I'd come down to see you in your little *den of spies*. I 'ave to be at the House later and you're on the way. So make us a cup o' tea, Sir Mansfield, and let's be doin'. We've brought our own milk, ain't we, Thompson?'

'Yes, Prime Minister,' the young woman said and duly produced a screw-top jar from her briefcase.

Despite the fact that Kingsley had gone to prison in protest at policies for which this man was now ultimately responsible, he could not help but enjoy this quite extraordinary encounter. He had always voted Liberal and the incredible energy of the little Welsh Wizard, as he was popularly known, seemed to fill the whole room with electricity. And his voice was as musical as he had heard it said to be, even though he seemed so far to have said nothing of consequence. It was exciting to be in the great man's presence. Kingsley could quite understand why women found him so appealing.

Cumming had returned to his little gas ring and was boiling more water.

'Uhm, perhaps Miss Thompson might be more comfortable in the adjoining room, Prime Minister,' he said.

'What? Do you think so? Oh well. Shame, there never was a room that wasn't improved by 'aving a *lady* in it. Still. Run along, Thompson. I shall call you when I need you.'

The Prime Minister gave her a big friendly wink and the secretary gathered up her equipment and scuttled from the room. Kingsley could not help but wonder what the full extent of this personable but exhausted-looking young woman's duties might be.

185

'Now then, Prime Minister, I was just . . .' Cumming began, but Lloyd George interrupted him and turned to Kingsley.

'This Abercrombie business, do you see? We want you to clear it up. Either prove the Bolshevik is guilty so we can shoot 'im fair and square without 'avin' George Bernard bloody Shaw writin' to the papers about it, don't you know, or else find out who *is* guilty so that we can shoot *'im*. I don't care either way. What we need is the *truth*, do you see? *The truth*. Can't have a *fudge*. Otherwise it's goin' to blow up into a real bloody scandal. You know that Abercrombie's dah's Tory Chief Whip in the Lords, don't you?'

'Yes, sir, I did,' said Kingsley, speaking for the first time since the Prime Minister had entered the room.

'Imagine that, the Tory Party on one side and the trades union movement on the other, and grim murder the cause of it. If I wasn't stuck in the bloody middle I'd be *laughin'*, so I would. We have to nip this in the bud. They say you're the best detective in Britain. If anybody has a chance of sortin' it out, it's you. The Home Secretary agreed. "Get that swine Kingsley," 'e said, but of course you weren't available, were you?'

'Uhm . . . No, sir. I was . . .'

'In prison. Yes, I do read the papers, Inspector. That's why we had to have Cumming here *produce you*. Couldn't just haul you out of the Scrubs, you're too bloody notorious! I'd never have heard the end of it. HM Government using convicted felons and known traitors to sort out its affairs. The King would 'ave chucked me out and called for Bonar Law before you could say *dissolution*! 'E might even 'ave 'ad Asquith back, God forbid.'

'Hence my death while escaping.'

Lloyd George put his fingers in his ears in an exaggerated pantomime of innocent ignorance.

'Don't want to hear about it! Don't want to know! *Men of Harlech come to Glory!*' he roared, affecting to cover the sound of Kingsley's voice by singing. 'I shouldn't even *be* 'ere! In *fact*, there is no *'ere* to *be* as it 'appens because, as I think you know, Cumming and this whole department don't exist any more than you do! Never 'ave done, never will, 'Is Majesty's Government does not *stoop* to *spying*, do you see? I just couldn't resist 'avin' a look at you. You've caused quite a stir yourself after all.'

'I am flattered, sir.'

'So. Are you going to 'elp us out then, lad?'

Kingsley had been hooked anyway but had he not been it was unlikely he would have held back now. Lloyd George was not a man it was easy to say no to; he could turn a hostile crowd or a lady's head with a wink of his eye. The power of his voice and the content of his oratory had changed the social face of Britain. He had risen from poverty in Wales to control the interests of the British Empire. Kingsley, like much of the country before him, had been utterly seduced.

'Yes, Prime Minister. Of course I shall help.'

'Good. Quite a *lark*, eh? A dead man takes a job that don't exist from a man who's never met him, in a room of which we deny all knowledge! I *love* politics, so I do! Now then, I have 'ad my look at you and I should be getting to the 'Ouse. We'll 'ave that cup of tea another time, eh, Sir Mansfield?'

'Of course, sir.'

Lloyd George jumped up from the chair.

'Thompson!' he cried as he headed for the door. 'We're off!'

And the great man was gone.

A moment later he was back.

'Forgot my milk,' he said, snatching up his jar before once more departing.

It was as if a whirlwind had passed through the building and for a moment or two both Kingsley and Cumming could do no more than catch their breath.

'Well?' said Cumming finally.

'Well,' Kingsley replied, 'I wonder if you have anything stronger on offer than tea, Sir Mansfield?'

'Good man! What is it, nearly noon?' Cumming consulted his wristwatch. 'Twenty past! Good lord, positively late in the day. Almost evening! And damn it, we've earned a snort. Not every day the Welsh Wizard casts his spell on you, is it? Scotch all right? Better be, that's all there is.'

Cumming opened the steel drawer of a filing cabinet and produced a bottle of Black and White, from which he poured two generous measures.

'I think you're all out of your minds,' said Kingsley, lighting another cigarette while Cumming filled his pipe.

'Why do you say that?'

'Well, think about it. This war is costing us on average a thousand casualties a day and we are discussing the fate of just two men, one of whom is already dead! You're mad, Captain. The Prime Minister is mad, the Labour Party, the unions, the Tories and the army are all mad. The whole world is mad and I am a dead man brought to life to discuss a living man who is about to die. Clearly I must be mad also.'

'A man has been murdered and another faces execution. You are a policeman. What's mad about wanting to uncover the truth?'

'Because the only "truth" that matters is that this war has so far accounted for upwards of three quarters of a *million* casualties in Britain alone. Civilization is now entirely villainous, murdering its own, murdering all it sees. If I save this Private Hopkins, he'll be executed anyway, in battle. If Abercrombie had not been murdered he would almost certainly have died in battle too. It does seem like something of a farce that the British army should hold a *murder* investigation, don't you think? That any army or government involved in this lunacy should even *consider* such matters as innocence and guilt.'

'It's politics. Now then, let's get you kitted out.'

Taking up his drink, Cumming led the way into the map room. There on the big central table lay the uniform and kit of a captain in the Military Police.

'We measured you up while you were unconscious in Folkestone. Can't send you to France in ill-fitting boots, eh?'

'Very thorough,' Kingsley commented. 'You must have been pretty certain that I'd play ball.'

'And we were right, weren't we, Captain Marlowe?'

Kingsley put on the uniform. It felt good, he could not deny it; it felt very good to be in uniform once more. Yes, it was a soldier's uniform, but it was the uniform of a military *policeman* and that was what mattered. All he had ever wanted in life, professionally, was to be a policeman. Three days earlier he had worn the uniform of a convict, now he was a policeman once more.

'Very smart,' said Cumming, nodding his approval. 'Now, how about a spot of lunch?'

34

Lunch at Simpsons

Cumming proposed that they venture across the river into south London and find an out-of-the-way chop house or perhaps a small Chinese establishment. Not unreasonably, he saw no sense in running any more risk of Kingsley's being recognized than was necessary.

'Once you get to the front,' he said, 'I do not anticipate any problems. People there have better things to do than worry about recently dead detectives but here in London many people know you, particularly in the West End and the City. There's always the chance of you bumping into an old acquaintance.'

Kingsley would have none of it.

'We shall not skulk about, Sir Mansfield. I should have thought that you above all people would understand that no bluff is effective unless delivered with *absolute* conviction. The skulker will always be detected and fortune will always favour the brave. If I do not have the confidence to stroll along the Strand then I am not safe anywhere. But I *do* have the confidence, you see, Captain. Because Inspector Kingsley is dead, Captain Christopher Marlowe, bearded, bespectacled and splendidly uniformed officer of the RMP, no more resembles him than does General Haig. But even if I were clean-shaven and put amongst my former peers I can assure you that they would not know me, for I do not *wish* to be known and therefore I shall not *be* known. A successful deception is about *inner conviction*, Captain, not facial hair and hats.'

'Hmmm. Well, quite frankly that sounds like absolute balls to me but I have to admire your side, Inspector . . .'

'Captain.'

'Yes, Captain. Besides, I do agree that got up like that I cannot imagine why anybody would recognize your old self, even strolling along the Strand.'

'They will not and I suggest we put it to the test by lunching at my favourite restaurant, where I have dined many times. Simpsons-in-the-Strand.'

Together the two men strolled out into Whitehall and back through Trafalgar Square towards the Strand. The revolutionary peace demonstration was over and in its place a military band was playing.

'*Pack up your troubles in your old kit bag and smile smile smile*,' Cumming sang along good-humouredly. 'They appear to be playing your song, eh, Marlowe?'

They walked past Charing Cross Station, outside which as usual ambulances stood amongst the ranks of wounded awaiting dispersal. Those able to walk sat about miserably in groups, smoking their fags and drinking tea which was dispensed free from a small stall run by the Salvation Army. All the men were utterly filthy, still caked in the mud of northern France and Belgium, their eyes staring out from blackened faces as they scratched at the fleas and bugs that tormented them. The less fortunate were laid out in rows on stretchers; some groaned, others lay very still. Kingsley had never got used to sights such as these in the heart of London. Some of the men appeared to be dead, but he knew that the army did not go to the trouble of shipping back soldiers who were certain to die, for the spaces were needed for those who stood a chance. Male medical officers and female nurses were attending them. Some of the nurses had clearly come direct from France and were nearly as dirty and desperate as the wounded. Other young women had come over from Charing Cross Hospital and were clean and smartly turned out. Not much more than girls, most of them, newly trained and very nervous-looking. One or two, Kingsley noticed, were smiling shyly towards him and Sir Mansfield as they passed. He thought this most uncommonly forward of them until he realized that Shannon had sneaked up behind them as if from nowhere and was winking and waving at the girls.

'Morning once again, Kingsley,' Shannon said with irritating bonhomie. 'Morning, sir. Splendid sight, eh? British nurses, all starch and powder. Jolliest in the world, say I. Think I'll pop back after lunch, they'll have seen a lot of hellish sights by then and will no doubt be *most* upset. They'll need some comforting.'

'Be quiet, you odious man!' Cumming snapped angrily. 'We are not interested in your wretched obsessions.'

'As you wish, sir,' Shannon said, but his manner was insolent.

They arrived at Simpsons and it was, as Kingsley had expected, very crowded. Nonetheless he strode straight up to the maître d' and, addressing him by his name, loudly demanded a table.

'I am shortly to depart again for France, Ridley, and wish to dine once more at my favourite watering hole. Come now, I'm sure you can find room for us.'

The maître d' did not recognize Kingsley though he clearly felt he should have done, and he ushered them immediately to a booth.

'We always try to accommodate our brave officers, sir,' the maître d' assured them, 'especially such distinguished ones.'

Both Shannon and Cumming wore impressive medal ribbons and whoever had organized Kingsley's uniform had seen fit to invest him with a DSO.

'Capital choice,' Shannon said as the three of them settled into a booth. 'Do you know, I think the reason we chaps like Simpsons so much is because it serves very posh school dinners. Two four six eight. Bog in. Don't wait!'

He grabbed a bread roll and pushed almost all of the butter into it.

Both soldiers ordered beef cut rare from the big joint that was brought to them on a trolley but Kingsley had a piece of fish. He was by no means a vegetarian but after the sights he had just seen at Charing Cross Station he had temporarily lost his appetite for red meat. The wine, however, he was grateful for, as clearly was Shannon, who drained his first glass in a single gulp.

'Of course the war's playing absolute merry hell with the French wine industry,' Shannon observed. 'God knows what rubbish we'll all be drinking in ten years' time. Not that most of us will be around to try it, of course. Not anyone worth serving a decent vintage to, anyway. Rather a pleasing thought that, when all the sound, brave chaps are dead and only the cowards, smug old men and shitty conchies remain, at least they'll only have war vintages to drink.'

Kingsley drank his wine and ate his fish in silence. He was thinking about the mission they wanted him to perform. He had been thinking about it all the way along the Strand.

'Sir Mansfield tells me that you have been to France and spoken with the relevant witnesses in the Abercrombie case, Captain Shannon,' he said finally.

'Briefly, yes.'

'Sir Mansfield mentioned a nurse.'

'Yes, Nurse Murray. The last person apart from the killer to see Abercrombie alive,' Shannon replied. 'Very sweet girl, very, very sweet.'

The man's voice made Kingsley's skin crawl. He thought once more of sixteen-year-old Violet on Folkestone beach.

'Did you manage to apply your rule?' Kingsley asked coldly.

'Rule? What rule?' Cumming enquired through his roast beef, Yorkshire pudding and tobacco smoke.

Shannon smiled the most charming of smiles.

'Oh, just something Kingsley and I have been discussing, sir. A matter of no consequence. But yes, as it happens, Inspector, I did

probe the witness *most* thoroughly. I felt it my duty to do so.'
Shannon let this hang in the air for a moment before adding, 'And
she told me that she saw an officer hurrying from Abercrombie's
room but she did not see his face or his rank.'

'How did she know he was an officer?'

'Cap and boots. We don't issue riding clobber to privates, they
get canvas leggings.'

'What about the other witness to this mysterious officer?'

'McCroon?'

'Yes. Did he get any more detail?'

'Sadly not. Again he caught only a fleeting glimpse. The
château is a large one, a sort of stately home, lot of corridors, lot
of shadows.'

Once more Kingsley took out his notebook.

'Were McCroon and the nurse together when they made their
sighting?'

Shannon drew heavily on his gasper and lit a second one from
its glowing end.

'No. In different parts of the same corridor, which turns a
number of corners and contains numerous wards. Nurse Murray
saw the figure leave Abercrombie's room as she emerged from
Hopkins's ward, which is next door to it. She saw him hurry off
in the opposite direction to her. McCroon was further along the
same corridor, in a different ward, and says he had left it to relieve
himself. He claims that the mysterious officer pushed past him
and hurried on in front.'

'So McCroon's sighting of the officer would have taken place
moments after Nurse Murray's?'

'Yes.'

'And both witnesses saw only the back of this man?'

'Unfortunately, yes.'

'So if this mystery man shot Abercrombie, Nurse Murray
would have been next door in Hopkins's ward at the time. Did
she hear a shot?'

'She may have done but it's impossible to say.'

'Why is that?'

'Because, dress it up with as much Not Yet Diagnosed balls as you wish, this place is a loony bin and loony bins are damned noisy, especially at night. I know, I've been there. There are bangs, shrieks and much rattling of chains. Most unsettling. Also, the walls and doors of the château are thick. It would be quite possible for a shot to go unnoticed at any time in such a place.'

'So nobody heard a shot?'

'Oh, they all heard shots, any number of shots. I've told you this is a loony bin, a loony bin for victims of shell shock. Some of them hear very little else *but* shots.'

'What about timings?' Kingsley enquired. 'Do you have any?'

'We have Nurse Murray's timings, which are very clear. She filled in bed reports for all the patients in the ward, reporting on their status as she left them. She did Abercrombie at nine twenty-five and then went next door to Hopkins's ward. She spent an hour in there, what with changing dressings and the like, and filled out her last report at ten thirty-two. She would have left the ward and spotted the mystery officer moments after that.'

All three men ordered trifle and cream from the dessert trolley and called for more cigarettes.

'So that places McCroon's nocturnal visit to the lavatories at approximately ten thirty-three,' he said.

'Yes, but of course he cannot confirm that because he doesn't own a timepiece.'

'Imagine that?' Cumming interjected. 'Not having a watch. I can't live without knowing the time. Feel absolutely naked.'

'What time was the body discovered?' Kingsley enquired.

'Later. Between eleven forty and eleven forty-five.'

'And when was Hopkins found with the gun?'

'Moments after that.'

'Who discovered the body?'

'The night nurse who went on duty at ten forty-five, replacing Nurse Murray. She was the one who raised the alarm,' Shannon answered, before adding for Kingsley's benefit, 'I didn't

195

apply the rule there, by the way, face like a German general.'

Kingsley ignored him.

'I presume that there has been an appeal made for the mystery officer to come forward and explain himself?'

'We are assured that the local Military Police have made inquiries but so far with no result.'

'And Hopkins was arrested because he was found with the murder weapon?'

'Yes, Abercrombie's own service revolver.'

'Abercrombie retained a gun even at a centre for shell shock?'

'It would seem so. After all, he had not yet been diagnosed.'

'You are sure that this gun *was* the murder weapon?'

'Well, Abercrombie had been shot, and Hopkins was found in the next room with Abercrombie's gun, which had very recently been discharged.'

'Yes, I can see that it is *probably* the murder weapon but are you *sure*? The bullet has been checked against the gun?'

'I doubt it, they are fighting a war out there, you know. Lots else to do.'

'But for heaven's sake, Shannon, you must have proof! You can't hang a man on weak circumstantial presumptions. There are an awful lot of guns in France.'

'Well, that's what you're here for,' Cumming said. 'It's your job to find some proof.'

They had moved on to the coffee and cigars. Shannon, true to style, had also ordered cognac.

Cumming, who clearly had other business, rose to go.

'Your papers are being prepared as we speak. I shall leave Shannon to organize the details of your departure. Good luck, Kingsley, and don't let me down. Sort out the bill, Shannon, get a receipt and *don't* go ordering a pocketful of cigars to take away with you.'

With that, Cumming left. Shannon rolled the big balloon of cognac in his hands to warm the spirit and inhaled deeply of its vapours.

'Do you know the Hole in the Wall pub at Waterloo?' he asked.

'Yes.'

'I'll meet you there at six with your identification papers and movement orders.'

'Why there?'

'France, Inspector Kingsley. The night troop train to France. You're on it.'

'And I am free until then?'

'Why wouldn't you be?' Shannon said easily. 'You're a captain in the RMP. We have no authority over you. But I wouldn't go making any more trips to Hampstead if I were you. That was a very foolish trick you played.'

Kingsley was surprised, and inwardly most embarrassed. He had always trusted himself to know when he was being followed and yet Shannon, or at least his people, seemed to have shadowed him in complete anonymity.

'The special constable?' Kingsley asked.

'Yes. One of ours. I recruited her myself, as it happens. *Lovely* girl. Thought I ought to have your house watched, but I couldn't believe it when I read her report this morning. Did you really break in?'

Kingsley was pleased to realize that they had at least not shadowed him all the way from Folkestone and right across London, but had only picked him up at his house.

'I'm afraid I did. Don't worry, I was not detected. I should not like to drag my family into the world you inhabit.'

'Your ex-family.'

'My family, Captain.'

'Well, can't blame you really, wanting a last look. Mrs Beaumont is certainly a cracker. Absolutely gorgeous hair, eyes, fabulous top shelf. You're a lucky man – or at least you were.'

Kingsley's blood ran cold.

'You've met my wife?'

'Oh yes. Held her hand and told her you were dead, old boy.

Not surprised you miss a filly like that. Still, your misfortune will no doubt some day be another lucky fellow's gain, look at it that way. She's fair game now, old son ... Steady on, Inspector, crowded place and all that. Wouldn't want to cause a scene.'

Kingsley had raised his hand to strike Shannon, but now he lowered it.

'You've been to my house?'

'Popped in before following you to Folkestone. Only decent thing to do, I thought. She took it well, but was obviously pretty shaken.' Shannon smiled unpleasantly. 'Glad I was there really ... You know, when a girl's upset what she needs is an experienced and sympathetic shoulder to cry on.'

Kingsley leaned forward until his face was close to Shannon's.

'If ever you were to lay a hand on her . . .'

'Oh do come on, old boy. Just making small talk.'

'I'd kill you.'

'Fine talk for a pacifist.'

'I am not a pacifist. I believe killing can sometimes be justified and would consider myself perfectly justified in killing you, whether you'd personally hurt me or not. Remember that, Captain Shannon.'

'Oh, yawn yawn *yawn*. Nothing more embarrassing than nice fellows pretending to be nasty. I'd stick to snooping if I were you, *Captain Marlowe*. Leave killing to professionals.'

'Captain Shannon, as with most things in life you'll find that the gifted amateur who is *really inspired* to do the job will always triumph over the paid professional.'

35

A show, then off to France

Kingsley decided to take a good long walk. It had been a heavy and rather alcoholic lunch and he knew that he would soon be cramped in a train for many hours. First of all, he strolled along the Embankment watching the traffic on the Thames, and then all around the streets and alleyways of Waterloo. There was an afternoon music-hall concert advertised at the Old Vic to give some distraction to the hordes of troops milling about the area who were awaiting entrainment back to France.

Kingsley bought a cheap ticket to stand at the back and went inside.

The songs were mainly the old ones to which everybody could sing along: 'The Old Kent Road', 'Any Old Iron', 'When Father Papered the Parlour', even the ancient and creaky 'Come Into The Garden, Maud'. The audience sang along lustily with the girls on stage.

> 'It's a long way to Tipperary, it's a long way to go,
> It's a long way to Tipperary to the sweetest girl I know!'

All of the songs were familiar to Kingsley. Agnes and he had loved to visit the music hall. She in particular was very fond of popular music, and bought all the sheeted scores from the street vendors outside the theatres so as to play the songs at home on her piano.

Then a pretty soubrette came on and announced 'In The Twi Twi Twilight'. This was too much for Kingsley and he left.

He missed Agnes dreadfully. In some ways he took comfort from the fact that the investigation he had agreed to undertake must be conducted beneath the shadow of the guns. What witnesses there were would be soldiers engaged in battle, and the mysterious missing officer likewise. If Kingsley was to find them he must needs go into battle too, or at least do his work in the midst of it. That appealed to Kingsley in his current mood. He was going to France in the pursuit of truth, a cause to which he had devoted his life, and if he were to lose his life in its pursuit then perhaps that was so much the better. No one would mourn him; those with a mind to were already doing so. He had no future and no past. Why not fall in the war that had ruined everything?

Kingsley met Shannon at the appointed location and, in an upstairs room, was given his new identity papers, travel documents and French money.

'Have a nice trip,' Shannon said. 'Do send us a postcard if you solve the case.'

'Remember what I said,' Kingsley said quietly.

'My dear fellow, London is full of skirt. I really have no need to pursue it as far as Hampstead Heath. And speaking of skirt . . .'

Kingsley and Shannon had descended into the public bar and there, across the crowded room, stood a young nurse from Charing Cross Hospital.

'I told you I'd pop back and grab one,' Shannon explained. 'Vera! You found your way here all right, I see.'

'Yes, I did,' said the nurse, clearly delighted to see Shannon. It wasn't a comfortable thing for a woman to be alone in a pub, particularly one near a mainline station.

'Well now, what *shall* we do with our evening?' Shannon said with a charming smile, putting his arm around her. 'Oh, this is Captain Marlowe, by the way, Vera. He's just leaving. Off to France, eh? Poor you, and I get to take a ravishing young lady to dinner and a show.'

'Oh, *stop*!' said Vera, her eyes shining.

Kingsley felt sorry for the girl but there was nothing he could do. At least she was older than Violet. He could only hope that, as Shannon himself would put it, she knew the score.

Kingsley left the pub and, shouldering his kitbag, made his way to the great entrance of the station. It was awash with civilians, packed four deep on the pavement and spilling over on to the street. It was always like this when a big push was on in France. Kingsley recalled two or three occasions when chases he had been involved in were thwarted as the prey ducked in amongst the crowds of gawpers who waited about to watch the wounded being bussed out of the station. Kingsley knew from conversations he had had with Tommies that no soldier appreciated the attentions of sightseers.

'They thinks as how just because they chucks a few fags at us that they's doin' their patriotic bit, boostin' our morale with a cheer an' all, but they ain't. They ain't doin' it for us, they's just curious an' lookin' for a cheap thrill. Probably goes 'ome afterwards thanking Gawd it ain't them sittin' there all bandaged up and bleedin' like a bunch o' fuckin' mummies in a jam factory.'

Kingsley pushed his way through the crowd and into the station. Pandemonium reigned. The arrival of a large transport of wounded had clashed with the impending departure of a couple of trainloads of Tommies bound for the front. Kingsley got his back up against one of the numerous stalls providing a French money exchange to 'officers and men in uniform', and smoked a cigarette before attempting to board his train.

It was jam-packed but at least there were seats. He wedged himself into a second-class compartment in which a dozen other officers were lodged and tried to sleep. It was impossible; he was too uncomfortable, and his mind was racing with thoughts of Agnes and George and the case that he must investigate.

Nonetheless, this first part of the journey turned out to be luxurious in comparison with the Channel crossing to Boulogne, which was unpleasant in the extreme. On its previous trip the boat had carried horses, of which the army employed many thousands. A small effort had been made to clean the ship for its human cargo but in reality all this meant was that the horses' straw had been swept over the horses' shit.

The crossing was a rough one, with high winds and driving rain, and there was mass seasickness. In the crowded conditions, the smell of vomit mixed with horse manure was not one any of the men on board were ever likely to forget. Despite the enormous number of casualties it had taken, the British army had continued to grow throughout the war, partly because the Royal Army Medical Corps was getting better and better at patching up the wounded and sending them back to the front. Millions of men were now under arms and it seemed to Kingsley as if all of them were on the same boat as him.

On arrival in Boulogne, any romantic illusions that new recruits might have harboured about experiencing a little of France were soon shattered, as they were moved directly from the boat to the railhead. And if the boat had been vastly more uncomfortable than the train from Waterloo, then the train from Boulogne was to prove far worse than the boat. The train which Kingsley's movement order directed him towards was quite the longest he had ever seen: forty carriages. Thirty-six of them were horse trucks, or, to be more precise, horse or human trucks because, like the boat, the trains were used to carry both. Each truck bore the legend 'HOMMES 4O. CHEVAUX 8'.

'Is that forty men *or* eight horses or forty men *and* eight horses?' Kingsley enquired of a harassed railhead marshal.

'Very funny, sir. I wonder 'ow many times I've 'eard that one.'

It had actually been a genuine question. Fortunately, further investigation showed that the army did not expect the men to travel with the horses. It was difficult to be thankful for this small mercy. There were four trucks reserved for officers but a brief inspection revealed that these were not much better than the horse trucks; many doors were missing and although there were seats they were wooden, badly in need of repair and already grossly overcrowded. Kingsley was of course an officer, but he had discovered on the boat that ordinary soldiers hated military policemen in a way that only criminals hated civilian police. His red tabs and cap had marked him out instantly and he had decided to remove them, along with his badges of rank, until they were required. Kingsley was anxious to learn something of the mind of the soldiers amongst whom he must conduct his investigation and he was unlikely to learn anything if he was treated as a leper.

He decided to throw in his lot with the enlisted men and climbed aboard one of the troop trucks. It was without furnishing of any kind, unless a sprinkling of straw could be considered furnishing. The only distinguishing feature was a great burn mark in the middle of the wooden floor, where at some point freezing soldiers had clearly improvised a little central heating. Large signs warned against this practice on pain of imprisonment.

'Is it always this spartan?' Kingsley asked a man crushed next to him, whose weathered face suggested he was a veteran of the trenches.

'Always. Never changed, not since 1915 at least, when I first come here. Always cramped, always crap.'

Kingsley could hardly believe that this was how the British Empire treated its heroes. Men who were travelling willingly towards probable death in the service of their country were packed into horse trucks. The only blessing, he reflected, was that the journey would be a short one, for it was less than a hundred miles to their destination. He made this point to the man beside him.

'You've had an easy war so far, mate, haven't you, if this is your first go up the line?'

'I confess that it is.'

'Well, settle down, my greenhorn pal. Settle down for a long trip.'

The train lurched forward about three or four yards and then stopped. There it rested for several hours, during which the men remained packed into the trucks. Eventually it moved, although only at walking pace, and after a mile or two it stopped again. So began a process of crawling and stopping that continued for the following eighteen hours.

'It's always like this,' the old hand beside Kingsley assured him. 'I was in transit three days once. That's thirty miles a day, not much more than a mile an hour. We don't move no faster than Wellington's lot did. Mind you, when we gets there we dies a lot bleeding faster.'

36

A communal interlude

Once during one of the endless halts a discussion developed about the war's origins, amongst a group of men who were taking the opportunity of a predicted sixty-minute stop to empty their bowels. Kingsley had never defecated in front of anyone before but the men he was travelling with – all experienced soldiers and comrades of old – thought no more about it than if they were pissing up against the same wall.

'You needs a bit of time to take a shit,' Kingsley's companion advised him, 'leastways you do on army rations. You need time to 'ave a smoke and relax a bit, get things moving, so to speak. Time to let it drop comfortable and finish off neat. Nothing worse than hearing the whistle blow an' having to pinch it off all in a hurry and ending up with an 'orrible sore arse and flies buzzing round it. Good army tip that, mate, take it from a bloke who's already long overdue a bullet. Look after your arse. Always make sure you've got time to do the right thing by your arse.'

The train had halted in a pleasant field. The rain had stopped and all up and down the track fires were lit, fags rolled, pipes filled, tea brewed, a scratch made in the ground with a bayonet and the whole army settled down for a shit.

Kingsley joined the group that had formed around his new

friend. Fifteen or so men, grouped by a fire, squatted down with their trousers round their ankles, some leaning forward on their rifles for support. The men chatted idly, as if they were in the pub. Kingsley, who had expected to feel self-conscious, found it curiously convivial. Everybody smoked, of course, and Kingsley drew contentedly on his Players Navy Strength, listening as the talk turned to the origins of their current misery.

'The question I always asks is, why did anyone give a fuck about this bleeding Archduke Ferdinand what's-his-face in the first place?' one fellow said. 'I mean, come on, nobody had even *heard* of the cunt till he got popped off. Now the entire fucking world is fighting 'cos of it.'

'You dozy arse,' another man admonished, 'that was just a bleeding spark, that was. It was a *spark*. Europe was a *tinder box*, wasn't it? Everyone knows that.'

'Well, I don't see as how he was even worth a spark, mate,' the first man replied. 'Like I say, who'd even *heard* of the cunt?'

A corporal weighed in to settle the matter.

'Listen, it's yer Balkans, innit? Always yer Balkans. Balkans, Balkans, Balkans. You see, yer Austro-Hungarians—'

'Who are *another* bunch we never gave a fuck about till all this kicked off,' the first man interjected.

'Shut up an' you might learn something,' the corporal insisted. 'You've got your Austro-Hungarians supposed to be in charge in Sarajevo but most of the Bosnians is Serbs, right, or at least enough of 'em is to cause a t'do.'

'What's Sarajevo got to do with Bosnia then?'

'Sarajevo's *in* Bosnia, you monkey! It's the capital.'

'Oh. So?'

'Well, your Austrians 'ave got Bosnia, right, but your Bosnians are backed by your Serbs, right? So when a Bosnian Serb shoots—'

'A Bosnian or a Serb?'

'A Bosnian *and* a bleeding Serb, you arse. When this Bosnian Serb loony shoots Ferdinand who's heir to the Austro-Hungarian throne, the Austrians think, right, here's a chance to put Serbia back in its bleeding box for good, so they give 'em an ultimatum. They says, "You topped our Archduke so from now on you can bleeding knuckle under or else you're for it." Which would have been fine *except* the Serbs were backed by the Russians, see, and the Russians says to the Austrians, you has a go at Serbia, you has a go at us, right? But the *Austrians* is backed by the *Germans* who says to the Russians, you has a go at Austria, you has a go at us, right? Except the *Russians* is backed by the *French* who says to the Germans, you has a go at Russia, you has a go at us, right? And altogether they says kick off! Let's be having you! And the ruck begins.'

'What about us then?' the first man enquired. The rest of the group seemed to feel that this was the crux of it.

'Entente bleeding cordiale, mate,' the corporal replied. 'We was backing the French except it wasn't like an alliance – it was just, well, it was a bleedin' *entente*, wasn't it.'

'An' what's an entente when it's at home?'

'It means we wasn't obliged to fight.'

'Never! You mean we didn't have to?'

'Nope.'

'Why the fuck did we then?'

'Fuckin' Belgium.'

'Belgium?'

'That's right, fuckin' Belgium.'

'Who gives a fuck about Belgium?'

'Well, you'd have thought no one, wouldn't you? But we did. 'Cos the German plan to get at the French was to go through Belgium, but we was guaranteeing 'em, see. So we says to the Germans, you has a go at Belgium, you has a go at us. We'd guaranteed her, see. It was a matter of honour. So in we come.'

Kingsley could not resist interjecting.

'Of course it wasn't really about honour,' he said.

'Do what?' queried the corporal.

'Well, we'd only guaranteed Belgium because we didn't want either Germany or France dominating the entire Channel coast. In

207

the last century we thought that letting them both know that if they invaded Belgium they'd have us to deal with would deter them.'

'But it didn't.'

'Sadly not.'

'So what about the Italians, an' the Japs, an' the Turks, an' the Yanks, eh? How did they end up in it?' asked the original inquisitor.

'Fuck knows,' said the corporal. 'I lost track after the Belgians.'

For a while conversation lapsed as the soldiers concentrated on their bowels.

'You lot make me laugh, you really do,' said a man who had not spoken yet, a thoughtful-looking fellow in steel glasses who up until then had been staring at a book whilst he did his business.

'Oh, that's right,' the corporal sneered, ''cos you'd know better, wouldn't you, Price?'

'Yes, I would, Corporal. I most certainly would. This war, like all bourgeois wars, is the inevitable result of capitalism.'

'Oh Gawd, here we go.'

'A bayonet is a weapon with a worker on both ends.'

Kingsley had heard this Socialist slogan before and had always thought it rather neat.

'War creates new markets and generates new investment,' Price continued. 'It also provides a nice distraction to idiots like us who might otherwise notice that we live in a constant state of near-starvation while the owners of the means of production are too fat to get out of their Rolls-Royce cars. War is the last stage of the capitalist cycle and as long as we have capitalism we'll have wars. If you want to get rid of war you've got to get rid of capitalism.'

'What, and there wouldn't be wars if your lot was running things?'

'Course not. Why would there be? The workers of the world are all comrades. Truth is, you've got more in common with Fritz and his mates having a shit just east of Wipers than you have with your own officers.'

Some men protested at this and angrily warned the Socialist to shut his mouth. Others looked more thoughtful.

'You are a Marxist then, my friend?' Kingsley enquired.

'It's just common sense. Why work for a boss when you can form a collective and work for each other in mutual cooperation?'

'What if people don't work?'

'They don't eat. To each according to his needs, from each according to his means.'

'More like "What's yours is mine and what's mine's me own",' the corporal sneered.

A warning whistle blew and it was time to leave socialism and the origins of war behind. Men began grabbing clumps of leaves and grass to clean themselves with, grateful for the rain that had fallen, for it aided their ablutions enormously.

Back on the train Kingsley asked the Socialist if he had any views on the death of Viscount Abercrombie.

'What, you mean apart from being happy that there's one less aristocratic parasite to leech upon the working man?'

'Yes, apart from that.'

'I heard he didn't die in battle. That he was shell-shocked. Maybe he killed himself, who knows. One thing's for certain, the army has something to hide.'

37

At home with the nervous

Finally the troop train crawled into the railhead, which was the dispersal point for the whole Ypres salient. The men had arrived at the place they called Wipers, arguably the most loathed destination of any part of the British line, certainly the wettest, a place around which there had been nearly continuous fighting for the entire war. As the train approached, a fellow with a harmonica began to play a mournful tune. A number of the men took it up in gentle, sombre tones. Like so many soldiers' songs, this one had begun life as a hymn but it was a hymn no longer.

> *'Far, far from Wipers I long to be*
> *Where German snipers can't get at me.*
> *Dark is my dugout, cold are my feet.*
> *Waiting for whizbangs to send me to sleep.'*

On disembarking, Kingsley parted from the soldiers with whom he had entrained. They were heading directly up to the front, towards Ypres, whilst he must begin his investigation at the scene of the murder, the NYDN centre at Merville on the River Lys, some six kilometres from the front line.

Despite the fact that the war was already some three years old and the areas of combat had not changed significantly since the early autumn of 1914, transportation and communications to the rear of the fighting remained primitive and highly inefficient. Kingsley watched, astonished, as men who had just been subjected to a day and a night crammed into horse trucks were formed up with full kit and ordered to march immediately to the front, over what he could see was the most appallingly broken ground. Like most civilians, Kingsley had grown used to the numerous photographs published at home of cheery Tommies loaded into double-decker buses, waving to the camera as if on a spree. The reality was very different. The army of Sir Douglas Haig, like every army before it, travelled up the line on its feet, and in this most modern of wars the armies of the great industrialized nations arrived at their trenches exhausted.

Kingsley was more fortunate. He had put his red tabs and captain's pips back on and was able, with the authority they gave him, to find transport to Merville. This was, after all, the dispersal centre for the whole line and Kingsley was heading for a Royal Army Medical Corps facility. It did not take him too long to find an ambulance that was heading his way.

'Hop in the back if you want,' the medical orderly at the wheel shouted down, 'but don't expect much conversation.'

Kingsley climbed into the back of the canvas-covered truck and found a place amongst the patients. For a moment he almost wished that he had walked. The atmosphere was stifling but it was not the fug of unwashed men sitting about him caked in mud and blood that oppressed him so; it was their faces. It was their eyes.

Kingsley had known instantly that things were not right when not a single man returned his greeting as he climbed into the truck. The silence that met him was far more intimidating than the sound of the guns, which had been clearly audible ever since he had got off the train. Kingsley should have been expecting it, of course; he knew exactly what kind of facility it was towards which he was heading and he knew that many shell shock victims were mute. All the same, these silent men who had withdrawn inside themselves, staring at nothing with their empty, startled expressions, unnerved him. It felt to Kingsley, as they bumped along the cobbled road in their ill-sprung vehicle, that he was sitting amongst the living dead. He was ashamed to realize that these poor wretches scared him.

Suddenly, there was a scream.

Kingsley nearly jumped through the roof. One of the silent men was silent no longer: he screamed and screamed, bawling incoherent commands at the top of his voice, scratching at his face with his nails before falling to the floor of the truck and writhing at the feet of his impassive comrades. In a moment the fit was over, the man lay where he had fallen, and there were no further disturbances for the duration of that most uncomfortable ride.

When the journey ended, Kingsley had never been so glad to leave a truck in his life. The eighteen hours in the horse truck had been far preferable to the hour he had spent with these lost men, and he resolved that at the end of his investigations at the NYDN centre, when the time came for him to return to the railhead, he would either find a place in the front of a truck beside the driver or he would walk.

'Warned you they weren't very sociable,' the orderly remarked as he dropped Kingsley off at the front of the château.

It was a magnificent building, the first beautiful thing that Kingsley had seen in France and the first truly French thing as well. Even Boulogne, what he had seen of it as the train rode through, had been more like an extension of Britain than a French town, with its hotels bearing English names and signs offering fish and chips and India Pale Ale. Now, though, Kingsley felt that he was truly in France and he could not help his thoughts turning to Agnes, who had loved France, adored it, or at least she had adored Paris. Or at least she had adored the shops and cafés in Paris and of course the Eiffel Tower. She had *quite* liked the art galleries and could stomach Sacré Coeur but she thought Notre Dame simply the gloomiest place on earth and had declined even to ascend the towers, saying that she had no desire to seek out the company of gargoyles. Kingsley smiled at the memory of their trips together to that most beautiful of cities and how they would clash over the day's itinerary at breakfast each morning. She would vote for shops and cafés, he for art and history. He missed her terribly.

He looked about him. Two games of football were under way in the grounds of the château and a drill sergeant was taking a gentle PT class. Lawn tennis and croquet were being played, and a course in motor mechanics appeared to be in progress around and underneath a magnificent Renault limousine. In spite of all the activity, there was something strange and listless about it all, as if the participants, or most of them at least, were simply feigning interest whilst waiting for some other thing of which only they were aware. Kingsley watched a fellow in striped shirt and footer bags kick the ball to a similarly dressed teammate: although the pass was good (if rather slow), the second man simply let the ball roll by without even attempting to block it.

'Not what you'd call spectator sport, is it, Captain?' a woman's voice behind him said. 'But then I imagine the very best players might be put off their game a bit by spending a year or two in hell before kick-off.'

Kingsley turned to find himself facing a woman in her early twenties wearing the uniform of an RAMC staff nurse.

'Murray. Staff Nurse Murray,' she said, offering her hand as if challenging Kingsley to shake it. 'I presume you are Captain Marlowe?'

'Yes. Yes, that's right.'

'We were warned to expect you. You're here to speak to me about Captain Abercrombie, the famous hero who died in battle who didn't die in battle, and Private Hopkins, who murdered him except he wasn't murdered. Am I right, Captain?'

'You are right. They were patients of yours, I believe?'

She was not tall, in fact she was quite short, but she definitely had presence. What she lacked in height she made up for with a kind of tense energy that seemed to exude from her even in what one might have imagined were relatively relaxed circumstances. Her uniform was neat but she was not wearing her cap, which strictly speaking was an offence. Her hair was rather modishly bobbed, like a shiny black helmet with a severe fringe cut straight across her forehead about a half-inch above her eyebrows. She wore tortoiseshell glasses and had on not even the faintest hint of rouge. She was very pretty in a schoolgirlish sort of way. Both bookish and sporty at the same time, like a head girl at a seaside boarding school. The sort of girl who would think nothing of taking an early morning dip in the middle of January before rushing enthusiastically to her first Latin class.

'Yes, we had them here,' Nurse Murray said. 'Like all these fellows they were NYDN, Not Yet Diagnosed but Nervous. *Very* nervous. Don't you just love the army? They take a fellow who's been turned into a catatonic mute by being shelled from here to Christmas and say he's not yet been *properly diagnosed* but he seems *a bit nervous*. The army know these men have been driven crazy, the question we're supposed to answer is *how* crazy. Or to put it another way, can they still hold a gun? The only diagnosis the army's interested in is how soon can we shove them back in the trenches. No jolly wonder they're nervous.'

'And how soon would Abercrombie and Hopkins have been returned?'

'Very soon,' Murray replied. 'They could stand, they could walk, they had regained sufficient speech to answer to and give a command. What more do you need to fight in this war? Most of the men you see here will be sent back to fight within a month or so.'

Kingsley looked once more at the desultory activities taking place on the beautiful lawns around him. These strange, abstracted men did not appear to have much fight in them.

'Captain Marlowe?' Nurse Murray said, a frown wrinkling her brow. 'May I speak plainly?'

'But of course.'

214

'You will probably think me very rude but I must speak my mind. I always speak my mind and I make no exceptions for military policemen.'

'I would expect nothing less, nor desire it.'

'A lot of men seem to find it irritating when women speak their minds, intimidating even, but I can assure you that has never stopped *me* from speaking my mind.'

'I am sure that it hasn't.'

'The woman who does not speak her mind is worse than the man who does not give her credit for having a mind in the first place. *He* merely lets *himself* down, *she* lets down her whole sex. Women have a duty to speak their minds and that is why I always speak mine.'

'Uhm . . . right. So. Would you like to sit down somewhere?'

'I am quite happy to stand.'

'Right-ho.'

'I am not a weakling.'

'No.'

'Perhaps you are used to women who swoon in the presence of policemen?'

'Not really.'

'Female stamina is in fact universally proven to be greater than the male's. In some societies women not only produce and raise the children but also do all the work.'

'Yes, I believe that is true.'

'Do you know why women swoon, Captain?'

'Well, I . . .'

'It is because their corsets constrict their breathing. Imagine that, Captain, women abusing themselves in an attempt to change the shape of their bodies in order to be more attractive to men. How appalling. How pathetic. Only society women swoon; working women do not wear corsets.'

'Mmm, well anyway, Nurse Murray, you mentioned that you wished to speak your mind. What was it that you wished to say?'

'That I don't like military policemen.'

215

'I see.'

'In fact I don't like any policemen.'

'Well, I suppose there's not much I can . . .'

'I loathe them with a furious and righteous passion.'

'. . . do about that.'

'There are no words to describe the contempt in which I hold every single policeman on this earth. British policemen may be better than some but not by much, I think, and they are still policemen in the end.'

She clearly meant it, and although her youthful intensity had a certain charm about it Kingsley decided that he would be wary of Nurse Murray. Something beneath the amusingly severe exterior suggested to him that here was a young woman who was capable of real anger. Clever too, he thought, and probably brave; after all, the RAMC on the Western Front was not a place for sissies and although he knew her to be only twenty-two she had already achieved the rank of staff nurse.

'If you do not wish to sit, would you mind if we walked a little?' Kingsley asked. 'I've been travelling for a couple of days now. A boat, a horse truck and an ambulance. I'd really love to stretch my legs in these beautiful grounds, if that's all right? Particularly since the rain's holding off.'

Nurse Murray shrugged.

'Walk, stand, sit, jump. Just so long as I have made it absolutely clear that I don't like policemen.'

Nurse Murray set off at a brisk, no-nonsense pace, leading Kingsley towards a little elm wood that promised a real comfort to Kingsley's eye after the grimness of his recent journey.

'Nurse Murray?' Kingsley enquired after they had walked together in silence for a few moments. 'I have heard reports of your account of the night on which the murder took place and I confess I found it rather short on detail. Do you think that there is any way that your judgement or your memory might be affected by your attitude to the police?'

'Well, you're a blunt sort of chap, aren't you?'

'Like you, I speak my mind.'

'You mean am I lying?'

'Yes.'

'The answer is no, of course not. I am a soldier, I know my duty and I saw what I saw, Captain, and what I saw was all I saw.'

'And remind me again, what did you see?'

'Very little.'

'But what?'

'I do not think that I can tell you any more than I told your colleagues. I was on the final round of my shift. I had first visited Captain Abercrombie and then the ward next door, where Hopkins and five other enlisted men slept. I was some time in the ward because some of the patients have physical injuries as well as mental ones and their dressings needed changing for the night. Also one of the patients was having a particularly noisy fit and I was required to ring for assistance and administer a needle.'

'Your colleague left before you?'

'Yes, I had the rest of my work to do in the ward. When I had finished and walked as much as halfway back to my room, I remembered that I had left the needle and dish in the ward. Obviously I couldn't leave something like that lying about with the men in the state they were, so I returned and as I was doing so I saw a British officer walking briskly away from Abercrombie's room. I saw only his back and he quickly disappeared up the corridor, in the opposite direction from me.'

'Would you say he was in a hurry?'

'Yes, I would definitely say he was in a hurry.'

'Did he appear in any way what you might call furtive?'

'Well, yes, as a matter of fact I think that perhaps he did.'

'Please be good enough to explain to me how it is possible for the back of a man to appear furtive.'

'Well . . . I don't know.'

'Did he stoop? Did he skulk? Did he hover in shadows and wear a big cloak?'

The young woman's face flushed with anger.

217

'You are being facetious.'

'You said he looked furtive. I would like to know what gave you that impression.'

'He was in a hurry.'

'And that's all?'

'Yes, that's all. I didn't say he *was* furtive, I said that perhaps he *looked* a bit furtive.'

'And you think he killed Abercrombie?'

'I don't think Private Hopkins did.'

'Why?'

'Because in his moments of lucidity he swears he didn't and in my experience shell shock does not induce murderous leanings. Suicidal certainly, but not murderous.'

'On the other hand we know very little about shell shock, do we not?'

'As a matter of fact we know a good deal about shell shock, Captain,' Murray replied angrily. 'It's just that most of what we know the army refuses to acknowledge because they wish they did not know it. They seek to deny it, or at least to deny it in all but the most extreme cases when a man's fists are so clenched that his fingernails are growing through the palms of his hands.'

'You think that the army does not treat shell shock sympathetically?'

'I have told you, the army's sole ambition is to return men to the front, or, better still, to prevent men from leaving it.'

They had left the elm copse now and arrived at the edge of the château's grounds. Beyond them lay the enchanting valley of the River Lys. Wild flowers were still in bloom in the fields, the leaves on the trees were still rich and green, and from where they stood three church spires were visible. Kingsley thought of July 1914, when the whole world had been like this and George had been one year old and he and Agnes the happiest people on earth.

The estate was bounded by nothing more than a low fence, which they walked along until they came upon a stile.

'Shall we cross over or have you walked enough?' the nurse enquired.

'I don't think I could ever walk enough in such a place as this,' Kingsley replied.

Nurse Murray put a foot upon the stile. For a moment Kingsley's instincts nearly led him to take her arm and assist her but fortunately he remembered in time that this would scarcely be a welcome gesture. Instead he stood back and let her climb the obstacle unaided.

'You don't seem much like a military policeman to me,' Nurse Murray said.

'And what are military policemen like?' Kingsley asked.

'Bastards,' she replied. 'Swine. Poor donkeys, how could they be anything else? After all, it's their job to keep the army at the front, isn't it? That's your one rule. Tommy must be more scared of you than he is of the Hun, isn't that right?'

'Yes, I suppose it is.'

'So why aren't I scared of you?'

'I don't know, perhaps I'm not very good at my job.'

'I think you're probably very good at your job, which is why they have sent you. Perhaps General Staff are not as stupid as I've always assumed.'

'Were you scared of the military policemen who came before me then?'

Murray paused. She clearly did not want to admit it.

'Yes, I suppose so. They were rather a rough bunch. It was after midnight, I'd been called from my bed after Abercrombie was found dead. Poor Hopkins was just sitting there in his bed, not speaking, swaying back and forth with that awful gun still in his lap. We took it off him and he did not seem even to notice. It smelt of cordite. Then very quickly they arrived, four enormous men, a sergeant and three corporals. Smart as paint, boots gleaming, stamping and shouting. They marched in, took the gun and then grabbed Hopkins, pulled him bodily from the bed. That broke his trance and he screamed and soiled himself all at once.

I've never seen such terror. I tried to stop the MPs from being so rough, I told them there was a procedure and that I would accompany the prisoner.'

'And how did they react to that?'

'They reacted like all rozzers in my experience, like bloody animals. Male bloody animals. Just told me to shut up and dragged the poor man away, naked and screaming, into the night. I can still hear him pleading with me to stop them. Anyway, it was over as soon as it had begun and we went in to deal with Abercrombie's corpse.'

'You mean the police didn't secure the scene of the crime?'

'They took a look at it before coming for Hopkins. That was all. What was there to see? The captain was dead.'

Kingsley's mind reeled at the sheer incompetence of it.

'And did you look about you at all? Were any notes taken? Any photographs? I presume you carried out an autopsy?'

Nurse Murray looked at him as if he was insane.

'Captain, this is a military hospital, we are concerned with the living not the dead. When they die, we send them for burial, full stop, that's it, toodle-oo, goodbyeee. Then we prepare their beds for the next poor wretch in a queue that seems to contain every young man in Europe. That's what we did that night and I hope you won't think me callous if I tell you that as we sewed Abercrombie up in his blanket I thought that at least he'll pen no more poppycock about the honour and glory of war. "Forever England", ha! What rot. What utter rot. Forever nothing, except dead. Forever dead, that's all you can say about poor old Viscount Alan Abercrombie, forever *very* dead.'

They were walking back towards the château now.

'You did not like Abercrombie then?' Kingsley enquired.

'Oh, I wouldn't say that. Of course I didn't know him very well and he wasn't in the most communicative of states, which was why he was with us in the first place. But I won't say I didn't like him, I just didn't like his poetry.'

'You discussed poetry?'

'I discuss poetry with lots of them. I run a little group for patients and their friends. The doctors think footer and cross-country runs do more good but they let me have a bash in my spare time. Personally I think it helps some of our fellows a bit, you know, to get it out. Often I find writing things down is easier than saying them.'

Kingsley thought back to Shannon's contemptuous assessment.

'*Everybody's a bloody poet these days*,' he whispered beneath his breath.

'Pardon?'

'Nothing. Just something a . . . colleague of mine said to me. You know the fellow actually, Captain Shannon.'

Nurse Murray paused for a moment.

'Ah yes, Captain Shannon,' she said, and then added, 'Did he tell you he ended up in my bed?'

'Uhm . . . well. Good lord. I suppose he may have intimated . . .'

'Ha. And they say we women are gossips.'

'Well, he didn't say much really . . .'

'I should imagine he did not. Captain Shannon is not a man whose sexual tastes are calculated to endear him to women.'

Kingsley had never before met such a frank and outspoken woman.

'Yes. Uhm, we were speaking about your poetry group?'

'Yes. It's been rather a success in a small way. We meet and I encourage them to try to express themselves on paper. I run a little occasional magazine, just a sheet or two with what I think is the best stuff. I'll show it you if you like. I've even managed to get a couple of bits printed in the *Manchester Guardian*.'

'Did Abercrombie contribute to the group?'

'Well, he wasn't here long. He attended the one session I had before he was killed but he just sat in, said he had nothing to show me. Said he didn't feel like writing at the moment and hadn't for some time. Hardly surprising when you consider the sort of utter tommyrot he wrote before. I think that perhaps he was also intimidated by his own reputation. I imagine that when you've been such a huge success it must be quite hard to have another bash.'

'Yes, probably.'

'The only thing he really wanted was to know if I could get him a green envelope, which of course I couldn't; I have no authority over that sort of thing. I suggested that the Chief MO might be able to help.'

'A green envelope?'

'Yes, a green envelope.'

Kingsley had been on the verge of asking her what a green envelope was but realized in time that it must be to do with the military and therefore, as an MP, he should know about such things. That piece of information would have to wait.

Instead he watched as she hopped nimbly back over the stile. She was a graceful, athletic creature and Kingsley liked her fire and her passion. He would have liked to confide in her. But he couldn't, so he asked to be taken to look at the room in which Abercrombie had died. They made their way back past the half-hearted games and exercises that continued in the grounds. In front of the château the croquet had finished and in its place a little stage was being erected.

'We are to have a concert tonight if the rain holds off,' Murray explained. 'The 5th Battalion are pulled back resting and they have a theatre company. They're using our grounds to mount their show. We're all invited.'

'The 5th was Abercrombie's outfit, was it not?'

'I believe so. Quite frankly all battalions are the same to me.'

Nurse Murray led Kingsley into the château, the interior of which had clearly once been grand and glittering but was now filled to bursting point with dull khaki. Everywhere he looked there were drab, shuffling figures. Kingsley was instantly oppressed by the place; even the air seemed heavy and rich with nightmares. As he breathed he felt he could smell the fear. Men were everywhere, hobbling, limping, staggering, standing.

Staring. Staring was definitely the most common occupation of the men in that place. This was basically an enormous clearing station; most of the men wandering the corridors had been in action only days before.

Having ascended the magnificent main staircase, they arrived by a series of twists and turns at the corridor on which both Abercrombie and Hopkins had been billeted. The same corridor in which the mystery officer had been sighted.

'That's the ward Hopkins was in,' Murray remarked as they passed one doorway, 'and this, briefly, was Abercrombie's private room.'

She turned the handle of the door and entered. Inside, a man was lying on the bed. He was masturbating furiously. Kingsley paused at the door but Nurse Murray walked in. The man himself did not seem to notice either of them.

'He does that till the shaft bleeds and still he pulls at it,' Murray said quite matter-of-factly. 'He doesn't seem to register that he's worn the skin away. He doesn't seem to register anything at all really. Fascinating, isn't it? The MO who sent him down said he'd been doing it in the trenches and just wouldn't stop. The other chaps couldn't stand it – well, not pleasant, I'd imagine, having a chap doing that at such close quarters. Have you heard of Freud?'

'Of course.'

'I wonder what he'd make of it?'

'I imagine he'd take it as proof of all his theories.'

'Yes. Probably say the poor chap was dreaming of his mother.'

Kingsley was quite taken aback at this spectacularly rude joke but he could not help but laugh.

'This is where we found Abercrombie,' Murray said, looking down at the man on the bed. 'Just where this fellow is, with a bullet in his head. From what I remember there were no signs of a struggle.'

In Kingsley's long and varied experience as a police officer he could not recall having ever attended a murder scene in which a naked man lay on a bed masturbating while the investigation was conducted. He tried to put it from his mind but it wasn't easy, particularly as the man was grunting and moaning as he pumped away.

'*Urgh, urgh, urgh.*'

'Bullet in his head, you say? It had not passed through?'

'No, there was a lot of blood on the bed but nothing like what there'd have been if the back of his head had been blown off. When he was moved I recall that there was no exit wound.'

'*Urgh, ahh, urgh, ahh.*'

'He must have had a very tough skull. How long had Abercrombie been occupying the room?'

'He'd been with us for a week.'

'How had he been? What was his demeanour? His mood?'

'*Aaargh, uuurgh.*'

'Well, he wasn't lying about in a trance-like state abusing himself like this fellow. I'd say he was more emotionally exhausted than actually shell-shocked. He was very quiet but lucid. My guess is that we'd have given him a week or two's rest, a spot of retraining and back he'd have gone into the line. Contrary to what the public believe, we actually manage to send over three-quarters of them back, you know. Can't have malingering in the British army.'

'*Aaaaaarrghh!*'

The man on the bed let out a cry, and they both turned just in time to witness his ejaculation.

'Don't know where he finds the stuff,' Murray said. 'He seems to have an endless supply.'

She found a towel and cleaned the man up.

'Thank you, Maud, that was lovely,' the man on the bed muttered.

'He always thanks Maud,' Nurse Murray explained. 'I don't know who Maud is but she sounds like a very obliging sort of girl.'

There seemed to be nothing left to discover, the murder scene having been thoroughly cleaned and reoccupied several times since, so they left the moaning man to return to his memories of Maud.

'Who collected his personal effects?' Kingsley asked when they were once more outside the room.

'I did, sent them back to England care of the House of Lords. There wasn't much, of course. Not a lot of room for kit in the trenches.'

'To your mind was there anything of interest?'

'Not really. All very dull. Two shirts, two long johns, two pairs of socks. Comb, toothbrush. That sort of thing. Oh, one thing was a bit strange. One of his boots was missing.'

'Really?'

'Yes, I could find only one and I presume he'd arrived here in two.'

'He might have lost one in the mud, a lot of men do.'

'Yes, but he'd been here a number of days.'

'Had he any other footwear?'

'We issue them with plimsolls if they haven't got any, because of all the sport. Perhaps he'd been wearing those and wasn't bothered about his boots.'

'Yes. Perhaps. Anything else?'

'Of interest? No, I don't think so.'

'And don't you find that interesting?'

'What?'

'That this fascinating celebrity poet, envied and lionized by most of the nation, should have nothing of interest in his personal effects at all. No notes, no jottings. No poems.'

'He'd given up writing.'

'Yes, so I believe he told everyone.'

'There was blank paper.'

'But nothing written?'

'No.'

They continued along the corridor to what had been McCroon's ward, pausing to inspect the water closets that he had been visiting when the mystery officer rushed past him.

'Where is McCroon now?' Kingsley enquired.

'We sent him back to his mob.'

'Still alive?'

'I would not have the faintest idea. That's the sort of thing you're supposed to know, isn't it? You're the military policeman, aren't you?'

She was looking at him rather inquisitively.

'Well, aren't you?' she repeated.

'Of course,' Kingsley replied.

'Perhaps you'd like a cup of tea?' Murray said. 'We don't have a canteen here but I have a little spirit stove in my billet. I'm afraid I've no milk.'

Nobody seemed to have any milk these days, Kingsley thought, except the Prime Minister. No wonder the great man had guarded his so jealously.

Nurse Murray led Kingsley down through the labyrinth of corridors, the richly papered walls of which were punctuated with the marks of absent works of art that had been removed for the duration. They progressed to where the steps became narrower and the passages meaner – the part of the house no doubt once occupied by the servants – before arriving finally at a little door that bore in French the legend '*Third assistant scullery girl*'.

'This is me,' Murray said. 'This is where I close my eyes and dream of one day being promoted to second assistant scullery girl.'

It felt good to be in a woman's room, even the poor garret that the RAMC saw fit to provide for its staff nurses, although Kingsley could not deny that he felt a momentary distaste imagining the odious Captain Shannon making a beast of himself in this very place. Kingsley liked Nurse Murray and for some reason felt rather protective of her, an emotion for which of course she would have despised him. She had a little bed and a dressing table on which stood a mirror and a hairbrush. There was a small chest of drawers but no wardrobe; Murray's dresses were hung from a hatstand. Just like George's dressing-up costumes behind which Kingsley had hidden what seemed like a year before but which in fact had been only a few days ago. Above a small basin hung a clothes line on which were pegged out three or four stained, rust-coloured rags. Kingsley saw Murray's eyes flit towards them and for a moment an expression of extreme embarrassment passed across her face; however, he was not surprised to see it followed by one of indignant resolve.

'Boring being a woman sometimes,' she said, angrily pulling the rags from the line and stuffing them into a drawer. 'Menstruation definitely *not* the Almighty's best bit of design. The only thing that makes me doubt Darwin – I'd have thought such a palpably awful arrangement would have been naturally deselected centuries ago. I suppose it's just one more of nature's clever little ways of keeping women in their place. Now then, Captain. Tea.' She lit her little stove and then, with the same Lucifer, a Capstan Full Strength cigarette on which she drew hungrily. 'Last one, I'm afraid,' she added.

'I have plenty. Take a pack.'

He gave her a box of twenty-five Black Cat and took another from his cigarette case for himself.

'Do you have a first name?' he asked.

'Yes,' she answered.

'Mine's Christopher.'

'Bully for you, Captain. I do not wish to be on first-name terms with policemen. I've told you, I don't like them. I don't like them as a class. You seem all right but you're still a rozzer and that's enough for me.'

"This all sounds rather personal, Nurse Murray. Do you have a *reason* for hating the police so much?'

She looked at him for a moment, the smoke curling up around her nose and eyes, which seemed suddenly to shine more brightly through the tobacco fug.

'Don't miss much, do you?' she replied finally.

'Not much as a rule.'

'Can spot an old con, eh?'

'You've been arrested?'

'Oh, many times, Captain. Many, many times.'

'You must have started your life of crime rather young.'

'I did. I was eighteen. Scarcely more than a child, but that didn't stop you rozzers from assaulting me.'

All at once Kingsley realized to what she must be referring. He felt a guilty fool.

'Cat and mouse?'

'Yes, cat and mouse.'

The infamous Temporary Discharge for Ill Health Act of 1913, commonly known as the Cat and Mouse Act, in which hunger-striking Suffragettes were released and then rearrested on regaining their health. Mrs Emmeline Pankhurst herself had suffered twelve successive incarcerations.

'Of course,' said Kingsley, 'I should have guessed. You were a Suffragette.'

'I *am* a Suffragette, Captain. Even though we're British women and can see that currently we must pull together with the men for the good of the whole team, we are still *women* and one day soon women *will* vote. And when we do, we will make laws that shame the kind of bullies who beat us and abused us for having the temerity to state that half the population of Britain had a right to a say in how the country was run.'

'How many times were you rearrested?'

'I was in and out seven times. They tied me down and forced a rubber tube down my nose and my neck and into my stomach. I still feel the pain in my throat to this day.'

And as if to prove it, having taken a huge pull on her cigarette until the glowing end threatened to creep back and burn her fingers, she succumbed to a coughing fit and hacked away most mightily for a spell, her small frame shaking, dislodging her glasses and causing the bed on which she sat to shake too.

Kingsley looked away, ashamed. He well remembered the terrible policy of Cat and Mouse: it had been a grim time to be a policeman and a period which had tested his conscience sorely.

He had been a servant of a government that denied any power or influence whatsoever to every mother and sister in the country. What was more, as a policeman he had been called upon to attempt to police the increasingly violent terror tactics which the Suffragette movement, in its anger and frustration, had felt onliged to adopt. Kingsley had never himself subjected a hunger striker to force-feeding but he had worn the same badge as the men who did.

As Nurse Murray coughed, Kingsley once more found his mind flashing back to his own time in prison when the big red-haired trades unionist had accused him of having allowed all sorts of iniquities to pass him by without protest. The man had been right. Abuse of the poor, abuse of the Irish, abuse of women, as a policeman he had connived directly in them all. Why had it taken the war to make him recognize his duty to his conscience? Once more the only answer he could come up with was that of scale. The war was just too wicked to ignore. But now he looked at this young woman who had been so abused and yet was serving her country with the same courage as any man. Reflected that this splendid person *still* had no vote. Agnes, the mother of his child, *had no vote*. Emmeline Pankhurst, a brilliant strategist and fighter, *had no vote*. Every woman who laboured in the munitions factories and on the land *had no vote*. It was truly incredible. Kingsley concluded that his conscience should have troubled him earlier.

'I apologize unreservedly for my offensive assumption,' he said, before adding with a smile, 'and also, for what it's worth, for men in general.'

'Not worth a lot really, Captain,' Nurse Murray replied, but she smiled. 'Ta very much all the same, though.'

38

Cassoulet and much grumbling

During the afternoon Kingsley returned to Merville, where he had been assigned a billet above a small bar or *estaminet* which lay on the outskirts of the little town and was patriotically named Café Cavell after the martyred British nurse.

Kingsley was aware of the urgency of his mission. The Third Battle of Ypres was fully under way a few miles up the road and whatever might be left of the case he was investigating must surely by now be in danger of sinking into the mud of Flanders. Who could tell whether this mystery officer, if indeed there *was* a mystery officer, had not already been dealt his punishment by fate in the shape of a German shell or bullet? Perhaps McCroon, the Bolshevik comrade who had been present at the château on the night of the murder, might also already be dead. However, Kingsley had chosen the Military Police Headquarters at Armentières as his next point of investigation, and since he had no chance of getting there and back that day he decided it would have to wait until the morning. He took comfort from the fact that the 5th Battalion in which Abercrombie and Hopkins had served were at rest and so whoever was left who might be of use to him was unlikely to be killed in the immediate future. McCroon might even be at the concert that evening. As might the mystery officer.

Despite being only a few miles from the front, Merville was fortunate in that it was outside the range of normal field artillery and had so far been untouched by shelling. Two or three miles up the road, in the area immediately behind the front line, the story was very different: some villages had been quite literally wiped off the map, as if they had never existed at all. War had of course come to Merville in other ways, principally in the form of commerce. The town was full of Tommies and equally full of French peasant entrepreneurs anxious to profit from them, selling eggs, bread, wine, livestock, pots to piss in and any other comfort that they might hope to unload at a ruinous price.

As Kingsley walked through the central marketplace he heard many raised voices as Frenchman and Briton alike haggled over a few francs. Very few British private soldiers spoke any French and the vast majority of French peasants had no English. Therefore, even after three years of living cheek by jowl, all conversations between soldier and local were conducted in sign language accompanied by loud cursing. Kingsley noticed that his MP uniform had a markedly calming effect on the Tommies as they saw him approach but that the shouting began again the moment he had passed.

It started to rain as Kingsley explored the cobbled streets that the Tommies cursed so. The British soldiers who had to march on them loathed the cobbles, for they were all large and rounded with big dips between them that continually threatened to turn an ankle. They offered no opportunity to develop a regular marching rhythm, for no step landed the same way twice. At the railhead that morning, as the men from the horse trucks had formed up for their march up line, many unflattering comparisons had been made between British road-building and French. Walking through Merville, Kingsley could see their point: a seven-mile march with full pack up the line on roads such as these would require the equivalent exertion to twenty-five or thirty miles on decent paving or tarmacadam.

He passed a large house with a number '1' painted on it. This he knew to be a brothel, a Number 1 Red Lamp establishment as licensed by the French government. His companions on the train had warned Kingsley against these places; the fear of venereal disease was almost pathological amongst the soldiers.

At the Café Cavell, Kingsley was shown his billet by the French matron who owned it. It was a small bare room with a crucifix on the wall and an uncomfortable-looking cot with a straw mattress. The blanket seemed clean enough but there were no sheets. The matron explained that the room was her son's but that he had fallen at Verdun, along with half the sons of France. Her husband, although over fifty, was a soldier also and was paid very little and so she had turned her house into an *estaminet* in order to support herself and no fewer than three surviving grand-parents. When Kingsley asked for a bath he was shown to the pump in the back yard, where he washed himself down as best he could with pump water and in the pouring rain, under the mildly contemptuous eye of a pig and a few chickens. Then he went back inside and ordered an early supper. Since Abercrombie's battalion were to attend the concert at Château Beaurivage that evening he had decided to attend also, and he doubted that food would be provided.

The ground floor of Café Cavell consisted of one large room with a biggish table in the centre and two or three smaller tables set against the walls. The bar itself was little more than a kind of lectern arrangement upon which stood *vin blanc*, *vin rouge* and a jug of what Kingsley presumed must be beer. It smelt vaguely hoppy although he could not detect the faintest hint of a head on the still, dark surface of the liquid.

'Stick to the wine,' a voice spoke up from the group who were sitting at the large centre table. 'The beer comes straight out of Madame's pig.'

'I wouldn't be surprised if it don't come straight out of Madame,' a second soldier remarked. 'They try to sell us every other stinking thing they produce.'

Kingsley had taken the precaution of removing his police

insignia. He knew that had he been wearing them none of the men would have spoken to him, or to each other in his presence. In fact they probably would have left the room.

Kingsley sat at an empty corner table. He was approached by an ancient gentleman who he assumed was one of the three surviving grandparents whom Madame was struggling to support. Kingsley enquired in French if he could order some food; the man was clearly surprised to be so addressed by a Tommy and suggested that he might like to try the chicken cassoulet.

'What have you besides cassoulet?' Kingsley asked.

'More cassoulet,' the man replied.

Kingsley ordered cassoulet and a glass of *vin rouge*. The other men in the room were naturally interested in hearing an Englishman who did not appear to be an officer so fluent in French, and fell into conversation with him. They were part of a group taken out of the line for a period of rest, in fact part of the same 5th Battalion who would be attending the evening's cabaret. They had clearly been making the most of their days off and Kingsley reckoned that, if they were anything to go by, the audience that night would be a drunken one.

'I don't mind dying for bleeding King and Country,' one of them was saying, banging his glass of wine down on the table. 'None of us minds dying for King and Country . . .'

'I fucking do,' another interjected.

'Well, all right, yes, we all *minds*. Granted, we all *minds*, but we dies if we *has* to 'cos we ain't cowards neither. What I *does* object to, and I objects to it with knobs on, is getting *paid less* to die for King and Country than some cunt what joined up a year *after* me! Paid *half* as bleeding much.'

This was an obsession of army life that Kingsley was already very familiar with. The illogical and inexplicable disparities in pay and conditions were a source of more passion to the Tommies than the alleged frightfulness of the Hun, a frightfulness which obsessed the civilian population back home but that Kingsley had never once heard mentioned at the front.

'What about leave?' another soldier added. 'Never mind pay, what about leave?'

'What about it?'

'*Exactly!* Exactly. My very point. What a-fuckin'-bout it, eh? We've 'ad none. That's what about it. This caff's the furthest I've got from the front in *eleven months* and my cousin wiv the Gloucesters down at Plug Street just got a ticket after six.'

Kingsley began to jot down notes. He sympathized with these men enormously; he felt, like them, that it was one thing to suffer terrible hardships and quite another to have to deal with the frustration of apparently arbitrary decisions. He had been in France only three days and yet it was already glaringly obvious to him that the inability of the army to standardize pay and conditions was undermining morale up and down the line. The notes that he began to take were in the form of a memo to Sir Mansfield Cumming and the SIS, explaining that if they wanted to avert mutiny in the British ranks they might dispense with cloak-and-dagger work altogether and simply lobby parliament to put an end to such a manifestly unfair system. A system where staff officers and men who saw no fighting at all were paid more and got considerably more leave than their comrades who were dying in the trenches.

'Can't say nuffink though, can yer,' the man who had had no leave for a year added. 'Can't go complaining in case you meets an officer what got out of his puddle the wrong side that mornin' and gives yer what for.'

'But we have to make our grievances known, surely? Nothing will change if we don't say anything,' a quieter voice suggested.

'And nuffink ain't gonna change if we do neither, 'cept we might end up on Field Punishment Number One like that stupid cunt Hopkins.'

Kingsley's ears pricked up at this.

'What happened to him?' he enquired.

'Lashed 'im to a limber wheel in the flies and the rain, that's what. And why? For talkin', that's what, just talkin'. Nothing more than that.'

The soldier next to him did not feel that Kingsley was being given the full story.

'Talkin', Jack! He was doin' more than talkin'. He was *incitin'*, that's what he was doing. Refusin' to obey an order in the field.'

'In the field! In the fuckin' bath'ouse, more like.'

Kingsley's cassoulet arrived, a very decent bean stew with quite a lot of meat in it, although Kingsley suspected that the meat was rabbit and not the promised chicken. With bread and a half-bottle of wine the meal cost him four francs, which was very steep.

Whilst Kingsley ate, the men around the big table continued to discuss the unfortunate Hopkins.

'D'ye fink 'e did murder Captain Abercrombie, then?'

'Abercrombie died in battle,' a younger man said.

'That's what the army *says* but don't you believe it, son.'

'Why the 'ell would anybody want to murder Captain Abercrombie?'

'Abercrombie was in charge of the punishment detail that lashed Hopkins to that wheel.'

'Yeah, but he didn't order the punishment, did he? I mean, Abercrombie had no more choice in the matter than the lads what tied the knots. If he'd 'a refused, the colonel would have had *him* tied to the wheel instead.'

'Do officers get Field Punishment Number One then? I've never seen that.'

'Dunno, but he'd have got something, that's for sure. Officers can't go disobeying orders any more than us. Not even viscounts.'

'Well, you an' I know Abercrombie had no choice, but don't forget Hopkins was doolally. He'd joined Fred Karno's army. 'E might have just seen Abercrombie and thought, right, you bastard, and popped him one.'

'Abercrombie died in battle,' the youngest man insisted once more. 'It was in the papers, I read it.'

'Well, maybe he did,' the quieter man said, 'but if he was

murdered, Hopkins never done it, I swear. Hopkins knew all about what a lot of rubbish this war is and he wasn't afraid to say it. *That*'s why they're going to shoot him, to get rid of a Bolshie, just like the French did.'

'Well if he is a bloody Bolshie then I reckon they *should* shoot him. Them lot in Russia have left us in the lurch.'

'They had the right idea, getting out of this mess!'

At this, the conversation suddenly grew heated; the drink was having its effect and voices got louder. Kingsley noted that the Socialist was in a minority of one and that, for all their grumbling, the other soldiers were fierce patriots and would hear no talk of walking away from the war.

Finally the loudest of the gang turned to Kingsley.

'What do you think then, mate? You look like an educated sort of bloke, what with your writing stuff down and speaking French and all, so come on, what do you think?'

'Well,' Kingsley said, finishing the last of his wine, 'I do not believe that victory for either side in this war is worth the destruction it is causing and it is beyond me that none of the belligerent governments can see it. However, I also do not believe that the British military authorities are so morally corrupt as to seek to frame an innocent man for murder simply to kill a Communist. If they want to do that, they need merely send him over the top in the first wave of the next big push. And now, gentlemen, I must leave you. Oh, one other thing: if you are attending the concert tonight you may see me again, but dressed in my uniform as a Military Police officer . . .'

The men around the table went white.

'Please do not be alarmed, I regard our conversation as entirely off the record.'

With that, Kingsley gathered up his things and left.

39

Amateur theatricals and a nocturnal stroll

That evening Nurse Murray had sufficiently mellowed in her attitude towards policemen to allow Kingsley to accompany her to the concert.

'Not *escort*, you will note, Captain. Accompany.'

'Of course.'

'I do not need *escorting* anywhere.'

'I did not imagine that you did.'

'Very few women do, if you bother to ask them.'

'I shall remember.'

The weather was terrible but the three hundred or so khaki-clad men who had assembled on the groundsheets that had been spread upon grass in front of the big château were not about to let a little rain spoil their enjoyment of the cabaret. They lived in rain, they slept in rain, they ate in it, fought in it and died in it, to them it was natural that they should watch a show in it. Some effort had been made to provide covered seating for the officers and nurses but the canvas awning that had been erected was already bowing alarmingly under the weight of water. Every minute or two a corporal would come and poke the bulge with a broomstick in an effort to displace some of the contents but this in itself was so distracting and created so much splashing and dripping, particularly for those sitting at the edge of the enclosure, that the colonel eventually ordered the whole thing dismantled.

'We'll *all* sit in the bloody rain,' he announced, to much cheering from the troops. 'If it's good enough for Tommy Atkins it's good enough for me. Ladies may raise umbrellas if they wish.'

Kingsley was a little late and joined Nurse Murray at the place she had been saving for him just before the concert began. He had been asking the company sergeant major if Private McCroon was present but had been disappointed to find that he was not.

'I'm sorry that I have no box of chocolates to share with you,' Kingsley said as he sat down, remembering how Agnes would always insist on chocolates when they visited the theatre.

'I came prepared,' Nurse Murray replied, producing a block of Cadbury's Dairy Milk from her apron pocket. 'Must have treats. Can't see a show without treats. Want some?' she said, offering Kingsley a chunk. Kingsley declined, noting privately that, Suffragette or not, some things united all women and a love of chocolate was one of them.

The rain poured down, the little four-piece orchestra struck up the overture and the show began. It turned out to be rather good, in Kingsley's opinion; all written and produced by men of the 5th, with songs, sketches and jokes that reflected the sardonic wit of the British Tommy.

'Soldiers' superstitions!' a man dressed as John Bull announced.

'It is unlucky for thirteen to sit down at a meal when rations have been issued for only seven! . . . If the sun rises in the east it is a sure sign that there will be stew for supper! . . . To drop your rifle on a green second lieutenant's foot is bad luck for him; to drop it on a sergeant's foot is bad luck for you!'

The audience, in great good spirits, laughed and cheered each line despite the rain. They were clearly overjoyed just to be out of the line. As the compère conceded, 'I'm so happy to be here, mates. But quite frankly, the way the Staff is directing the war I'm happy to be anywhere.'

The crowd roared at this, the officers sitting around Kingsley most of all, for they were front-line soldiers and as frustrated at what they perceived as the ineptitude of the General Staff as the men they had to lead.

'Superstition number four,' the compère announced. 'To hear a lecture on the glorious history of your regiment indicates you will shortly be going over the top. Number five. If a new officer tells you he has learned all he knows at cadet school, this is a sign that he is very soon going to get a big surprise. And finally, it is most unlucky to be killed on a Friday!'

Many of the men shouted out this last 'superstition' along with the compère, having heard the joke many times before. This did not seem to prevent them from enjoying hearing it again and everybody roared with laughter.

When the compère had finished he announced that the 5th Battalion Players had only one rule, unlike the 5th Battalion which had millions. The one and only rule of the evening was that the 'ladies' of the company were strictly out of bounds to all ranks. This of course provoked much booing, over which the compère had to shout in order to introduce the 'ladies' in question.

'I wonder what Freud would make of this?' Nurse Murray whispered to Kingsley as the three artistes tripped on in their wigs and dresses, heavy with make-up, to sing 'Three Little Maids From School' followed by 'Oh We Don't Want To Lose You'.

'The middle fellow's not bad-looking,' Kingsley replied. There was no doubt that he was the soldiers' favourite, showing considerable feminine grace and making much of his elegant, stocking-clad legs.

'He was a friend of Abercrombie's,' Nurse Murray replied. 'He came here to visit. Rather a weedy sort of chap. *Terribly* limp. Definitely makes a better girl than a man.' She dropped her voice to a whisper. 'I rather suspect he's *one of them*, you know.'

Kingsley studied the female impersonator. It certainly was a convincing performance. The soldiers clearly thought so and cheered him loudly, suggesting in no uncertain terms that he get his drawers off. Kingsley thought that this might spoil the illusion.

'Another case for our friend Freud if you ask me,' Nurse Murray giggled. 'A man pretending to be a woman, with a whole lot of other men wanting to see him naked even though they know damn well he's a man? *Very fishy* in my opinion.'

'Oh, I don't know,' Kingsley said. 'I think it's all just good clean fun.'

'Ha!' said Nurse Murray.

An officer behind them went shush and Nurse Murray made a naughty-little-girl face.

'If he does get his togs off,' she whispered, 'I hope he gives me his silk stockings. Can't *think* where he got them.'

'Where did they get any of it, wigs, dresses, pearls?' Kingsley whispered back.

'Well, these concerts mean a lot to the men. Everybody chips in, and of course the drag acts are by far the most popular part. Personally I hate them with a passion.'

'Really, why?'

But the officer behind them shushed again and Nurse Murray did not explain further. The concert progressed through numerous patriotic songs, dance displays, sketches about regimental sergeant majors and the inevitable Charlie Chaplin impression, which, unlike most such impersonations, had real charm and captured something of the grace and pathos of the Little Tramp's persona.

'That's the same chap who did the drag act,' Nurse Murray whispered. 'Damned good, isn't he?'

Kingsley agreed wholeheartedly. He *was* damned good.

After the show the colonel lumbered forward on his stick – he had been wounded earlier in the week – and made a brief speech in which he thanked all those involved for a ruddy splendid effort.

'Do you know, I've seen shows in London that weren't half so

240

good,' he said, to considerable cheering. 'And the girls weren't as pretty either!' at which the cheering redoubled.

Afterwards tea was served for NCOs and men and a small reception was held for the officers, with whisky donated by their mess. Nurse Murray, the youngest and prettiest of the female nurses in attendance, was a major centre of attention. However, she seemed happy to stick by Kingsley's side.

'So why do you hate female impersonators?' he enquired.

'Because they're not female impersonators at all,' she answered loudly, clearly happy, in fact even anxious, for as many men as possible to hear her views. 'They don't *impersonate* women, they represent a *male fantasy* of women. If they were impersonating women they might show them making shells or staffing the buses as they now do – and do every bit as well as the men, incidentally – or discovering radium like the wonderful Madame Curie.'

'Hmm. Yes. Might be a trifle dull. I mean theatrically speaking, collecting fares and staring into a microscope.'

'I don't see why. Certainly no duller than kicking your legs about and pretending women are coquettish, brainless, ankle-flashing idiots. That's not what women are, it's what men *want* women to be.'

'Surely that's the point, isn't it? I mean this entertainment is *for* men after all.'

'But is that what men *really* want us to be? Is that the sort of women they claim to be dying for? Brainless fools concerned only to make themselves pretty for men?'

'Here here!' one of the officers enjoined. 'It'll do for me!'

'I'll drink to that,' said another, raising his glass. 'I say, you fellows. The ladies. Bless every one of them!'

There followed a small toast, during which Nurse Murray quietly fumed.

'Bloody idiots,' she muttered under her breath, which drew an admonishment from a lieutenant colonel who was hovering in the vicinity.

'Never liked to hear a woman swear, my dear,' he said. 'Can't abide it.'

'I'm sorry if my language offends you, Colonel,' Murray replied tartly. 'I can assure you I hear a great deal worse from your men when they're screaming in the night, imagining themselves breathing gas and calling out for death or Jesus or their mothers. Perhaps I've picked it up from them.'

Kingsley really liked Nurse Murray. Of course she was rather earnest, as he had found many Suffragettes to be, but he had to admit that they had a great deal to be earnest about. Anyone who had been a victim of Asquith's appalling Cat and Mouse Act had every right to be angry about men's attitude to women.

A nervous, polite voice intruded on Kingsley's thoughts.

'Hello, Nurse Murray.'

A young subaltern had approached the group. A slim, sensitive-looking young man, despite the absence of the heavy make-up he had worn he was easily recognizable as both the sweetest of the show 'ladies' and the excellent Charlie Chaplin.

'Ah, Lieutenant Stamford,' Nurse Murray replied. 'Well done on the show, most amusing.'

'Did you really enjoy it? Honestly? I call my girl Gloria, after Gloria Swanson. I love playing her. Do you know, one or two of the fellows have actually asked me out!'

'I don't jolly well doubt it.'

'Jokingly, of course,' the young man added quickly, reddening.

'Hmm. Yes. This is Captain Marlowe. He admired your Chaplin.'

Stamford's face lit up.

'Really? I say, that's splendid. I mean did you really? Honestly? I shan't mind at all if you're just being kind.'

'No, no,' Kingsley reassured him, 'I thought it was beautifully observed. You really captured the marvellous liquidity of his movements. I have always thought that the world lost a truly great ballet dancer when Chaplin became a clown.'

'Yes. Yes, you're right!' Stamford agreed eagerly. 'When I watch his films, all the fellows are laughing and rolling about and of course I think he's funny too, but what I'm really feeling is just how beautiful he is. Very, very beautiful . . . And Edna Purviance,' he added quickly. 'I mean, we're all in love with Miss Purviance, aren't we?'

'She has great charm. I wouldn't be surprised if Charlie wasn't a little sweet on her himself,' said Kingsley.

'Well, it certainly looks that way on the screen. What a marvellous life they must all lead. So glamorous and fulfilling. I should love to be an actor in the moving pictures.'

'A dream I think you share with every young man and woman on the planet.'

'Well, *I* should love to see one picture heroine who is not a helpless ingénue,' said Nurse Murray. 'Captain Marlowe is here to investigate the death of your friend Viscount Abercrombie, Lieutenant.'

Pain came into the young man's face.

'What would you investigate? He died in battle,' he said.

'Hmmm. Yes, I'm sure,' Kingsley replied. 'How well did you know the viscount?'

'Not *very* well but we served together, you know, just for a little while. He helped me a lot. I'm quite new, you see. Alan showed me the ropes and all that. And of course he was terribly famous.'

'You liked that about him?'

'Well, gosh, who wouldn't! I mean, to have met Ivor Novello! Gosh. That *is* something, don't you think? He told me that they'd dined together at the Savoy Grill and that as they entered, the band played "Forever England". I don't suppose anything gets much more thrilling than that, do you?'

'Not much, I imagine,' Kingsley agreed. 'You visited the viscount while he was here at Château Beaurivage, did you not?'

'Well, yes, I did actually. You know, just to be nice . . . you know, as a pal. I thought it might cheer him up. No sweethearts to visit a fellow here, are there?'

'Aren't there?' Kingsley responded, looking hard at Stamford.

'Lieutenant Stamford attended my poetry group with Viscount Abercrombie,' Nurse Murray said. 'That was on the afternoon of his death, wasn't it? Or perhaps I should say the last afternoon on which he was seen alive . . .'

'He died in battle,' Stamford said quickly.

'Quite.'

'I often think . . . I mean, if we'd only known . . .' It seemed for a moment as if Stamford would cry. 'It all just seems so terrible.'

'When did you last see Viscount Abercrombie?' Kingsley enquired.

'Oh . . . after the group, I suppose. Yes, after we'd finished with Nurse Murray.'

'Visitors have to be out by six,' Nurse Murray added.

'And you left?'

'Yes . . . Of course. What else would I have done?'

Kingsley did not reply but just kept staring at the young man. Nurse Murray broke the silence.

'Lieutenant Stamford is a poet too, aren't you, Lieutenant?'

Stamford reddened and shuffled his feet awkwardly.

'Well, you know. Sort of. I mean, I'd like to be.'

'And how is your writing coming along?'

The young man reddened further.

'Well, actually, Miss Murray, I *have* been writing. You know, like you said we all should.'

'Bully for you.'

'Yes. I think that what with Alan, I mean Captain Abercrombie . . . well, dying and all that, it sort of spurred me on. Did you mean it when you said that you would read something if I gave it to you?'

Stamford was carrying a small leather case, the sort that is normally used to carry sheet music.

'Of course I did.'

Stamford turned to Kingsley.

'Nurse Murray has got stuff published in the *Manchester Guardian*, you know. Isn't that thrilling?'

'Yes. Yes, I suppose it is,' Kingsley replied.

'Of course I'm sure that nothing *I* wrote would ever be published,' Stamford added quickly, still bright red. 'But it's nice to think about it, isn't it?'

'Oh, absolutely.'

'Well, uhm . . . I've actually brought one or two poems with me. Of course if you don't . . .'

'Bung them over then, Lieutenant. No good hiding your light under a bushel,' Nurse Murray said.

Stamford scrambled to open his music case. He reached inside and pulled out a small sheaf of neatly written pages.

'Here you are,' he said. 'If you like them I can send you more.'

'I'll look forward to it,' Murray replied. Kingsley found her lack of enthusiasm glaringly obvious but Stamford did not seem to notice. He was thrilled, and having stammered more thanks he made his farewells and left.

'Well, there's a bit of reading I shan't be looking forward to,' Murray opined. 'What an absolute Gawd'elpus. I think I shall get another drink.'

After that Nurse Murray was quickly besieged on all sides by officers clearly anxious to spend a few moments in the company of a woman, even if she was an uncompromising Suffragette. Kingsley took the opportunity to try to gather a few more opinions of Abercrombie from his brother officers.

'Nice chap, much quieter than I'd have expected,' seemed to be the general impression.

'He came to us after the London Regiment (Artists Rifles) got ripped to bits at Plug Street, so we didn't know him long,' said one man.

'Yes, we were expecting someone rather grand, putting on airs and all,' another officer added, 'what with him being famous and a viscount, etc., etc. Father's Tory Chief Whip, you know. But actually he was quite withdrawn. Well, let's face it, he ended up here, didn't he? Not Yet Diagnosed, eh? But pretty "nervous" nonetheless.'

'I think his old outfit getting mauled so badly they had to break it up hit him pretty hard,' said a third.

'Still can't quite work out how he managed to get himself killed in battle though,' the second officer added. 'Last we all heard, he'd been sent down here.'

It was not long before the party began to wind down. The men had long since departed, looking forward to a sleep undisturbed by shells or something stronger than tea at an *estaminet*, or maybe even a trip to the No. 1 Red Lamp. The officers too were drifting off, the whisky having run out and the nurses all gone to their rooms. Kingsley had not seen Nurse Murray since he had left her cornered by officers and so he set off to walk back to his billet. He had not slept in a bed since his night in the hotel at Victoria and he was looking forward to the poor little cot at the Café Cavell as if it were a feather-stuffed four-poster.

The rain had stopped earlier and the night was not cold. There was a fullish moon and the way was clear, so Kingsley decided to take a short cut across the lawns. It was not long, however, before a light rain began to fall once more. The clouds covered the moon and the night suddenly became very dark. Kingsley was forced to walk with his hands held out before him and he very much regretted his decision not to stick to the gravel paths.

Just then a voice behind bid him stop.

'I love the feeling of rain, don't you?' It was Nurse Murray. 'I mean, I know it's hellish for the troops but back here, in this beautiful château filled with nothing but pain and sadness, I sometimes think it's the only clean thing there is left.'

She must have followed him from the house, and he had not heard her because of the soft, springy turf on which they were walking. She had waited until he got amongst the first trees before approaching him. He could scarcely make her out in the darkness.

'Private Hopkins did not murder Viscount Abercrombie, Captain.'

'How can you be so sure?'

'I just know it.'

Still he could not see her but he sensed that she was close. The rainclouds were thick around the moon now and the darkness was almost impenetrable.

'You should go back to the château,' he said. 'Shall I esco— I mean accompany you to the door?'

'I told you I like the rain. Besides, it's too dark all of a sudden. We should wait for the clouds to pass or we shall lose our way and break an ankle.'

It was certainly true that the night was now darker still and the rain heavier. It seemed that they were fairly stuck.

'Is there any smell more exquisite than fresh rain in a wood?' the voice enquired, and now it was directly in front of him. She could not have been more than a foot away.

'Why did you follow me?'

'You interest me. Come on, we should get beneath the trees.'

'I could not tell you where they were.'

'I can, I eat a lot of carrots.'

He felt her take his hand in hers, a tiny hand but a confident one with a firm grip. Kingsley allowed himself to be led until he felt the rain no more, save for the occasional bigger drops that plopped down as the water filtered through the leaves which he knew must be above them.

'How is it that I interest you, Nurse Murray?' Kingsley asked, as once more they stood still together in the darkness. She had not let go of his hand.

'Well, as I said, you don't seem like a military policeman to me. I don't really believe you are one. Perhaps you're a spy.'

'A spy? What sort of spy?'

'Oh, just any old spy. There's more to this mystery than meets the eye, I think. First Captain Shannon came. Then we had the murder and the police said they'd solved it, and now you turn up, a seasoned military policeman who doesn't salute when he's supposed to, doesn't stamp about like they all do *all* the time and doesn't know what a green envelope is.'

It took a moment to sink in and then Kingsley felt ashamed. He was astonished that his face could be read so easily, and by a girl of twenty-two.

'Ah,' was all he could say, knowing that there was no point in denying the ignorance in which she had caught him out.

'For your information, a green envelope is the only avenue by which a soldier may send a letter home which will avoid the eye of the censor. All post sent from the front is routinely read except that which is contained in the much-coveted green envelope. The troops get about one a month if they're lucky.'

'And anything contained therein is not read?'

'That is the *theory*.'

'Thank you,' Kingsley said quietly. 'I was wondering.'

They were silent for a moment while the rain grew more noisy. Still Nurse Murray held his hand but it did not make Kingsley feel uncomfortable. Normally it would have done but for some reason it did not.

'So you're a civilian then?' she asked.

'Let us say that my commission . . . is a recent one. Very recent.'

'Good. That means I haven't broken my rule.'

'What rule is that?'

'Never to feel kindly towards a copper.'

'I'm afraid that I am a copper, Nurse Murray, just not a military one.'

'Damn. Oh well, exception and rule and all that, eh? My name's Kitty, by the way. Short for Kathleen.'

'May I call you Kitty then?'

'I hope you will.'

Had she squeezed his hand? He thought perhaps she might have done, but oh so lightly.

'What sort of thing is normally put in a green envelope?' he enquired.

'Two things. Sex and moaning. That's what a man keeps private. His erotic thoughts and his opinion of his superior, who tends to be the person who censors his letters. Of course mainly it's sex. Sex. Sex. Sex. That's all anybody seems to think about out here.'

'I see.'

The rain was falling ever harder and the leafy canopy was affording less and less protection from it.

'You will be wet through,' Kingsley said. 'Will you take my coat?'

'If you insist,' she replied.

Finally disengaging her hand, Kingsley took off his greatcoat and held it before him. He felt her feel for the coat. With one hand she took it but regained hold of Kingsley's with the other. Then he heard the coat falling to the ground. She had dropped it as she pulled his hand towards her in the pitch blackness. Then she drew it inside her blouse, which she had clearly unbuttoned in anticipation, and placed it upon her naked breast.

'Modern girls,' she whispered, '*so* forward.'

It was small but wonderfully firm and springy. The skin was very wet and the nipple that nestled in the palm of Kingsley's hand had grown big and hard in the night air. Kingsley did not withdraw his hand. He had not expected this and he had not sought it, but now that it had happened he was intoxicated. His throat was dry and his every nerve had sprung alive. He did not pause to consider as suddenly he reached forward with his other arm and pulled her towards him. She was at least a foot shorter than him and he had to gather her up off her feet in order to kiss her, which he did, holding her to him in one arm whilst with his other he kneaded at her breast.

Then, as quickly as he had clasped her to him, he disengaged himself.

'I'm . . . I'm married,' he gasped.

'Lucky Mrs Marlowe.'

'I love my wife.'

'Bully for you. I'm not asking you to love me.'

The voice now came from closer to the ground than before. He felt her fingers at his trouser buttons. Still he could see nothing, nothing at all. The night was like a cloak; perhaps it was the darkness that was weakening his resolve. It felt so anonymous, so secret.

'I can't,' he pleaded, but he was already surrendering.

He had been alone for so long.

'You can,' she insisted, struggling with the buttons.

'I love her,' he said, pushing her fingers away.

'And you can still love her tomorrow, unless you're dead,' she replied, putting her fingers back inside his fly. 'Only moments count in this war. Each minute is a whole new lifetime out here.'

This time he did not push her fingers away. He could not. The rain and the darkness and the smell of the sodden trees and the feel of that firm wet skin, that strong hard nipple and then her lips on his had intoxicated him.

He stood there, his head thrown back with the rain falling on his face, as he felt fingers reaching into his fly and searching for a way into his long johns. Murray was a nurse and used to undressing men; it was not long before she had found what she was looking for and liberated his straining manhood, and then he gasped out loud. The warmth of her mouth on him was almost too much to bear.

'Oh Jesus. Yes!' he gasped as her lips and teeth closed savagely around him and he felt the tip of her tongue poking and probing. Then, just when he was beginning to think that he must explode, her mouth was gone and in its place he felt her hands once more and he smelt the unmistakable smell of oiled rubber.

'Glad *this* wasn't hanging on the line to dry when you saw my room,' he heard her say. 'I think even I would have been embarrassed.'

She slipped the big thick rubber sheath over him and then pulled him down to her. Kingsley soon discovered that beneath her skirt she was wearing nothing. He felt the thick, luxuriant bush of soft wet hair between her legs and in a moment he was buried inside it.

'Ooh-la-la!' she breathed as he smelt the clean aroma of her short bobbed hair and the rain-sodden grass around it. '*Oooh*-la-jolly well-*la*!'

And so they made love together in the pouring rain, with Nurse

Murray emitting a stream of girlish exclamations which seemed to indicate that she was enjoying herself. 'Gosh', 'Golly' and, as things moved towards a conclusion, even 'Tally ho!'

When it was over she pushed him off, stood up and lit a cigarette. It was still too dark to see anything but the glow of the burning tip, and by the way that was moving about Kingsley sensed that she was buttoning herself up.

'Jolly nice,' she said, '*most* invigorating. Lovely. Gasper? They're yours anyway.'

'I'll wait a moment.'

'Suit yourself. Excuse me,' she said.

Then the little red dot descended and once more he felt her hand upon him.

'Just grab this if that's all right with you,' she said and pulled the sheath from his collapsed manhood. 'I forgot to take it back once, from an American doctor who was here studying our work. Had to go round and ask for it in the morning. Most awkward.'

'I can imagine. So you, uhm, do this often?'

'When I feel like it. I'm very fond of sex. Does that surprise you?'

'Not now.'

'It surprises some men, particularly Englishmen. They think that women don't really like it at all and just put up with it. What's the old joke? Marriage is the price men pay for sex and sex is the price women pay for marriage.'

'Yes, I've heard that one.'

'Load of tommyrot. Women need sex as much as men. Intellectually, of course, I'd definitely prefer it to be sapphic but frankly the idea revolts me. I love women in every sense except for sex and I feel *exactly* the opposite about men.'

'And when you meet a man who attracts you, you make love to him?'

'If he's interested and it's convenient and I've got my trusty baby-barrier handy.'

'Captain Shannon?'

251

'I did not *make love* to Captain Shannon. I was momentarily attracted to him but I very soon lost interest. Beastly fellow. There was an altercation.'

'An altercation?'

'He wished to stick it where I did not wish it to be stuck.'

'Ah.'

'We did not part as friends.'

'I imagine not.'

'Unlike tonight, I hope.'

'Oh, definitely. I should be honoured to consider myself your friend, Kitty.'

'Good, then that's done, Christopher . . . Christopher Marlowe,' she mused. 'Funny sort of name to choose. But then you're a funny sort of chap, aren't you? Toodle-pip.'

And Staff Nurse Kitty Murray disappeared into the night.

Kingsley lay on the grass for a little while, letting the rain fall on him. Perhaps hoping that it would somehow wash away his sin. For he was suffused with post-coital guilt. What had moments before felt ecstatic now felt miserable. He still loved Agnes, even though she was lost to him, and he felt the pain and guilt of having been unfaithful to her. Something he had never in his life intended to be. In vain did he argue with himself that Agnes had treated him cruelly and failed to stand by him in his hour of greatest need. He didn't care; he loved her. She was his Agnes, the sweetest girl he ever knew, all the sweeter perhaps because she was not perfect and never pretended to be. He missed her terribly and now he had betrayed her utterly. He found himself caressing the wedding ring that Agnes had returned to him at Brixton Prison and which he had worn upon his little finger ever since. The rain on his face mingled with sudden tears.

40

The Military Police

The following day Kingsley set out for Armentières, to visit the
Military Police station that had responded to the emergency at
the château on the night of Abercrombie's death. There was
plenty of motor transport on the roads and once more Kingsley's
captain's pips guaranteed him a lift, but it was heavy going. Every
possible byway was swollen with military traffic. The enormous
British offensive was continuing unabated, despite the startling
lack of progress.

'We were supposed to be in Passchendaele on the first day,'
Kingsley's driver said. 'It's been a fortnight and we aren't there
yet.'

The troops considered Armentières to be an unattractive, dirty
little town but that did not stop them visiting it, and over the
previous three years it had become little more than a military
camp. On occasions it had been within range of the German guns
and had suffered accordingly, but the house in which the Military
Police unit was accommodated was undamaged. Kingsley had
managed to telephone ahead and so he was expected. The most
senior soldier in the unit, a sergeant, greeted him at the door.

'Sergeant Bill Banks, Royal Military Police, sah!' he said,
coming to attention, saluting smartly and stamping loudly.

'At ease, Sergeant,' Kingsley replied. 'We shan't be able to chat very comfortably with you stamping and saluting the whole time.'

'I don't do it all the time, sir. Only when it's prescribed.'

'By the book?' asked Kingsley, remembering his prison doctor.

'Yes, sir, by the book.'

Kingsley was shown into what had once been the parlour of the house but was now the sergeant's office. He was given a most welcome mug of sweet tea, served with fresh milk. The Café Cavell had had coffee only, and it was coffee that resembled no coffee he had ever drunk.

Kingsley got straight down to business.

'So, Sergeant. You attended the scene of the murder?'

'That's right, sir, I did.'

'So might I see your scene-of-crime report?'

'My what, sir?'

'Your report. The report you and your men assembled at the scene of the crime.'

'Do you mean the Incident Notification, sir?'

'Possibly.'

The sergeant reached into a cabinet and produced a sheet of paper.

'Here are you are, sir,' he said proudly. 'There's a copy with Division and two here on file. In my filing drawer, which is where I keep my files. I have considered destroying them, seeing as how the incident which they describe has been officially designated as not having happened, but I would not wish to destroy an official file without having filed an official request to do so. But I can't file this request since the file describes an incident which officially did not happen and hence clearly cannot be on file. It's all most confusing, sir.'

Kingsley glanced at the sheet. Beneath the date and time, the report was brief:

Attended Château Beaurivage RAMC NYD(N) Facility after being alerted to incident over telephone by Medical Officer in charge.

Discovered Viscount Alan Abercrombie in bed, shot in the head. Called to next-door room where Nurses had discovered patient Private Thomas Hopkins in possession of Abercrombie's service revolver which had recently been discharged. Arrested Hopkins for murder.

Kingsley handed back the piece of paper.

'That's it? That's all you wrote?'

'That's all that happened, sir.'

Kingsley sighed. There was no point getting angry; it was not his business to teach the Military Police rules of procedure that would have been obvious to an eight-year-old who had read *The Hound of the Baskervilles*.

'I visited the crime scene myself yesterday. There was no bullet hole in the bed or the floor so I'm presuming that the bullet did not pass through his head.'

'That sounds right, sir,' Sergeant Banks replied rather doubtfully.

'No autopsy was performed on the corpse, I believe?'

'Not that I know of, sir. We certainly never asked for one. What would have been the point? We could see he was dead.'

For a moment Kingsley wondered if the man was joking. But he wasn't.

'Besides which, the following day we were told that the viscount's death was to be reported as "killed in action" anyway, sir. So that was sort of that.'

'The bullet, I presume, is still in the head of the corpse?'

'Very likely, sir.'

'And where is the corpse?'

'I think they buried it, sir. In the grounds of the château. They have a small cemetery, I believe.'

'Well, what I want you and your men to do, Sergeant, is to unbury it. Dig him up.'

'Very well, sir,' the sergeant said, clearly uneasy. 'I shall prepare a letter of instruction for you to sign, sir, if that's all right. Just so things are done by—'

'The book, yes, I expected no less of you, Sergeant. Now, though I dread to ask, do you know the whereabouts of the gun that fired the bullet?'

'Yes, sir!'

'Wonderful. Where is it?'

'Back in the line. We returned it to the Brigade.'

'Returned it. You mean for service?'

'Yes, sir. Guns after all are guns, sir, and we need all of them we can get. There's always a shortage, you know.'

'You gave the *murder weapon* back?'

'Yes, sir. To the Brigade armourer.'

'Right, well, I want you to get on your field telephone immediately and find out who the armourer gave it to, all right?'

'As you wish, sir.'

'Also I want you to locate the witness McCroon. The private soldier who claims to have seen an officer in the corridor on the night of the murder. I believe that, like the murder weapon, he has been returned to the line. Please find out if he is still alive and, if he is, where he is.'

'Very good, sir.'

'Now then, I should like to meet your prisoner.'

'Yes, sir!'

The sergeant rose to his feet, came to attention, stamped his foot, spun around, stamped his foot again and then marched from the room.

Kingsley had not expected to learn much from the unfortunate Private Hopkins and his pessimism proved well founded. The man was being held alone in a makeshift cell in the basement of the house. He was thin and haggard and at first appeared not to notice Kingsley's presence, continuing instead to sit fidgeting with some invisible irritant that appeared to be located on his trouser leg.

'Stand up when an officer enters the room, you little shit!' the sergeant barked and Hopkins rose slowly to his feet.

'Thank you, Sergeant,' Kingsley said gently. 'That will be all.'

When the sergeant had stamped his way out of the room Kingsley offered Hopkins a cigarette and, lighting one himself, asked the prisoner to talk about the evening of the murder.

'Nothing to t-tell,' the man replied. He had developed a stutter since his experiences on the first day of the third battle. 'Me and McC-C-Croon played a bit o' cards, that was all. Did our b-basket-making. Nice of him to sit with me. I was f-feeling very low. What with the bangin' in my head and all.'

'Did you know that Viscount Abercrombie was in the next room?'

'I didn't even know there *was* a next room till that evening. Mind you, I'd have known th-then because whoever it was was having a terrible row with s-someone. They was shouting and everything.'

'A row? Are you sure? Nobody's mentioned this to me before.'

'Well, m-maybe they never heard it. I was n-next door after all.'

'Do you know who the row was with?'

'No, never saw him. L-l-ike I say, I never even knew it was Abercrombie, the bastard that l-lashed me to a g-gun limber.'

They sat and smoked together for a moment, listening to the sound of the not-too-distant artillery.

'So you did not shoot Viscount Abercrombie then?' Kingsley said, breaking the silence.

Hopkins finished his cigarette and cadged another before replying.

'Course I f-f-fucking didn't,' he stammered. 'What would I w-want to f-fucking do a silly thing like that for?'

'He was an aristocrat. I believe that you are a Bolshevik.'

'If every Bolshevik shot an aristocrat we'd have had a revol-l-lution long ago.'

'I suppose that's true.'

' 'Sides, we ain't going to sh-shoot the gentry, we're going to put 'em to w-work 'longside us.'

Kingsley had read enough Lenin to wonder whether this would in fact be the case, but he was not there to discuss politics.

257

'I reckon they'd r-rather be shot than work though,' Hopkins added, finishing his second cigarette and asking for a third.

'You were found with Abercrombie's gun.'

'That's what they say. I d-don't remember.'

'You should try to remember. It might save your life.'

'How could I? I was asleep. I woke up when they all came in shouting. The g-gun was in my lap.'

And try as Kingsley might, Hopkins could tell him nothing more.

When Kingsley returned to the sergeant's office he discovered that the policemen he was dealing with were not entirely useless; given proper guidance they could get things done quickly enough and Kingsley was informed that Abercrombie's revolver had been located. It had indeed been returned to active service and issued to a Captain Edmonds, who was currently in a trench in the middle of the Ypres salient. McCroon had been pronounced fit for duty and returned to the line; he too was on the Ypres salient, where currently there was a brief lull in the battle except directly around Passchendaele itself.

The sergeant had only two constables available to him and there were of course other duties to be carried out, so Kingsley decided that the sergeant should organize the exhumation of Abercrombie's corpse while he himself would go in search of the alleged murder weapon. McCroon would have to wait.

'Oh, by the way, Sergeant,' Kingsley enquired casually, 'were you aware that the viscount had requested a green envelope?'

'No, sir, I was not.'

41

Going up the line

In order for Kingsley to go in pursuit of the missing gun he had to make his way from Armentières to the town of Ypres itself, and beyond that into the forward trenches of the British attack. It was a hard journey indeed: there was no vehicle available for him to commandeer and even had he been able to do so he would have got no further with it than he managed aboard the various lifts that he found. The roads were swollen with a massive and continual traffic of men, machines and horse-drawn transportation, all rattling over those same crippling cobbles that the Tommies cursed with such venom. In fact the going was shortly to get much rougher, but if anyone had told Kingsley this during the first mile or so of his travels he would have asked how it *could* get any rougher.

Axles broke, horses slipped, men shouted and swore like the troopers they were. The entire army seemed to have taken to the roads but to have no particular idea why they had done so or what their hoped-for destination might be. Road marshals were everywhere attempting to impose some order on the chaos, but their efforts appeared to be entirely ineffectual. They were not, of course; slowly but surely men and equipment were moving up the line and a lesser trickle of the same was moving back from it. But for a detective in a hurry it was frustrating indeed.

The famous town of Ypres was no longer a town at all but simply a pile of rubble. The Cloth Hall, a proud symbol of medieval commerce that had for so many centuries embodied the quiet, civilized prosperity of the region, had been almost totally destroyed. Kingsley had in his desk at home (or at least it had still been there on the day he left for gaol) a postcard which his brother Robert had sent to him in 1915, when he had been engaged in the Second Battle of Ypres. It was a French print showing the Cloth Hall half destroyed and partially covered with scaffolding. Above the photograph was printed *La Grande Guerre 1914–15 – Aspect des Halles d'Ypres après le bombardement*. Now the war was two years older and the Cloth Hall had ceased to exist at all. It was strange for Kingsley to think of Robert traversing this same ground, pistol and swagger stick in hand, touching these same bricks as Kingsley himself now stumbled over. He had survived it too and lived to fight another day. Not many more, but some.

Beyond what had once been Ypres there was nothing. Nothing at all.

Kingsley had never dreamed of or imagined such desolation. There were names upon a map, names of places through which he was passing and towards which he was heading. He had heard these names many times – what Briton, Canadian or Australian had not? Menin Road and Château Wood were places in which Allied forces had fought and died for nearly three whole years, but now that he had arrived at them, there was nothing. Not a single feature left save the vaguely discernible pathways across the desolation that the brave sappers had made and remade so many times over the years. Nothing else: no tree, no house, no hedge, no wall. Not one single stone or brick stood upright upon another. Not one single leaf or bud was attached to a twig. Only mud and water, and in amongst it men and horses, making their way along the barely existent pathways. Walking on the bones of last year's battalions, who slept just beneath the surface of the mud with the battalions of the year before beneath them.

Nineteen fourteen, 1915, 1916 and now 1917, every year a new crop of bodies sown across what had once been the pleasant fields of Flanders.

If you want the old battalion,
We know where they are,

Kingsley could not help singing that sad refrain beneath his breath as he made his way along the duckboards.

They're hangin' on the old barbed wire.

It was late afternoon before he finally found himself amongst the guns, rank upon rank of howitzers standing just behind the lines. Their job it was to pulverize the enemy's wire and trenches, to harry him constantly and, before a big push, to destroy him ahead of the infantry, laying down a creeping barrage just in front of the advancing men. As it was still light there was little obvious activity amongst the guns; almost everything that happened at the front happened at night, in an effort to conceal movements from the enemy's spotters. As Kingsley passed by, the artillerymen were to be seen inside their trenches and dugouts, some getting what sleep they could on the wet boards that were their home.

Now Kingsley exchanged mud at ground level for mud six feet beneath it as he entered the trench system proper and began his final approach to the front. First he descended into the reserve trench. There he found men who were either being rotated forward into the line or back towards their billets in the ruined villages and farmhouses immediately to the rear, or perhaps even for a proper 'rest' out of range of the firing line. Men tended to spend an average of a fortnight commuting between the billets and the front before being pulled back for six days' rest. It was not difficult to see, from the faces and condition of the men, which were going forward and which were heading back.

Kingsley was now only a hundred yards from the front but the going was very slow. First he had to traverse along the reserve trench in order to reach a communications trench that would take him up to the support line. The trenches were fashioned in a zigzag pattern resembling a series of cogs; viewed from the air, they would appear like a battlement stretched out across the ground. This design was to minimize the effect of the blast from a shell landing directly in a trench and exploding out along it, or of the enemy getting in and setting up a machine gun which could then rake all along the line. A sensible precaution indeed, but it made for heavy going. As Kingsley found himself constantly twisting and turning, rounding corner after corner, he felt deeply for the soldiers who had to navigate this labyrinthine swamp every day, carrying sixty pounds of kit. There were rats everywhere, as big as cats, swimming in the water, scurrying along the parapet, running across the men as they sat in their funk holes trying to get a little sleep before the exertions of the night. It was said that only three things lived amongst the trenches: rats, lice and men. Such was the company that man, with his divine inspiration, had arranged for himself to keep.

He eventually arrived at a communications trench and so turned away at right angles from the reserve and headed out towards the support trench that lay between him and the front. As he scuttled along this communication line Kingsley encountered an overpowering smell of chloride of lime mixed with excrement, and realized that he had not opened his bowels since he had taken part in the communal dump in the field beside his horse truck on the journey out. Perhaps it was the smell or the occasional whiz and crack of ordnance overhead, perhaps it was the advice he had been given 'never under any circumstances to miss the opportunity for a shit'; whatever the reason, suddenly he was overtaken by a desperate need to relieve himself, so he took a swampy detour into a latrine cutting. The sanitary arrangements consisted of a series of pits approached by a short trench cut out from the one he was traversing. In the pits were buckets and one or two large biscuit tins, all filled with the men's slurry, waiting to be emptied by the sappers under cover of darkness. Kingsley made his way along the slit and selected a bucket. Pulling up his greatcoat and undoing his trousers, he squatted down in the pouring rain. One or two other men were doing likewise.

'There's an officer sanitary facility just up at the reserve, sir,' a lance corporal said, having clearly noted Kingsley's captain's pips.

Kingsley could not help but smile at the incongruous use of language; if there was one word that did not apply to an inch of the Western Front, it was sanitary.

'I'm happy to use your facility if you have no objection,' he replied.

'You're very welcome, sir. But don't linger, eh? It never takes Fritz long to spot where we've dug our closets and this one's been here a week.'

The corporal left and, thus spurred on, Kingsley attempted to finish his business without delay. There was no paper or water to wash with save for the lime-rich puddles at his feet, so Kingsley had simply to pull up his trousers and belt and move on. He realized that men whose dugouts were often literally shorn up with the rotting corpses of fallen comrades soon got used to doing without the usual niceties, but for Kingsley it felt most uncomfortable not to wipe his backside or wash his hands.

After wading back into the communications trench and turning once more towards the enemy, Kingsley soon found himself in the support line. Here men were stationed whose job it was to supply, cover and replace the men in the front in the event of an attack by the Germans, or occupy the front in the event of an attack of our own. All was in quite good order: there were sandbags and decent boards to walk on, Kingsley noted, and rubbish chutes and gas alarms, rifle racks and properly supported funk holes. However, considering that the British line was supposed to be moving forward in an epic push, he thought that these were worryingly stable-looking arrangements and testimony to the lack of progress being made.

The men who were not still sleeping sat or stood about looking to their kit, cooking a tin of something (if they had any food, and fuel to warm it), cleaning up and engaging in the constant battle that was every bit as much a part of their lives as fighting the Germans: the war on lice. Lice were no respecters of rank, and officers and men simply crawled with them. Even in the short time he had been amongst these troops Kingsley could feel that he himself had collected the beginnings of the usual infestation. He watched as men ran matches and lighted cigarettes along the seams and folds of their garments, listening to the satisfying crackle of popping insects.

'You might kill a thousand,' a trooper said to Kingsley as he passed, 'but a million will come to the funeral.'

Kingsley smiled.

'I'm looking for Captain Edmonds,' he said.

'Keep going,' the man replied. 'Him and his mob is up the sharp end. Moved back up yesterday.'

Kingsley thanked the man and was about to move on when a shell burst some ten yards behind the trench. Kingsley ducked down but the men around him scarcely moved.

'Don't mind about that, Captain,' the lice-killer said with a smile. 'I reckon he chucked two or three hundred of those over yesterday and not a man scratched. He's looking for the latrine, see – don't half help you get your shit out.'

Kingsley pushed on, turning the corner of another zigzag tooth in the trench, leaving a platoon of around fifty men behind him. Then almost immediately there was another tremendous explosion, such as Kingsley had never experienced before. The concussion thudded into his eardrums like a sledgehammer in the side of the head and he felt a searing pain. The bang was followed by a brief silence and then came the screaming.

Kingsley turned back to look into the section of trench through which he had just passed. Had he not turned a sandbagged corner, he would surely have been a part of the terrible sight that now he witnessed. A high explosive shell had got in amongst the men and the carnage was beyond belief. Of the fifty men whom Kingsley had just passed through – men who had been cooking, cleaning and killing lice five seconds earlier – at least ten were dead, fifteen more were dying and scarcely a man amongst them had escaped a serious wound. The walls of the trench were crimson with blood, body parts were everywhere and, glancing down at his uniform, Kingsley discovered that he had been showered with what the soldiers called 'wet dust', the flying flesh and brains that a moment before had been a part of living men. He could see what was left of the man who had given him directions. He had taken a dreaded 'abdominal'; his guts were blown away, and the surgeons would not even attempt to treat him. The man was pleading with a comrade to shoot him there and then.

'Let's wait for the MO, eh?' Kingsley heard the comrade say, but it was obvious to all that no good news could be expected from that source.

As whistles blew and stretcher teams began to hurry past him, Kingsley struggled to resist the temptation to turn and run. To get out of that appalling place as fast as his legs could carry him. He was terrified, terrified in a way that was new to him. Kingsley's courage had always been based on the quiet confidence – *arrogant* confidence, he now realized – that he had in his own abilities. He was a man who could think and who could fight and, what was more, he could do both at the same time better than almost any man he had ever met. His survival instincts were taut and honed and if any man was equipped to triumph over danger it was him. But that was all very well in the usual way of things, when men made choices and planned their actions. But this, this utterly arbitrary killing over which no intellect, no matter how mighty, could exert the slightest influence had revealed a huge gap in Kingsley's armour. This was a situation in which genius and fool were reduced to levels of complete equality. Brave man, coward, cautious, reckless, it did not matter, for here men were truly swatted like flies. The only thing in that trench which determined whether a man would live or die was fate.

'Every bullet has its billet,' the boys would say.

You simply had to trust to luck.

Nothing could have been more alien to Kingsley's character.

Struggling to contain his rising nausea and master his churning bowels, he turned away from the dreadful scene and moved on in the direction he had been heading, in search of the last communications trench that would deliver him into the front line. It was there, as night fell on the waterlogged army, that Kingsley finally found Captain Edmonds. He was sitting in a small dugout along with two lieutenants, eating bully beef which a servant was warming for them over a spirit stove.

'Good lord, Captain,' Edmonds said, looking at Kingsley's bloodstained greatcoat, 'what happened to you?'

'A shell burst in the support trench I'd just passed through.'

'Yes, we heard that go off. Whiz-bang, eh? Rotten business. Normally Fritz can't shoot for toffee.'

The three officers munched in silence for a moment, considering the tragedy that had occurred not more than fifty yards from where they sat. But clearly they considered it only briefly before returning to the immediate present. Kingsley had noticed that nobody dwelt on death for long in that place.

'Do you know,' Edmonds said, 'when this war's over I shan't mind if I never see a tin of bully beef ever again. We had quite a decent stew yesterday but can't get it at all today. Fruit cake to follow though, and cheese,' he added cheerily. 'Got a parcel. God bless Auntie Joanna, say I. She does better by me than my own mater. So now, what brings a captain of the Military Police up so close to the Boche? No offence, Captain, but we don't normally see many red tabs hereabouts.'

'I am investigating the death of Viscount Abercrombie.'

'Good lord. Poor old Alan Abercrombie – killed in action, they said, didn't they? Mighty rum, that. We all thought he was safe back at Beaurivage.'

'May I come in?'

Edmonds was most pleasant and hospitable and bid the

266

younger of the subalterns give up his place on the little bench that had been built inside the dugout.

'Cup of tea? Tastes of onions, I'm afraid, we've only got the one pan at present. Damnable business when an Englishman no longer has a pot to brew up in, eh? Ha ha! Eh, Cotton?'

Cotton was clearly Edmond's batman, a small, wiry fellow who was making himself busy cutting the cake.

'We has one pan, sir, and we also has one old petrol can.' Cotton sounded rather hurt, as if the captain was somehow implying that the lack of a decent kettle was his fault. 'So you can have your tea tasting of onions out of the pan or you can have it tasting o' petrol out of the can. It's all the same to me, of course, but I thought as how you'd prefer onions.'

'Quite right, Cotton. Well done. Carry on. And let's have a spot of Auntie Jo's tinned fish paste on a biscuit too, go down well with the cheese. Nothing like a savoury after pud.'

Kingsley accepted a cup of tea but declined a slice of cake or any fish paste. He did not intend to remain long in the trench and felt it churlish to take any part of what small luxuries they had there.

'I shan't keep you, Captain,' he said.

'No rush. Always happy to entertain company, aren't we, lads?'

The two subalterns agreed enthusiastically.

Kingsley could see that the two young men, neither of whom could have been more than nineteen, were somewhat in awe of Captain Edmonds, who was a tough, weather-beaten soldier of at least twenty-five.

'Did you know the viscount at all?' Kingsley asked.

'Well, not really. I mean I spoke to him, you know, just over a snorter in the officers' mess when we were back at rest, but he wasn't with us long. Of course we were all rather excited when we heard he was joining us, what with him being famous and all, but to be frank he was a bit of a disappointment. Very quiet, withdrawn, not what you'd expect from his poems at all. I'd heard he was an awfully effusive bloke, quite the bon viveur. But not with us, didn't seem interested in very much at all really. Well, of course he was on the verge of shell shock, wasn't he? That's got to change a fellow. Beyond that I'm afraid I can't help you. I'm sure there's fellows who knew him far better than me.'

'Well, actually, Captain, what I really want from you is his revolver.'

'What's that?'

'You have been issued with a replacement sidearm. It previously belonged to him.'

'I say, are you pulling my leg?'

'Not at all. The circumstances of Abercrombie's death "in action" remain puzzling to the authorities. We have reason to believe that his own gun may have been used against him. However, the gun was returned to service and you got it.'

'Good lord, what a lark. Are you really telling me that's Viscount Abercrombie's own gun? And that he might have been killed with it?' Edmonds was pointing to where his servant Cotton had been laying out Edmonds's kit. The batman was oiling the pistol, using the rag, oil bottle and pull-through that were a part of every soldier's kit.

'Well, we think it is possible and it is most important to us that we find out. That is why I need your gun.'

Edmonds looked thoughtful.

'You want my gun?'

'Yes. I have brought you a replacement.'

'A replacement?'

'Yes.'

'Fine. Good. All right, Captain Marlowe, I shall send Cotton back with the pistol in the morning.'

'I'd rather take it now if that's all right with you.'

There was a slightly uncomfortable pause.

'Well, no, actually it isn't. Sorry and all that, but no can do. I shall send it back tomorrow morning.'

'Why do you not wish me to take it now?'

'Because I don't want you to.'

'I'm afraid I'm going to have to ask you for a considerably better reason than that, Captain, because I must have that gun.'

'Well now, Captain,' Edmonds replied, his manner still polite but no longer jovial, 'I rather think you should remember that this is *my* trench and that *I* am in charge, hence I do not need to explain my decisions to you, nor are you in a position to make demands. However, as a courtesy, because you are my guest and since you are probably the first copper who's ever been in a front-line trench, I shall tell you that tonight I have been ordered to lead a raiding party across no-man's-land.'

Kingsley tried to interrupt but Edmonds pressed on, languid but firm.

'We appear to be in something of a lull in the main battle and our colonel does not like to see men idle. He thinks that since we're sitting about the place we might as well have a biff at the Boche. Harry the fellow, prod him, keep him on his toes. I have therefore been briefed to take a party over, under cover of darkness, and give him a bloody good kick in the arse. Good fun, say I, and we're all jolly keyed up and raring to go. Isn't that right, Chamberlain?'

'Absolutely, sir!' one of the young subalterns piped up with genuine enthusiasm.

'Bad luck, Jenkins,' Edmonds said to the other, who was looking rather downcast. 'You'll get your chance. Can't have two greenhorns out there in the dark on the same fox hunt. Got to blood you one at a time, eh?'

'Of course, sir. I do understand, it's just I am awfully keen to have a go.'

'Stout fellow. Well done you. It'll be your turn soon enough so don't fret about that. Plenty of war left for all of us, I think. Anyway, Captain,' said Edmonds, turning his attention once more to Kingsley, 'the thing is I've been soldiering in France since the off. Don't wish to swank but I was a subaltern with the BEF at Mons, don't y'know, and I've been in it ever since. That's *three years*, Captain, in almost every show. Dardanelles even. I only missed out on the Somme because of trench foot, when my tootsies were the size of barrage balloons. Now the only reason I'm boring you with this is because when a fellow's had as many near misses as I've had, you come rather to trust your luck. Silly little things become important, routine and all that. I hate to call it superstitions – I read chemistry at Balliol and I can't abide mumbo-jumbo of any sort – but nonetheless, until they find a better word for it, superstitions it is. I like to go over the top *my way*, d'ye see?'

'Not really, no.'

'I smoke a fag, I take a good long look at my kit, check it, check it again and then hand it over to my fellow. Then he checks it, polishes it, oils it, pampers it and treats it with a damn sight more respect than he ever gives me, ain't that right, Cotton?'

'I don't know what you mean, sir.'

'Ha ha. Then he checks it one more time and hands it back to me. I check it. I smoke another fag, finish my tea and then go and kill as many Germans as I can. As of this moment, we're nearly through our routine. I've smoked my gasper, checked it all, hatchet, knobkerrie, pistol, checked it again, given it to Cotton, he's checked it, oiled it, polished it, pampered it. In a minute he'll check it again, give it back to me, I'll check it, have another fag, finish my tea and we'll be ready to go.'

'Yes, I understand that—' Kingsley tried to interject.

'And what I am saying to you, Captain, is this.' Edmonds's voice was now very firm and steady. 'I'm *not* going to arse about with my routine. That is the pistol I was issued to take with me on this raid and it is the pistol which I intend to take. It's the gun *God gave me*, do you understand? I've checked it, it's ready. Call me an old woman if you will but I do *not* change my routine, is that clear? I shouldn't do it for General Haig himself and I certainly won't do it for the Military Police.'

'Captain Edmonds. I want that gun. I have brought you a perfectly good gun to replace it. You may imagine that fate has sent me if it makes you feel any better but I must ask you to hand over the pistol I seek and let God give you another one.'

'I have told you, Captain Marlowe. You may have it in the morning.'

'Sir, if you take that pistol with you, you know very well that there is every chance neither you nor it will return.'

'Well, thank you for the cheery thought, Captain.' Edmonds had risen to his feet, stooping of course since the dugout was no more than five feet high. 'Do give our regards to all the boys *behind the line*, all the other coppers and staff wallahs having it cushy. Tell them they're welcome to join us up here at the front any time. For the moment, though, I shall have to ask you to leave as we real soldiers of the Poor Bloody Infantry have fighting to do.'

Captain Edmonds walked out into the trench and strapped on his Sam Browne belt, on which hung the holster containing Abercrombie's gun. He took the weapon out and studied it. The subaltern who was to accompany Edmonds also began to don his equipment.

'Give me the gun, Captain,' Kingsley snapped.

'Sergeant!' Edmonds called out, having looked at his watch. He was completely ignoring Kingsley.

A sergeant appeared, his face blackened.

'Sah!'

'Is the raiding party assembled?'

'They are, sah. Raring to go!'

Edmonds began to apply blacking to his face.

'Sergeant. This is Captain Marlowe of the Royal Military Police. He has asked that *when I return* from the raid I give him my pistol. I have agreed. Is that clear, Sergeant?'

Kingsley emerged from the dugout.

'I want that pistol now and I am ordering you to hand it over!'

'Is that clear, Sergeant?' Edmonds repeated.

'Captain Marlowe requires you to give him your pistol *when you return* from the raid, sah!'

Kingsley could see how the land lay. It was useless to protest further. He was in Edmonds's trench amongst Edmonds's men.

271

They clearly loved and respected their commander; they were a band of brothers, of whom Kingsley was not remotely a part. They would close ranks around their captain be the enemy German soldiers or British military policemen. Kingsley was in no doubt that, if Captain Edmonds were to suggest to his sergeant that Kingsley should fall victim to the arbitrary killing that could be the fate of any one of them at any time in such a trench, the sergeant would arrange things accordingly.

'I see that I am outflanked, Captain Edmonds.'

'I am very much afraid that you are, Captain Marlowe,' Edmonds replied before turning to address the group of twenty men drawn up behind the sergeant.

'Now then, you men,' he said. 'You have all been fully briefed and know what we are about this evening. British army policy on no-man's-land is very clear: *there is no such thing as no-man's-land*. It's ours, we own it and we wander about in it as we please. What is the German wire?'

'The British front line, sir,' the men replied.

'Exactly, the German wire is the British front line. Not theirs. Ours. Now then, if the artillery have done their job there should be some decent holes in the sausage-eaters' wire. If there aren't, cut yourself a path and be bloody quick about it.'

Kingsley peered through the darkness, reviewing the shadowy group of men whom Edmonds was addressing. They looked a wild, violent bunch, with blacked faces and bludgeons, axes and knives on their belts, all tied with rags so as not to clink together. Some were also hung with Mills bombs and grenades. They carried no rifles; clearly the combat would be entirely at close quarters.

A Very light exploded overhead, briefly illuminating the scene. Kingsley saw flashing eyes and teeth, the odd glint of uncovered metal. These soldiers looked as if they were about to invade hell.

'Now then, you fellows,' Edmonds said, 'I know that each one of you will do your duty to King and Country and to the girls we left behind.'

'If only I had one, sir,' a trooper piped up cheerfully.

'Well, do your duty to mine and I'll show you a picture,' Edmonds replied, and everyone laughed. 'Cotton! There is almost a whole fruit cake in my kit. If by any chance I am not with you tomorrow, you are to divide it amongst the men who do return to have with their morning rum.'

'Quite right, sir. See you in the morning.'

'Good. Well done. Sergeant, the ladders if you please.'

The sergeant issued his orders and ladders were leaned against the parapets. Then Kingsley watched as Captain Edmonds led his men silently up the ladders and into no-man's-land. Kingsley's blood was up: he knew exactly what he had to do. He had come to gather evidence and he intended to do just that. As the last man disappeared over the top and the men who remained were about to remove the ladders, he stepped forward.

'One moment, Private.'

Despite the protests of the assembled soldiers, Kingsley ran up the ladder.

42

A raid on the enemy trenches

A few feet in front of him, Kingsley could make out the crouched figures of men as they made their way forward, creeping from shell hole to shell hole across the blasted landscape. The ground was sodden, for it had rained pretty continuously since the storm of the previous night, the night in which he had watched a show and lain on a soft bed of wet grass with Kitty Murray. On that occasion, Kingsley had felt fully the sensation of living a totally different life to the one he had lived before. Making love to a stranger on a lawn in front of a French château seemed as far away from the life of a happily married London policeman as he could possibly get. But now, crawling in Belgian mud towards German machine guns, he felt doubly dislocated from the life he had known. Every day now seemed to herald the beginning of another new life.

He remembered that he had not blacked up his face as the others had done. It was true that he was bearded but he felt that he should take all precautions; after all, it would be foolish to die and perhaps cause the death of others because of a bead of sweat on a pale cheek. He plunged his hand into the dirt to gather up some earth. The next moment he was gasping and swallowing, trying to retch as silently as possible, realizing that he had stuck his hand through the body of a maggot-ridden corpse. After a few seconds he regained control of himself and, wiping his stinking, maggoty hand on his already gory greatcoat, he continued to creep forward. Only for a moment, however, because almost immediately a flash in the sky signalled that another star shell had gone up. A split second later the whole area was bathed in a curiously flattening, silvery light. Ahead of Kingsley, the men of the raiding party froze. Kingsley froze too, understanding by instinct what most soldiers had to be taught: when the star shells burst, the way to save oneself was to become motionless. Instinct tempted a man to hurl himself to the ground but it was movement, above all, which alerted the observer to your presence. Edmonds's well-drilled company understood this and every man became a statue, then as the light faded they were able to resume their progress undetected.

Captain Edmonds led at a goodish pace. He and his men clearly had some knowledge of the terrain because there were numerous holes and obstacles that Kingsley would have most certainly blundered into had he been finding his own way. It was obvious that this raid had been very well scouted; Kingsley was learning just how much time the British spent in no-man's-land during the still watches of the night. The German wire was indeed their front line.

In scarcely twenty-five minutes they arrived at their destination and assembled before the German wire. Kingsley remained unnoticed at the back of the group. Captain Edmonds was signalling his silent orders: the shells had not done sufficient damage to the wire and they must needs cut more away in order to get through. This two or three of the men did, working in near-complete darkness and with the enemy now only yards away. The tiny pings that rang out as the cutters did their work were agony for the attackers; if they were detected at this point they would be the proverbial sitting ducks, and death a near-certainty. The German soldiers' voices were clear and Kingsley, who spoke German like a native, had no problem understanding their

275

conversation. For the most part, little of any interest was being said. The sentries were clearly too tired and numbed by the rain and the tedium to bother with much more than observations about the weather and requests for tobacco, but two fellows were engaged in animated talk, although they kept their voices low. It was not a dissimilar discussion to the one that Kingsley had taken part in while defecating at the side of the railway line.

'I tell you, this war is a war between two ruling classes. And *we're* fighting it, more fool us! I'm a tram driver from Frankfurt. What has any of this to do with me? It's so stupid it makes me weep.'

The other soldier disagreed.

'The English started this war,' he said.

'Why?' the first man replied. 'Why would they start it?'

'Because they're bastards, that's why, and they're in the pay of the Jews. And that is also why the Americans are in, because they are all Jews.'

Ah yes, Kingsley thought to himself, that was an element of German nationalism which thankfully was far less prevalent in Britain. The Germans always loved to blame the Jews.

'It's got nothing to do with the Jews. It's about capitalism, you prick.'

'Ah-ha! Exactly! And who invented capitalism?'

'I suppose you think the Jews did.'

'Of course they did, just like they invented communism.'

'But communism is the opposite of capitalism.'

'You see how clever they are? They have it all. Both ends and then the middle.'

The last wire had been cut and Edmonds's men were now gently bending back the strands to create a pathway. It seemed impossible to Kingsley that they had remained undetected for so long, but they had and now the hour had come. Three gaps had been formed; the men in front of Kingsley gently took up their weapons and crept through. As he followed, Kingsley could see that this was to be a battle as old as man himself, a desperate hand-to-hand struggle. The men carried hatchets and clubs. Some of the weapons they had clearly fashioned themselves during idle hours in the trenches; he saw maces studded with spikes, sometimes with a short stabbing blade protruding from the end. Stone Age man had done battle in exactly this way, leaping upon his opponent and attempting to slash, stab or bludgeon him to death.

The section of trench to be attacked had been carefully chosen. It had been scouted on three previous nights and the Royal Flying Corps had taken a number of photographs. A complex including two large dugouts where men were quartered, it was approached by single slit trenches on either side, and if the British could once get into the complex a small force could hold its perimeters for a short period while the main battle was joined in the middle.

And so Kingsley watched, as with a mighty yell the attack began. Having crept forward beyond the wire to the lip of the German trench, twenty Britons rose up and hurled themselves over it and down on to the heads of the soldiers chatting within. Kingsley followed as the first thuds and screams began, peering over the parapet into the darkness below where the crunch of metal on bone punctuated German cries of panic and blood-curdling yells of pain.

'Bombs in the hole! Sharp now,' Edmonds's voice cried out, and Kingsley watched as men approached the dully glowing patches of light that marked the entrances into the underground complex. One or two Germans were already stumbling out, attempting to raise their rifles, but as they did so they were stabbed or shot. Then Mills bombs and grenades were hurled into the dugouts, and almost instantly great bangs beneath the dirt were followed by a chorus of screams and pitiable whimpering.

Now a flare went up and the whole scene was suddenly bright as day. The British were laying about themselves with wild and savage fury, and the Germans to whom Kingsley had listened only moments before were all dead or dying. At the edges of the battle the Germans were clogging up the approach trenches, attempting to get at the British but being held at the perimeters by those

Tommies whose job it was to secure the area of attack. Kingsley could see Captain Edmonds in the midst of it all, with two dead at his feet, in the process of emptying his revolver into a third, a large man who appeared to be brandishing a cook's ladle. Kingsley lay flat on the parapet, watching Edmonds's gun.

Now stunned and wounded Germans began to emerge from the smoky darkness of the bombed-out holes. They were attacked instantly and the dead piled up, blocking the entrances and muffling the cries from within.

'Carstairs, Smith! Look to the edges,' shouted Edmonds. Kingsley glanced to left and right and could see what Edmonds had already spotted: the perimeters were being squeezed, two or three Tommies were already dead and the Germans were pushing the remaining defenders back into the mêlée.

'Warm work, lads! Too damn warm, prepare to withdraw!' Edmonds shouted.

Kingsley thought that this excellent officer might have left his order to retire a minute too long. The Germans who had come to the aid of their comrades were nearly in amongst the British now, and the fighting was shocking in its violence and frantic energy. For a second Kingsley was reminded of those ridiculous scenes in American moving pictures when entire Wild West saloons erupted into fighting, with every single person furiously thrashing away at everyone else. The trench was now a seething mass of flailing humanity.

Looking down, Kingsley could see Edmonds draw breath to shout further orders, when a German buried his bayonet in him from behind. Instead of words, blood blurted from his open mouth. He fell forward to the boards, and in so doing dropped his revolver.

Kingsley sprang forward over the parapet wall and leaped into the mob below. He did not hesitate. He did not think at all. Right from the first moment when he had accepted the assignment from Cumming he had known that it would almost certainly place him in enormous physical danger, but only a danger that millions of

278

other men were facing every day. Since arriving in France he had taken a certain grim satisfaction in the prospect that he would now be able to give the lie to those who called him a coward; finally he would be able to share the dangers that his countrymen faced without compromising his conscience.

Kingsley had almost *sought* this chance to see action. Now that it presented itself, he hurled himself into it.

He had the advantage of having had an aerial view of the fighting, so he knew the current make-up of the struggle. He dropped in between two Tommies near where their captain had fallen and was about to duck and pick up the gun when suddenly a German loomed up in front of him, raising his Mauser pistol to shoot. Kingsley had in his hand the gun he had hoped to trade with Captain Edmonds. He had not intended ever to fire a weapon in this terrible war, but now he had no choice. His arms snapped into the firing position he knew so well from the pistol range at Met Small Arms, and he took aim and squeezed the trigger. The German fell back, shot between the eyes. As the soldier fell away, Kingsley saw another one directly behind him and a third and fourth approaching from either side. Kingsley shot them all, each between the eyes, turning his hips from left to right, his upper-body firing position never altering: left arm up and crooked, barrel across the sleeve, gun held high, eye behind the hammer. Whenever Kingsley fought, he remembered the advice of his first fencing tutor: 'It takes about as long to panic as it does to think. In a fight, think quickly but always *think*.'

As the fourth man went down, Kingsley was looking about himself for Abercrombie's gun. He had marked well where it had been dropped and there it should have been, next to the body of Captain Edmonds, but it was gone, kicked away in the movement of the fight, perhaps slipping off the boards or between them into the mud, perhaps still nearby but impossible to see amongst the skidding, thumping crowd of scrambling legs and boots. Fully forty men were upright in a space no bigger than half a rackets court. Another twenty must have been beneath them, dead or dying, trampled under the struggling soldiers. Kingsley could see that it was hopeless to try to find that gun now: in another few moments the Germans would overwhelm their attackers, and it was already a moot point whether any of them would get out alive. In front of him Kingsley saw the young subaltern with whom he had drunk tea spin round with half his head blown off. Both officers were now gone, the raid was being overwhelmed.

Then Kingsley remembered the fat man Edmonds had shot. Where was he? Rolling away one of the men he himself had dispatched, he found the corpse of Edmonds's victim, the cook's ladle still between his fingers. Was his body fat enough to stop a bullet? By rights a service revolver fired at point-blank range should send a bullet through one man and then perhaps another before drilling into the mud behind. But this had been an exceptionally fat man, wearing a big greatcoat, heavily webbed with leather and buckles. Kingsley dropped to his knees and rolled the man over. There was no exit wound.

For the second time in less than half an hour Kingsley found himself burying his hand in a corpse. A fresh one was not so easy to penetrate, and he was forced to take a hatchet from the man's belt and hack the dead cook open with it. The bullet had entered the chest, so whilst above him three dozen men stabbed and bludgeoned their lives away, Kingsley chopped at the man's ribs, then took a knife and delved beneath. Having created an enormous incision, he put his hand inside and felt for the bullet. Sure enough, there it was, wedged between the man's back ribs. Kingsley plucked it out and slipped it into his pocket, then stood upright in the mêlée to consider his position.

'Order them back,' he heard a voice beneath him say, 'or they'll fight till they die. No officers left. Someone must give the order.'

It was Edmonds, who much to Kingsley's surprise was still alive.

'For God's sake get them out, man.'

Kingsley took in the scene at a glance: the perimeter of the field of battle was within moments of collapse. More Tommies now lay dead at either end along with twice as many Germans, and it seemed to Kingsley that only the logjam of piled bodies was preventing the Germans beyond from coming to the aid of their embattled comrades.

'Mills bomb!' Kingsley shouted at the top of his voice. 'Mills bomb here this instant! Captain Edmonds is fallen, I am in command. Mills bomb, if you please!'

He put every ounce of calm and clarity into his command and it had the desired effect; even the Germans seemed to stop for a moment.

'Mills bomb, sir!' a trooper said, presenting himself as the fighting around them redoubled.

'Thank you, soldier.' Kingsley took one of the man's explosives. 'Now kindly oblige me by blowing up that end and I shall blow this.'

The trooper understood what he intended.

'Yes, sir!'

'Throw it just beyond the fighting,' Kingsley shouted, 'into the fellows beyond. Steady now. One-two-three, throw!'

Together he and the trooper pulled the pins on their bombs and hurled them into the crowded trenches just beyond the fighting. There could be no doubt what the result would be: at least half a dozen more dead bodies blocking the way and a lengthy moment of panic and bloody confusion. Two almost simultaneous explosions signalled the last chance for the British to make an escape.

'Raiding party withdraw!' Kingsley shouted. 'Fall back in good order!'

'Sir! The captain!' It was the trooper who had thrown the other bomb, reminding Kingsley that Edmonds was still alive.

Kingsley looked down at the seriously wounded officer.

'Never mind me. I'm done for. Get our fellows back,' Edmonds said.

But Kingsley was not sure that Edmonds was done for. The bayonet wound was midway down his trunk, and Kingsley reckoned there was a good chance that the blade had gone in between the heart and the stomach, missing both those vital organs.

'All right. Up with him,' Kingsley said, 'over the parapet.'

Together he and the trooper were able to manhandle the captain's bleeding body up on to the ridge of the parapet. The German trench was so well constructed that it provided firm walls for them to scale. Others in the British troop saw what they were about and covered them from above. Once clear of the trench, Kingsley was able to shoulder Edmonds in a fireman's lift.

'You spread the wire, Private,' he ordered. 'I shall carry him through.'

The British withdrew through the German wire, leaving about a third of their number behind them along with five times as many Germans. Kingsley was able to get Edmonds halfway back at a stooped run, blundering from waterlogged shell hole to shell hole, before the Germans in the trench behind him had recovered sufficiently to begin firing. After that, more star shells went up and he and the men around him had to fall on their faces and crawl the rest of the way on their stomachs, creeping now from hole to hole, dragging their wounded with them, waiting ten or fifteen minutes between each move until finally they reached the safety of the British line.

The violence of the raid had been clear even from afar and medical orderlies were waiting to tend the wounded. Kingsley was happy indeed to unload Captain Edmonds from his back and place him in the care of a stretcher party. Edmonds could no longer speak for loss of blood but he squeezed Kingsley's hand and gave him a weak thumbs-up before he was carried off.

Kingsley was a vain man and he knew that he had done exceptionally well, but he took no pride or pleasure in Edmonds's thanks. The truth was flooding in on him with horrifying clarity. He had joined the combatants, he had fought in the war. The thing for which he had sacrificed everything and thrown his life away to avoid had happened anyway. In vain could he argue to himself that he had killed in self-defence; if he had not been there, he would not have needed to defend himself. He had been pursuing evidence certainly, but for what? A murder trial? There was only one defendant facing the death sentence, while he had personally killed four men in his first moments in the trench. He had ordered the tossing of the Mills bombs. He himself had thrown one, thrown a high explosive into a metre-wide mud corridor packed with men. How many had he killed with that single action? Six at least, perhaps more. How many had he maimed?

Kingsley staggered along the trench, sickened by the realization of what he had done. He had killed at least ten Germans. The majority of servicemen would not kill anything like so many in their entire service, and he was a *conscientious objector*! The perverted irony of his position filled him with horror.

Just then a soldier scurried up behind him and called respectfully for his attention.

'Sir? Please, sir? If you please, sir?'

Kingsley turned wearily.

'You got us out, sir. You saved half the troop. Without you we'd have been slaughtered for sure.' It was the soldier who had supplied him with the Mills bomb. 'I hope you won't mind me saying as how I shall never look at a copper in the same way again.'

Was this some comfort? Kingsley wondered. Some moral salvation? It was true that he had played the crucial role in saving the Tommies who had made it back. There had been many capable men on that raid but no one else with the authority to order a retreat. Could Kingsley find some comfort in his actions in bringing the party home? He had killed Germans, he had saved Britons. He had done so whilst defending himself and in the pursuit of criminal evidence.

But try as he might, he could not argue that his conscience was clear. Looking at it from whatever angle, he still emerged a hypocrite. Having lost everything on a point of principle he had then tossed that principle aside in his desire to be a good detective, and probably also to prove his own courage to himself. Whether he saved Hopkins from the firing squad or not, the blood of at least ten Germans, innocent conscripts in a wicked war, would always be on his hands.

43

Further investigations

Back in the reserve trench, Kingsley sat for a long time on an upturned ammunition box. He thought hard about chucking it in. Returning immediately to England and facing whatever fate might await him. Slowly, however, he began to change his mind. The element that influenced him most was the same one that guided all his steps. Logic. After all, the Germans were dead; what possible use could there be in abandoning his investigation because of them? He had retrieved the evidence, in what was definitely a fine bit of police work. If he did not use it, the men he had killed would, in a way, have died in vain. The bullet in his pocket had been fired by the weapon currently assumed to have killed Viscount Abercrombie. It was his duty as a policeman to ascertain if it had.

Such were the musings of a man who knew in his heart of hearts that he could never abandon an investigation. Once he had the bit between his teeth, it simply was not in his nature. And so, instead of heading back to England, he set off to seek out Abercrombie's commanding officer, the colonel whom he had seen address the audience after the concert party the night before.

Kingsley had already learned that when he wasn't in the front line Colonel Hilton made his headquarters in a ruined farmhouse a mile or so behind the guns. Wearily he trudged back up the Menin Road until he found what he was looking for. It was now nearly dawn and the colonel had just had news of the trench raid. To his surprise, therefore, Kingsley was greeted like a hero.

'Good God, man! You brought the platoon home!' Hilton said, saluting him. 'Saved the life of one of my finest officers. Tophole bit of soldiering. Absolutely splendid effort! I intend to recommend you, Captain. No! I shan't hear another word about it. I absolutely intend to recommend you in dispatches. If last night's show ain't worth a gong then I should like to know what is. Why, I've been told your blood was so up you were *tearing the very innards* out of the enemy, hacking him open with a hatchet! Now *there's* an example to set. I always say to the chaps, if you've got no ammo and your bayonet's broke, *bite* the bastards! Eat his Hun head off! And there's you organizing an orderly withdrawal under heavy fire, calm as y'please, *and* ripping Boche hearts out with your bare hands to boot.'

'Actually, sir, I was retrieving evidence,' Kingsley replied.

'Eh? What's that?'

'I am investigating the death of Viscount Abercrombie.'

'Abercrombie? I thought it had been established that he died in action?'

'Oh yes, sir. It has. Nonetheless, I am looking into it.'

'Oh. I see,' the colonel replied with a knowing look.

'The gun Captain Edmonds was using once belonged to the viscount. It is believed to have been the weapon which killed him.'

'In action,' Hilton added.

'Yes, sir, if you wish, in action. I need to know for sure whether it was, so I was attempting to retrieve the gun. In the mêlée, however, the gun was lost and I was forced to retrieve one of the bullets it had fired instead.'

Kingsley reached into the blood-caked pocket of his greatcoat and produced, with a small flourish, the bullet he had removed from the body of the fat German cook. Despite all his doubts and the terrors of the previous few hours, Kingsley was still Kingsley and his vanity and sense of theatre were now getting the better of him. He could not resist playing up to the drama of the moment and was gratified to note that the colonel and others present were open-mouthed with surprise and admiration.

'Well, I'm *jiggered*!' the colonel said finally. 'That is as rum a bit of business as I can recall in twenty-five years of soldiering. Do you mean to say that while you were taking part in a trench raid, killing hordes of Huns and beating a damn fine retreat, you were also *conducting a police investigation*?'

'Yes, sir. I was.'

'Well then, I think it's high time we drank your health.'

Hilton pushed Kingsley into a chair at his map table.

'No fizz, I fear, but we have a tolerable cognac. Probably better in weather like this anyway. We were just about to have a snort. Mornings are our evenings, don't ye know. We're all owls these days.'

Kingsley accepted a glass of brandy and also some toasted cheese that the colonel's batman was preparing. Just then a soldier appeared at the farmhouse door, announcing that there was a private who wished to see Captain Marlowe. It was Cotton, Captain Edmonds's batman.

'Beggin' your pardon, sir, I followed you back,' he said. 'Been tryin' to catch you all the way but you certainly can travel. We thought as how you ought to have a bit of this, you know, just for fellowship.'

The man opened up a small oilskin parcel to reveal a generous slice of fruit cake.

'The captain's got a Blighty, sir, and they say he's going to live, thanks to you. And all the boys wanted to say as how we're very grateful and we swears we'll never call coppers what we usually calls 'em ever again.'

'And what do you usually call them, Private?' the colonel demanded.

'Cunts, sir.'

'Ha ha! Good man! Well done! Although personally I'd say

287

they were the opposite, because while I can't normally *abide* a military policeman I've never met a cunt I didn't like! Well done, Private. Carry on.'

Kingsley took the cake from the little batman.

'Thank you, Private Cotton. I am very touched.'

The slice of cake was sufficient to be sub-divided and went down very well with the cognac and cheese, just as Edmonds himself had said it would. When the little victory feast was over, Kingsley said that he would be obliged if he could ask the colonel one or two questions.

'Of course, of course. Fire away.'

'When did you last see Abercrombie alive?'

'I visited him at Beaurivage two days after he was invalided back.'

'That was very good of you, Colonel. Do you visit all your injured officers?'

'Well, one tries, you know, one tries. Besides, he was most concerned about his leather case – it had been with him in the forward trench and he wanted it back, so I took it with me.'

'Do you know what was in that case?'

'Well, papers, I suppose.'

'You did not look inside?'

'Good lord, Captain! What a suggestion. I say, you peelers do have a horrid view of people. As if I'd go fossicking about in another chap's kit.'

'Only blank paper was found in his room when he died.'

'Well, perhaps that was what he wanted. Blank paper. I've known stranger things, believe me. Fellahs who are convinced they've painted bloody great canvases and it turns out to be two dots and a splodge. Shell shock is very delusionary.'

'Yes, that's true, I suppose,' Kingsley conceded, 'although he was not thought to be suffering very severely.'

'He probably wanted to write more poetry.'

'No poetry was found, and the staff nurse there, a woman named Murray, claims that he'd given up on poetry anyway.'

'Hmm. Well, he certainly has now.'

Hilton drained the last of his cognac.

'It's a bad business all round but look here, Captain, I really do need to turn in now, battle going on and all that. We'll be back in the thick of it again soon, no doubt. Is there anything else I can tell you?'

'No, not at present, Colonel. Thank you for your time and also for the meal.'

'Well, thank *you* for bringing the raid home. I meant what I said, you know. I'm mentioning you in dispatches. You, sir, shall have a medal.'

44

Under the magnifying glass

Kingsley's journey back to the Château Beaurivage took him all the rest of the morning and it was late lunchtime before he finally stood once more in front of the beautiful old house. He was surprised to discover how much he had been looking forward to seeing Kitty Murray again, and how disappointed he was when he discovered that she was not at the château. She had left in order to accompany some severely distressed men back up to that same railhead where Kingsley had first arrived at the battle zone.

'Will she be accompanying them to England?' Kingsley enquired of a medical orderly whom he met in the great entrance hall.

'I hope not, sir. Things would be a lot less jolly around here without her.'

Kingsley very much agreed with the man, which rather disturbed him. The last thing he needed was any emotional complications clouding his judgement and he resolved to dwell on the diminutive Suffragette no longer.

Kingsley had returned to the château in order to see the military policemen whom he had ordered to exhume the body of Captain Abercrombie. An order which had not endeared Kingsley to the staff of the Château Beaurivage.

'Digging up corpses is *not* the sort of thing we need around here,' the senior medical officer complained as he scurried after Kingsley through the château towards the stairwell that led down into the cellar where the autopsy was to take place.

'I'm sorry, sir, but I need that body,' Kingsley insisted.

'My patients have just come from a place where bodies pop up out of the ground continually, and they're supposed to be safe from that here. If one of them was to see . . .'

By this time they had arrived in the cellar, where the sergeant from Armentières was waiting for him with the corpse. It had been removed from its coffin and placed ready on a makeshift operating table built from boards and packing cases.

'All present and correct, sah!' the sergeant said, stamping the stone floor so hard that sparks flew from the nails on his boots. 'One body. Dead. Previously belonging to Captain the Viscount Abercrombie, sah!'

It seemed a strange way to describe a corpse but Kingsley let it go.

'I have run an extension cable to a portable generator which I have placed outside, sah, as I does not think you can do delicate stuff such as this by candlelight, sah!'

The sergeant had indeed wired up a sixty-watt electric light bulb above the corpse, which made the sallow whiteness of its skin positively glow in the otherwise darkened cellar. It was a truly macabre scene.

'Thank you, Sergeant. That was extremely sensible of you.'

'Sah!' More sparks flew.

'Right,' said Kingsley, 'this won't take long.'

He approached the body stretched out upon the planks, naked save for a loincloth.

'You buried him like this?' Kingsley enquired of the senior medical officer.

'Yes. His friend Lieutenant Stamford informed us that he had expressed a wish not to be buried in uniform.'

'Really? I did not know that.'

'We saw no reason to deny the request.'

Looking down at the corpse, Kingsley recalled the verses he had read in the newspaper in Folkestone library. He repeated them now.

> 'To mark the sacrifice I gave
> Put "Forever England" on my grave.'

There was silence for a moment.

'Funny that the man who wrote that did not wish to be buried in uniform, eh?'

Kingsley bent down and looked at the wound in Abercrombie's head. A single bullet hole almost exactly between the eyes. The wound had been washed, much to Kingsley's annoyance, but still he inspected it.

'Do we have a magnifying glass?' he asked.

'I anticipated that, sah!' the sergeant said, producing one.

'Good, well done. You know, Sergeant, when you find yourself demobbed, you should apply to Scotland Yard. You would be an asset to the murder investigation team.'

'Thank you, sah. I shall remember that.'

'Of course you'd have to give up the stamping.'

'I only stamps 'cos it is required, sah. Civilians are not required to stamp.'

Kingsley studied the wound. The magnification afforded by the glass was not great, nonetheless he detected specks of black at the entrance that he would not have expected unless they had been deposited there by the bullet.

'Sergeant, you wouldn't by any chance have—'

'Tweezers, sah?'

'Yes, exactly, Sergeant. Tweezers.'

The sergeant produced a pair.

'Well done, Sergeant.'

'Borrowed them off a nurse, said I had a splinter. Best not tell her what you're actually using them for, she does her eyebrows with 'em.'

Kingsley set to work with his magnifying glass and tweezers, picking tiny bits of residue from the jagged flesh of the wound and depositing them in a saucer which the sergeant had also thought to provide.

'I must say, Sergeant, you think of everything.'

'Thank you, sah.'

'And this exhumation has also been most efficiently carried out. Well done.'

'Sah!'

Kingsley was crouched over the corpse, talking as he worked. Were someone to have entered the cellar at that point they might easily have thought that Kingsley was imparting some urgent wisdom to the dead body.

'I can't help asking myself,' Kingsley continued, 'and I know that you'll forgive me for saying this, Sergeant, how was it that such a thorough fellow as you could make such an unholy mess of the initial scene-of-crime investigation?'

'Well, sah . . . I assume you are aware that we was called off.'

'I don't know what you're talking about. Who called you off?'

'Staff. The same Staff what put us on in the first place. We was in bed at Armentières when we received a call from Staff to attend a murder here at Château Beaurivage and to arrest Private Hopkins.'

'They told you who to arrest, before you'd even attended the scene?'

'Yes, sir. Well, he had been found with the gun after all.'

'Who was this person from Staff?'

'A Colonel Willow, sir. I don't know him personally. Anyway, shortly after we attended the scene we received another call here at the château, which, as you may know, is on the telephone, saying that we should take our prisoner and depart without causing further disturbance to the medical work of the centre.'

'Did that not seem strange to you?'

'Well, no, not really, sir. The case was pretty cut and dried, and we do make a bit of noise when there's a bunch of us.'

'Sergeant, when we are finished here I would like you to get in touch with Staff HQ and enquire after this Colonel Willow. I should very much like to speak to him.'

The sergeant assured Kingsley that he would, and for a few moments silence fell on the grim scene as Kingsley worked away at the entry wound between the eyes of the corpse. Finally he was satisfied that he had picked up all the evidence he could from that source.

'Were you aware, Sergeant,' Kingsley said, 'that amongst Viscount Abercrombie's effects only one boot was found?'

'No, sir, I was not.'

'Well, that was the case, and I know what happened to the other boot. It was used as a silencer. The killer put his gun down the leg of one of Abercrombie's boots and shot the bullet through its heel. I have found rubber, leather and what I think are wool fibres too. Possibly the killer had filled the boot with socks. He must have taken the boot away with him when he made his escape.'

'Well I never,' the sergeant said.

'Quite extraordinary,' the senior medical officer added.

'Which also accounts for the fact that the bullet did not exit Abercrombie's skull: its velocity had been reduced by the impact with the boot heel. And speaking of bullets, let us retrieve it.'

Using a scalpel and the tweezers Kingsley dug into the wound, delving deep between the eyes to extract the thing he sought. Having done so, he washed it off and took it upstairs to where there was more light. There, with the help of the sergeant's magnifying glass, he compared it with the bullet he had taken from the German cook the night before.

'Dear me,' he said after a moment or two of investigation, 'I had thought that I might require a microscope but this is as plain as day.'

'What is, sir?' the sergeant enquired.

'Every gun is different, Sergeant. Not very different but different enough to leave its own particular signature on every bullet it fires. These two bullets were fired from different guns.'

'No, sir!'

'Yes, sir! The gun which was found on Private Hopkins, the one which fired this bullet,' and Kingsley held up the one he had brought back from the trenches, 'did not fire *this* bullet, the bullet which killed Viscount Abercrombie. That fact and that fact alone clears Private Hopkins, for he was arrested on no other evidence than his possession of Abercrombie's gun. Sergeant, you must release him.'

45

Back into battle

That evening, despite the fact that he had not slept at all the previous night, Kingsley returned to the trenches. He did not feel he needed sleep now; the puzzle was beginning to show tiny signs of resolution and in Kingsley's mind the hunt was on.

As he battled his way along the waterlogged duckboards that constituted the communications system of the Ypres salient, he saw a man in front of him, bowed down with barbed wire, slip and drown. Down or suffocate, all in an instant. Even as he watched, he knew there was nothing to be done, no time to do more than note such a gruesome example of the arbitrary barbarity of this war.

Eventually the duckboard pathway came to an end and Kingsley descended into the forward trenches, struggling up the communications slits towards the very front of the British line.

'You there! You men!' he shouted at the groups of soldiers carrying breakfast, fresh water and rum for the men who crouched beneath their parapets counting seconds. ' "C" Company. Where can I find "C" Company?'

Some men pointed up the line, others merely shrugged. Some pretended not to hear and others genuinely could not, for the barrage hurtling through the air above them was intense.

'I must find a fellow named McCroon. Private McCroon,' Kingsley shouted through the rain and thunderous noise.

'Who fucking cares?' a voice shouted back.

What sanction could Kingsley threaten that would be worse than the sentence already passed on the tens of thousands of men scuttling about and skulking in those forward muddy holes? Men who were expected shortly to emerge from that mud and proceed in good order towards the German machine guns? Kingsley's shoulder tabs gave him little authority here. He was alone and the man who shouted at him with such contempt was with his mates. The pre-dawn was dark, the rain torrential, the mud and water waste deep, thousands of cannon were firing, the noise was appalling. No one would miss one bastard copper who had made the mistake of venturing too close to where the real killing was done.

Besides, Kingsley reflected as he hurried past, the man was right. Who fucking *did* care? Why should the hunt for any individual matter in the middle of this terrible war? Particularly on a morning such as this one, when battle was once more to be joined in the Ypres salient which all the boys called Wipers? In an hour or two's time most of the men whom Kingsley was passing would be dead. Nobody cared that Kingsley wanted to find a man called Private McCroon, and Kingsley knew that he of all people should care least. But he did care: some unanswerable compulsion drove him on and so he struggled, sometimes chest-high in water, along the crisscross of stinking and fetid mini-canals that made up the communications network of the British forward position.

The going was horrendously hard but the distances were no longer great and it was not long before Kingsley arrived in the most advanced excavations of the line. Beyond this point there was a thin ribbon of mud and wire and beyond that the German Empire. It had been thus at the time of the First Battle of Ypres and also at the Second, and it was thus once more in the Third. Nothing had changed in that dreadful place for years. The shells currently exploding just ahead of the line were rearranging the bones of the men who had died in the battle before, and the battle before that.

Some wag had chalked *Savoy Bar and Grill* upon a board.

'McCroon!' Kingsley called out. 'Private McCroon!'

As he struggled along, he scanned the faces of the men he passed. He knew that McCroon's unit was in the vicinity and he had some idea of what the soldier he sought looked like, but the minutes were ticking by and still he had not found him. The soldiers all looked the same, every one caked in mud, every one with his fag burning between his lips, every one hunched over his tot of rum, waiting, the water dripping from his helmet brim. Every one with an expression sitting somewhere between elation and terror.

'Five minutes,' an officer called out. 'Fix bayonets.'

Even the shelling could not cloak the unmistakable sound of shearing steel being drawn en masse.

'Remember, lads,' a company sergeant major called, 'not too deep now. No sense wasting good steel on a Hun. Three inches is plenty, in the neck or the chest, then pull it out and go find another one.'

' "C" Company? Is this "C" Company?' Kingsley appealed to the sergeant.

'It is indeed, sir. Have you come to arrest the Germans for us?'

The men about him smiled and raised their mugs of rum. A good CSM could turn nervous wrecks into heroes simply by being steady.

'McCroon, I'm looking for a man called McCroon,' Kingsley shouted.

'With respect, sir, it's less than five minutes to zero. I think you should look for him some other time.'

'Some other time may be too late!'

'Sir, we are about to attack. This is no place for any man not ordered in the first wave. Not even military policemen. So I suggest you take your leave, sir, or grab a rifle and spike and give us a hand.'

The boys gave a ragged cheer at this.

'Sergeant, this is a matter of life and death!'

The CSM actually laughed. The men laughed also.

'You hear that, lads? Officer says it's a matter of life and death and there's me thinking it was something important.'

Kingsley left them and waded further along the trench, pushing past the crowded men, every one now with eighteen inches of bright steel attached to the end of his rifle, the only shining thing in the dark grey of that wet and miserable pre-dawn.

'McCroon, I must find a Private McCroon!' Kingsley cried out and suddenly he could hear himself speak, for the thunder of the guns had stopped. It was like the moment in the Underground when a man raised his voice above the rattle of the wheels and the train stopped and he was left shouting over nothing but silence. Many heads turned at once.

'Yes?' a soldier replied, looking up from his cigarette.

'ONE MINUTE!' an officer cried out, staring at his watch as if all the world existed on its face – which for him, of course, it did.

A man stepped forward.

'I'm McCroon. Who are you?'

'I need to speak with you. Fall out.'

For a moment an expression of joy flooded across McCroon's face. Was he to be granted a last-minute reprieve? But zero hour was upon them and it was too late for any reprieve. The officer who had just called out the time looked up from his watch in fury.

'You, sir! Who are you and what the hell are you about?'

Kingsley might be wearing the uniform of a captain in the Military Police but by this time he looked like just another anonymous creature of the mud.

'I am a policeman and I am taking this man out of the line. I wish to interview him.'

'The devil you are, you bloody fool. You will do no such thing. There are no interviews here and no bloody policemen either. This is "C" Company and we are about to attack!'

'I must speak with . . .'

The officer raised his pistol and pointed it at Kingsley.

'Stand aside this instant or I shall shoot you down. This company will do its duty. Every single man will do his duty.'

He glanced down at his watch.

'Zero hours, boys, and the best of luck to every one of you!'

'See you in Berlin, sir!' a voice called out.

The officer blew his whistle, and all up and down the line other officers looked up from their watches and blew their whistles also. A chorus of whistling cut through the silence that had descended so suddenly. Then with a roar the men began to swarm up the makeshift ladders propped against the parapet walls, scrambling and gripping at the mud as the wooden posts sank down under their weight. As the first British heads emerged above ground a new sound was heard, which to Kingsley's ear felt almost like a massive swarm of bees: the German machine guns two hundred yards away across the mud opened up.

The officer who had confronted Kingsley advanced a step or two, stick in one hand, pistol in the other, before staggering back under the force of the bullets that hit him and tumbling down into the trench on top of the men who were following. He was still trying to speak but there was blood geysering from his neck and chest and if he made a sound, Kingsley could not hear it. He fell back head first into the mud, with only his legs and boots to be seen.

'Up, boys! Up, damn you!' cried an NCO, and now the whole body of the trench seemed to heave itself over the crumbling lip of mud. McCroon went too: there was no question of staying. Army discipline did not allow men to hesitate once the whistle had blown. You got up and got on with it. A kind of hysteria gripped the men who had stood in the mud so long. They were finally to attack, to do their bit, to engage those bastards who had ruined everything with their frightfulness.

Kingsley felt he had no choice but to follow. He had come to speak to McCroon and McCroon was advancing in good order towards the enemy. Kingsley gripped hold of the ladder and launched himself up into the maelstrom.

He was later to ask himself what it was that caused him to follow McCroon over the lip of that trench and into the teeth of the German machine guns. He would very swiftly conclude that of the many emotions which crowded in on him as he ascended the rough ladder to the killing grounds, the foremost was the same desire that drove a million other men up those fateful steps.

The simple desire not to funk it.

Time and again Kingsley had heard soldiers speaking of just this fear. Not the fear of death but the fear of being found wanting, of having *let the side down*. Robert, Kingsley's brother, had spoken of it often in his letters. 'I am afraid of fear,' he had written, 'I only want to do my best.' They all wanted to do their best. Indeed, after a yearning for home, Kingsley had read, the fear of letting the side down was the principal emotion expressed by the doomed generation that sat in ditches in France. Comrades living cheek by jowl in fear and squalor, dependent only on each other for comfort and support, and in each man's heart the deep-seated desire not to let his mates down and the secret fear that when the ultimate test came, he might.

Kingsley was of course not bound by any ties of group loyalty to the men he followed over the top; he had not lived with them and suffered with them. He had not drawn ever closer to them as one by one they died. They were not his pals. Nonetheless they were his brothers, fellow men who faced appalling hardship and danger because they considered it to be their duty. There was a job to be done and it was up to them to do it. Kingsley knew that he too had a job to do, a different job but still a duty.

Here, as with the trench raid of the night before, was his chance to 'do his bit'. To stand shoulder to shoulder with his dead brother but to do so without compromising the beliefs he held so deeply. He would *not* fight their war but neither would he shirk his duty. In his own way and by his own volition, he would *do his bit*.

The first thing that Kingsley focused on as he breasted the lip of the trench was clouds of blue, yellow, black and green smoke hanging over what he presumed were the enemy trenches. For a nervous second or two he feared that these different-coloured clouds must be gas; whether German or British was irrelevant to Kingsley, for he had no respirator. In almost the same instant that the panic had begun it subsided, for all around and ahead of him Kingsley could see experienced soldiers whose masks still hung from their belts or remained in their packs. Kingsley was thinking clearly, as he always did when in danger, and he knew immediately that this was not gas but the curious multicoloured residue of shellfire that was now all that remained of the British barrage which had lifted moments previously to allow the troops to advance.

Ahead of him Kingsley could still make out McCroon, although how long he would last was anybody's guess. In fact how long any of them would last seemed a moot point as all around him men began to fall, blown to bits by the shrapnel from German artillery (artillery which supposedly had already been destroyed by the British cannonade) or mowed down by machine guns. Kingsley's one hope was speed. The battalion were advancing at a slow trot, as they had been instructed to do, in order for the assault not to break up in a helpless scampering mêlée but to arrive at the enemy trenches as a body. Kingsley marvelled at the courage of these men as they moved forward in good order into the eye of a storm of exploding steel. Men fell continually but no comrade stopped to help them. Later perhaps, but for the present every man was instructed to advance and keep on advancing as long as he had blood and breath in him to do so.

Kingsley did not trot. This was not his battle and he was not under military command. He was a policeman in pursuit of a witness and so he sprang forward at a crouching run, leaping ditches and craters and dodging the corpses that were already beginning almost to blanket the ground.

'You there!' a voice screamed. 'Steady pace, you bastard! Hold the line.'

Kingsley ignored him and ran on, past other men, some of whom also called upon him to quit his ill-disciplined personal assault. Kingsley ignored them all as he ignored the shrapnel exploding overhead and the streams of bullets coming in at waist height. Once more he had no choice but to trust to luck, and in so doing there came upon him a curious and illogical feeling of exhilaration.

When trying to describe it later, Kingsley realized that it was not necessarily bravery or foolhardiness either, but rather a feeling of helpless invulnerability. Fate was in motion, the dice were spinning in the air, he could do no more than trust his luck. And in the meantime to be part of such a body of men, moving forward together amid these awesome, cataclysmic forces that made the air and the ground explode with primeval power – it did have its own mad excitement. He felt an intense sense of *being*.

In retrospect, Kingsley was to conclude that this madness did not *replace* the terror but numb it. A tingling numbness, like the helpless exhilaration of a dream. Or perhaps it was simply the concussive sledgehammer of the exploding ordnance that bludgeoned men into becoming momentarily careless of their fate.

Whatever the reason, madness lent Kingsley wings and within a minute or two he had come level with the man he was seeking.

McCroon, like all the soldiers still upright, was moving towards the enemy line with a fag in his mouth and a bayonet-mounted rifle held before him. No shield at all from the German fire.

'McCroon!' Kingsley shouted, falling in beside the man. 'I must speak to you.'

McCroon turned in surprise.

'Who the fuck are you?' McCroon shouted back.

'My name is Marlowe. I am investigating the murder of Captain Abercrombie. It was I who found the evidence that freed your friend Hopkins.'

'Hopkins!' McCroon shouted above the din. 'You want Hopkins?'

'No, not Hopkins,' Kingsley roared in reply, 'it's you I seek.'

'Hopkins is here!'

And before Kingsley had time to reply McCroon had pulled at the arm of the man marching beside him, who turned to face them.

And there, beneath the dripping rim of his steel helmet, behind the glowing ember of his fag, was the grim face and staring eyes of the man whom Kingsley had met only once but whose fate was inextricably entwined with his own. The man whose release from military prison Kingsley had brought about just one day earlier. Whom Kingsley's brave and careful detective work had saved from the firing squad.

And they had sent him straight back into the line.

Even in the midst of battle Kingsley felt the shock of it. Here was a man falsely accused of murder, who had been awoken from a shell-shocked sleep and dragged bodily from his hospital bed to face arrest for a crime of which he knew nothing, who had been held in brutal incarceration in fear of his life – and yet they had not given him even a day to recover from his ordeal. The smile that Hopkins must have smiled on hearing that he was to be released without charge must surely have disappeared instantly from his lips as he learned that he was to proceed directly from prison into battle.

The argument Kingsley heard later went like this: Hopkins had always protested his innocence, and since it turned out that he *was* innocent he must be in a lucid and steady state of mind. Or, to put it another way, not sufficiently shell-shocked to be excused duty. In the midst of this most desperate of battles, with the body of the British Army haemorrhaging men as if from every artery, each extra man who could fight must fight. And so poor, bewildered Private Hopkins had been tossed from the temporary safety of gaol into the fierce heat of battle.

Hopkins turned to see why McCroon had pulled his arm.

Kingsley noted no spark of recognition in his eyes – eyes that, like every man's in that cauldron of exploding sulphurous mud and smoke, were red and watery. Perhaps Hopkins's vision was too blurred to see, perhaps a muzzle flash from the German fusillade had momentarily bedazzled him. For whatever reason, he was never to greet again the man who had cleared his name because just as he had turned to look, drawing upon the thin, bent cigarette clamped between his lips, just as the ember glowed hot, he died. He was blown into countless pieces of 'wet dust' by a German mortar shell.

Once more Kingsley was coated with the remains of a British soldier, but this time it was the remains of a British soldier *whom he had killed*. Kingsley understood it all in an instant. Even as the man disintegrated in front of him. Even as his suddenly dead flesh splattered into Kingsley's face, coating his mouth. Even as Kingsley *tasted Hopkins's blood*, he knew that he had killed the man. For had he not proved successful in his investigation of the murder weapon, had he not retrieved a bullet from the chest of a German cook, had Kingsley never come to France at all but instead refused and returned to prison, facing the fate he had chosen for himself, then Hopkins would still be in his cell. Safe for a few more days at least.

Kingsley had lifted the shadow of the death sentence from this man only to witness a different death sentence being passed upon him instantly.

The guilt and the confusion of these momentary reflections would return to haunt Kingsley many times, but for the moment they were literally blown from his head by a second mortar shell, which briefly concussed both him and McCroon and hurled them together into a shell hole.

It was fortunate indeed that the concussion was brief, for the hole into which they had been flung was at least five feet deep and, like every other indentation upon that blasted plain, was entirely full of water. Kingsley, half drowned when he regained consciousness, spluttered and puked his way to the surface and was then able to reach down and pull up McCroon. He had swallowed even more water than Kingsley and was in a poor way. Kingsley held the man's head above the water, jammed him against the side of the hole and attempted to revive him with a slap. The moment that Kingsley perceived the signs of returning consciousness in McCroon's face, he turned once more to the task that had led him into the battle.

'Tell me about visiting Hopkins on the night Abercrombie died,' he shouted.

For a moment there was total incomprehension on McCroon's face.

'What the fuck . . .' he said finally, coughing up the filthy water he had swallowed.

'Tell me about your visit to Hopkins,' Kingsley shouted a second time.

McCroon stared at him in amazement.

'Hopkins is dead, you fucking lunatic. He just *fucking died*, didn't you see?'

'What did you hear going on in the ward next door?'

'This is a battle, you mad bastard! Do you hear me?'

A third voice intruded, loud and commanding. That accent again, the one which ruled the world.

'You men! I say, you men down there! Attend to me! Are you hurt?'

Kingsley looked round to see an officer standing on the edge of the shell hole staring down at them.

'You don't look hurt,' the officer said. 'Get out of there this instant, you bloody cowards, and do your duty!'

'I am a police—'

The officer levelled his pistol at Kingsley. He was clearly in no mood for a debate and what was left of Kingsley's military policeman's uniform was concealed below the surface of the water.

'This instant, you malingering swine! Advance towards the enemy immediately or I will shoot!'

Kingsley saw the man's finger whiten on the trigger. He knew that the British service revolver, once cocked, responded to very little pressure.

'I shall count to three!' the officer shouted. 'One . . . !'

Kingsley could scarcely believe it but he was going to have to rejoin the assault.

'All right!' he cried, and began to search about himself for a way to climb out of the hole.

Just then, however, the officer disappeared, or at least his head did. Something had blown it clean off at his shoulders. The headless body stood where it had stood a moment before, the gun still in its hand, and then it toppled forward into the shell hole, splashing down beside Kingsley and sinking beneath the murky surface under the weight of its kit.

Once more Kingsley turned his attention to McCroon.

'Tell me what you heard the night you made baskets with Hopkins.'

'*He's dead*, you lunatic. Don't you understand? It doesn't matter. We're all going to die!'

Kingsley slapped McCroon again across the face, and even in that moment he reflected that this was the first time in his career that he had ever laid a hand on a witness during an interrogation.

'Just answer my question, Private!'

Kingsley could feel his feet sinking into the mud beneath him. McCroon was also slipping, sliding down the side of the hole against which Kingsley had jammed him. Only their heads were above water and it was becoming a struggle to breathe. Just in time Kingsley found a firmer footing. It was soft but solid, and without much emotion he realized that he must now be standing upon the body of the headless officer.

'Answer my question!'

McCroon tried to focus his thoughts.

'There was a row. Next door, Abercrombie and another officer. That's all I know.'

'You have spoken before of having sighted an officer in the corridor when you visited the water closets. When was that?'

'I don't know, I don't have a watch. It was on my way back to my own ward from Hopkins's.'

'On your way back? That was before Nurse Murray had finished in the ward then?'

'She'd only just started . . . Look, what does it matter, you fucking fool!'

'It definitely matters. Are you sure?' Kingsley shouted. 'Think, man, think.'

'Yes, I'm sure. She'd only just come in.'

'Describe the officer you sighted.'

'I only saw him from behind. He pushed past me.'

'Describe exactly what you saw.'

'He was an officer! You're all the same, all cunts!'

'Describe what you saw!'

Suddenly Kingsley had the man by the throat. McCroon responded to the threat.

'He had a sort of briefcase! Not a big one, a soft, thin little one.'

'A music case?'

Kingsley knew that this was leading the witness but the circumstances were peculiarly urgent.

'Was it a music case?'

'I don't know what the fuck a music case is. It was an old, thin little brown leather case. That's all I know.'

Just then an enormous piece of ordnance exploded overhead. The battle was showing no signs of abating and Kingsley decided he had probably got as much from the witness as he could. He had discovered something new and highly significant: McCroon had left Hopkins's ward *before* Kitty Murray had done so.

Kingsley let go of his witness's throat so that the man briefly slipped below the water. He instantly emerged, spluttering.

'Good bye, McCroon, and good luck,' Kingsley said.

'What?' the man replied, as bewildered at the sudden ending of their acquaintance as he had been at its beginning.

'I said good luck,' and with that Kingsley scrambled and slithered his way up over the lip of the shell hole, facing back towards the British line.

There were more and more Tommies rising up out of the trench from which Kingsley had himself emerged a few minutes earlier and it was eerie to see so many of them fall the moment they reached the surface. Kingsley had been fortunate indeed to get as far as he had done. Now he had to get back.

He put his head down, held up his warrant card and ran. This was not his battle; he had merely visited it. He had a case to solve and the rest of the puzzle lay elsewhere. Fortunately for him, the water in the shell hole had washed a great deal of the mud and gore from his uniform and so his red police tabs were visible once more.

'Police! Police!' he shouted as he scrambled through the on-coming men.

Perhaps they heard him, perhaps they saw his warrant card. Either way they did not shoot or bayonet him and he made it back to the line from which the British had begun their assault. For a moment he crouched on the edge of the trench as men pushed past him, moving up into the battle. He could not resist turning back to take one final look at the scene.

The dead were piled high right across the sea of mud, but the first of the British assault had arrived at the German trenches. He could see them struggling to pass the wire, which the bombardment had failed to destroy entirely, and the German machine-gunners were pumping lead into them at point-blank range. The Germans were suffering heavily too. In order to gain a field of fire their gunners must needs expose themselves, and they were continually being shot from their seats. Another gunner would leap up instantly to take his place. Both sides were fighting like cornered wild animals. Kingsley had never seen such blind courage and on such a scale. It was an awe-inspiring sight.

Just then he saw McCroon. In the grey light he was raising himself from the shell hole. He had his back to Kingsley and was facing the enemy, clearly intent on rejoining the battle. He had had some time to catch his breath and had no doubt reflected that, being unharmed, he must fight on or risk being shot later for cowardice. He hauled his trunk above the lip and, struggling to bring a leg over, managed to extricate himself from the hole. Then, taking up the rifle of his fallen comrade Hopkins, he advanced once more towards the German guns.

46

A literary discussion under pleasant circumstances

Kingsley made it back as far as the artillery line before he collapsed. He had had scarcely any sleep for two nights and during that time had been involved in a ferocious trench raid and a full-scale infantry assault. So far the accompanying adrenalin had kept him going but now, in relative safety behind the forward line, he succumbed suddenly to complete exhaustion. The guns were silent for the moment and men and horses of the Royal Artillery lay about him under whatever shelter they could find from the rain. Kingsley had just sufficient energy left to kick apart some ammunition boxes, the broken boards of which he laid upon the mud. On this poor bed and with the cold comfort of a torn and sodden gas cape to shield him from the pouring rain, he slept for two hours.

On waking he was able to cadge a mug of tea from the gunners, who of course viewed him and his red tabs with the greatest suspicion, and then he began to make his way back to Merville. Having interviewed McCroon, he now had some idea of the direction in which his investigation was heading, but he was also aware that he desperately needed further rest, a wash and some dry clothes if he was to continue to function effectively.

The ordered chaos in the immediate vicinity of what was a

fairly fluid front line, a line constantly vulnerable to enemy counter-attack, was breathtaking in its scale. Everywhere men and horses struggled against the mud and the confusion. Some moved forward, some back. Some were wounded, some whole. All of them, to Kingsley, seemed lost. In search of destinations and formations which had all melded into one in the thick porridge of mud and corpses to which two mighty armies clung.

It took Kingsley the rest of the day to struggle the few miles back out of the battle zone and towards his billet, and darkness was falling once more when, shivering and exhausted, he fetched up at the Café Cavell.

Utterly done in though he was, he knew at once that something was up when he saw the faces of the men sitting round the table. They had not fought that day and so had the strength and spirit for sport, and they were smirking and nudging one another as Kingsley called for Madame in the hope of arranging for hot water.

'You have a visitor,' the woman said. 'She said she would wait in your room.'

Even in his cold, sodden and exhausted state Kingsley could not help but feel a surge of excitement. He knew only one woman in all of France and Belgium, and only one woman knew him.

Staff Nurse Kitty Murray.

Kingsley went upstairs and opened the door. She was sitting on his bed, reading some papers she had brought with her.

'Gosh,' she said, looking up at him. 'Well, I must say, you *are* in a state.'

'Hello, Kitty,' Kingsley said, and he knew how pleased he was to see her.

'I had thought that when you came I should leap up and kiss you whether you wanted me to or not but I'm very much afraid now that I shan't. I have on my nicest blouse and you look as if you've just crawled out of a very nasty hole.'

'I have.'

It *was* a nice blouse. Pale green silk and daringly open at the collar. She was smiling so prettily too. He wished she would kiss him.

'Where have you been?' she asked. 'When I got back yesterday I heard you'd been at the château digging up corpses. I came here looking for you and waited till nine but you didn't come.'

'I was in pursuit of a witness. Why were you looking for me?'

'Aren't you pleased?'

'I'm very pleased. I just wondered.'

'Well, actually, I do sort of have a proper reason. I have a message from that Military Police sergeant. I must say he seemed much nicer than when I first met him.'

'He gave you a message for me?'

'Well, he wanted to deliver it himself, of course, but you weren't there and he couldn't wait all day so he gave it to me. Aren't I the lucky one? He told me to tell you that there is no record of a Colonel Willow at Staff.'

'No, I had rather suspected there wouldn't be.'

'It all sounds fearfully sinister. What witness were you pursuing?'

'A soldier, McCroon.'

'Ah, Hopkins's Bolshevik pal.'

'That's right. I followed him over the top. I must say, I've had easier chases.'

'You've been in the battle for Passchendaele?' she asked, her eyes growing wide with surprise, and also, it seemed to Kingsley, with some excitement.

'Yes.'

'Coo, you jolly well don't make life easy for yourself, do you? I heard we took a fearful mauling.'

'Yes, I rather think we did.'

'Well, you'd better get your togs off, Captain.'

'My togs?'

'Yes, and be quick about it too. Look at you, you're shivering pretty badly, and here's us standing round chatting. If you're not careful you'll develop a fever. So come on, chop chop. I'll get some water.'

Nurse Murray marched smartly from the room and Kingsley began to undress. He *was* shivering and he had not remotely the strength to consider the social niceties. He was in his wet and filthy underwear when Murray returned with towels and a basin of hot water.

'*All* your togs, Captain. Those long johns are dripping wet and besides, they look like they could march into battle on their own. Coo. Pretty lively on the nose too! *Pongo!* Come on, look sharp now, I am a staff nurse, you know.'

Feeling only slightly self-conscious, Kingsley did as he was told and removed his underwear. Nurse Murray dipped a towel into the hot water and began to wash him. For Kingsley, who had recently experienced nothing but extreme physical discomfort, it was a wonderful thing to be cleaned and ministered to by such a deft and charming young woman. He had just closed his eyes and begun to luxuriate in the unfamiliar tenderness of the sensation when she brought them open again, wide with surprise.

'Golly. That *is* a big one, isn't it?' she said, while with absolute confidence and candour she began to flannel his private parts. Kingsley could think of nothing to say in reply.

'Quite *scary* really, now that I see it in the light. Did I really get that in my mouth?'

'Uhm . . .'

'Gosh. I think I should get a prize!'

'Kitty, I don't think I have ever in my life met so frank a girl as you.'

'Woman, Captain. I'm twenty-two and a *woman*. One of the ways men diminish women's status *and* our contribution whilst simultaneously entrenching their quasi-paternal male authority is to call us *girls*. *Girls* go to school, Captain. *Women* tend the wounded, make the shells and drive the ambulances.'

And, occasionally, brazenly wash the private parts of near strangers, Kingsley thought to himself.

'Well then,' he said, 'you're a very frank woman.'

'And you're a very handsome chap. Did you know that,

314

Captain? I expect your wife has told you. Has she? Don't be modest. I've thought about you heaps since the other night when we made the beast with two backs outside in the soft refreshing rain. Do you think I'm pretty? Do say you do even if secretly you don't.'

'I think you're very pretty.'

'Good-oh. I shan't ask again, I just wanted you to say it.'

'You don't have to ask me, Kitty. I'll say it anyway, happily. I think you're very, very pretty and also rather splendid.'

'Ta very much.'

He meant it too. He could not help himself. She *was* splendid. Perhaps it was the awful experiences he had been through; perhaps also there was a touch of the 'quasi-paternalism' of an older man for an idealistic young girl, a notion that Kitty no doubt would have resented hugely. Perhaps it was simply because she was beautiful and funny and entirely refreshing. Probably all those things and more, for there was no doubt that at that moment Kingsley felt an enormous affection for Kitty Murray. He did not love her. He could not love her, for he loved Agnes and Kingsley did not believe that a man could ever truly love more than one woman at a time. To love someone new it would first be necessary to cease to love one's old love and Kingsley had certainly not done that, and he believed he never would. But he *liked* Nurse Murray enormously, so very much indeed that the sensation was rather like love. And she *was* very, very pretty.

'Shall I get my togs off too then?' she asked. 'Just to make it even Stephens?'

She asked it with her usual chirpy brashness but Kingsley could see that she was blushing. The last time they had been in such a situation it had been in near-total darkness. Kingsley was charmed and perhaps slightly relieved to discover that even the surprising Nurse Murray had some limitations to her candour.

'I don't know that you should,' Kingsley replied hesitatingly.

'Thought you said I was pretty?'

'You are, extremely.'

'Well then,' she replied.

And then, eschewing further discussion, she undressed in front of him, not slowly or seductively as Agnes was wont to do but briskly, almost officiously, folding her garments quickly and neatly as she removed them. Nonetheless she avoided meeting Kingsley's eye and it seemed to him that, despite her aggressively modish disregard for the accepted norms of behaviour, beneath it all Kitty Murray was as shy and self-conscious as anyone might be in such a situation, and that she resented herself for it.

As she undressed she talked.

'I heard that you have managed to prove Private Hopkins didn't do the deed,' she said, taking off her shoes. 'I was so pleased. Told you he was innocent, didn't I?'

'Yes, you did.'

She was unbuttoning her blouse now.

'Terribly clever of you, comparing the bullets like that. Who would have thought it?'

Under her blouse she wore a delicate, cream-coloured silk slip. Crossing her arms and gripping the hem she pulled it up over her head. She had on no corset or brassiere, and Kingsley saw everything as the lacy garment rose. First her navel, then her small shapely breasts, then the hair under her arms as she raised her elbows above her head. He wanted to put his nose into it and breathe deeply.

'So will they release him?' she asked, draping the silky slip across the back of a chair. She was now naked from the waist up, fine-boned and exquisite. Her bobbed hair fell no further than just below her ears. Kingsley had never before seen a woman's neck, shoulders and breasts thus exposed. Always in his past experience there had been unpinned, cascading hair partially obscuring the view, which was lovely too, of course, but this clearer, starker style was undeniably erotic. Kitty's petite frame, with its small, dainty breasts, slim shoulders, distinct collar bone and delicately curved neck, seemed to have been made to be crowned with just such a spartan coiffure.

'They've released him already,' Kingsley answered, 'and now he's dead. Killed in action before Passchendaele this morning.'

'Coo. How's your luck, eh? Poor chap.'

She pulled up her skirt and began to unfasten her drawers. She leaned forward slightly to do so and her little breasts hung down before her. Kingsley wanted to reach forward and take one in each hand. He did not do so, although it would have been idle for him to pretend that he was not aroused; he was naked himself and the evidence stood out before him.

'I wanted to ask you,' Kingsley said, 'did you ever read those poems that Lieutenant Stamford gave you?'

'Actually I did,' Kitty replied, wriggling out of her drawers and unfastening her belt. 'Very strange. I was expecting all patriotism and naïve glory and in fact it's the opposite – mud, blood, disease and death, really gloomy, disillusioned stuff.'

Now she undid her skirt, letting it fall to the ground, and stood for a moment naked save for her gartered stockings. Then she picked up the skirt and placed it neatly on the chair.

'Shall I leave my stockings on?' she said. 'Some chaps really like that and I must say I think it's rather a jolly look. Terribly French, don't you think?'

'Kitty, how many "chaps" have there been?'

'Twenty-four. I keep notes. I *am* a bad girl, aren't I?'

'A bad woman.'

'It's all right if *I* call myself a girl, that's totally different from when a man does it. What about you then? How many lucky, lucky, lucky little flappers have you pleasured, monsieur?'

'I don't know. Five or six, I think.'

'Does it bother you that I've rutted with so many chaps?'

'Yes, I think it does a little, if I'm honest. I suppose I should like to have been more special.'

'You are special. I'm here, aren't I? And I *very* rarely order the same dish twice. If I didn't believe that romantic love is a myth I think I could fall in love with you.'

317

Kitty took from her bag the big rubber sheath.

'There certainly isn't anything romantic about the way you go about *making* love, is there, Kitty?'

'Ah-ha. That's a man talking, you see. How would it be if I got preggers, eh? I'd be in a fearful fix. You men don't think about that very much, do you? Not your problem.'

With that, Kitty reached up and, taking his face between her hands just as she had done beneath the trees, she kissed him long and fiercely, pulling him down on to the bed beside her.

When Kingsley had arrived at the café he had thought himself good for nothing and ready to drop but the sensation of Nurse Murray's taut young body against his had totally revitalized him. Despite the ever-present guilt, he was incapable of not returning her kisses with equal intensity.

Then they made love and afterwards they fell asleep.

Kingsley awoke again shortly after dawn, once more consumed by the guilt that had beset him after the last time he had made love to Kitty Murray. She did not even open her eyes but it was as if she'd read his thoughts.

'Don't worry,' she said, 'the war means different rules. Nothing that happens out here goes home and nobody who wasn't here will ever know what it was like, so who are they to judge us?'

'Shannon made that point to me once.'

'I don't want to talk about Captain Shannon,' she said quickly. 'Anyway, you must promise me you won't tell your wife about this; she doesn't need to know and she wouldn't understand anyway. Out here we need to take our comfort where we can. Besides, I should simply *die* if I ever thought I was being loathed by some poor woman I had never even met.'

'My wife and I . . . She left me.'

Kitty sat bolt upright in bed, the sheet falling from her naked shoulders.

'No! Really? I say, that *is* jolly news. I mean, sorry and all that but well . . . More fool her, say I.'

Kingsley did not reply. He was thinking of Agnes. Kitty also fell silent, looking thoughtful and saying nothing for as long as it took her to smoke a cigarette.

'Look here,' she said finally, 'how about this? What say you and *I* be sweethearts? Wouldn't *that* be fun? Sometimes I *long* to go legit, life can get so *jolly lonely*, can't it? So do say yes, it would be *such* a lark and I'm sure we'd have *heaps* of fun.'

Kingsley looked at her. She was trying so hard to appear breezy and casual as she lit her second cigarette but he could see that she meant what she was saying.

'I'm sorry, Kitty,' he said gently, 'but I'm afraid I still love my wife.'

'Bother!' she said, bringing her clenched fist down hard on his chest. '*So* inconsiderate of you to be so jolly fascinating!'

'I thought you hated policemen?'

'I do. I hate them *especially* now.'

There was a catch in her voice and she was looking away, smoking furiously. It was obvious to Kingsley that in the short time they had known each other this young woman had begun to imagine herself in love with him. It made him feel wretched. As if he had now deceived two women about whom he cared.

'I'm sorry,' he said.

'Oh, *do* put a sock in it,' Nurse Murray replied.

Then, grinding out her cigarette, she threw herself on top of him once more and pressed her mouth angrily against his. Kingsley had definitely not been intending to make love to her again, particularly now she had revealed herself as far more emotionally vulnerable than she pretended. However, as she pulled at him with deliberate roughness, tugging him towards and inside her, he realized that in part it was her pride which was making her rush so ostentatiously to return their relationship to a purely physical plane. She had momentarily opened her heart and now she wished to show that she had not been hurt in the process. Her body was *demanding* that he make love to her once more, to set the record straight, so to speak, and so that they might part on equal emotional terms. Kingsley did not feel he could deny her.

And of course she was very, *very* pretty.

When they were done, once more Kingsley returned to a subject that he had intended to return to hours earlier, before sex and sleep had got in the way.

'You say that Stamford's poetry is angry?'

'Oh yes, terribly intense. Absolutely stuffed with regiments of ghosts, gas-corrupted lungs, unforgiving guns sowing death where once golden wheat had grown and all the general hell of war.'

'Rather strange for a man who had yet to see action, don't you think?'

'Well, when I was at school I wrote a poem about being a hand-maiden to the Queen of Sheba and I hadn't experienced that.'

'All the same, it does seem rather presumptuous to write about the hell of war before you've even dipped a toe in it.'

'Well, that's how poetry's going at the moment, nobody wants the glory, glory stuff at all. Particularly since Siegfried Sassoon sent his letter to *The Times*. I reckon poor old Abercrombie's lucky he died when he did. He's totally out of fashion now amongst the smart set. I suppose Stamford's just aping his betters; lots of aspiring writers do.'

Kingsley looked up at her. She was still sitting astride him, so very sweet and, for all her numerous lovers, so very innocent.

'I must say, for such a clever young woman you're being rather dense, Kitty,' he said.

'Ta very much, I'm sure. And how do you make that out?'

'Because it's absolutely obvious that Stamford did not write those poems.'

47

Confessions of a plagiarist

Kingsley and Nurse Murray rose and got dressed.

'Fresh bloomers,' said Kitty, producing a pair from her bag. 'Fresh bloomers and a toothbrush, the new woman's survival kit for an evening on the tiles.'

'That and your trusty rubber sheath.'

'Ah yes. I'm *always* forgetting that,' she said, taking it from the bed and rinsing it in the basin of water with which she had washed Kingsley the night before. 'Wash it properly later but it's *so* much easier if you can give it a quick rinse before all the semen dries. *Such* a bore if you don't.'

Kingsley felt that he did not really need to know the details; charming though Nurse Murray's candour was, at times it could get a little much. They went downstairs together and had breakfast in full view of the Tommies who had gathered for the same purpose. Kitty had been horrified at Kingsley's suggestion that she might like to breakfast upstairs and depart discreetly.

'Petty moral strictures are what keep women oppressed. Men go whoring when they please but insist that women be ashamed of sex.'

'I've never been whoring.'

'All right, *some* men go whoring. Anyway, I am a *new woman* and I have nothing to hide. *Particularly* from *men*.'

And so they had gone downstairs together and Kitty had ordered bread, ham and eggs in a loud, bossy voice.

'Got to refuel after a *really* vigorous night, what!' she said.

Kingsley wished he could disappear under the table.

He had decided to accompany Kitty back to the château. He felt it would be discourteous not to do so. In addition, she had told him that Lieutenant Stamford would be joining her for lunch and bringing her more of his poems.

'Aren't his lot in battle at the moment?' Kingsley said.

'Yes, they moved back up the morning after the concert and he copped a bullet in the arm. Might even be a Blighty, lucky so-and-so. He's waiting for orders, that's why he's so anxious to see me. He's acquitted himself well, though. I spoke to his medical officer: apparently he made the first German line in the original assault, the one which proved too much for Abercrombie.'

'A good actor and a good soldier,' Kingsley said, 'but my guess is *not* a poet.'

They walked back to the château through the pouring rain, passing beneath the trees under which they had lain together four days previously. Kitty suggested that they might pause a while and relive the moment, but Kingsley declined. The revelation that she had so quickly developed feelings for him had redoubled the guilt he felt over their relationship. He had not only betrayed Agnes but he was also toying with the emotions of a woman who, for all her tough exterior and considerable sexual experience, was very young and vulnerable.

When they arrived at the château, Stamford was there waiting, his right arm in a sling.

'Captain Marlowe also has an interest in poetry,' Kitty said. 'Would you mind if he joined us, Lieutenant?'

'Heavens, no!' said Stamford. 'The more the merrier.'

Kitty excused herself to go and change out of her wet clothes, suggesting that Kingsley and Stamford wait for her in a small conservatory. They sat down together in front of the elegant French windows that overlooked the scene of Stamford's thespian triumphs a few nights earlier.

'I suppose it will be a while before you're swinging your Charlie Chaplin cane again, Lieutenant,' Kingsley opined.

'Well, I still have my left arm and, do you know, looking at his films I rather think the little tramp is ambidextrous.'

'I hear you had a good battle?'

'I don't know about that. I just tried not to funk it and things turned out all right. This time they did, at any rate.'

Kingsley lit a cigarette and offered one to Stamford.

'Actually I'll have one of my own if that's all right,' he replied, and produced from his box a long pink cigarette with a gold filter. 'They're called Harlequins. Rather jolly, don't you think? They come in every colour except boring old white. The fellows do rib me about them but I don't care. Just because one has become a soldier doesn't mean that one can't still have a bit of style. Don't you agree, Captain?'

Kingsley conceded that Stamford had made a good point.

'My favourite ones are the black ones,' the lieutenant went on. 'Terribly sinister and sophisticated. I'd show you one but I'm all out – smoke them first, you see. Can't resist.'

Kingsley nodded.

'Black and gold. Wonderful. When I have my own house I shall have my bedroom curtains all in black and gold.'

Kingsley paused. It was time to change the subject.

'I believe you visited Viscount Abercrombie on the day he died, Lieutenant?'

Stamford was clearly somewhat taken aback, and his face clouded.

'Yes. Yes, I did. I wanted to . . . you know, cheer him up. Fellow officer and all that. He'd been kind to me on the eve of the battle.'

'And having cheered him up, when did you leave him?'

'I don't know . . . Whenever one is supposed to leave, I imagine.

323

I must have gone when they chucked us out. At the end of visiting time.'

Stamford was an appalling liar and his face had turned bright red.

'He was heard having a quarrel with someone, another man, in his room considerably after the time at which visitors are required to leave.'

The long pink cigarette was shaking between Stamford's fingers. Ash was falling on to the polished tiles of the floor.

'Really?' he said. 'Who could that have been, I wonder?'

'I thought perhaps you might know.'

'Good lord, why on earth would I . . . ? No, I have no idea.'

'The man was seen.'

Stamford gulped audibly and tiny beads of sweat appeared on his brow. Kingsley could not remember a suspect who was so easy to rattle. This man would not make much of a poker player.

Just then, and to Stamford's obvious relief, Kitty Murray returned, allowing him a moment to collect himself. She was not the sort of person to dawdle over anything so mundane as changing her clothes, particularly if something exciting was going on elsewhere. Nonetheless, Kingsley thought she now looked rather splendid: her hair and skin shone and her fashionably short calf-length skirt showed off her shapely ankles to perfection. Such health and vitality were a genuine tonic after the many terrible sights of the last few days. There was such a terrific energy to Kitty that a room felt more alive simply because she had entered it.

'Haven't missed the fun, have I?' she asked.

If Stamford wondered what she meant by this he did not pursue it, preferring to concentrate his attention on Kingsley.

'You say that the man was seen, Captain? Do you have . . . a description?'

'Only details. He was carrying a little case apparently. A music case . . .' said Kingsley, staring at Stamford, whose eyes revealed his shock.

'A music case, you say?'

'Yes, a soft, old, brown leather music case . . . Rather like the one I saw you with on the night of the concert. I see you have it with you now.'

Kingsley left the words hanging in the air. The silence that followed crackled with tension as Stamford struggled to find a response.

'Right then,' Kitty said after an awkward silence. 'These poems you gave me to read, Lieutenant. Gosh. They're pretty strong stuff.'

'You like them?' Stamford asked, and despite his discomfort he could not help but pounce on the possibility of literary praise.

'Yes, I think they're rather moving, although I don't know if *like* is exactly the right word,' Nurse Murray replied. 'They certainly grab one's attention.'

Kitty produced the sheafs of paper that Stamford had given her and began to pick out some quotes. '*Young men bent double, coughing like hags . . . Foul stew of limb and gut/Painted on the parapet wall . . . Charming girls who sing "Forever England"/ And send brave men to scream in Hell.* How old are you, Lieutenant?'

'Nineteen.'

'And how many days have you spent in forward trenches?'

'Fifteen.'

'Yet you write about gas, shelling, bayonets, trench raids, dressing stations . . . Good heavens, there's scarcely a single aspect of military life which you haven't experienced and, what is more, come to loathe. And all this *in fifteen days?*'

'Well, I talked to the other fellows . . . I . . . used my imagination.'

'In fifteen days, Lieutenant?'

Now Stamford was silent, staring at the floor.

'Who is the Golden Boy?' Nurse Murray asked.

'Just a figure. I made him up.'

'He seems to have meant a great deal to you.'

325

'Not really. It's just poetry.'

'Oh? You didn't seem to feel that way when you wrote about him. By far the most moving passages of the poems you gave me concern this Golden Boy and his death in action. It's a theme to which you return over and over again. It seems to me, reading between the lines, that all the hatred of this war that screams out from your poems emanates from the anger and grief that you feel at the dreadful loss of this fallen comrade, this *golden boy* whose . . .' Nurse Murray searched for a particular passage, '*Precious blood fell full and flooded/On that foul tunic belonging to the King,/Washed it and made it pure.*'

'I don't know anything about the Golden Boy,' Stamford mumbled. 'He's a metaphor.'

'A metaphor? For what?'

'Well . . . all of us . . . They're just poems.'

Then Kingsley spoke.

'Yes, and as a matter of record, they are in fact *Viscount Abercrombie's* poems, aren't they?'

The young man did not speak but instead miserably massaged his cigarette case between his sweating palms.

'You stole them from him, didn't you?' Kingsley insisted.

This aroused Stamford from his anguished silence.

'No!' he said, looking fiercely at Kingsley. 'They're mine!'

'You wrote them?'

'He . . . gave them to me.'

'Gave them to you to claim as your own?'

Stamford turned to Nurse Murray, shouting now.

'They're mine! Give them back!'

Suddenly he lunged forward and tried to grab what papers he could from Kitty's lap.

'Steady on!' she exclaimed, pushing him away. 'No shenanigans now, Lieutenant!'

Stamford, denied the poems, panicked. He leaped up and rushed the French windows, setting his good shoulder against them and bursting through. Kingsley had noted at the concert how agile the young man was, and despite his wounded arm Stamford was through the windows almost before Kingsley had scrambled to his feet.

'Hold hard, you bloody fool!' Kingsley shouted but Stamford was already tearing across the lawn, dashing through the middle of a desultory, rain-sodden football game and setting a course for the woods. Kingsley set off in pursuit but Stamford was only nineteen and had a dancer's fitness. What was more, fear gave him speed.

'Stop that man!' Kingsley shouted at the footballers, but whether they thought him mad or simply were not minded to respond to the voice of authority, the players made no more effort to chase Stamford than they had been doing to chase the ball.

Then, just as the panic-stricken lieutenant had reached the comparative safety of the edge of the woods, he stopped and sank to his knees.

By the time Kingsley came up beside him, the young man was curled up in the long wet grass, weeping.

'He said he didn't want them,' Stamford stuttered.

'So you took them from him?'

'He gave them to me. He told me to burn them.'

Kingsley, who until he had attempted a two-hundred-metre dash had not realized how exhausted and out of condition his body was, sank down in the grass beside the sobbing man.

'But you decided not to burn them?'

'I couldn't do it. They were too good, too special.'

'And besides, you had already decided to copy them out in your own hand and take the credit for them.'

Stamford looked up at Kingsley, tears rolling down his face and mixing with the rain and the sweat. His face shone like a waxwork.

'They're wonderful poems. They should be seen!'

'Under your name?'

The young man hung his head.

'I couldn't resist it. After he died I thought, why not? It doesn't matter to him, he'd disowned them, and perhaps I could be famous too . . . And anyway . . . I wanted to punish him.'

'Punish a dead man? Why?'

There was a long pause before Stamford replied.

'For not loving me the way he loved that damned Golden Boy! For not loving me *at all.*'

'Was that why you quarrelled with him, that night in his room? The night he died?'

'I told you it wasn't me . . . I'd left . . . I wasn't there . . . I . . .'

Kingsley waited. It was clear that Stamford was about to break and, sure enough, moments later the young man gave up all pretence. He might have been a good actor on the stage but in a real-life drama he had neither the wit nor the spirit to dissemble further.

'Yes. I was there. And we quarrelled. I tried to keep my voice down but I was so . . . *angry* with him.'

'Because he didn't love you?'

'He *used me.*'

'No, I don't think so.' It was Nurse Murray who spoke. She had followed them and stood looking at them now, wiping the rain from her glasses on her nurse's apron, squinting short-sightedly as the rain dripped from the tip of her nose. 'You gave him what it was that he wanted from you but he was incapable of giving you what you wanted from him. That is not the same as using someone.'

'He didn't give me anything!'

'He gave you his poems,' Murray replied. 'And it appears to me that the man who wrote those poems had nothing more to give to anybody, Lieutenant. He was hollow inside. *An empty cup*, as he wrote himself, *drained to the dregs.* A man with a broken heart.'

'*But not about me*,' Stamford wailed. 'His heart wasn't broken about me! I worshipped him. He was my hero.'

'He didn't want to be *anybody's* hero, Stamford,' Nurse Murray explained. 'Can't you see that? You've read his poems. It's obvious that he'd come to hate the very *idea* of heroes. He hated the fact that his poems had played their part in making people want to *be* heroes.'

'He was *my* hero. That's different. I loved him.'

'And is that why you shot him?' Kingsley asked. 'Because he didn't love you back?'

'I did not shoot him! I never would have hurt him! I tell you, I loved him.'

'In my experience love is easily the equal of hate when it comes to provoking murder.'

'No!'

'You wanted to steal his poems.'

'No. Never! That came afterwards. After I left . . . After he'd gone. I wanted revenge because *he'd left me!*'

'Stamford, he was *murdered*,' Kingsley pressed.

'*I know that!* Who was in his room? *Why* was there another man in his room? Had Alan been looking for comfort again? That was his taste, Captain Marlowe, a new fellow, no strings, no attachments – believe me, I know it. Loveless comfort! That was what he took from me. Perhaps he went looking for loveless comfort again? Not every man is as obliging as I was!'

'You think Viscount Abercrombie was murdered by an angry lover?'

'Yes!'

'But not you?'

'No. It was a private, they say. Hopkins. Some poor shell-shocked fellow. I expect Alan couldn't resist him. Or perhaps Hopkins was blackmailing him and they fought. Alan was in terror that anyone would ever know that he . . . that he was . . .'

'The love that dare not speak its name,' Nurse Murray said quietly.

'Yes,' Stamford replied, 'the love that dare not speak its name.'

Stamford was shivering now and he began to sneeze, snot adding to the mix of rain, tears and sweat on his waxen face. Nurse Murray was shivering too.

'We should talk inside,' she said, 'get some tea.'

329

The three of them returned to the conservatory, wet through yet again. Kingsley reflected that no one was ever truly dry in Flanders.

Once towels had been brought and tea made, it seemed that Stamford had collected himself somewhat. At least he had stopped crying.

'Private Hopkins did not kill your friend,' Kingsley said.

'Well, it wasn't me, I swear.'

'You were the last person to see him alive.'

'Except his killer.'

'Unless you are his killer.'

'I'm not!'

'Look at it from my point of view, Stamford, the point of view of the investigating officer. You visit Abercrombie, you have a furious row with him, you are seen sneaking out of his room long after you were supposed to have left the building. Shortly there-after he is found dead, and now you turn up claiming his work as your own. It doesn't look good, does it?'

'No,' Nurse Murray chimed in, 'it jolly well doesn't.'

Stamford's face had gone from ashen to deathly.

'Tell me exactly what happened on the night of Abercrombie's death,' Kingsley said.

'I came to visit him during normal hours,' Stamford said. Then he added defiantly, 'We had been lovers before, you know.'

'Yes. I think I had gathered as much.'

'At first he was friendly. He asked me to stay and for a while I think it helped him that I was there. He was quite shell-shocked and we . . . we hugged.'

'But then you quarrelled?'

'Yes, because I felt used, and also because he had asked me to burn his poems. It made me so angry! I hated the way he'd turned against his writing. Then Nurse Murray made her rounds and I hid under the bed until she had gone. After that I tried to make up with Alan and asked to stay the night, but he was too angry and strange by then and he made me leave.'

'And you did?'

'Yes, I did. I swear I did, I swear I never hurt him.'

Kingsley looked long and hard at the shivering young lieutenant.

'No. No, I doubt that you would. You don't seem the type to me, not for violence. Besides, my witness recalled that he saw you carrying a music case. He would have noticed if you'd been carrying one of Abercrombie's boots as well.'

'I beg your pardon?'

'Nothing. It's not your concern.'

'Can I go then?'

'Just one other thing. Did Viscount Abercrombie ever mention a green envelope to you?'

Stamford's eyes widened in surprise.

'How did you know . . . ? Yes. Yes, he did. But I didn't have one to give him . . . I said I'd do my best to get one, but they're non-transferable, you know, you can't swap them around.'

'Very well then, Lieutenant,' Kingsley said. 'That will be all for the time being.'

Stamford rose to leave.

'May I have my poems back?' he asked Nurse Murray.

'No. No, I don't think so,' she replied.

'But he . . . he gave them to me.'

'He gave them to you to burn. You didn't do it when he asked you to and I don't believe I can trust you to do it now.'

'Surely you can't mean that you're actually going to burn them yourself?'

'Of course.'

'But they're beautiful, they're too good . . .'

'And they are also the work of a man who trusted you to dispose of them. It was, as it turned out, his dying wish. I intend to honour that wish.'

Defeated, Stamford walked to the door.

'It's funny,' he said. 'Do you know, if Alan had let me stay that night, when I asked him, perhaps he'd be alive today.'

'I rather think not, Lieutenant,' Kingsley said. 'You're a good Charlie Chaplin but I doubt you'd be much of a bodyguard. If you had spent the night with Abercrombie, I believe you would have been killed alongside him. Look at it that way, if you like. He saved your life.'

48

A rough ride

After Stamford had left, the first thing Kingsley did was to visit the château wireless office and send a telegram to Sir Mansfield Cumming in London:

I believe that the case is drawing to its conclusion. I intend shortly to produce your murderer. Please advise all interested parties.

Having seen this safely dispatched, Kingsley returned to the main entrance hall intent on once more beginning the weary journey up to the front. On his way out he encountered Nurse Murray, all dressed up for heavy weather in rubber boots and an ankle-length oilskin coat.

'I presume you're off investigating again?' she said.

'I have to visit Abercrombie's colonel,' Kingsley replied. 'If he tells me what I think he will tell me, then I believe the case will draw to its close. I have telegraphed London to tell them so.'

'Well, the battalion's back in the line, as you know, so time is of the essence,' Nurse Murray said, and with that she handed Kingsley a leather helmet and goggles. Having donned a similar set herself, she led him round to the stable block of the château, where stood a magnificent 500cc BSA motorcycle.

'Yours?' Kingsley enquired.

'Of course it's mine, you oaf,' Nurse Murray replied. 'You don't suppose I go about the place pinching bikes, do you? I'd pretty soon be collared – girls stand out like sore thumbs around here anyway, especially girls on bikes. Besides, if I *had* pinched it, do you really think I'd tell *you*?'

'No. I suppose not.'

'Don't like coppers. Told you that. Never have. Her name's Jemima –' she indicated the motorcycle – 'I can't take her out much any more because she's a thirsty girl and these days petrol's dearer than champagne and a damn sight harder to come by. Just let me get her started and then hop on.'

She mounted the machine and after only a couple of tries managed to kick-start it. No easy thing to achieve with a cold, wet, 1911 machine, Kingsley thought, particularly for a person of Nurse Murray's small size. It was obvious she was a fairly experienced rider, a fact which occasioned him considerable relief since the weather conditions were appalling and Murray's goggles were already thickly filmed with rain.

'Come on!' Nurse Murray shouted above the roar as she revved the engine in neutral to warm it up.

The bike had no passenger seat but there was a small luggage rack on which Nurse Murray had placed a rolled-up blanket to create an improvised pillion. Kingsley climbed aboard. As there were no handles, he leaned forward and put his arms around Murray.

'When I lean, you lean, all right?' she shouted. 'Now hang on!'

The engine roared and they were off down the gravel drive. Suddenly the wind and the rain flew into Kingsley's face and for a third of a mile or so they made quite the fastest progress Kingsley had done with any means of transport since disembarking from the Waterloo boat train. Soon, however, the gravel road ran out and they found themselves riding over the dreaded French cobblestones.

'Keep your teeth together,' Nurse Murray shouted as they bounced along, 'or you'll bite your tongue off.'

The BSA was bumping and slipping about on the deeply indented wet cobbles and Kingsley could feel the tension in Murray's body as she struggled to maintain a steady course. She certainly was an athletic type and, although not hugely strong, she clearly knew how to control the power of the machine and harness its erratic and ungainly motion to her best advantage. The road was of course very crowded, and Murray had constantly to stop or swerve to avoid parties of soldiers engaged in what seemed to Kingsley to be the same meaningless two-way scurrying that had continued without pause since first he arrived at the front. There were also numerous potholes and huge puddles to negotiate and Kingsley felt that they would be upset at every moment, but somehow Murray kept the machine upright. Before long, to Kingsley's great relief, for he had been rattled and shaken to the point where he feared that his joints would be dislocated, they came to the end of the cobbled road.

'Fifth Battalion East Lancs,' Murray shouted at a road marshal, who looked as if he had been constructed entirely from mud. 'Colonel Hilton commanding.'

The man could only wave them forward towards the guns, for the battle was still raging and the confusion everywhere within its orbit was considerable.

Kingsley was about to dismount and thank Nurse Murray for having got him thus far, but before he could do so she had twisted the throttle and launched the machine off the end of the cobbles and on to the chicken wire and planking which was all that lay between the army and the glutinous, sucking mud beneath it.

'You can't take this thing any further!' Kingsley shouted.

'Captain,' Murray shouted back, 'if they can get nine-inch howitzers further forward than this, I think Jemima should be able to make some progress.'

And sure enough, with Kingsley hanging on to Murray with all his might, they slithered, slipped and roared their way forward, forcing a path through trudging men and weary horses, constantly in danger of leaving the road (such as it was) and descending into the swamp on either side.

They passed a tank, the first Kingsley had ever seen. Wiping the mud from his goggles (as he and, more particularly, Nurse Murray had constantly to do), he could see that it had thrown one of its tracks and was now hopelessly bogged. In a ditch, almost upended, its nose was in the air and its two side-mounted guns pointing impotently skywards. It was like some great beached whale in armour plating, at once mighty and pathetic, its very size and strength mocked by its hopeless position. The eight-man crew, filthy, wretched troglodytes, were desperately attempting to commandeer horses in an effort to drag the helpless iron beast out of the hole into which it had sunk.

Finally they came upon the artillery line, those sombre rows of cannon amongst which Kingsley had snatched a few hours' sleep two nights before. The line was now a hundred yards or so further east, having crept a tiny step or two towards Germany. The men and horses of the Royal Artillery had laboured mightily to move their massive guns forward over the corpses of the infantry in order to consolidate the gains that those dead men had made. At the rate they were progressing, Kingsley realized, the exhausted gunners would not reach Berlin for several hundred years.

'This really is it for Jemima, I'm afraid,' Murray said, bringing the machine to a halt. 'Not even horses move beyond here, only men and rats.'

They both dismounted and could not help but laugh to see each other so entirely and utterly caked in mud. When they removed their goggles, Nurse Murray laughed even more.

'You look like a panda,' she said. 'A very nice but rather startled old panda.'

Artillerymen turned to look at her. Neither laughter nor a woman's voice was commonly heard in that terrible place. She waved at them and some returned her salutation with a grin, but they looked too exhausted to engage in further communication.

'You'll have to wait here till dark,' she said, turning once more to Kingsley. 'Can't move forward in the light. Ping! Bang! *Dead!* Boche snipers are the most dreadful cads but awfully good at their job, you know. Our boys too, of course.'

'Of course.'

There was a pause. Then Nurse Murray continued.

'I don't suppose . . . I don't suppose you'd let me come with you? You know, to find Hilton? I'm sure I could make myself useful.'

'I'm sure that if anybody could, you could, Kitty,' Kingsley replied. 'But I don't think the colonel would appreciate me arriving with a woman in tow.'

'Not the done thing, eh?'

'No. Not the done thing at all.'

'You know there's two Englishwomen in Ypres who've been running a dressing station there since 1915, right through all the battles? Organized it all themselves and everybody's jolly glad they did.'

'Kitty, I can't take you.'

'Righty-ho. Only asking.'

Nonetheless, as there were about three hours of daylight remaining, she insisted on staying with Kingsley for at least part of the time.

'Damned cold,' she said. 'We can cuddle.'

They parked the motorcycle and crawled beneath an ammunition limber, huddling together against the chill and damp.

'So who did it then?' Murray asked, having struggled for some minutes to light a cigarette for them to share. 'Who killed Abercrombie?'

'I'd rather not say at the moment,' he replied. 'Not until I have gathered all the information that I can.'

'Don't you trust me?'

'It has nothing to do with trust.'

'If you get shot, which the chances are you will, no one will ever know the truth.'

337

'That's a chance I shall have to take. Quite frankly, I'm not sure that it matters very much anyway.'

The two of them smoked in silence for a while.

'Christopher,' Murray said finally, which confused Kingsley for a moment. 'I just want to say something and I shan't say it again so don't worry.'

Although Kingsley's considerable vanity did not stretch to matters of the heart, he could tell what was coming and he wished fervently that it wouldn't.

'The thing is,' Murray continued, 'I know you love your wife and all that, and I think that's terrif'. No, honestly, I really do. I *love* love. But you know, damn it all, she's *left you*, silly thing that she must be, and well, here *we* are and . . .'

'Kitty . . .' Kingsley began.

'No, let me finish. I've told you I shan't say it again, so you have to listen this once. The awful thing is that I've fallen in love with you. Stupid, I know, and dreadfully soppy of me, but there it is. Can't be helped. And what I wanted to say was . . . please *do* let's give it a try. I mean, why not? We have fun together, you must admit, and you did say you think I'm pretty, which I'm sure I'm not but you said it all the same and when you made love to me I rather felt that you meant it, and even if you're not *in* love with me surely we could just . . .'

'Kitty, please. You're twenty-two, I'm thirty-five.'

'Ha! That's about right then. It's well known girls mature earlier than chaps. I could never love a boy.'

'Look . . .'

'I'm sure that girls aren't supposed to be as forward as this but I am a new woman, you know, and I *told* you that I always speak my mind and . . .'

Kingsley was so very sad to cause her pain.

'If I were ever to love a woman other than my wife,' he began, 'it would be . . .'

'*Please, Christopher.* I know you like me, I felt it.' She turned to him and there were tears running down her cheeks.

338

'Don't run away from this. *I love you.*'

'Kitty. *I love my wife.* I told you. That's the point. You're right, I do like you, I like you hugely. I like you far too much to deceive you.'

She threw her cigarette into a puddle.

'Fine. Enough said,' she replied, attempting to sound as if they had been discussing nothing of great importance. 'No need to dwell. Just wanted to get things straight, that's all.'

'I think you're wonderful, I really do, and . . .'

Nurse Murray struggled out from under the limber.

'Look, sorry and all that, but I really should be getting back now. Don't want to do that journey in the dark, do I? You *will* come back and tell me how it went with the colonel, won't you? And that you're all right?'

'Yes, of course.'

'I'm part of this investigation too, you know. I want to see it through.'

The tears were still rolling down her cheeks but she was aggressively ignoring them.

'Right,' she said, pulling on her leather helmet. 'Toodle-oo then. Chin chin.'

'One thing, Kitty,' Kingsley said. 'I don't want you to burn Abercrombie's poems. I know how you feel about it but for the time being I want you to keep them safe.'

'All right,' Nurse Murray replied. 'Whatever you say.'

She mounted her motorcycle, kicked down with angry force, the engine leaped into life and she was gone.

49

Once more unto the breach

As night fell all along the British line, the usual feverish nocturnal
activity began anew. Kingsley knew that the Royal Artillery
would be anxious to discover the layout of the new British
positions in order to prepare for the next series of cannonades.
The infantry had advanced the previous day under a creeping
barrage, in which the artillery had laid down fire which moved
slowly forward, theoretically just in front of the troops, clearing
a way for them. Of course, as the battle had progressed and the
assault was slowly broken up by the German resistance, the most
forward positions had become lost in the mud and the smoke.
Now was the time to discover what was left of the most advanced
battalions and where they all were. Observation officers were
preparing to go forward along with stretcher teams and water-
bearers. Kingsley determined to accompany them.

'Is anybody looking for the 5th?' he enquired of the various
darkened figures moving about amongst the guns, and was
fortunate to find an artillery spotter who was preparing to do just
that.

Together he and his guide crept out beyond the artillery line.
Immediately they began to pass men both living and dead. The
skin of the dead, Kingsley noted, had turned slimy and black,

making them difficult to see (and hence avoid). Their rate of decomposition suggested that they had been buried by previous shelling and that last night's shells had merely exhumed them. The living men were all wounded, or else they were carrying wounded, men who had lain all day waiting for an opportunity to attempt to stumble back without being shot. All, of course, were desperate for water.

'It's tempting to offer a swig,' Kingsley's companion observed as they pushed their way past men in obvious need, 'but believe me, pretty soon we'll be in their position ourselves and we both have work to do.'

Water, Kingsley had heard, was perhaps the greatest of all the problems that bedevilled the soldiers in their swampy holes. They lived in it and drowned in it, it rotted their feet to the point where amputation was sometimes required and yet they yearned for it day and night, because once battle had been joined there was *never* enough of it to drink. Often there was none at all. Sometimes it was possible to drink the foul, filthy soup in shell holes, but frequently it was poisoned by rotting corpses and gas or else it was too thick with clay to drink.

Every man Kingsley passed pleaded for fresh water. In this rain-sodden landscape, the agony of thirst was a torment. The only good thing that could be said about it was that at some point it became so all-absorbing that it diverted men's minds from the other appalling discomforts they suffered. The constant imminence of death, the misery of sleeplessness, the rats, even the lice were forgotten once a raging thirst had set in.

Kingsley had also noted that, despite the numerous brilliant feats of organization that the army had achieved during the past three years, it had never managed to provide suitable water containers. For the soldiers of the Western Front, water came to be universally associated with the foul taste of petrol, for it was always delivered to the forward positions in fuel cans.

The artillery officer led Kingsley first along the communications trenches up to what had been, before the battle began, the British advance trench. Now these same poor slits from which the British and Australian armies had launched themselves a few weeks earlier were transformed into forward dressing stations. Within them, the stream of wounded were first jammed in order to be assessed. Here, just as Kingsley and his guide were passing, in the mass of blood and confusion some dog-tired sentry, half asleep, saw several men approach wearing German coal-scuttle helmets which they had taken as souvenirs.

'Counter-attack,' the sentry shouted. 'They're upon us!'

Instantly, and before the obvious mistake could be rectified, the dressing station exploded in a mass panic, with shocked and hollow-eyed men scurrying in all directions. Officers and NCOs shouted themselves hoarse in an effort to re-establish order, while wounded men were trampled underfoot, precious water was upset and a great deal of time and equipment lost.

Kingsley and his guide skirted the bloody confusion of the dressing station and moved on into what had once been no-man's-land but was now Allied territory. As they went, they asked constantly for the 5th Battalion and, more particularly, its colonel. In due course and by good fortune they came upon a runner who had been sent back by Colonel Hilton himself in order to re-establish contact with Staff and plead that water be got up swiftly to his decimated forces.

'They got as far as the third German line, sir,' the runner explained, 'and have dug in, in Fritz's trench. They's comfortable enough but awful exposed. The colonel don't think the 3rd to his right got so far, nor possibly our own boys on his left, and so he believes he has at least one open flank and possibly two. Go easy, sir, because there could very likely be Boche now 'tween us and them.'

Onward Kingsley and the artilleryman went, struggling over the most appallingly broken country. Ruined equipment and corpses lay everywhere, and everywhere scurrying men crept through the darkness. To what end? Kingsley wondered. But no doubt his own intentions appeared as pointless to the men whom he encountered as theirs did to him.

They had been heading down a shallow slope and at the bottom of it they came upon some walls. Of what had once been a farmhouse, only the cellar remained, open to the elements, and in it Kingsley could make out one or two shadowy figures.

'Battalion HQ,' said the artillery officer. 'By rights that's where Hilton should be, but it doesn't surprise me that he's up at the front. Damn stupid, of course. No point being a colonel if you act like a subaltern, but you have to admire his pluck.'

They moved on past the ruined cellar, cursing under their breath as they descended into one shell hole after another. At one hole they thought they had had a stroke of luck when they encountered a radio operator with all his equipment set out and his earphones on his head.

'If this fellow can give me an accurate fix, old son,' the artillery-man whispered, 'my job's done and you're on your own.'

The officer crept up to the lip of the shell hole.

'You there,' he demanded, having to raise his voice, for a fusillade had begun once more overhead. 'Have you established a frequency?'

The operator turned his head slowly and mouthed a pitiable plea for help. Blood had drenched the lower part of his tunic and he could not speak or move his lower body. The officer stepped down into the hole and plucked the earphones from the wounded man's head, placing them on his own.

'Nothing. Totally dead. Battery gone, I suppose,' he said bitterly, casting aside the headset. The operator just stared: it seemed that he was beyond pain, and Kingsley thought he had probably taken a morphine tablet.

'Sorry, Corporal,' the artillery officer said, 'but I have to move on. If I encounter a stretcher party I shall let them know you're here.'

Then the operator managed a single word.

'Water,' he croaked.

'That's an abominable, soldier,' the officer replied, indicating the man's bloody tunic. 'Nil by mouth, I'm afraid. One swig would kill you in a minute.'

Both he and Kingsley knew that, water or no water, the operator would be dead long before any stretcher party could be found.

The artillery officer clambered back out of the shell hole and together they went on their way. Such was the rapidity and apparent calm of their progress (with the exception of the shelling overhead) that Kingsley's mind began to fix upon the details of his case once more. Suddenly his reverie was shattered when there loomed out of the darkness those same coal-scuttle helmets that had so frightened the sleepy sentry at the dressing station. The men who wore them this time were not souvenir-hunting Tommies but German infantry. They were only yards away and had seen Kingsley and his companion at exactly the same moment that Kingsley and the artillery officer had seen them.

There were three of them, all in field grey. The rain and darkness made visibility difficult but the distant flashing of the fire curtain that was being laid down by both sides' artillery provided just enough light to illuminate the scene. The front German held a bayoneted rifle in his hands and had stick grenades bristling at his belt. The two men behind him were struggling with a heavy machine gun, for which they appeared to be searching for a suitable emplacement. The little team were further burdened by the ropes of ammunition draped across their shoulders. Kingsley and the artillery officer had been carrying their sidearms at the ready and for a moment the five men stood still, each party staring at the other shadowy grouping. Then, as if by common consent, both sides melted away. The Germans disappeared backwards into the night and the British did likewise, without a word.

'More important that I get an accurate range for our guns,' the artillery officer whispered, 'than that I attempt personally to take on the Prussian Guard.'

The presence of Germans suggested to both men that they must be close to the limits of the British advance. Sure enough, shortly thereafter and without further incident, the two men came upon what they were seeking: the most forward position of the remnants of the 5th Battalion of the East Lancs.

A fierce voice called out a challenge.

'Who goes there? Friend or foe?'

The two men froze and called out their replies in hoarse semi-whispers.

'Friend. Pilby. Subaltern. Field Artillery.'

'Friend. Captain Marlowe. Military Police.'

'Advance, friend, and be recognized.'

They crept towards the sentry's voice and, as they did so, a burst of machine-gun fire raked the ground around them. Kingsley heard a shout and Lieutenant Pilby, whose name he had only just learned, fell to the ground beside him. As he did so, fire began to pour from the area towards which they had been heading. It was directed at the attacking machine gun, which meant that the British were putting up covering fire.

Kingsley grabbed his fallen companion and dragged him towards the British entrenchment. Fortunately they were only yards away, for dragging a grown man over deep mud in the dark under fire was no easy task.

Moments later, Kingsley and Pilby tumbled together down the sides of a deep shell hole, Pilby crying in pain. The clatter of machine-gun fire subsided and relative peace returned, with the exception of the intermittent shellfire overhead.

'We'd flushed out that nest hours ago,' said a voice that Kingsley recognized as Colonel Hilton's. 'They must have managed to get a new team into it. Good bit of soldiering, damn them. Who's this now?'

Peering through the darkness with an electric torch, the colonel was most surprised to see Kingsley, but first he had to deal with the wounded artillery subaltern. A corporal was already inspecting Pilby's wounds and applying field dressings.

'Both legs, sir, two bullets in each,' he reported.

Colonel Hilton had noted the Royal Artillery insignia on the subaltern's shoulders and knew exactly why he had come visiting.

'Well, you won't be reporting our position to your rangefinders in a hurry, will you, lad?'

Kingsley, surprised to hear Hilton refer to Pilby as 'lad', took a proper look at the man and realized that his guide of the previous hour was probably no more than twenty years old. He had seemed so experienced that Kingsley had followed him without question.

'No, sir,' Pilby replied, grimacing in pain and trying not to look down at his shattered legs, 'but you're awfully far forward and well in amongst the Hun. We had you placed a good hundred yards back.'

It did not take a military strategist to divine the young subaltern's meaning. The 5th were in direct contact with the enemy and dug in considerably beyond their designated objectives. Without information to the contrary, there was every possibility that Staff would assume this territory was occupied exclusively by Germans and begin to shell it.

Colonel Hilton was reloading his pistol.

'Well, it's time I was getting back anyway,' he observed. 'Got what I came for. Scouted about pretty comprehensively after we knocked out that damned nest over there. Sergeant Walker!'

'Sir,' said a burly man emerging from the gloom.

'I think we have about a third of our original strength dotted about in various holes but we're properly mixed up with Fritz and no mistake. We need either to be reinforced or to withdraw. Can't withdraw because we're pinned down, can't be reinforced because nobody knows we're here. And if this young fellow's mob start shelling us it'll all be academic anyway because we shall be singing "Tipperary" with the heavenly choir.'

'Yes, sir,' the sergeant replied. 'Bit of a pickle.'

'A bit of a pickle, as you so rightly observe, Sergeant. Now Subalterns Longley and Smith are still with us and also Captain Greyshot, all in various holes, but apart from that, I am afraid to say, all our officers are down, along with the majority of the NCOs. I intend to make my way back now. You are in charge of

346

this section, Sergeant, and your job is to sit tight and, if attacked, to give a good account of yourselves.'

'Yes, sir.'

Hilton made ready to leave the shell hole, then almost as an afterthought he turned to Kingsley.

'Had you been hoping to speak to me, Captain?'

'Yes, sir, I had.'

'Still snooping about?'

'That's right, sir. Still snooping. Although I hope shortly to draw my conclusions.'

The colonel lapsed into thought for a moment. A soldier was warming a can of meat on one of the pocket-sized oil stoves the troops called a 'Tommy's cooker'. Hilton waded across the mud, leaned forward and sniffed the contents of the can. Grimacing slightly, he turned back to Kingsley.

'Did you ever look about yourself, you know, at all of *this* and wonder, does anybody really give a damn about a police investigation?'

'Yes, sir, many times.'

'You're an excellent soldier by all accounts, why don't you transfer? Do something useful.'

'I prefer being a policeman, sir.'

The colonel looked genuinely perplexed.

'Extraordinary,' he muttered under his breath, then added, 'Can't talk now, you understand. Busy.'

'Yes, sir. I can see that. Would you mind if I followed you back?'

The moment the artillery officer had been hit, Kingsley had known that his investigations would be delayed. He fully understood that he would not be able to conduct an interview with Colonel Hilton while the fate of two companies of the colonel's battalion hung in the balance. Wearily, Kingsley concluded that he would have to trust once more to luck and retrace his steps to the artillery line in the hope that, once Hilton had done his duty by his men, he would be able to speak to him. Assuming, of course, that he and Hilton survived the trip.

347

'Well, you're a useful fellow,' Hilton replied. 'I know that from how you took command of that trench raid the other night. But are you any good at keeping quiet?'

'Yes, sir. I'm very good at keeping quiet.'

'You'll need to be. The damned shelling's dropped right off, just when we could have done with a bit of noise cover. Always the same with shelling – like taxis, when you don't need one, you see hundreds. The moment we leave this hole we're a very easy mark for that damned machine gun. There is a covering ridge but it's a good fifty yards back. Until we reach it we shall have to make our way very, very slowly.'

The colonel meant what he said. He and Kingsley crept out of the shell hole and began to inch forward, lying flat on their faces, chins resting in the cold mud. Scarcely daring to breathe, and agonizingly aware of every tiny sound they made, including their own heartbeats, which seemed to thunder treacherously in their chests like kettledrums. Knowing that any noise that attracted the attention of the ever-vigilant Germans, peering into the night from within their sandbagged machine-gun nest, must bring instant death.

In many places the British and German trenches were barely fifty yards apart; nonetheless, Kingsley knew that Staff insisted that the area between the two armies should be regularly occupied and charted. And so, on every night of the war, that long, thin stretch of mud that ran south through Belgium and France was alive with young British, Canadian and Anzac officers lying flat on their faces, reconnoitring a strip scarcely two hundred yards long, and yet the terrifying task took almost all night to complete. If, indeed, it was completed.

On this occasion Colonel Hilton was forcing the pace some-what, although it did not appear so to Kingsley as he inched his nose and chin through the mud. They crossed the fifty yards of swamp to the covering ridge in less than ninety minutes, at a fairly reckless speed considering they were under the nose of a German machine gun, but they needed to move fast if they were to have any chance of reaching real safety before the dawn light made further movement impossible.

Beyond the shallow ridge they were able to raise themselves up into a crouch and begin to make their way back up the blasted slope and across the Langemarck–Gheluvelt Line. They were moving at a stooped scuttle now, gaining in confidence with every step, pausing only when the Very light star shells forced every living thing either to freeze or die. The ground was becoming a little more populated. They came across stretcher-bearers and retreating wounded, so they knew they must be approaching the British lines proper.

Just then, almost within sight of home, the German guns opened up once more in earnest.

'Take cover!' Hilton shouted and together they dived into the nearest hole.

50

Waiting it out under fire

There now began one of the most miserable days of Kingsley's life. Like thousands of other men hiding in thousands of other holes on that mutilated plain, he was forced to sit tight in the midst of a full-scale artillery bombardment. Most of the shells were landing further up the slope from where Kingsley and the colonel had been heading, but enough were dropping short to make movement impossible. In a hole a man was pretty safe from everything except a direct or near-direct hit, but if he were to venture above ground he would be putting himself in the path of the lacerating side-blasts of every shell that landed within a hundred metres. He would be slashed to pieces within moments. There was nothing to do in such circumstances but to dig one's hole as deep as possible, jam one's helmet on low and sit it out. This Kingsley and Hilton did, scooping down into the puddle in which they stood and clawing up handfuls of sopping mud. With some effort they managed to extend their shelter to about three and a half feet in depth, before settling down together, waist deep in water, facing each other, knee to knee, to wait for the storm to lift.

Fortunately, for the time being at least, the rain had stopped.

Sitting out a bombardment was one of the most testing

experiences of all for a soldier, and one that in itself left many strong men no longer in full command of their senses. To lurk within the stinking earth while all around it shook and moved; to be constantly showered with broken metal, rock and clods of clay, conscious that at any moment one was likely to be buried, possibly alive, and confined to oblivion: such an arbitrary threat came close to defeating Kingsley's courage. The cannonade grew more swollen with the dawn and the whistles, bangs, throaty roars and constant clatter and clanging of falling debris seemed to shred his nerves by degrees with the coming of the day.

It was not a hurricane barrage of the kind known to the troops as drumfire, rather a plodding, heavy bombardment which grew slowly in intensity as the day progressed. Some conversation was possible between the most immediate blasts, and the colonel, who could see that Kingsley was shaken, took the opportunity to try to comfort him.

'You mustn't think about it, Captain,' he said. 'That's the way we old sweats get through these things. Don't dwell. If you dwell, you go mad. Fellows sit stewing, getting obsessed with meaningless rituals. They start thinking that if they don't complete some silly song a hundred times or tap their knees a certain way, or get so many pulls at a cigarette before it burns their lips, then the next shell will be theirs. I've known men disobey orders just so they can get through some insane mental task they've set themselves, thinking it's all that stands between them and the next blast. Don't think that way, old boy. Drives a man nuts. Believe me, I have sat in holes just like this one and watched men go mad in an afternoon.'

Kingsley was shocked at the colonel's perception. He had indeed begun to count the beats between blasts of certain types and distance, imagining that an order was developing which was known only to him and which he was bound to follow. The notion lacked all logic but nonetheless he could feel himself being drawn into the obsession, thinking that if he did not construct the pattern between each shell in his head, then the one he failed to note would kill him. It was like the times when he had flown in aeroplanes and had become convinced that if he personally stopped concentrating on keeping the machine aloft, it would fall out of the sky.

'You're right, colonel,' Kingsley said. 'I was beginning to . . . dwell. Thank you.'

'Have to try to think about something else. And don't let anybody see that you're scared, that's the most important thing.'

'Why?'

'Making the effort to look brave takes your mind off being scared. Everybody feels it. Same as whistling a happy tune.'

'Are you scared, sir?'

'Me? Scared? Of course not. I'm in a small, shallow hole under heavy bombardment from a battery of German howitzers, why on earth would I be scared? Ridiculous notion!'

The colonel smiled and they both laughed and Kingsley felt grateful to his older companion for sharing a little of his courage.

'Shall we sing together?' the colonel suggested. 'I fancy a sing-song.'

'Well, if you wish. Certainly.'

Kingsley was still deeply unnerved by the shelling all around him and was happy to try any method that might help him get through the ordeal.

> 'It's a long way to Tipperary,
> It's a long way to go,'

the colonel began in a rich, full tenor.

> 'It's a long way to Tipperary
> To the sweetest girl I know!'

Kingsley took up the tune and together they sang 'Pack Up Your Troubles', 'Fred Karno's Army' and 'The Quartermaster's Stores'.

Soon they could faintly hear other voices joining in. Kingsley was struck by the strangeness of it all: a landscape full of little holes in which men crouched, singing cheerful songs, while death fell all around them from the sky. He found his mind drifting back to the conversation he had had with Captain Shannon at the Hotel Majestic about the bizarre nature of modern war. It would be difficult to imagine a more bizarre situation than the one in which he currently found himself.

Eventually they sang themselves hoarse. It had certainly made Kingsley feel a little better, and so, in a conversation interrupted constantly by massive blasts of ordnance, he turned his mind once more to his investigation.

'Sir,' he began, 'seeing as how we're stuck here for the time being, perhaps I might speak to you again about the death of Viscount Abercrombie?'

'What? Still harping on about that, eh? I wondered why you'd turned up again,' the colonel replied. 'Oh well, Abercrombie's as good a topic as any, I suppose. I was going to suggest we discuss cricket.'

'Colonel, were you aware that, while he was staying at Château Beaurivage, Viscount Abercrombie had tried to lay his hands on a green envelope?'

'Really? No, I hadn't heard that, but then I don't issue them.'

'Why do you think he might have wanted such a thing?'

'To send a letter that he didn't want the army to read, I imagine.'

'As colonel, you would have the job of censoring your soldiers' mail, is that right?'

'Just the officers', not the men's. Horrible job. Loathsome. Can't stand the idea of reading another chap's letters but it has to be done. You've *no idea* the indiscretions some of these lads blurt out. They tell their girlfriends positions, strengths, battle orders! As if any decent girl would be interested in that sort of thing anyway.'

'Did you ever have cause to censor Captain Abercrombie's mail, colonel?'

'Well, yes. As a matter of fact, I did.'

'You never mentioned it to me.'

'You didn't ask.'

'Did you not think it might be relevant?'

'Not really. I consider it absolutely central to my duties as censor *never* to discuss the contents of the letters I am forced to read. It's quite bad enough having to look at someone else's private correspondence without chatting about its contents afterwards. Imagine what a cad I'd feel.'

'I should like to ask you about that letter now.'

'You can ask. Let's see how far we get, eh?'

'Was it because of this letter that you visited Abercrombie at Beaurivage?'

'Yes, it was. I wanted to tell him personally that I'd blocked it. I wanted him to withdraw it voluntarily, otherwise I'd be compelled to refer it to Staff.'

'Refer it to Staff. I thought it was your policy never to discuss the contents of the mail you read with anyone?'

'Unless it involved matters affecting security. I would have thought that was pretty bloody obvious, Captain. Otherwise what would be the point of censoring the letters at all?'

'You felt Abercrombie's letter represented a breach of security?'

'I found it . . . disturbing and I wanted him to withdraw it voluntarily.'

'And what did he say to that?'

'He told me to go to hell. First thing he *did* say, as a matter of fact.'

All this conversation was punctuated by the fearful blasts of high explosives that were going off above and all around the scratch of ground in which they sheltered. Kingsley was grateful that he had something solid to occupy his mind, for he felt that he had never in his life been in a more nerve-racking situation.

'I'm afraid I'm going to have to ask you to tell me what was in this letter, Colonel.'

'I'd really very much rather you asked them at Staff. They have it now.'

'I have reason to believe that they don't any more, Colonel. It's my supposition that Abercrombie's letter has been destroyed.'

'Good thing too, if you ask me. The chap wasn't himself. Shell-shocked. It would be a rotten shame if he were remembered only for some damn-fool notions knocked into him by German shells.'

'What damn-fool notions, Colonel?'

The colonel shrugged.

'Well, you're a policeman, so I suppose I have to tell you. He wanted to resign his commission.'

'To go into the ranks?'

'Don't be ridiculous! The man was a viscount, how could he possibly have gone into the ranks? No, he wanted to chuck the army altogether. He'd *turned against the war*. Do you understand, Captain? The man who wrote "Forever England" wanted to resign his commission because he was against the war! Decided it was wrong and wicked and *all* the usual stuff which we *all* feel most of the bloody time, but that still leaves three million German soldiers sitting in France and trying to get to Britain! What did he expect us to do about *them* while we're all chucking it in just because we lost a pal or two?'

'Was that in his letter? The loss of his friend?'

'Oh, the loss of every damn friend. A generation! A generation of *golden boys*. All the usual bloody clichés. Did he think we'd honour them by giving up? I've lost a son, we've all lost sons, and the best memorial we can build for them is to kill as many Germans as we can and to win the war they died in.'

Kingsley was about to reply but instead he waited. Throughout their talk each of them had been entirely alive to the shrieks and whistles of descending shells all around them. Kingsley had very soon learned to identify which noise signalled an approach that would land more closely than the rest and what sort of blast would follow. He and Hilton were listening to just such an approach now, both of them knowing that the whistle which their minds had picked out unbidden signalled that this time they were well and truly underneath one.

355

Hilton drew his knees in close to his chest and put his fingers in his ears. Kingsley did likewise and held his breath through the long, plodding seconds that marked the passage of the descending shriek. He thought he heard Hilton wish him luck and then the missile struck.

Kingsley found himself lifted up and somersaulting, but not through air, rather through earth. It was as if the ground had become a solid but shifting sea and Kingsley was being sucked under by an approaching wave. He rolled over and over inside the mud, entirely helpless, one small element in a mighty cataclysm.

Then the movement stopped, at least outside Kingsley's body it stopped. Within himself, every nerve and cell seemed to be in violent motion. He had been utterly shaken as if by some giant's hand, and now he was so disorientated that he had no real sense of his own form.

And yet he knew he was alive. And that he was buried. Buried alive.

Struggling to concentrate his rattling brain whilst his trapped body convulsed with the mud that filled his mouth and ears, desperate to expel it from his throat but having nowhere but solid mud to expel it into, Kingsley understood one thing. He must somehow ascertain which way was up. In the few seconds of struggle that remained to him, in which direction should he attempt to force his body?

Kingsley had been fighting the dirt, trying to push each of his limbs in a different direction, but now he forced himself to stop. He remembered his fencing master: 'In a fight, *think*.'

He had been holding his breath when the blast had occurred, and there was still some air in his lungs. He had perhaps ninety seconds left to him. He forced himself to count out ten of them in stillness.

Surely there must be some means of ascertaining which way was up?

Those few seconds saved his life for in them, even through his blocked ears, he could make out a sort of thudding, a heavy pattering, like a rain of mud. Kingsley knew that he was listening to a great balloon of mud and rock that had been hurled into the air by the blast and was now falling back to earth. That way was up, and it could not be far, for the earth in which he was entombed would dull the sound in no time.

Twisting with all his might, Kingsley was able to turn his body towards the thudding and then to claw and push at the mud with his arms. For what seemed like the longest while, although it could only have been a few seconds, he felt he was getting nowhere. But then suddenly his fingers encountered nothing: they had burst through the fearful resistance of Flanders mud, and seconds later Kingsley had his face through and was coughing and puking and breathing all at once, trying to empty the earth from his body whilst simultaneously gasping for air.

Hilton was dead. He had not been buried but instead, by some accident of fate, he had been thrown upwards into the blast and then shredded by the hurtling shrapnel. Kingsley could see a part of his upper chest and shoulders with their colonel's pips lying quite close by; the rest of him was lost, disintegrated.

The bombardment was still very much under way and Kingsley knew he must find cover again, and quickly. Flat on his front once more, he crawled in the direction of the British line. As luck would have it, he soon came upon a ruined trench. This must have been an excavation from an earlier stage of the war, he realized, as before the current battle it had been in no-man's-land. Kingsley was further fortunate in that the slit, or what was left of it, must have been a communications trench, for it was running roughly east to west and so he was able to follow it in the direction he wished to go.

By this means Kingsley was able in quite good time to reach the British line. This did not mean he was free of the bombardment, for this line was its target, but it did mean he could once more move quickly from trench to trench. He did not, however, do what every straining nerve in him wanted to do, which was run as fast as he could to beyond the reach of the guns. He had a duty to perform to Colonel Hilton and to the stranded men of the 5th Battalion. The British guns would no doubt be shortly commencing their reply to the German bombardment and Kingsley knew that before he did anything else he must inform their rangefinders of the exposed positions from which he and Hilton had crawled so many hours before.

'I have no idea if they are still where we left them or whether they've perished under this current fusillade,' he informed the first artillery officer he could locate, 'but I can tell you where they were last night.'

Kingsley made as full a report as he could concerning the whereabouts and disposition of the 5th and also delivered news of the death of its commander. Then, finally, he was able to make his way from the line for what he prayed with all his might would be the final time. Men were laboriously tugging an empty ammunition limber back towards the stockpiles located beyond Ypres and Kingsley used his rank and status as a military policeman to throw himself up on to it, whereupon his entire nervous system instantly shut down and he fell into deep unconsciousness.

51

A confrontation

Captain Shannon had been with Sir Mansfield when Kingsley's
message regarding his anticipated conclusion to the investigation
had reached London. It had been quickly agreed that Shannon
should return to France and find out what, if anything, Kingsley
had discovered.

He had an easier journey to Flanders than Kingsley had done.
After allowing himself the diversion of a night in Paris and then
commandeering a staff car to take him up to the line, he had
arrived at the Café Cavell when Kingsley was hiding in his shell
hole with Colonel Hilton. Having found his quarry absent he had
left a note requesting Kingsley to contact him at the police station
at Armentières.

Late that same afternoon Kingsley finally arrived back at his
billet and, exhausted though he was, he gave himself only the
briefest time to clean himself up before setting off to make contact
with Shannon. The café had no telephone but Kingsley had an
idea which establishment in Merville might be sufficiently
wealthy to afford one, and so he made his way to the Number 1
Red Lamp establishment. Stepping up to the rather forbidding
front door, he rapped upon it and demanded entrance. Dirty and
drawn though he might have been, he still wore the uniform of a

captain in the Military Police, which commanded enormous respect from an establishment that depended for its survival on its relationship with the British Army. Kingsley was immediately ushered inside, and so caused a mighty panic amongst the sheepish-looking soldiers hovering in the reception area.

'Easy, lads. Easy,' Kingsley said. 'I've no interest in you. This is a licensed place, it's all tickety-boo. I just want to use the telephone.'

A thickly painted Frenchwoman of indeterminate age shuffled forward and, having made a bow and explained how honoured her establishment was by his visit, led him to a little cubicle. As he passed, Kingsley could not help but notice the two or three girls sitting amongst the soldiers, either hoping to be selected or perhaps waiting for a room to become free. Tired and thin, they were a miserable group indeed. The excessive paint they wore gave them a slightly ghoulish appearance, like marionettes. Kingsley felt that Tommy Atkins would find little comfort with these poor used-up creatures whose life expectancy was surely not so much greater than his own.

Kingsley made two telephone calls from Madame's little cubicle, one to Armentières and one to the château. He spoke first to Sergeant Banks at the police station, who confirmed that Captain Shannon had billeted himself upon them.

'He's a *fast* sort, isn't he, sir, and no mistake?' Banks whispered down the crackling line. 'Brought a trunk full of wine in the boot of his staff car, although he don't mind sharing it, I'll give him that. But you won't believe it, sir, he's brought a *girl* with him as well. Bold as you please! All the way from Paris. Says he's promised to show her some action and I think he means it!'

'Yes, that sounds like Captain Shannon,' Kingsley replied. 'Could you please inform him that I have returned from the front and that I shall expect to see him at the Château Beaurivage at six o'clock this evening.'

Having concluded this phone call, Kingsley rang the château

and made suitable arrangements for his meeting with Shannon. When he emerged from the little booth the ageing proprietress was waiting for him.

'What do I owe you, madame?' he asked in French.

The old painted woman waved a hand and mouthed the traditional French 'Bof', as if to say that such matters were of no consequence to her, before adding with a pantomime wink that she was always most happy to oblige the Military Police. Kingsley made his way back through the village and then on to the château, thinking of the sad establishment he had just left and of all the misery and suffering he had encountered in his life and then passed by. He thought of 'Red' Sean McAlistair in the prison canteen, taunting him for his apparent indifference to the condition of the poor. He thought of Kitty Murray, still a girl when she was brutalized by the police force that he served and loved. He thought of the Germans he had killed whilst 'not participating' in the war. His mind reeled at the daily compromises a man must make with misery and injustice simply to muddle through. He remembered that it had been only the sheer scale of horror that the war had brought which had caused him to take a moral stand. Kingsley reflected that in 1917 the twentieth century was not yet two decades old, but the quantity of human misery it had already witnessed was unparalleled in all history. He wondered what scale of suffering and injustice future generations would find it practical to accept before they took a stand. Or if, in fact, they would find it practical to take no stand at all.

This was why he knew he must complete his case.

Brutality, it was clear, had a cumulative effect on the people who perpetrated it and on those who witnessed it, numbing their senses to decency, until in the end it was difficult to remember what decency was. No matter how inconsequential his investigation might be within the wider picture, justice must be done. The concept that there *was* such a thing as right and wrong had to be maintained.

Then Kingsley wondered whether he was fooling himself with

361

these grand and sombre thoughts. A part of him strongly suspected that his dogged pursuit of evidence had more to do with vanity and pig-headedness than grand ideas of justice. Logic dictated that he would be doing more good by joining a stretcher party, as many other conscientious objectors had done. Whatever his reasons, however, Kingsley intended to see the case through to the end, and the end was approaching.

As he neared the now-familiar house, he could see a splendid staff car parked outside and concluded that his acquaintance of London and Folkestone had arrived. At the front steps Captain Shannon came out to meet him. To Kingsley's relief, Shannon appeared to have left his new girlfriend elsewhere.

'Well, well, old boy,' he said, 'you *have* been in the wars, haven't you?'

'Yes, I have,' Kingsley replied.

'Enjoy it?'

'I beg your pardon?'

'Simple question, chum. Being in the wars. Did you enjoy it? A lot of us do, you know. We're not all Sassoons by any means.'

'I haven't noticed many people enjoying it.'

'Oh, not being shelled, of course, no one much likes that, or sitting in a puddle, or eating filthy rubbish and all the other dull business. But a battle, eh? Can't deny there's something about a battle . . .'

'There is something absolutely hellish about a battle.'

'Hmmm,' Shannon replied, looking at Kingsley with a thoughtful smile. 'I wonder.'

'I should like to talk to you, Captain. The rain's holding off, shall we take a stroll?'

'By all means, Captain, by all means. Did myself rather well in Gay Paree, I'm afraid. Too many rich sauces, too much *foie gras*. Could use a little exercise.'

Together they went back down the gravel drive towards the woods, Shannon swinging along with his usual arrogant gait, splendid, as always, in his perfect uniform, looking as if he owned the whole estate.

'I'm not saying war isn't hellish, of course,' Shannon remarked, swishing his swagger stick at the hedges that lined the drive. 'Absolutely hellish, as you say. But there is an *exhilaration* too, surely? The point where you become blind to your own fear. It's almost *primeval*, like being a beast of prey amongst other beasts. I mean, that's where we came from, isn't it? It must still be in us somewhere. I sometimes think that to feel truly, absolutely and completely *alive*, a chap has to be charging pell-mell into the teeth of death. Of course, no one who hasn't done it could ever remotely understand.'

'So you often observe.'

'Not boring you, am I? I'd hate to think I was repeating myself. But, come on, Kingsley, you must admit that—'

'Marlowe.'

'Oh, shove that rubbish, will you, Kingsley? I *know* you and, what's more, I'd be prepared to wager that somewhere in the midst of the battles you've been through, you too felt *alive*. I mean really and truly alive in a way that you could never feel back home.'

Kingsley did not answer. He did not wish to give Shannon the satisfaction of admitting that he had a point, for there was no doubt that the man had struck a chord. There *was* a curious and terrible thrill to being in a charge, Kingsley knew that now; he had felt it as he breasted the parapet and followed McCroon towards the German line. He had felt it as he leaped into the trench in pursuit of Abercrombie's gun. He had felt it as he emptied his own gun into four Germans in succession and then managed to get the raiding party out in relatively good order. It was not that he remotely enjoyed killing, but to be a part of a furious mêlée, to be in the thick of a life-and-death struggle, to be an *animal* once more, existing exclusively on one's animal instincts . . . It was in some ways *exhilarating*, and Shannon was right, primeval was a good word to use. However, one thing

363

was certain, he had not *enjoyed* it, as Shannon was claiming to do. And so he determined not to discuss the idea further.

'I want to talk about the Abercrombie case. I want to finish it so that I can leave this damned place.'

'Ah yes, and sneak off to Botany Bay with a new name and passport, eh?' Shannon replied. 'Your message to Cumming said you were reaching your conclusions. Fire away, I must say I'm agog.'

They were approaching the trees now, the same trees under which Kingsley and Nurse Murray had first made love.

'I knew it would be you who came,' Kingsley replied. 'When I sent my message I knew that you'd come.'

'I'm your contact. Who else would come?'

'All the same, I knew that it would be you.'

'Missing me, I expect. I have that effect on all the girls.'

'You are, of course, aware that Hopkins did not kill Abercrombie?'

'Of course. They released him. Bullet didn't fit, sensational bit of news. Sir Mansfield assured me that Lloyd George was thrilled, no more class war. The union's satisfied, MacDonald and all those self-righteous novelists and playwrights happy as larks. The Tories have been forced to stop Red-baiting. The only sour note is Lord Abercrombie's not unnatural interest in who actually *did* kill his bloody son, but that's not a political issue after all.'

'Isn't it?'

'Ah-ha. So Sherlock Holmes has surprises to reveal. Well, come on, man, spit it out, I can see you're dying to. What of this shadowy officer who was seen? I presume it was him who did it.'

'I know who that was. A young subaltern named Stamford. Abercrombie's lover.'

'*Lover?* I say, that is juicy. So the people's hero was a bugger, eh? Bloody poet, you see. Should have guessed.'

'You mean you didn't know?'

'Why would I?'

'Well, what with you being Secret Service and all.'

'We don't know everything. In fact the truth is we know very little. It's all show with us.'

Now they were well amongst the trees, Kingsley felt that they must be nearly at the exact spot where he had made love to Nurse Murray. Involuntarily he found himself wondering for a moment what Agnes was doing.

'I saw your lovely wife again,' said Shannon, almost as if he had been reading Kingsley's thoughts. 'Felt I ought to, you know, since it was me who arranged your death. See how she was and all that. She's a fine-looking woman though, isn't she?'

Kingsley remained silent but he could feel his fists clenching as a surge of rage swept through his body.

'Don't you want to know how she was? How I was received and all that . . . ?' Shannon sneered.

'We are discussing my assignment, Captain.'

'. . . Not warmly, as it happens. Proud piece, your missus. God knows why, considering she married *you*. What she needs is a proper breaking-in. Damned if I don't fancy the job myself.'

'We are discussing,' Kingsley said, struggling to keep his voice steady, 'the Abercrombie murder.'

'I thought you just said Stamford killed him? Lovers' tiff, I suppose. God, this'll be a nasty one to explain away to the press.'

'Stamford did not kill Abercrombie.'

'I thought you claimed he was the shadowy officer?'

He was *one* of the shadowy officers.'

'There was more than one?'

'Yes. There were two. McCroon and Nurse Murray saw two *different* officers.'

'Ah yes, Nurse Murray. Top-hole little filly to take over the jumps. More fire than a furnace, more spirit than a distillery.'

'We are discussing the—'

'Did you have a crack at her? More your type than mine, I imagine, at least intellectually. All that politics, not for me, *so* dull. Not that I bed a bint for her conversation. And too skinny, of course. Why *do* girls these days want to look like boys?'

'Captain Shannon, you are trying my patience!'

Kingsley blurted it out and knew immediately that he had dropped his guard. Shannon leaned languidly against a tree, a sneer upon his face.

'Oh dear, have I touched a nerve? I rather think I have. Perhaps the good captain has taken his comfort where he could find it? She don't half scratch, eh? And bloody strong, considering she's practically a midget.'

Kingsley struggled to master his rage. He understood very well that Shannon was deliberately making him angry.

'The mistake that was made in the early part of this investigation,' Kingsley said, slowly and clearly, 'was to presume that the two eyewitness reports regarding an officer leaving Abercrombie's room referred to the *same man*. They did not. I know this because McCroon told me that Nurse Murray was still in the room with Hopkins when he left it. Hence the man with the music case who pushed past McCroon immediately thereafter could not have been the same man that Nurse Murray saw when *she* left the room some time later. Abercrombie was visited by *two* officers on the night of his death. Subaltern Stamford was the first of them and it was he whom McCroon sighted.'

Shannon shrugged and then, as was his habit, lit a fresh cigarette from the burning stub of the previous one, as if to say that, much as he would like to, he could not get overexcited about Kingsley's revelations.

'You interviewed McCroon in the field, didn't you?' Shannon drawled.

'Yes, I did. We shared a shell hole for a short time.'

'Cool bit of work, I must say. Well done. You've made quite a soldier, haven't you? I saw the medal citation that Colonel Hilton submitted after you shot up that Hun trench. Cumming and I shared a smile when that came through. Nice work for a conscientious objector, we thought. So much for all that bloody "offended logic" you used to bang on about ad nauseum. How many blameless, innocent Germans do you think you killed, by the way?'

Now it was Kingsley's turn to chain-light a cigarette. He was rarely rattled by anybody but Shannon had a curious ability to get under his skin.

'So the obvious question is—' Kingsley began, having drawn deeply on his fag.

'Do they bother you,' Shannon insisted, 'those dead Germans? Do you dream about them at night? Can you still see their faces? Bet you can.'

'If Nurse Murray did not see Stamford—'

'I mean, what an appalling moral balls-up for you, eh? You ruin your life, let down your beautiful wife and desert your son so as *not* to kill Germans, and within days of arriving in France you're slaughtering them by the bloody trenchful. Damned strange way to claim the moral high ground, if you ask—'

'If Nurse Murray did not see Stamford,' Kingsley continued, calmly and firmly, 'who did she see? And I think we both know the answer to that question, don't we, Captain Shannon? Because the officer Nurse Murray saw was you.'

Shannon smiled and stepped away from the tree on which he had been leaning. His stance was no longer quite so nonchalant; the cigarette still hung lazily from his lips but nonetheless he looked *ready*.

'Me? Inspector Kingsley,' Shannon drawled, and this time Kingsley did not bother to correct his name, 'why would she have seen me?'

'I should have spotted it earlier – in fact Nurse Murray gave me the clue without knowing it on the first day I met her, but I only understood its significance when I realized that there *had* to have been two officers sighted.'

'And what did the delightful but rather violent Nurse Murray tell you?'

'She said, "First Captain Shannon came. Then we had the murder and the police said they'd solved it and now you turn up." Do you hear that, Captain? *First Captain Shannon came.* You did not *go* to France to interview the witnesses in the case, you were already there.'

The ash was growing longer on Shannon's cigarette but he did not flick it off.

'I never denied it. I'm a soldier, where else would I be but France?'

'But you weren't in combat. You had already been seconded to the Security Service. You were here on spy duties, looking at the likes of Hopkins and McCroon, weren't you?'

Shannon shrugged once more and the ash fell.

'Yes, I was, as a matter of fact, and I would have told you so had you asked. Now that Kerensky's gone in Russia and Lenin's in, our number-one fear is Bolshevism in our own ranks. But what, if you'll forgive me for asking, has any of that to do with Abercrombie?'

'Well, Abercrombie may not have been a Bolshevik but he was no longer quite the standard-bearer for British arms that he had been, was he?'

'Wasn't he?'

'I think you know he wasn't. Abercrombie was totally disillusioned with the war. His view was graphically described in his recent poetry and, what is more, he intended to do something about it.'

'You seem to know rather a lot about a chap who died before you had a chance to meet him. Have you been consulting a spiritualist?'

'No, no. Just reliable witnesses. In the last days of his life Viscount Abercrombie had been anxious to secure a green envelope, whereby he might send a letter home that would escape the eye of the censor.'

Shannon's hand was resting on the leather cover of his holster now. Kingsley had not seen Shannon's arm move towards it but, nonetheless, there his hand was, fingers toying with the little button that secured the flap. Shannon smiled a patronizing smile.

'Amazing how soldiers believe that "green envelope" rubbish,' he drawled through his cigarette smoke. 'For heaven's sake, if we want to read a man's letters we read them, whatever colour the envelope is.'

'Abercrombie had already had one letter refused him. His colonel had picked up the one in which he was attempting to resign his commission and refused it passage. But this wasn't a letter to the *army*, was it? Otherwise it would have been an internal matter. So to whom was Abercrombie writing? Not his mother, I think. What possible help could she be in the matter? His father perhaps? Hardly, I doubt the Tory Chief Whip in the House of Lords would be very sympathetic. No, my view is that he was writing to a newspaper. He intended, in fact, to follow directly in the footsteps of Siegfried Sassoon. Colonel Hilton, perceiving the disastrous effect that this change of heart would have at home, came to see Abercrombie here at Château Beaurivage and attempted to get him to change his mind. Furthermore, he explained that if Abercrombie would not reconsider, the colonel intended to forward the inflammatory letter to Staff HQ. This he did.'

'And you think that the letter came to me?'

'I cannot imagine who else they would give it to other than the senior security officer on the ground. Your brief was to deal with mutiny and here was mutiny indeed, and of the most inflammatory kind. A decorated officer refusing to serve? The author of "Forever England" denouncing the war as stupid and wicked? It would take a far less astute mind than yours, Captain, to deduce that this was a very dangerous letter indeed.'

Shannon had flipped the button on the cover of his holster, so that the leather flap was hanging loose.

'Here was a man,' Kingsley continued, 'who could do far more damage to morale than working-class Socialists like Hopkins and McCroon could ever do. They had *always* been against the war. Abercrombie, like Sassoon, had been *turned against it*, which is far more corrosive. And Abercrombie was a much worse case than Sassoon: certainly they had both been decorated for valour, but Abercrombie had been a celebrated

369

jingoist, he was the son of a senior Conservative politician, *a British aristocrat . . .*'

'He was a lily-livered swine, that's what he was,' Shannon snarled, for the first time losing something of his sangfroid. 'A damned turncoat about to let the side down with a bloody almighty clunk.'

'Except that you did not intend to let him, did you? So late one night you crept into the château, that same château which housed the revolutionary troublemaker Hopkins, one of the very men you had gone to France to deal with. What a happy coincidence, simply too good to miss. Two birds with one stone, eh? Dispose of a national embarrassment and frame a Bolshevik into the bargain.'

For all that Shannon had tried to provoke Kingsley, it was now Shannon who was the angry one. He spoke with bitter venom.

'How do you think the other fellows would have felt? The ones still in the trenches doing their duty? How would they have felt to learn that national bloody hero Abercrombie thought they were all *sheep*, cattle! Fools making a pointless sacrifice?'

'So you entered the viscount's room, took up one of his boots to act as a silencer and then shot him through the heel of it as he slept.'

Something in Shannon seemed to change. He had made a decision and so once more was his old, relaxed, arrogant self.

'Yes, as a matter of fact, I did,' he said with a shrug and an easy smile. 'I rather liked the macabre little detail of there being only one boot left at the scene, like in a novel. You know, the thing that defies all logic and baffles the investigation. Not that I intended there to be any investigation.'

'Because you planned to pose as a staff officer and call off the Military Police.'

'Yes.'

'A Colonel Willow.'

'Mmm. Don't know why I picked that. Constance Willow was the first girl I tupped – that must have been it, although God knows why. A servant, don't you know. Often the way, I've found, talking to other chaps.'

'So you shot Abercrombie and no doubt intended to plant your gun on poor deranged Hopkins, but then you noticed that Abercrombie still had his gun amongst his kit. A most unusual circumstance for a hospital patient, I'm sure.'

'Yes, I hadn't expected it.'

'But having seen it you couldn't resist the added detail. It would always have appeared strange that Hopkins had had a gun available to him, but to have snatched up Abercrombie's *own* gun in a moment of madness, that was *much* more plausible. An added touch which seemed brilliant at the time but which was, of course, to lead to your undoing.'

'Well, obviously I never dreamed that a ridiculous figure like yourself would think to go sneaking about the place digging up corpses and comparing bullets. Too clever for my own good, I suppose.'

'No, Captain Shannon, you are not. I am. Because it was only your plan to frame Hopkins for Abercrombie's murder that sparked the political row which brought me into the game in the first place. If you had just sneaked in and killed him, you probably would have got away with it.'

'Oh, I think you'll find that I *did* get away with it, old boy.'

Whilst still maintaining his same easy smile Shannon lifted the leather flap of his holster and rested his hand on the butt of his gun. Kingsley had on an officer's greatcoat, and there did not appear to be anything so large as a weapon secreted within it.

'So you pocketed your own smoking weapon,' Kingsley continued, 'took up Abercrombie's and fired it once, no doubt out of the window. I'm sure that if we searched for long enough we should find a bullet lodged in one of these trees hereabouts, or perhaps a slaughtered squirrel.'

'Probably,' Shannon agreed, affecting a yawn. 'I'm such a damned superb shot that I'd probably hit *something* even at random in the dark.'

'You then took up the ruined boot and Abercrombie's smoking pistol, crept into the next-door ward and deposited the incriminating gun on Hopkins's bed. Having done that you made a hasty exit, walking away from the ward up the corridor. It was then that Nurse Murray returned, having forgotten to take away the needle she had administered to a patient earlier. She saw your back as you made your retreat. Later on, when she heard about the murder, she of course drew the mistaken conclusion that the mystery officer had departed from Abercrombie's room, when in fact it was Hopkins's ward that you had just left.'

'Ah, the lovely Nurse Murray.'

Shannon's hand closed around the butt of his gun.

'Yes, the lovely Nurse Murray,' said a voice from within the trees.

Nurse Murray stepped out from the foliage in which she had been hiding, holding in front of her, in both hands, a German officer's magazine-loaded Mauser pistol, cocked and in the approved firing position.

'Take your hand away from that holster, Captain, or I shall shoot. You know very well that I have good cause.'

'Well, well, well,' Shannon drawled, 'what's this, Kingsley? An accomplice?'

Shannon had not yet moved his hand away from his gun. Perhaps he was about to, or perhaps he was going to draw it. Nurse Murray was clearly in no mood to wait. She lowered her sights, pointed the gun at Shannon's groin and squeezed the trigger.

As the report of the shot rang round the surrounding trees, Shannon stood for a moment, his face a mixture of shock and horror, then he looked down. Already a dark crimson stain was growing at his fly.

'Think about what has just happened to you, Captain,' Nurse Murray said calmly. 'Think about what a bullet there *means*.'

Shannon sank to his knees, his head bowed, contemplating the ruination of his manhood. Then he raised his face to Murray, agony etched in every line, agony and blind fury. He screamed, a long, cold, blood-curdling scream. A scream that was both horrified and horrifying.

'You'll rape no more,' Nurse Murray whispered and then cocked her gun again.

'No!' Kingsley cried.

It was too late. Nurse Murray shot Shannon through the middle of his forehead, so that his whole body lurched backwards and spread itself upon the ground. Stone dead.

Kingsley was lost for words. Nurse Murray spoke first.

'He was a rapist and a murderer. Any English court would have hanged him if they had the chance. I have just saved everybody a whole lot of trouble.'

Kingsley found his voice.

'An English court might well have hanged him, Kitty, but they would have tried him first.'

'This is war. We just had his trial and heard his confession and he's met a damn sight fairer fate than is afforded to most poor fellows out here.'

'When I asked you to follow us and to cover him . . .'

'Look, I didn't set out to shoot him but when I heard him confess to murder *and* saw him go for his gun, or very nearly go for it, quite frankly I thought, why not? He *raped* me, do you understand that? And, what is more, in a most appalling and unnatural manner, if one rape *can* be considered more unnatural than another, which I don't know that it can. However, one thing is certain, Captain Shannon was a *very, very bad man*.'

'Yes,' Kingsley admitted quietly, 'I know that.'

'Of all the Englishmen who will die in France today or on any day, I think, his is the *best death*. The only good one.'

'Yes. I believe that is true.'

'So you approve of what I did?'

'No . . . I don't.'

'Well, that's just bloody stupid. But then, from what Shannon said, you seem to be a bit mixed up over your morals in general.'

373

Nurse Murray stepped forward and inspected the corpse for a moment.

'I'm going to get my bike,' she said.

'Why?'

'Because I can't carry that bastard all the way to Ypres, can I? I'm going to wrap him up in an army blanket, sling him over the pillion and go and dump him in a shell hole.'

Kingsley joined Nurse Murray by the corpse, bending down to remove Shannon's gun from its holster and pocketing it, together with his papers.

'I think that's too risky. A body on the back of a motorcycle so far from the action might attract comment. It'll be dark in twenty minutes, we'll put him in his staff car.'

'You'll help me?'

'Yes, I'll help you. Justice has been done.'

And so, under cover of the night, Kingsley and Murray loaded the corpse of Shannon into the boot of the big staff car that Shannon had arrived in and took it as far up the line as they could get. Then Kingsley shouldered the corpse, and walked with it in a fireman's lift out along the duckboard pathways. He had not gone far when he came upon a dressing station. There was a steady stream of stretcher-bearers and walking wounded approaching it and nobody took any notice of the fact that Kingsley was coming from the opposite direction to the rest of them. As Kingsley had guessed, a man carrying a wounded comrade in whatever direction caused no comment whatsoever in the dark confusion to the rear of a massive battle. The one thing on earth least likely to provoke interest in Flanders that cruel autumn was a dead body.

Kingsley approached the front of the large tent where an RAMC orderly was making initial assessments of the wounded, the dying and the dead. Kingsley put the body down on the ground and the orderly glanced at it.

'I'm sorry, sir, but he's dead. Nothing we can do for him.'

Kingsley shrugged. The orderly summoned a passing stretcher-bearer and nodded towards Shannon's corpse. The bearer picked it up and took it to a large horse-drawn limber upon which were piled at least twenty other mutilated, lifeless bodies. Kingsley watched for a moment. The medical orderly had already turned away to assess another bloody human ruin, and the stretcher-bearer, having deposited the corpse, also moved on to his next weary job. Kingsley turned away too, leaving Captain Shannon to be buried as one of the many unidentified casualties of the Third Battle of Ypres.

Kingsley returned to the car, where Nurse Murray was waiting.

'Just as a matter of interest,' she enquired as they began their journey back, 'if I hadn't shot him, what were you intending to do with him?'

'I was going to have him held at Armentières until I had made my report to his superior.'

'And what do you think would have happened then?'

'I think probably they would have quietly court-martialled him and shot him.'

'You really think so? For obeying orders? I think they would have quietly shot *you*.'

'I do not believe Shannon's superiors ordered him to shoot Abercrombie. I believe he acted on his own initiative.'

'Ha!'

'That is what I believe.'

'Ha!' Nurse Murray repeated.

They drove on in silence for a little while.

'So your name is Kingsley then? Not Marlowe?' Murray asked.

'Yes.'

'And you're not a military policeman either, are you?'

'No, I am not.'

'There was a detective called Kingsley, wasn't there? A very famous one, but he went to prison and he died.'

'Yes. That's right, he died.'

Again there was silence.

'This is a rum business, isn't it?' Nurse Murray said finally.

'Very.'

'I've never killed anyone before, you know.'

And then Nurse Murray burst into tears. Kingsley drove on while she wept.

'You mustn't cry, Kitty,' he said eventually, 'because you were right. It *was* a good death. The right result. The *logical* result.'

'I don't want to talk about it any more,' Nurse Murray replied, trying to dry her eyes and light a cigarette all at once. 'I don't want to talk about it ever again.'

52

Back from the dead

Kingsley took Nurse Murray back to Château Beaurivage, where he asked to be allowed to collect Abercrombie's poems. Having now learned of the viscount's ambitions to resign his commission, Nurse Murray agreed to hand them over to him.

'Perhaps we shall meet again some day,' Kingsley said.

'Oh, I expect I shall pretty soon meet some marvellous chap and forget all about you,' she replied. 'Whoever you are.'

She turned and ran back up the steps into the château, clearly fearful that she would cry again. Kingsley drove the staff car to the nearest civilian main-line station and, having telegraphed Cumming to announce his return, began his journey back to Britain.

One week later, a cab drew up outside the Kingsley household in Hampstead and a smartly dressed officer emerged into the evening gloom.

The officer had written:

Darling Rose,
You will know by this ring which I am returning to you that I am alive and well. I have had an adventure and now it is over. I am returning to you but I return under another name, that of Robert my brother . . .

In his letter Kingsley told his wife the whole story, from the moment she had left him in Brixton Prison to the point when he and Kitty Murray had dumped Shannon's body and he had retrieved Abercrombie's poems. He was almost entirely frank, leaving out only certain details concerning Nurse Murray. Kingsley had agonized considerably on his journey home as to whether he should tell Agnes the truth about his relationship with Kitty. He had never deceived Agnes before and he hated to do so now. In the end, however, he had decided that he must never speak of it. It had happened, that was all. It had happened at a time when he thought Agnes was lost to him (although he knew Agnes would not consider that fact to be remotely mitigating), and he intended to bury the memory of Nurse Murray deep in his heart forever. Apart from that, he related his adventure with absolute candour, knowing that this was the only time the story would ever be told. He concluded:

I returned to England last week and met Sir Mansfield Cumming at my hotel in Victoria. There I told him of Shannon's guilt and also that Shannon was now dead. Here, I embellished the truth a little, not wishing to incriminate Nurse Murray. I told Cumming that Shannon had resisted arrest, that he and I had exchanged shots and that he had lost. Cumming seemed genuinely shocked at what I had discovered and I still honestly believe that he knew nothing about Shannon's crime until I revealed it to him. I told him that I had proof of Shannon's guilt in the shape of Nurse Murray, a corroborating witness to his confession, and that I also had Shannon's gun, which I was sure would match the bullet that killed Abercrombie.

I offered Cumming a deal. I told him that if the true facts were ever known, his department would be finished and he along with it; Abercrombie's father would see to that. I offered to cover up my discoveries and submit a confidential report stating that whilst I had been able to clear Hopkins of the murder, I had been unable to ascertain who had done it. This, of course, meant that the 'killed in action' story could stand without further complications. I told him, however, that I would only do this if two conditions were met. First, a small selection of Abercrombie's last poems must be published posthumously in order that the world might learn of that great hero's disillusionment. Secondly, that I be allowed to assume the identity of my dead brother. I told Cumming that it must be announced that Robert had in fact been a prisoner in Germany for the past year but that he had now escaped and returned to Britain. Robert and I shared a distinct resemblance and, although he was three years my junior, prison camp would surely age a man. Most of his friends are dead, and of course he never married; you will recall how often you tried to matchmake for him, without success. Darling, please agree to this unusual deception! This way George will have a father who was brave enough to protest the war and an uncle who was brave enough to fight in it. Ironically, the father died and the uncle lived, an uncle who very much wishes to be a father to his nephew.

He signed his letter 'Douglas. *For the last time.*'

There had been an agonizing wait of twenty-four hours before Agnes had replied. Kingsley clutched her note in his hand as he paid the cab driver and made his way up the path of the home that they had once shared.

My dear Robert,

I was overcome with emotion to hear of your survival and safe return to England. You know by now of course that Douglas is dead. You know also how completely I loved him.

Am I to presume that your letter was by way of a proposal?

Your affectionate sister-in-law, Agnes

She answered the door herself. It was past eight and George was in bed as she had decided he should be. She had also given the servants the evening off, so she and Kingsley would be alone.

For a moment the two of them stood motionless, staring at

each other, she inside the house, he on the step. Then she reached out and drew him inside, closing the door. Kingsley almost leaped forward, enfolding her in his arms, kissing the lips he had thought lost to him forever.

For quite some minutes no word passed between them.

Then Agnes disengaged herself and, as suddenly as she had embraced him, she hit him. The savage slap to the face actually made Kingsley stagger. Agnes looked as surprised as he was.

'I didn't mean to do that,' she said. 'I didn't plan to.'

'I don't mind,' Kingsley replied.

Suddenly she was shouting.

'You could have found a way to tell me. You *should* have found a way! I went to your *funeral*! It was so . . . so . . . cruel!'

'What can I say to you?' Kingsley stammered. 'I'm truly sorry. I was dealing with very dangerous people. The stakes were high. I couldn't put you at risk. I did it for us, you know. I did it all for us.'

'Ha!' she snapped. 'And also, I've no doubt, for the thrill of your precious investigation! You forget how well I know you!'

Once more there was silence between them, although this time without the pleasure of kisses.

After a little it was Kingsley who spoke. Something had occurred to him.

'You say you went to my funeral?'

'Did you doubt it?'

'Well, I . . .'

'Of course I went to your funeral! Perhaps I am wrong,' she added with angry sarcasm, 'but I rather thought it was customary for a wife to attend the funeral of her husband.'

'I was disgraced. Buried within the confines of the prison.'

'And what has that got to do with anything? You were my husband! I loved you! I hated you but I loved you. I told you as much when I gave you back your ring. I read Kipling's "If" over your grave! How could you *think* I would not attend your funeral?'

Kingsley was very moved.

'Shannon told me you did not go.'

'And you *believed* him?'

'Well . . .'

'I cannot credit that you believed that man! He was obviously an utter cad. I knew it the first moment I saw him.'

'But you received him again, more than once. He visited you.'

'He may have visited me but I did *not* receive him. He came to my door but he was informed that I was out. I know *his* sort.'

Once more Kingsley was reminded of just how much he loved his wife. Her intuition was faultless.

'Agnes,' he said, 'will you marry me?'

'Yes.'

Once more they embraced and this time she did not break away. Instead she took Kingsley's hand and led him towards the stairs.

'*Most* improper before our wedding night,' she said as they stumbled together into their bedroom.

After they had made love, Kingsley went into George's room and stared awhile at the dear face of his sleeping son. When he returned to the bedroom, Agnes was sitting at her dressing table, looking thoughtful.

'This Nurse Murray,' she said, with just the faintest hint of acid in her tone. 'She figures rather prominently in your story, doesn't she?'

'Nurse Murray? Oh . . . she was a fine young woman, a . . . a great help in the investigation.'

'Really?' Agnes replied, and there was a wealth of meaning in that single word.

As Kingsley endeavoured to change the subject, he could not help wondering whether Agnes's intuition might be just a little *too* faultless.